The insidious power of the drums was pulling at him. Giddiness swam in his head.

From somewhere the sleek, slim body of a girl sprang into view. Stark naked like the others, arms writhing sinuously above her head. Against the background of leaping flames her skin shone a golden amber. Her eyes gleamed like liquid fire. A red flower was pinned above one ear in the mass of her wild, tossing hair. She danced closer, blood-red lips parted around shining white teeth.

"Do you wish me to dance for you, *docteur?*"

Céleste! Only by her voice would he have recognized her because of the shadows and fiery reflections rippling across her face. He rose to his feet and moved toward her. The raging drums were deafening. Everything was a crazed blur. . . .

"Come. . . ." She was leading him by the hand. The drums were suddenly silent. In the shadows he saw couples wrestling on the ground.

They sank down into darkness.

"I knew you would come," she whispered.

Creole Surgeon

Mitchell Caine

A FAWCETT GOLD MEDAL BOOK

Fawcett Books, Greenwich, Connecticut

For my two loves, Ren and Alisa

CREOLE SURGEON

Produced by Lyle Kenyon Engel

© 1977 Lyle Kenyon Engel and Mitchell Caine

ISBN 0-449-13924-7

Printed in the United States of America

10 9 8 7 6 5 4 3 2 1

PROLOGUE: St. Louis, 1831

THE mountain man was drunk. He offered to whip any, or every, man in the tavern. He said he was half hoss and half alligator and claimed acquaintance with the notorious Mike Fink. He bragged that he had kicked old Mike half to death one day. The other patrons suffered in silence, putting it down to booze and brag, until finally the host showed the mountain man a bung starter and gave him three choices—calming down, getting out, or a busted head. It was then that the mountain man, who allowed his name was Seth Anderson, rummaged through the pack and produced the buffalo bladder.

The bladder was packed with rich dark soil. Spilling some on the planks that served as a bar, the hunter spread it around with his fingers.

"From right near the Little Sioux," he said. "Near a hundred miles from Fort Atkinson. I was up and down the river, after beaver, and I got me a passel of samples. This here is pure bottom, and it runs both ways from the river. Maybe fifty, seventy-five miles of it. I brung this back to show my brother-in-law. If the lazy hoss ever gits here. He's got a mind to farm out here, and wants me to jine him. Might do it, too. Man gits a mite old for beaver and Injuns and walking in freeze water up to his tailbone."

John Dixon, standing at the man's elbow and nursing a noggin of rum and water, reached to take a handful of the soil and spill it between his callused farmer's fingers. It was better than good soil. It was the best he'd ever touched or smelled. Better than anything back in Indiana, and there was good soil in that state. But this was prime. This was bottom—the hunter wasn't lying about that. As he sniffed and fingered the soil again, John Dixon could feel greedy excitement swelling in his chest. He could almost see the corn growing nine feet tall.

The landlord, a crotchety man who didn't much like farmers, and who could read and liked to show it off, said,

"You ain't never heard of the 1807 Act? The govermint don't want no farmers in the Territory. Riles the Injuns."

There was general laughter at this and the usual potshots at the Federals. What the hell did they know in Washington about anything? Anything at all that had to do with a man making a living for his wife and little ones? A man paid about as much attention to Washington as he did to the wind blowing down the Mississippi. If a man wanted to go into the Territory and settle some of that prime virgin land, as much as he reckoned he could handle, then it was purely his own business. And his own hair. Anyway, there weren't enough soldiers to stop you if you were really set on it. Come down to it, the government didn't seem to give much of a damn. All talk. Talk and laws they never really had a mind to enforce. Let them worry about the Injuns.

John Dixon, hot with his new land dreams, stuck close to the fur hunter. He bought him drinks and let the hunter do most of the talking, and drinking, while Dixon just nursed his noggin of rum, listening and drawing him out with questions.

When he left the tavern, Dixon had a crude map. That night around a campfire he showed it to the Salters and the Fletchers. The three families had come all the way from Indiana in their Conestoga wagons and were camped a mile or so north of St. Louis. It was the middle of April 1831, and the Mississippi was swollen with fast-sliding brown water.

After handling and smelling the handful of earth Dixon had brought back from the tavern, Harry Salter and Jake Fletcher agreed it was prime. They pored over the map and began estimating time and distance.

Salter spat tobacco juice into the fire. "Three weeks, a month, maybe a leetle more an' we'd be there," he said. "Barring breakdowns. What we waitin' fer?"

Jake Fletcher nodded. "We git there the middle of May or thereabouts, we could still git some kind of crop in. Start building. Lay us enough by to git through the winter. Maybe git to the fort and see what's to be had."

"We'll be illegal," Dixon pointed out. "That land ain't officially open to settle."

The other men laughed. "Let's worry about that when the cows come home," said Salter.

That night under the canvas roof of the wagon, while their two-year-old Paul slept, John Dixon discussed it with

Elizabeth. He lightly stroked her stomach, which was just beginning to round out with another child, and said, "We'll want to be settled before he gets here."

Elizabeth smiled and patted his cheek. "There you go again, John Dixon—saying *he!* Thinking that all a farm needs is boys. But I told you, I'm bound and determined this one's to be a girl."

Dixon chuckled. "I was forgettin'. Of course, if you've made up your mind then I reckon the Almighty won't interfere. Just like there ain't nothing going to interfere between us right now. . . ." He reached for her in that bold way that sometimes made her blush.

After they had made love and Elizabeth nestled to him before sleep, she said, "You reckon we might run into Kit out there?"

Dixon, half in and out of sleep, had been counting the chores ahead of him tomorrow. There was a mountain of things to be got through before they could start.

"Ain't likely," he told her. "That's a big country out there, like no end to it, and from what I hear, the trappers got to keep moving west all the time for the beaver. Land gets hunted out pretty quick. If you run into your kid brother, it'll be plumb accidental. Might be we could hear something about him at the fort, though. If we ever get in there."

She sighed. "Seems funny, and wrong somehow—not being able to see your own brother when you know he's somewhere around."

Dixon stared at the canvas ceiling and let it pass. Lizzie worried too much about young Carson. That was because she was five years the older and had near mothered the boy to death back in Indiana. Even after Dixon married her and they had gone to farm out on Polk's Run, Lizzie fretted about young Kit.

Dixon smiled wryly. Young hellcat was more like it. Whiskey-drinking and dancing all night to the fiddles. Brawling every time a body looked cross-eyed at him. Running away at sixteen to be a mountain man. Only two letters home in four years. How old would the young scamp be now? Twenty?

He drifted into sleep with the thought that if anyone could outsmart the Injuns and take care of himself, it was Kit Carson. Anyhow, Dixon had his own worries. Like tomorrow he had to go to town and spend the last of their money on salt and meal and powder and a whole list of other

necessaries. It was going to be root hog or die on the new
land the first year. But they would make it. Somehow they
always did.

The warmth of Lizzie slipped from his embrace, bringing
him just enough awake to know she'd gone to tend young
Paul. Two years old and bright as a button on a soldier's
suit. Too soon to be worried about the boy's schooling. The
country out there was going to open up fast. Bound to be a
school started by the time the boy came of age.

Lizzie settled back on the pallet. Seeing him stir, she
kissed his cheek and whispered, "Paul was fussing. It ain't
like him not to sleep right through the night. I sure hope it
ain't the colic."

ii

The trek took six weeks. They went northwest, guiding on
the Missouri River to their left, the wagons rolling and
creaking day after day up and down the grassy swales, over
prairie stretching to infinity. The pace was slowed because the
Salters had only oxen to yoke to their wagon, but Dixon
and Fletcher, grateful enough that they had horses, didn't
complain. There was time enough and the weather was kind.
Almost every day bright sun glimmered blindingly on the
river, danced amid the luxuriant green leaves bursting from
the trees. Marveling at the height of the grasses and weeds
so early in the season—taller than anything he had ever
seen back in Indiana—Dixon said, "Man could make out
real good on land like this, but I figger the kind of bottom
land we're headed for, everything grows at least twicet as
big."

Fletcher laughed. Their optimism was high. Even the food
problem would soon be eased because now, barely three days'
trek from the Little Sioux River, they began to see buffalo.

What they didn't see was the Indian sign that was everywhere. Had the drunken, bragging mountain man Seth
Anderson been there, he would have known instantly.

But these men were farmers. Stalwart, toil-hardened, as
brave as the next man, but farmers. They did not see the
pony droppings, or notice the sudden absence of buffalo.
The char of dead fires meant nothing to them. They had no
dogs with them, trained to scent Indian.

iii

They may have been Sacs or Fox—Chief Black Hawk was at

the moment harrying the western Illinois settlements—or
they might have been Sioux or even Mandans, Rees or
Kiowa. They were a small party, not more than twenty, and
it is doubtful they were looking for trouble. They scouted
the little wagon train carefully, following it for an entire
day without being spotted, their minds on loot, and all
through a fireless night they palavered. The older braves
were suspicious. It was too easy, too inviting. No soldiers,
no hunters, no long rifles or knives. One of the braves had a
white man's "looking glass," taken long ago from a yellow-
leg officer, and he lay on his belly in the tall grass and
studied the wagons with great care. His nostrils flared with
anticipation.

Before the attack they palavered again. The younger braves
were openly scornful of their elders. Why did they hesitate?
When the Great Spirit offered such a bounty, was it not to
be accepted? Were there old women among them, that they
feared to attack three white men, their three women, seven
children and one infant? *Hoeeee*—was such a gift from the
Spirit to be disdained? There were but twenty soldiers at
Fort Atkinson, and they fifteen suns away. Why did they
wait?

It came at dawn. Salter was on watch, sleepy and yawning
one moment, a human quiver the next. With arrows studding
him like one of his wife's pincushions, he still managed to
scream and discharge his piece. And die.

Fletcher was next. He fired once from his wagon before
he was dragged out and knifed and tomahawked. The Indian
party had but three rifles and were stingy with powder and
ball.

Elizabeth shrieked as John Dixon blasted with his shotgun, a nigh useless weapon. Arrows zipped cleanly through
the canvas of the wagon. Snatching up young Paul, Elizabeth
clutched him to her breast.

Dixon, an arrow in his throat and another dangling from
a shoulder, threw aside the shotgun. There was no time to
reload. Grabbing his old horse pistol, a relic from his grand-
father, he lifted and snapped it at the whooping Indians. It
clicked dry. Dixon turned to shout at his wife.

"Hide the boy—!"

A covey of arrows took him then, slicing his lungs, and he
fell half in and half out of the wagon, spewing blood.

Elizabeth, in the last few moments before her death,
opened the old leather trunk and dropped Paul into it.

Frantic with terror, she was not thinking, only mothering, protecting to the end—even to wedging the trunk lid open with a Bible, the only book she had brought from Indiana, so the child would have air. Then, still screaming, she leaped from the wagon in the hope of drawing attention away from Paul.

One of the braves caught her as she leaped and, mindful of her luxuriant glossy-brown hair, did not use his hatchet. Slitting her throat and then the skin of her scalp, he ripped off the hair even as she was still kicking in her death throes. Of the three women, hers was by far the finest trophy.

After the Fletcher and Salter children had been dispatched—they were too young to scalp—a small cask of whiskey was discovered in the Salter wagon. They passed it around, drinking from the bunghole, and in much less time than it would have taken a paleface, every Indian was gloriously drunk. Drunk, elated, looting and bragging.

iv

It was this thorough looting that was to so puzzle Dr. Jeremiah Abbott. The Indians had taken everything remotely usable, and what they did not take they destroyed by smashing or burning.

How, then, had they overlooked the boy?

Dr. Abbott, who had taken a two-year degree from the Baltimore College of Surgery and Medicine, had come West five years before. Alcohol had much to do with his move. In St. Louis, after still another year of drunkenness, by tremendous effort and no little help from friends—for he was a likable man when sober—he finally managed to pluck himself from the gutter. For a time he practiced in St. Louis, neither thriving nor starving, and when offered a post as civilian doctor at Fort Atkinson, he took it. It was a salutary change, for he enjoyed hunting and fishing and found that he got along well enough with Indians. The garrison was small and his duties mostly routine.

On that day of discovering the tragedy, Dr. Abbott had been out with a meat-hunting party. Because of the Black Hawk war, both supplies and troops were being diverted eastward, and the fort was getting low on food. Noticing buzzards making dark circles in the blue air over a distant rise, and not having seen buffalo all day, their head scout, a man named Talbot, allowed that they might just as well take a look. Just might be buffalo. They proceeded cautiously because Talbot had been uneasy all day. There was Indian sign all over the place, but nary an Indian to be seen.

"Small parties," Talbot grumbled. "After buffalo, I reckon, same as us. Or anything they can steal or kill. No women, which means they'll fight if they figure to win, but they don't figure to tackle a party like us. Thing is—where in tarnation are they?"

As they neared the circling buzzards, they picked up the wagon trail—about as clear as a city street to a woodsman's eyes. "Could be some poor fools wandered into trouble," the scout said. "Ain't no way to keep the clodhoppers out. They're bound to settle, come hell or high water, war or no war. Black Hawk don't mean nothing to them settler fools. And there's no troops to prevent them."

Shaking his head in disgust, he added, "Hard to see how they could miss all the Injun sign. Plenty of warning. They got to be greenhorns if they've lost their hair."

Talbot was even more disgusted, and sorrowful, when they reached the scene of the massacre and had driven off the buzzards.

"Damned poor fools—wandering around like they was back in Ohio! Walked right into it. I doubt they knowed they was scalped till the Injuns showed them their own hair."

Salter's cow had been killed and half of it eaten. An empty whiskey cask lay near a dead fire. A halfhearted attempt had been made to burn the Fletcher wagon. The funky stench of charred debris still lingered.

One of the soldiers pointed at the empty cask. "By the time they found the likker, I reckon they just about forgot everything else."

Still, the looting had been thorough. Bodies had been stripped of all clothing. Since this was a hunting party not equipped for burial, Talbot advised that they leave the bodies to the vultures. In a day or so they would be cleansed to the shining bone.

The doctor and Talbot watched as the corpses were arranged in a neat row. A useless gesture, the doctor thought, but the least Christian men could do.

"Wonder who they was?" said Talbot. "Not a damned thing to tell."

"Might find something in the wagons."

"Not likely. You notice, Doc, how there ain't any arrows?"

Abbott had not, in fact, noticed. He was, even after four years in the Territory, far from being a frontiersman.

"Took the arrows with them," Talbot explained, "so we won't know which tribe of devils to blame. Brushed out their pony tracks, too. It's Injun nature to clean away any kind of clues. Don't let anyone tell you a drunk Injun can't think."

He added, " 'Course he'll still think like an Injun."

There was nothing in the Salter or Fletcher wagons to identify the owners. The doctor found this strange.

"Most folks carry Bibles with them. Might be the only book they ever have, usually is, but they'll have a Bible with names in it. Birth records and such."

Talbot shook his head. "You ain't been around long enough to know, Doc. Bibles is big medicine to Injuns. White man's magic. They're afeard of it an' try to steal some of it for themselves. You go in some lodges—and I been in more'n a few—you find near as many Bibles as scalps."

One of the soldiers gave a yell. "Hey—Adams found a baby!"

The doctor pushed his way through the little knot of men around the wagon. A soldier was handing out a child wrapped in a long flannel nightshirt. Not exactly a baby, Abbott thought. Year and a half, maybe two years old. He sensed something was odd, something missing, and in a moment realized what it was. The child wasn't crying.

Someone called, "What is it—cow or bull?"

The one holding the child peeked under the flannel. "Bull."

"You bummers take it easy with that boy!" Talbot said harshly. "Give him to the doc here."

The child was handed to the doctor. Warm, squirming, a bit dirty, staring up at him wide-eyed. Smoke-gray eyes, Abbott noted.

"I want Mummy," said the child.

The doctor could not help but glance at the naked, scalped women. Which one would it be? He patted the boy. "In a while," he said gently. "In a while, we'll see about your Mummy."

The curious soldiers and scouts watched as he examined the boy. He found nothing but slight emaciation. Buffalo stew would soon fix that.

Abbott looked at Talbot. "How long would you say it's been since this happened?"

Talbot shrugged. "Not a lot to go by. I'd reckon two, three days."

The doctor ruffled the boy's hair. "You hungry, son?"

The boy blinked, nodded, and clung to the doctor's hand. "Yes. I wan' din."

While food was being prepared, the doctor and Talbot took the boy to one side, well away from the corpses, and spoke softly and carefully.

"What's your name, son?" Abbott was seated on a fallen cottonwood, holding the boy on his knees.

"Pau."

"Pau?"

Talbot nodded and said, "Paul. He's saying Paul."

Abbott jounced the boy on his knee. "Paul, eh? Paul what?"

"Pau."

"He don't know his last name," said Talbot.

"You're probably right. Give him time, maybe he'll remember. He's been through a lot."

He put a finger under the boy's chin and lifted it. "How much do you remember, Paul? How long were you in that trunk?"

Talbot, displaying a sensitivity that surprised the doctor, had meanwhile gone to see that what remained of the wagon canvas was thrown over the bodies.

"I sleep," said the boy. "I want Mummy." Suddenly, and for the first time, he began to cry. In spite of the doctor's clumsy dandling and comforting, he kept bawling until a soldier brought him a large tin of succulent-smelling buffalo stew. Then he ate.

Watching, the soldier said, "Ain't nothin' wrong with his appetite. Little booger's nigh starved to death."

That night around the fire, as Paul slept with a full tummy, Talbot and the doctor discussed the matter. They had examined the trunk in which Paul had been found. It was empty, probably looted. There had been nothing in it but the boy.

"I just don't understand it," the doctor said. "Why didn't they kill him along with the others? They must have known he was there."

The chief scout spat into the fire and shook his head. "Ain't no sense in twisting our brains about that. We ain't never going to know. I been around Injuns for twenty years, living with them and killing them and trying to keep my hair, and all I know is that a man can't never exactly figure them. Only two possibles I see here is, they did git drunk and overlook him—of which I got my doubts—or they found him all right and for some Injun reason we can't figure just decided to let him be."

"Neither possibility makes sense to me," said the doctor.

"Might have had something to do with their religion. Good medicine, bad medicine—that's the biggest thing in their lives, you know. If I knew who they was, I might make a better guess, but I don't. Way they built fires, I'd say Mandan, but it ain't hardly likely Mandans would come all this way just to get in on Black Hawk's little war. Could be Sac or Fox, except most of them is already away with Black Hawk. If I got to guess, I'd say they came from one of the Sioux tribes. My advice, Doc, it's best you forget it. No way we'll ever know for sure why he wasn't kilt. Thing is, what happens to the boy now? Kind of rough country for a little kid with no kin."

"I've been thinking about that," said Abbott. "For the time being, I guess I'll have to be his kin."

He glanced over at the sleeping boy, snuggled down in one of the soldiers' blankets. "I think Paul will agree with me that it beats having no kin at all. Of course it'll be temporary. We'll have to see."

Talbot stretched for an ember to light his pipe. "That'll be fine for the little feller, but ain't you getting along a mite to be a daddy?"

The doctor ruefully scratched the dome of his balding head. "Forty isn't all that old, Talbot. That don't worry me. What does is that a child that age needs a mother."

The scout gave him a sly glance. "You could get married."

BOOK ONE

Edinburgh 1855

ONE: The Hanging

THE 28th of January did not so much dawn as insinuate itself; muffled in freezing mizzle and tatters of mist, it crept in like the most miserable of thieves, a beginning day as forlorn as one of the gloomier chambers of Hell. Through thick dank air the great clock at Clockmill House mournfully tolled out the hour of six.

The hanging was to be at ten o'clock.

Much of Edinburgh still slumbered, loathe to rise and face the dismal Scottish weather. So miserable was the day, so foul the atmosphere, that for once the crowd was slow to assemble. Ordinarily the thousands of morbidly curious who pushed and shoved to see an execution would have been on hand many hours before the event. Places of vantage from which one might gain a good view of the doomed man's last struggles would go at premium prices. The leaning, decaying tenements facing Calton Hills—some of them towering seventeen stories high—would have been crowded with those able to pay for the view. Many would bring spyglasses, the better to observe the final agony, and food hawkers would do a brisk business. Hastily printed pamphlets and broadsheets, purporting to be the condemned's "true last confession," would be cried in the streets. There would be the usual frenzied activity of pickpockets. Those so inclined and with the necessary pence would crowd as near the gallows as possible, hoping to purchase a two-inch segment of the rope.

The man to be hanged was Fergus McIlwain, an illiterate and somewhat daft cobbler who had grown up in the fetid slums of Tanner's Close in the West Port. As a young man, his sole investment in honest labor had been as a navvy on the Union Canal, then being dug between Edinburgh and Glasgow. Finding toil unsuitable to his temperament, he soon turned to the easier tasks of thievery and pandering.

Over the years—he was to reach fifty before the noose caught up with him—McIlwain was often in and out of the watch houses and Bridewell. Nothing of a capital nature could be proved against him—until his final misstep. Frantic for money and subtly encouraged by his betters, McIlwain committed a crime that shocked all Scotland and sent waves of fear and revulsion throughout the British Empire.

He murdered a prostitute and sold her body for dissection by medical students.

Not since the orgy of body-snatching in the twenties, during the terrible times of Burke and Hare, had there been such a furor. Anger and indignation ran high. People feared a return to those lawless days when, literally, a body was not safe in the grave. The panic, bordering on mass hysteria, was greatest in Edinburgh, a seat of medical learning where corpses were in high demand for dissection.

ii

In another part of town a young American heard the clock boom six from Castle Hill and shuddered with something that was not altogether from the cold. Perhaps more than any other resident of Edinburgh, save the condemned man himself, Paul Abbott had reason to be seized by fear on this foul morning.

He paced nervously, his tall lank figure casting a shadow first long, then short under the flickering gas light. His dark hair, in need of trimming, hung awry around his ears. His cheap suit was rumpled and his smoke-gray eyes were bleared. The high-boned cheeks were more gaunt than usual, for he had scarcely eaten in nearly a week. He was in the "wet room" in the lower level of one of the drear stone buildings lining Surgeons Square. Six marble slabs lined the center of the room, three of them occupied by the corpses of two men and a woman delivered only yesterday from the workhouse. A faint stench from the beginning decomposition of their flesh permeated the air. Ordinarily, in mild or warm weather, one of Abbott's numerous duties would be to keep the bodies doused with cold water. Today there was no need for that. It was almost as dank and cold within this flagged, high-ceilinged chamber of the dead as it was outside, where a mizzling rain was freezing into gray slush the moment it touched earth.

As he paced, the young man muttered and cursed himself and the others who had gotten him into this dilemma. Shivering, he tried to warm his hands by thrusting them beneath his jacket and under his armpits—he didn't own a great-coat—and moved his toes inside his worn and badly cracked shoes to increase the circulation.

Damn the cold, he thought bitterly; damn poverty and damn the miserable, dangerous situation he was trapped in!

Since that day twenty-four years ago when Dr. Jeremiah Abbott had found him as a two-year-old child—the sole survivor of a wagon train massacre—a lot of water had passed under the bridge. Much of it good, some of it bad.

But nothing as bad as it was now.

He paced past the cadavers, unnoticing of their stink. Where in hell and damnation was his friend Alex? Alex should have been here by now with the news, good or bad—and it was certain to be bad. Alex was his only hope, and a slim one at that, of keeping out of a Scots jail.

Pausing in front of a blackened fireplace, he rubbed his hands briskly before the grate, making an ineffectual effort to imagine a fire. He laughed humorlessly, remembering how only a few years ago there had always been cozy fires, a full belly and no problems to speak of.

A good, happy life. He had traded it for this miserable existence—which could well terminate soon at the end of a hangman's rope.

Those happy days of his youth had been spent around Council Bluffs, U.S.A., where he had virtually grown up in the saddle, accompanying his foster father, Jeremiah, on his rounds. At other times he roamed and camped in the woods with his constant Indian companion, Deerfoot. The two had trapped and hunted over half of Iowa.

Jere taught him the rudiments of rough frontier medicine. He assisted at operations on plank tables in log cabins, sometimes in the woods on the ground. Jere's cures were blunt. Once when a child was choking with diphtheria, Jere slit the throat to open the windpipe and kept the aperture from closing with fishhooks.

While still in his teens Paul became an expert at "hunting-knife surgery"—using the same knife he used for skinning and cleaning game he shot or trapped. By the time he was twenty, with no training other than raw experience, the teachings of Jere and an Indian medicine man and gleanings from a few medical lectures he attended in Iowa City, he was considered ready to take over half of Jere's grossly underpaid practice as a full equal—frontier doctors did not require licenses—and doubtless would have remained in Council Bluffs practicing crude medicine for the rest of his life, had it not been for a fateful meeting in St. Louis. . . .

There by chance he met Dr. Amos Goodloe. Goodloe had attended Harvard and later had studied for three years in Edinburgh. Impressed by Paul, the eminent physician spent hours with him discussing medical matters. It was an eye-opener to Paul. Goodloe recounted tales of astonishing new cures and successful operations that Paul would not have dreamed possible. For the first time he realized how primitive and lacking frontier medicine really was.

Afterward he could think and talk of nothing else but going to Edinburgh. Jere, who had married an extravagant young wife and who had again taken to drink, was too pinched for money to help much. But Dr. Goodloe had intimated that a poor student, by dint of clever managing and much scrimping, could make it through in Edinburgh. And certificates from Edinburgh colleges were the most honored in the medical world.

Thus with Jere's reluctant blessing and with barely enough money for the first year's tuition, Paul had gone abroad for advanced training in one of the world's most esteemed medical academies.

That had been nearly four years ago. . . .

He resumed his pacing. Where in Christ's name was Alex?

There should be some news by now. His nerves were getting jumpy from anxiety and waiting.

Now he knew how the animals that he and Deerfoot had trapped in deadfalls had felt.

Turning, twisting, pacing. Futilely seeking a way out.

Leaving the wet room, he went into an adjoining chamber, the operating theater. There was no fire there either, but ample kindling and a sack of coal by the grate. In a rush of rage and rebellion, Paul laid a fire. There was an ironclad rule, strictly enforced, against a fire when the theater was not in use. If one of the proctors came in, he would be in trouble. More trouble, that is.

He touched off the fire with a paper spill lit at the gas fixture, and as the kindling snapped and the Welsh coal began to glow, he rubbed his hands over the sparse flames and thought he might just as well be hanged for a wolf as for a sheep.

What the hell was holding up Alex?

Leaving the fire, Paul went to a dirty window and peered out at the rain and mud-colored sky. The mizzle was turning into soft blobs of dirty snow. The day was a total disaster, so steeped in gloom that a man could welcome the devil. He lingered for a few minutes at the window, watching the foul brownish fog mixing with poisonous black smoke from a hundred thousand chimney pots. The vile mixture of smoke and fog nearly always lay heavy in the ravines and flatlands of Edinburgh. Those who had to live and breathe in the city called it "Auld Reekie." On many occasions he had opened lungs to find them pathogenic with a residue of coal. He supposed his own lungs would soon be in like shape, though he had lived in the city only four years.

A bit less, actually, and that was the nub of his problem.

This was January. If he could stick it out until June he would get his Certificate in Surgery. Only four and a half more months.

But if his evil luck continued, it might as well be four and a half centuries.

To relieve his tensions, he plucked a scalpel from a case and went to a table in the center of the theater and removed the drape from a cadaver. He studied it. It was about half worked over, and what remained had once been a woman in her late twenties. Extending the scalpel, he made a slight incision to lift the Fallopian tube out of the way so he could get at the epoophoron, and beneath it, the ovary. Professor

Townshend had been well into the lecture when the bell rang, and the lower quadrants were open.

The woman had died of postpartum hemorrhage. She had been an imbecile confined to the workhouse, and no one knew or admitted guilt as to how she had become pregnant. Paul himself had compiled her history. Such histories and related records were among the chores for which he was paid a meager twenty English pounds a year.

It had been, he remembered as he spread the broad ligament with his fingers, a most interesting case. It had come to their attention early, as did many such cases in the prisons and workhouses, and she had been brought into surgery when her time came. Townshend had been prepared for excessive bleeding, and with Paul and Jack Fordyce assisting, made ready with the syringes washed and a supply of human blood at hand. In all his lectures Townshend reiterated that animal blood should never be used, though there were surgeons in the Royal Academy who still used sheep's blood.

The child had come healthy enough and was sent off to the nursery, but the mother's bleeding could not be halted. Transfusions were begun. Syringe after syringe of blood was pumped into the woman while students in the tiers watched and made notes. The blood was fresh and in copious supply from many donors.

Still, the woman died.

After the failure, Professor Townshend discussed it briefly with Paul and Jack Fordyce.

"The percentage of successful transfusions is not as bad as it might be," he'd said. "But still, lads, how can we say that it is good when we have even one fatality that can be attributed to the blood alone? The woman should not have died. The paradox is that she died for lack of blood, purely and simply that, and yet we had blood. In ample supply. You saw how we poured it into her and how she bled it away."

Jack Fordyce, a dullard and a sly enemy of Paul's, listened to Townshend with a feigned air of deep understanding, nodded wisely and said nothing.

Paul said, "I've been reading Magendie and Brown-Sequard, sir. And Landois. They have interesting theories. Landois claims that the serum of one species agglutinates and dissolves the corpuscles of another species. He confirms your own theory, sir, that animal blood should never be introduced into humans."

The professor nodded. "I certainly agree to that. Though many still disagree."

"I was thinking, sir," Paul went on, "that perhaps the same thing could be true of blood samples taken from different humans. Could there be such differences in human blood, sir?"

Fordyce couldn't resist giving his contemptuous opinion. "That's all bullcock! Blood is blood, one and the same thing. At least human blood is."

Paul ignored him. "In short, sir, if it were so that all human blood is not the same and as a consequence incompatible blood was used in transfusions, might that not account for fatal reactions?"

Townshend had given Paul a sharp look and a clap on the shoulder as he left. "I've heard that theory before, Abbott. I do not at the moment subscribe, or disagree. Certainly the theory is not proven. And just as certainly there is room for work there. Good day, gentlemen."

Jack Fordyce smirked. Having first made sure that Townshend was indeed gone, and careful to keep his distance across the chamber, he turned on Paul. "I have been thinking, sir . . . " he mimicked.

Paul showed no reaction.

"I have been thinking, Abbott," Fordyce continued in his usual whining voice, "how long your nose is and how far you've got it up Townshend's arse. How do you manage to breathe, Abbott?"

Paul carefully maintained his distance, not trusting his temper with Fordyce. The bad blood between them had started with an incident shortly after Paul's arrival in Edinburgh. Fordyce, a student proctor, had tried to haze Paul by ordering him to fetch and carry and serve. But Paul, reared on the rough frontier, would not for a moment suffer such treatment.

The fight was brief and bloody. Paul used frontier tactics—hands, feet, butting, biting—anything to put the other man down. It was not a gentleman's way of fighting, but there were few who sympathized with the badly beaten Fordyce, who was generally disliked.

Since then Paul had avoided Fordyce whenever possible. When he couldn't, he managed to control his temper when Fordyce tried to provoke him with jibes and insults. He had too much to lose and nothing to gain by beating the man senseless.

iii

Paul broke off with his thoughts of the past, which couldn't be mended now, and walked back to the fire. He put on more coals. To hell with being caught by a student proctor and reported. If he were caught, at least it wouldn't be by Jack Fordyce.

For Fordyce was at this very moment under arrest in the Queen Street watch house.

Spilling his guts out to the police.

The irony of it, Paul thought bitterly, was that if instead of restraining his temper he'd followed his natural instincts and given Fordyce a hard enough drubbing to land him in the infirmary for a month or so to mend, all this trouble might have been averted.

But he knew this was only quibbling with his own conscience. There was no escaping the blunt fact of his own guilt—the guilt of making the biggest blunder of his life that wild night back in October, when it had all started. . . .

On that night a cold rain had lashed Surgeons Square and an unearthly wind had hooted in the chimneys. Paul had been alone in the operating theater, opening the belly of a pauper child brought in that afternoon. When a loud knocking resounded on the stout oaken door opening on the inner court, he did not at first open it, calling instead to know who was there. Edinburgh had more than its share of murderous footpads and bully boys after dark.

"It's me, Jack Fordyce!" shouted the despised voice. "Let me in, mon!"

Though Paul hated the man, he did not fear him. He unbarred the door and through the murk saw Fordyce and another man. Both were drenched to the skin, lugging between them a battered tea chest. Damp leaves swirled about them in the gusting wind.

"Don't stand there like a great lump, mon," said Fordyce in his usual insulting whine. "Help me with this."

The two lowered the chest to the ground. The man with Fordyce was a stranger, not young, wearing a beaver hat and a sodden greatcoat reaching to his ankles. Fordyce dismissed him with a whisper and bent again to lift the tea chest while Paul got on the other end.

"Into the wet room," said Fordyce. "This one is prime and the professors will want it well kept."

As they opened the chest and lifted the body to the slab,

Paul recognized her: Mag Ferguson, a drab he'd seen around on occasion, sometimes whoring it in the taverns where he ate, because it was cheap, and at times pushing a barrow and selling old shoes. She was well figured, not unpretty, and when he thought about it, probably not as old as she looked.

"The less mentioned of this the better, you know," Fordyce said, fixing Paul with a belligerent look. "It is no great thing. If I hadn't taken the body, those bastards over in Nicholson would have. The old bugger you saw outside came to me of his own free will and told me of Mag dying. None of it is anything to get in a blather about, but for all that we're treading a wee bit on the toes of the law. You know that, Abbott, so keep your big gab shut."

Paul shrugged. "It's none of my affair."

"Keep it that way and no harm will come. You've a little time to go for your certificate and I doubt you'll be wanting trouble."

But trouble had come. Paul had forsaken his child cadaver and that very night carefully scissored out Mag Ferguson's stomach and analyzed the contents. Before the stormy night was over, he knew.

Antimony. A slow-acting poison. Someone had been feeding antimony to Mag for days. . . .

Paul took the poker and savagely stirred the fire. What a dull-witted fool he'd been! *It's none of my affair,* he had told Fordyce. The words had come back to haunt him.

In all truth, it had not at the time seemed an affair of any great moment. Paul didn't want to become branded as a spy and talebearer who ran to authorities with nasty stories about his colleagues and professors. After all, he had only a few more months to go for his degree in surgery and could ill afford to stir trouble that could rob him of what he had suffered so many grueling years to achieve.

In that frame of mind it had been easy for Paul to rationalize that Mag, a wretched creature with nothing to live for, had taken the antimony herself to end her miserable existence. Antimony, a common and easily obtained substance, was frequently connected with homicide and suicide cases. In any case, Mag was dead and nothing in this world could help her now. The matter was better left to rest.

But murder? That was something he could not condone but at the same time had not wished to think about. Now, three months later, he could think of little else.

As he replaced the poker he heard the resounding slam of a

door from somewhere down the maze of dank corridors leading in from the quad. Two sets of footsteps approached, clicking in rhythm.

A voice suddenly called out:

"Paul—hallo, Paul? Goddemn it, Paul, are you anywhere around?" The cavernous old building picked up the echoes and bounced them back and forth.

Paul took a deep breath, exhaled it with a resigned sigh.

"In here, Alex," he called.

iv

Alex, the first to enter, was more formally known as Alister Duncan Malcolm Ushant, fourth son of Lord Craiglockhart as well as the joy and despair of that distinguished gentleman. Though he was two years younger than Paul, they were of the same college class. He was a bright enough student, but his irregular attendance at the college, due to drink, doxies and the turf, would have caused his expulsion except for the high connections and remarkable patience of his father.

Alex approached with an outstretched hand. "What the hell's up, laddie—hiding in this demned morgue like one of them?" He jerked a thumb at the cadaver on the table, which Paul had redraped. "I went to your digs, straightaway I had some news, and that hag landlady hadn't seen hide nor hair of your shadow."

As he shook hands with Alex, Paul glanced curiously at the man who had accompanied his friend. He had hung back a bit, darting nervous glances at the body on the table. He had, Paul thought, a grubby look about him.

"I couldn't sleep," Paul said. "It was as cold in my room as here, but no matter. . . . I spent the night here trying to work. What have you heard, Alex?"

"No good news, to come straight to it. I'm afraid it's a pretty rum go, and I am demned if I want to get into the telling of it in front of that wench on the table. I say we all go have a good stout breakfast, hey? The Bull's Head is the place, I think, for both talk and food."

Paul frowned. It was easy to be impatient with Alex. In the three years of their acquaintance they had had many fallings out, but one could not, for long, remain angry with Alex Ushant. One was attracted to his happy-go-lucky manner and was tolerant of his penchant for wild living that only birth and breeding salvaged from vulgarity. As for Alex, he was endlessly fascinated by Paul's tales of the American frontier and red Indians. Still, Paul was annoyed at his friend's dilly-dallying.

"Christ, man, I'm not concerned with stuffing my face! Tell me, what's the news? What the hell's up?"

Alex stepped back in a show of mock fright at the verbal blast. "I'll not tell it in this fornicating place. Come along and have a bite and a drink, and forget your demned pride. I'll only tell you this much now—all is not yet lost, for I've a plan or two knocking around in my brain."

Paul shrugged and nodded, then looked over at the stranger, who was at the moment peering under the drape that covered the corpse. The man pulled back with a grimace of distaste.

Alex snapped his fingers. "Demned if I haven't forgotten my manners. This is Robert MacCampbell, Paul. Mr. Mac-Campbell is a gentleman of the Press and at the moment in my employ."

This told Paul that Alex had again been to his mother for money. Lady Craiglockhart had her own private fortune and, fortunately for Alex, a nigh inexhaustible fund of love and patience. As Alex often put it, in laughter and drink, "A man has only to choose his parents well and he will have good fortune all his life."

The man who came to shake hands wore a dented beaver hat and a plaid cloak that had survived better days. His stock and high collar were long outdated, and such of his linen as showed was far from clean. His hand was cold and dampish in Paul's, the fingers ink-stained, the nails badly bitten. Yet he spoke like an educated man in a pleasant deep voice.

"My pleasure, Mr. Abbott. Alex has explained something of your predicament. It is possible that I may be able to help. But later for that. . . . Just now I have a more pressing matter." His thin lips parted to show yellowed teeth in an ingratiating smile. "Pray direct me to the loo."

Paul sent him off to the privy and confronted Alex angrily. "Have you gone completely loony? The last thing in the whole damned world we need is a newspaper writer in on this!"

His friend held up a cajoling hand. "Wait till you've heard it all. When you have, I think you'll agree that this is one of my better brainstorms. Come on, laddy buck, you can trust old Alex."

Paul shrugged in despair, then smiled at the expansive

grin on his companion's face. A more unlikely pair of friends, he thought, had never existed. Alex, a young man of birth and breeding, a member of the Scottish aristocracy, of which there were none prouder or more aloof; Paul, a frontier-bred American orphan, a penniless, fledgling surgeon with no clue to his real parentage.

Their attire was just as different. Alex carried a silver-headed cane with which he frequently tipped his billycock hat to a more rakish angle. His cloak was of dark tweed with a velvet collar. He wore tight and tubular trousers, in the fashion of the day—for Alex was a dandy—and a high-collared jacket of a hound's-tooth check. His linen was always immaculate, and he wore a tie of a violent silk magenta figured with tiny replicas of boxing men, reflecting, despite his high birth, that he was a man of the turf and the ring and had a penchant for what his parents deemed low company. The contrast with Paul's thin and frayed cheap garb was like that of a peacock and a sparrow.

Stroking his mustache, which reached almost to his thickish sidewhiskers, all of a dark reddish hue, Alex said, "I could do with a Black Velvet. So could you, my friend. The day is lang and mirk and going to be langer and mirker before it's over. A man stands in need of some fortification on a day like this." One of his eyes, which were of pure cerulean and at most times twinkling and clear despite his drinking, winked broadly. "And mayhap a bit of fornication to cheer your spirits, laddie. . . ."

Alex's reputation with the ladies was well earned, and though he often went to the bawds, his health was as yet unimpaired. Paul, who had neither time, money nor inclination for whores, had long since given up trying to talk sense to Alex on the risks involved. Thus far Alex had been lucky, not having contracted either a clap or the pox.

"For God's sake, Alex, I've got hooks in my guts! I've got to know *something*. In a word—what are my chances?"

Alex twirled his cane.

"Take your choice of two words, my friend—bad or good. Or both. I think we can save your arse, and maybe your neck—if we're lucky. That's the good. The bad is that you may have to get out of sight, out of the country, and wait till the storm blows over."

"Leave school!"

"I know, laddie, I know—it's hard when you're so near to the examiners and your certificate. But it's a hellish sight better than a hemp necktie or walking the treadmill for the rest of your life. It could, Christ forbid, come to the noose if matters go badly wrong. The town is gone barmy crying for blood and revenge."

"But you implied I do have *some* chance."

"There's a great deal here that doesn't meet the eye, Paul. There is flummery here, mean and nasty flummery. And hypocrisy and fear. Where there's fear there's lying and false witness. I have been looking deep into it—and spending a lot of Mother's money in the bargain—and I find a sinister chain of events. A scapegoat is needed—and not just that poor daft fool who is to swing this morning. The mob, and what is worse, the authorities, are after blood and in no mood to trifle. Hanging Fergus McIlwain isn't enough to satisfy them. They've got Jack Fordyce now, got him in the watch house and before the investigating committee, and they're welcome to him, the fat-arsed bastard."

"Has Fordyce talked?"

"You can count on him to spill his guts all over the room."

"But I did nothing! Nothing at all but keep my mouth shut."

"Aye, and that was your mistake. That's what they will try to hang you with—guilty knowledge kept to yourself."

They heard a distant flushing sound, and in a few moments, the sound of approaching footsteps.

"So here comes our friend," said Alex. "We'll go now and have a good breakfast and a few drinks, and try to get a smile back on that dour face of yours."

Paul lowered his voice. "How much does he know?"

"So far, just enough to interest him. He has promised to help if he can—and if he's paid enough." Alex winked. "It takes a small sum only to buy him. You can see that he is not prospering. I've been told these chaps make only a penny a line for their scribbling. A demned lousy profession, I would swear."

The three men left the building. Paul bowed into the shrieking wind as they skirted Surgeons Square. He had no greatcoat, and his feet in their thin, cracked shoes soon felt like lumps of ice as they trudged through sodden, slush-covered streets. They continued through Teviot Row on to George Square and the Meadows. Alex brandished his cane at several cabs, which only ignored him and went clopping on.

"Demned fornicating cabs!" said Alex. "Never about when you need one. Like the fornicating bobbies."

He swore again as another cab ignored them. A lady muffled to the ears stared down at them haughtily as the cab splashed by close, forcing them to jump back from the foul gutter water. The man on the box, whip in a frozen hand, looked like a forlorn bundle of rags.

The wind off the Firth came gusting with greater force now, swirling fog and smoke and cinders in wreathing curls about them. The gray sleet, turning to snow, was building white patches here and there in the mud. Paul walked bent forward, holding his silence. Never had he felt so low—and plain scared. The coils were slowly but surely closing in.

There was no use trying to deny that he *was* guilty—not guilty of the crime but of the blunder of concealing it. Not deliberately concealing it, but simply failing to report what he'd discovered. In the eyes of Scots law he was as guilty as the criminal himself.

v

Comfortably ensconced in a private room at the Bull's Head, Paul ate ravenously. Alex was paying the score, and for once Paul did not mind. For two years there had been no money from Iowa. Times were hard. His foster father, Jere, was being paid mostly in kind, and you couldn't send a pig or a bushel of potatoes by post. As a result, Paul had developed a pauper's mentality. His pride suffered on the rare occasions he allowed Alex to pay. It was needless, for money mattered nothing to Alex, being in his eyes only paper and metal to be rid of as pleasantly as possible. Still, it stung him to be always on the receiving end of Alex's generosity, and only because of the grim dilemma he was in now was he able to subdue his pride.

The hearty meal, along with four cups of steaming tea, cheered him—he had too long lived on dark bread, sausage and gruel—and for the first time he began to feel a spark of optimism. All might not be lost after all.

Alex lifted his goblet of Black Velvet—a mix of champagne and stout—and said in his broadest Scots, "Gie a smile, laddie, to gae alang wi a wee dunkin duris."

Paul broke into laughter. "What a fool you are, Alex, wasting your money on a man headed for the gallows."

Alex grimaced and took another gulp from his goblet. "It's

no waste when we have you smiling now and laughing a bit. Come have a drink, laddie. A bit of a drink will keep the cheer going."

Paul declined. During the past week, in an effort to soothe his nerves, he had drunk more than ever before in his whole life. It had tended to bring on nightmares. Dreams of home and Jeremiah and his foster mother, Sarah—and that terrible night when she had come entreating into his bed. . . . She was much younger than his foster father, a former dancehall girl, and Jere had married her to provide Paul with a mother. Paul had never condemned her, knowing that her invasion of his bedroom during the dark of night was only because her hunger for a man had grown too great—and his own fierce virginal hunger for the exploration of female mysteries had been fully as great. But it had been shattering to his conscience, a betrayal of his foster father and the image of motherhood that had nurtured him. He strove never, never to remember or dream of that night, for it always plunged him into depression.

The newsman, MacCampbell, had all this time shown no inclination to talk. He had devoted himself wholly to eating well and drinking even better. Now, after the table was cleared and the cigars brought, he left the table briefly to draw the green baize curtains to shut off the room. Then, leaning back in his chair, he blew smoke, and regarded his cigar with approval.

"An excellent cigar, Alex."

Alex tipped his own cigar in Paul's direction. "I think we had best get to it, Bob. Tell Paul what we know for certain, and what you propose we do about it."

MacCampbell leaned toward Paul, who for the first time noticed the look of a ferret about the man—the long nose, the undershot chin, the slightly buck teeth.

"First of all, Mr. Abbott, you will understand that men of my persuasion have what are called pipes. After pipelines, ye'll ken. Methods of obtaining information that your ordinary person does not have.

"Now I have pipes into this sad affair. Informants. They must be paid, of course, and Alex has most generously supplied the siller. Their information is not, I must admit, always accurate or truthful, but a man learns to discount."

Paul glanced restlessly at Alex, who held up a hand to be patient.

MacCampbell emptied his glass. "At present I have a spy in the police, and I believe his information to be genuine."

"And—?" Paul's fingers drummed the table impatiently.

"To keep it brief, Fergus McIlwain was arrested for a simple robbing and bludgeoning, as I take it, and at first came under no suspicion in the case of poor Mag Ferguson. He might have stood mute forever, is my guess, but he had the bad fortune to run into Inspector Olgivie. That was the beginning of the end for Fergus. Olgivie's a fiend for getting people to talk against themselves. It is not proper police procedure, but Olgivie cares not a groat for that. He twists them and turns them and leads them in and out of lies until in the end they have slipped the noose about their own necks. Such, it is my information, is what he did with McIlwain."

Alex nodded. "I've heard this Olgivie is a de'il for tracking down criminals. An old Covenanter with a long face and a tight purse and a tighter mouth."

"Aye, that's the bastard." MacCampbell took a sip from a fresh glass of whiskey. "They say that when the new laws passed and he couldna hang children for thieving, he wept. Be that as it may, when he got McIlwain, it was not long before the poor fool was telling all he knew or had ever done against the law. There are some who say Olgivie works alone in the cells at night with clubs and whips and such, but I cannot vouch for that."

MacCampbell leaned back and smiled in superior fashion. "Fergus McIlwain confessed a good deal to Olgivie that was never printed—which brings us to the moment. . . . "

Paul tensed.

"Olgivie has rummaged thoroughly into the affair, as you might guess. And kept much to himself. They say an iceberg is ninety percent concealed, and in this affair likewise. Concealed, that is, until Olgivie is ready to air it. And that, by my guess, will be right after the hanging of McIlwain. Olgivie is canny and is set on gulling certain persons into believing themselves secure while he builds his case."

"What other persons?" said Alex in a vexed tone. "You make it sound like a conspiracy."

MacCampbell smiled and tapped his nose with a dirty finger. "You see? You are like the others who think that when McIlwain is hanged, there is the end to it. Not so!"

"What else could Fordyce tell that's not already known? McIlwain murdered the whore and sold her body to Fordyce. He disclaims any knowledge of the murder, though he admits his guilt in the transaction for the body. This is all common knowledge, Bob, not what I paid you for."

MacCampbell, face flushed from his generous consumption of whiskey, waggled a finger at Alex. "Patience. Ye'll get what ye paid for. I must tell the tale in my own way or not at all, for there's much to be kenned and 'tis hard to hold it all in the mind. Now then—

"Olgivie, the bloodhound, has a hatred of his betters. His origins are low, and that no doubt accounts for it. He's convinced of a conspiracy among the professors, the swells and the nobs, to the very top." His gaze shifted back to Paul.

"He thinks that through some student or students hard up for shillings, Fergus McIlwain was encouraged to murder. Promised that if and when bodies were produced, no questions would be asked."

Alex clipped the end from a fresh cigar. "Olgivie is out of his pumpkin."

"Be that as it may, Olgivie is certain that the antimony that poisoned Mag Ferguson came from the infirmary."

Alex seemed to choke a bit on his stout, and Paul too felt a sudden new shock of fright.

"Jack Fordyce and I alone among all the students had access to the antimony," he said. "If it was taken it must have been by Fordyce."

"Fordyce denies that he knew anything about the poisoning. He admits taking the body to the college. He admits paying McIlwain a pound for it. Since Mag had no relatives and would have ended in a pauper's grave in any case—a shameful waste of a good cadaver, he says, with all the colleges so hard up for bodies—Fordyce insists he committed no crime but only did a good service. And no harm to anyone."

Alex chuckled grimly. "No harm indeed—except to that poor drab. He'll be demanding a medal next."

MacCampbell shrugged. "What's important in the matter is that Fordyce stands firm to his story. He thought the woman died of natural causes."

"Has he tried to cast suspicion on me?" said Paul.

"Not in direct words—he's too sly a rascal for that. My guess is that he's protecting someone above—the person or persons who put up the money for the purchase of bodies in the first instance. Fordyce *has* to protect whoever it is in hopes that they in turn will help him get off. At least with a light sentence. If he peaches on the real culprits and brings them into the net, how can they help him? So what does Fordyce do? He sets the police off on a false trail. He claims no knowledge of any poison. It is beyond his ken to believe that even a dram of poison could have been in poor Mag, says he, because if so, *you*, Mr. Abbott, would have found it when you opened the corpse."

Feeling another clutch of fright, a dismal sense of sinking deeper into the mire every moment, Paul stared back into the newswriter's cavernous eyes.

"It's true I opened the body—but how does Fordyce know of it?"

"He claims he revisited the college very early the same day, having gone to his rooms only for a bite of breakfast and a wee nap. His story is that you were gone when he returned, but that he found the body open and Mag's organs in a jar. That is the rogue's story, Mr. Abbott, and he won't budge from it. It substantiates his claim of no poison. For had there been poison, says Jack Fordyce, you would have found it and reported it immediately."

MacCampbell paused to add weight to his next words: "And you did not."

All too true, Paul thought miserably. *It's none of my affair,* he had said, and now he was being hounded by it.

"Is that the sum of it, Bob?" said Alex. "That's all your pipes have to spill?"

"Aye, for the moment. But there will be more as the matter progresses. My pipe is very close to Olgivie, and he hears most of what goes on."

Paul gave him a puzzled look. "If McIlwain confessed everything, as you say, why did he not also accuse Jack Fordyce of supplying him with the antimony? It *must* have been Fordyce."

MacCampbell nodded. "Aye, sir, you have hit on a weak spot. As to whether McIlwain ever made such an accusation, my information stops short of that. However, I do have a theory of my own."

Alex interrupted brusquely. "I'm not paying you a hundred quid for theories, Bob."

"Hear me out, mon! I agree that Fordyce must have supplied the poison. But he hasn't confessed to it. As sure as the inspector may be in his own mind that Fordyce is the man, all he has is McIlwain's word for it that he, McIlwain, poisoned poor Mag. There is even the lack of the body for proof."

At this, Paul felt another icy, sinking sensation in his belly. Mag's body was gone—but not her bones. Her skeleton, a prime specimen, was wired together and hanging in his own lodgings, as Fordyce and other students knew.

After the corpse had been dissected and all the organs discarded, he had painstakingly scraped, washed and bleached the bones, then wired them together to make an anatomical specimen. With luck, some young doctor just setting up practice would pay as much as twenty pounds for such a skeleton, though of late business had not been brisk.

What more "proof" did they need? Mag's bones up for sale in his lodgings would certainly be considered as additional motivation for supplying the poison.

"So what we have is this," MacCampbell went on. "Fergus McIlwain is to swing in any case—in less than two hours now—and for the moment the law is satisfied. But not Inspector Olgivie. As I said, he hates his betters and seeks to bring them low. As of now Jack Fordyce is the key to that end. He is leaning heavy on him to get leads to the others involved, and at the same time he will be allowing some hope to Fordyce—but when the mulcting is done and Fordyce can tell no more, then I would not value his neck at a ha'penny. Nor the necks of any others he will soon be tangling in his web."

"If all you say is true, why haven't I been arrested, or at least taken in for questioning?"

"I do believe, Mr. Abbott, that you would have been taken in charge before now were it not for your friendship with Alex."

Alex's gloomy countenance brightened a bit and he fell into his broad Scots dialect. "Aye, he'll nae want to fash wi' the laird."

Paul thought that the writer was probably right. Lord Craiglockhart was a wealthy and powerful man. Though he didn't entirely approve of Alex, he would protect him. And, many would assume, his son's friend.

But not if a charge could be proved against him. Even a lord couldn't go against the laws of the country.

MacCampbell glanced sadly at the empty bottle and dry-washed his inky hands. Alex ignored the hint. MacCampbell continued, addressing Paul:

"There is another reason, sir, and you will forgive me if I cannot be delicate about it. About your status in life, sir. . . ."

Alex growled, "What has that to do with anything?"

"The facts must be faced. Mr. Abbott has no money. No social position. In short—and be sure that Olgivie has looked into all these matters—he sees Mr. Abbott as little better than a pauper medical student who can be handled at any time."

Paul had shrunk within himself. To hear himself described as a pauper and nonentity by such as MacCampbell was blunt reality indeed.

"The plain fact of it, Mr. Abbott, is that the inspector *will* get to you whenever he's of a mind to do it. His men will be keeping you under close observation until the time is right."

"What's that, mon!" Alex's voice rose in alarm. "You mean Paul's being followed? Spied on?"

MacCampbell smirked. He had saved this upsetting bit for the last and was evidently enjoying the effect.

"Aye. Olgivie trains his men well for such purposes. They will be following to see where Mr. Abbott goes, who he talks to. They will be watching the Bull's Head this very moment, you can wager on that, though I doubt you'll see them—until they are ready to be seen."

Noting again that no more whiskey was forthcoming, he pushed away from the table and stood up.

"It has been a pleasure, Mr. Abbott, and I trust I have been of some assistance." Turning to Alex, he went on:

"There's one other small matter, Alex. Olgivie will be very curious as to what we discussed here today. I am certain to be questioned and would do well to have my wits about me to protect your interests when that happens. Could I have a word with you in private?"

Alex and MacCampbell left the room together and Paul knew the writer leech would of course be asking for more money. He wondered what it was costing Alex. It gnawed at his conscience. Yet he had no choice but to accept all the help he could get. Without Alex Ushant, he would be behind bars at this very moment. The clock boomed a quarter to nine.

Alex came back shaking his head. "Yon's a sharp weasel. A reifing mon, as the laird would say. But all in all, I think worth his cost in this affair. It is no bad thing to have a friend in the newspapers. The idea being, my lad, that if you are taken and charged, you will receive fair play in the Press. All the same, I think we will not let it come to that. We must take steps, laddie."

Paul shook his head glumly. "What steps? With Olgivie's bloodhounds watching, what else can I do but sit and sweat and wait for the ax to fall?"

Alex beckoned for a new bottle, then turned to Paul with a grin.

"Bullcock to that, laddie. We're going to put our heads together and scheme a way of getting you out of this. You're going to make a run for it."

TWO: Flight

AFTER Fergus McIlwain had kicked his last and was lowered from the gallows, those appointed by the college came forward to receive the body.

Paul Abbott was in the vanguard, for the recovery of cadavers was one of his college chores. He was accompanied by two porters carrying a plain wooden box, and a carter was standing by to convey it.

Quickly the corpse was boxed and on its way to the wagon through the dispersing mob—in the main a sullen, disgruntled crowd because old McIlwain had died too speedily, without much kicking. To his last breath he had done all possible to spoil their entertainment.

As the box was being loaded on the wagon, Alex Ushant came shouldering through the mob to whisper in Paul's ear.

"I think I have twigged them—two of Olgivie's bully boys. Plainclothes and eyes like weasels. Taking a great interest in you, my lad, and trying to be sly about it. It's best you pay them no heed. Just follow every detail of my plan and we'll bugger them yet." With that, Alex slipped a few bills in Paul's side pocket and disappeared into the crowd.

Paul rode on the front wagon seat with the carter, with the two porters seated on the box behind. By now it was snowing heavily and the wind was shrieking in from the Firth in near gale force. The garments of all four men were soon plastered almost white by the driving wet snow. Paul's mood was almost as bleak as the elements. His friend's "plan," it seemed to him, stood about as much chance as one of these white flakes would on a hot stove, but what other choice did he have?

None indeed, except the very likely chance of ending up in another box—perhaps the same box—on this very same wagon.

Turning, he spoke to the other three. "There's a public house just ahead, and we're all half-frozen. I suggest we stop for a noggin of something hot." He produced the bills Alex had slipped in his pocket and held them up. "The score's on me."

A few minutes later, the four men trooped into the public bar, where they ordered rum and hot water, leaving the box containing the remains of McIlwain alone in the wagon to gather a mantle of snow.

Paul at once paid the score, then excused himself on the pretext of making a visit to the privy. Instead of going into that odorous cubicle, however, he continued down a short hallway to the kitchen and into a mews, and thence into a back street near the Cannongate.

At the first intersection, Alex was waiting in a hansom cab. "Quick now, mon—jump in!"

Soon the cab was clopping away at a fast clip. Alex removed his hat and greatcoat. "On with them," he ordered Paul.

The greatcoat was a bit large and the hat was ill-fitting. Still, the fit was not so bad that it couldn't be mended with strips of paper padded inside the sweat band. Meanwhile, Alex was producing a handful of pound notes and gold coins. Two hundred pounds.

"It's all I could lay my hands on at such short notice, laddie, but it will get you to the States and a little to spare. I enquired the steamer rates—not so high as I thought—and there will be the canal to pay, and then the train."

"The canal?"

"Aye, a clever fancy of mine come late. Canal boats are out of fashion these days, with the trains racing at forty miles an hour, and I'm wagering those bastards of Olgivie's will never think to look there. So you go by canal to Glasgow and then a train to wherever you've a mind. Or a boat from Glasgow, for that matter—though I wouldn't advise it, for sooner or later the good inspector is going to twig that he's been done, and then he'll set a watch on the near ports. Better to get far away, and fast."

Paul was beginning to shake off the nightmare and think for himself, but he could find no flaw in his friend's reasoning. Alex knew the ways and byways and conveyances of the British Isles far better than he did. He felt a new surge of hope.

"And by the way, laddie, I sent my father's man Hogg to your room to fetch your belongings, which weren't extravagant in number." His foot indicated a battered portmanteau and two small medical bags heaped on one side of the floor. The portmanteau would contain little but his few precious books, shaving gear, a few shirts, collars, socks and ragged underwear, all soiled. More important were the bags containing his medical kit and surgical instruments, as old and third-hand as they were. He had scrimped and saved enough to purchase the instruments at a pawnbroker's shop where some student, even more destitute than Paul, had "popped" them.

"You've forgotten nothing! I can't figure how you managed it all in so little time."

"A bit of coin of the realm helps, though it may take more than a wee bit of explaining if Hogg tells the laird. Which he may have to do. . . . Ah, well, I will face the laird when I must."

Knowing his friend's spending habits, Paul surmised that the money had probably been borrowed at the usual usurious rates from money lenders. Paul assuaged his conscience about being such an expense to his friend by reminding himself that his need was so dire. For Alex, lack of money was only a temporary inconvenience; he was, after all, the usufructuary of his mother's fortune.

But on reaching the canal terminus west of the city, having thought it prudent to avoid Leith and Grangemouth, Paul knew that in all honesty he must bring up the matter. He was by nature a taciturn man whose feelings ran deep, and was shy when it came to expressing them. Now, at a loss for words to articulate his affection and enormous gratitude, he took resort in wryness.

"I hope you will have no need of the money for a long while, Alex, for God only knows when I can repay. You know my situation—who better?—and knowing, it is doubly noble of you to lend. But for your help, I would more than likely, at this moment, be in a cell with less chance than a cardboard cat in a dog's hell. All I can give you, my dear friend, is my deepest gratitude and a promise to repay when I can."

Alex too had emotions he sought to hide. Falling into the broad cant he used at times to disguise his feelings, he said,

"Dinna fash yersel o'er it, laddie. I've nae need for the siller at the once, ye'll ken, and if I did, I'd go meeching to her ladyship for it. What the laird dinna know canna harm him."

With a comradely clap on Paul's shoulder, he picked up the battered portmanteau and led the way aboard the canal boat. Paul followed with his medical and surgical bags. Alex flung the portmanteau atop the narrow shelf bed.

"At least we got away with your traps."

"Not to mention my life," said Paul with a laugh. He slipped off the greatcoat and handed it to his friend.

"No, no," Alex protested. "You'll freeze your nuggets else. And I have a dozen such. I only wish there had been time to visit my place and outfit you properly."

So as horses were brought up and hitched to the bow rig, they parted with a handshake. Alex again patted his shoulder and punched him in the chest and said, "Ye'll ken, now, not to write for a time. A year at least. Give the scent time to cool and time for the hounds to tire."

Then with a final embrace, Alister Duncan Malcolm Ushant took his leave. Paul watched him walk to the waiting hansom where the patient, shivering driver was furred with snow. Alex turned to wave, and then in a slither of wheels and slipping hooves—the horseshoes were not calked for icy roads—the carriage disappeared into the swirling murk.

Had any man, Paul thought, ever known a better friend!

ii

He spent the whole of the long slow haul in his tiny cabin, only occasionally glancing out a diamond-paned, leaded window at the drab industrial countryside. The Union Canal snaked through a maze of mills and factories, in and out of locks, over water bridges and under road bridges, and at last into the suburbs to wind past the cots and crofts of country folks. The boat was hauling a cargo of green hides bound for the tanner in Glasgow, and the rotting smell invaded the cabin. Inured as he was to the more loathsome odors of the infirmary and morgue, Paul did not mind.

He retired early in the cramped bunk, at once sinking into a deep and satisfying sleep, the first such in weeks. He awoke at dawn, much improved in body and spirits, his belly rumbling with a wolfish appetite. Even this early there were food vendors at some of the locks, and it was a struggle to resist the promptings of hunger as the boat awaited its turn to pass through. He decided to remain in hiding in the cabin, for Inspector Olgivie might have sent out men to ask questions along the canal route.

He was relieved when the boat finally tied in near the ancient Boomielaw quay in Glasgow, where he at once hailed a cab to the Buchanan Street station, urging the driver to hurry. Within an hour he was aboard an express for London, four hundred miles to the southeast.

At one of the few stops made by the express, he purchased food at the station counter, gulping down scalding tea and carrying sandwiches back to the train. Famished as he was, the mediocre food seemed like a kingly repast. The tensions and strain of the past weeks were lifting and he was feeling a sense of renewal, almost elation, at having escaped the dark mess behind him.

With a new buoyancy of spirits, he detrained at Euston Station and set out strolling through London streets. The weather was much milder than it had been in Edinburgh, with a weak sun showing now and then and occasional spates of rain.

Having decided to discard the billycock—it did not fit properly even stuffed with paper—he stopped at the first hatter's shop and bought a beaver of moderate crown. He went next to a mercer's store and purchased a supply of shirts, socks and underwear. To these he added some ties of somber hue as well as a cravat and collars, and a pair of wash leather gloves. Going thence to a shoemaker's, he rid himself of his miserable old shoes, donned fresh new socks and was fitted with new shoes, paying dear for them, but good shoes he must have. People noticed shoes. If he was to set up as a respectable physician, he had to look the part and hang the expense.

At a street kiosk he purchased several London papers, and burdened with his purchases and bags, sought out a barber's parlor, where he had a shave and his hair shortened somewhat. The shorter hair was Alex's idea.

"Change your appearance all ye can, laddie, for when Olgivie finds the fox is gone, he'll be sure to have your description printed along with a polite little notice to the coppers to seek to interview ye about a small matter—meaning give yersel up, do yer duty as a law-abiding subject of Her Fat-Arsed Majesty and save Olgivie the inconvenience and expense of catching you."

He found no mention of himself in the papers, but much

space was devoted to the hanging of McIlwain. The more vulgar sheets had pulled a very long bow in describing the condemned's last agonies, though in fact he had died quickly and quietly.

Only the *Times* editorialized, expressing hope that the demise of the ghoulish murderer would nip in the bud any return to the terrible days of body-snatching and heartily approving the harshest measures to prevent such horrible crimes. The final paragraph hinted that there might be more fire than the present smoke indicated:

> . . . it is reported to us from Edinburgh that the execution of the malefactor, Fergus McIlwain, may not entirely close the matter. There are rumours, very ugly rumours, that the blame for this appalling murder and sale of a body may reach higher than has heretofore been suspected. We refuse to engage in speculation, for it is the duty of this newspaper to report only factual information. We put our trust in the police and the laws of our great country and hope, and know, that if there are indeed other malefactors, they will surely be brought to book.

Feeling a chill slither down his spine, Paul went through the papers a second time, seeking the name of Robert Mac-Campbell over a dispatch, but found nothing. Yet he was positive that MacCampbell could not be trusted to keep the matter secret for long. Such inside information was more valuable to sell now than it would be later. He might have already sold his scribblings about it to a news syndicate, which in turn sold such items to papers in many countries. Once Paul's involvement became known to the Press, his name would doubtless be published abroad. Along with his description.

With this discouraging thought he left the barber's, hailed a two-wheeler, and piled himself in with his bundles and luggage. Giving the jehu the address of a transient hotel on Portobello Road that he had gleaned from an advertisement as being very cheap, he settled back and tried to relax. It began to pour, and as the two-wheeler clattered through drenched London streets, he wondered if Alex, by seeking information from the sly MacCampbell, had not created a Frankenstein monster. Even if he escaped this damned mess in England, it could follow to haunt him no matter where he went in the world.

iii

The Half Moon Hotel was a dismal structure set back on a street of the dingiest collection of shabby buildings Paul had ever seen. A couple of dismal cats and a dismal dog slunk past as he debouched from the two-wheeler and pushed through a wicket gate into a melancholy little courtyard fronting the hotel. The windows in its upper stories were like empty, dead eyes, only a few boasting ragged curtains, and the whole building wore a coating of soot and smoke. Only because of the hard spattering of rain did Paul hasten his steps to the entry of this forlorn namesake of the moon.

Inside he was greeted by the dank smells of dry rot, wet rot and a whole melange of unidentifiable odors except for the vague pungency of unclean water closets. Inured as he was to odorous places, he hesitated, then reminded himself that the rates were cheap and he must conserve his dwindling cash.

A thin and grubby desk clerk eyed Paul sullenly when he asked the rate for the cheapest room.

"Our specialty is cheap rooms, an' one's as bad or good as the next. A shilling each for the night."

Though he thought the rate far from cheap, Paul didn't relish going back out in the rain to seek other lodgings that might be even more dear. Besides, the less he was seen on the streets, the safer he felt. Accordingly, he paid three days in advance, which mollified the clerk enough so that he tossed him a key attached to a wedge of wood inscribed with a room number.

"One flight up on the left."

The room was small and dark and had a musty smell. Placing his bundles on the hard and narrow bed, Paul went to the dirt-encrusted window to raise it for air. After a struggle in getting it up, he was about to put his head out when it came slamming down like a guillotine—the sash cord had rotted away.

What an irony that would be, he thought, chuckling—after all this trouble running from the hangman's noose, beheading myself in a hotel room!

Finally settled in, he got out his money and counted it, careful as any miser, and thought he had spent too much. Still, there was no help for it, and more expenditures were necessary. On the morrow he must find a clothier's and purchase a suit or two of a respectable material, not too costly.

Carefully he put most of the coins—nearly thirty pounds—into a sock and tucked them away into the portmanteau. They were too heavy and bulged too much to carry in a pocket. The paper notes were replaced in the worn wraparound wallet secured with a leather thong that he had carried since Council Bluffs days.

His plan was to let several days or a week elapse, to let the trail cool, meanwhile venturing out only after dark to purchase the other items he needed.

To that end, on the following morning, he took his breakfast in. It was served by a frowsy chambermaid with a smudge of soot on her nose.

"Tha'll be four an' a ha'pence," she said, putting down a tray that held a plate of fried kidneys and eggs, two hard rolls and a mug of steaming tea. " 'Tis robbery, if yer was to ask me, but I don't set the prices around 'ere, yer understand. Is there anything else yer'll be wantin', sir?"

"Yes. I'd like several of the early papers," he said as he paid her, giving her extra coins for the papers.

"In 'alf a mo', sir." She took the money and scurried out.

Before he had finished eating, she was back with the papers.

"That was certainly fast."

"I made 'aste for yer, sir. 'At's alwis bin my worst fault—'aste. Anything else, sir?"

He thought a moment. The stale air in the room was making his stomach a bit squeamish. "I would appreciate it if you could manage to find something to prop that window open to let in a bit of fresh air."

"Yes sir."

This time it took her considerably longer to return—doubtless because of personal grooming. Not only was the smudge gone from her nose and her face washed shiny and clean, but she had removed the frilly, soiled workcap that had half-hidden a mass of golden hair. For the first time Paul noticed that she was quite pretty and quite young, with eyes of brightest blue and very red lips. She had a bit of kindling wood.

" 'Tis the best I could find, sir."

Together they got the window open and the wood propped under it. Waves of outside air of another kind of staleness, redolent with street stink, rolled in.

"Anything else I can do fer yer, sir? Anything a-tall?" She smiled, one hand fussing with her hair.

He ignored her unmistakable meaning. "Not at the moment, Miss—"

"Marigold, 'at's me name. Marigold Clumm."

"Marigold, I'd like to arrange to have all my meals brought to my room for the next several days, and all the daily papers."

Her eyes scrunched thoughtfully. "Yer wouldn't be hidin' out from the coppers, would yer now?"

He felt rudely jolted. Was his fear so apparent? He forced a laugh. "Oh no—it's nothing so dramatic as all that. It's just . . . I'm recovering from an illness and I was advised by a doctor to spend as much time as possible resting."

"Yer look 'ealthy enough ter me, but if it is the coppers yer dodgin', yer got no worries from me. I wouldn't go narkin' on me worst enemy. Copper's have to kill me first. Sop me gob they would."

When she was gone, he began a diligent search through the papers for mention of himself, finding none, but in one news item about the McIlwain affair were a few lines that jolted him with new worries:

> . . . It has been revealed to us by reputable sources that London detectives have entered the investigation of the dastardly murder of Mag Ferguson and that a startling new development leading to another malefactor involved will soon be disclosed. . . .

Could they have trailed him to London? Were detectives even now combing all London hotels? He had registered under a false name, but of course they would have his description.

It was imperative that he leave London as soon as possible. But first he needed a decent suit.

He went back to the papers to look for a clothier's ad, but his attention was caught by an advertisement of a different sort:

> A Ship's Physician is wanted for a single (return) engagement to serve as *locum tenens* for a regular Physician who is ill. The undertaking to be a sea voyage from Southampton to New Orleans, with a call to be made at the port of New York. Remuneration will be agreed on at the time of interview. Any interested party may call at either the London or Southampton offices of the British and North American

Royal Mail Steam Packet Company, at which time all details
will be given. In the City, 12-1/2 Upper Thames St.—in
Southampton, 172 Empress Dock Road.

Eagerly he slit out the ad and tucked it in a pocket. What
a godsend it would be if he could obtain the position! Counting the new suit he needed, he would soon have spent about
fifty pounds, and steamship fare to America would be a large
expense, with no income in sight.

Anxious as he was to get moving, he decided it was safer
to wait for darkness before venturing out to buy a suit and
a ticket to Southampton.

He spent the rest of the day pacing about restlessly. Now
and then he went to the smeared window and stared out into
the miserable but busy street, listening to the cries of the
hawkers and sweepers. This is but a taste of what it must
feel like to be a caged prisoner, he thought.

When Marigold came with his supper—a fatty-looking
chunk of boiled beef and cabbage and a tankard of ale—she
looked at him with a commiserating smile.

"Yer look down in the mouth, yer do. Look's though yer
lost a tanner an' found last year's Derby sweep ticket. Ain't
good ter be cooped up all alone in this 'ere room. It'd give
anyone the monkeys. Wot yer need is ter get out an' wet
yer gob." Her smile turned coy. "If yer'd like me to show
yer around to a few pubs . . . "

Glancing at the unappetizing supper, he made a quick decision. After all, detectives wouldn't be so likely to pay much
notice to a young man escorting a girl.

"That's a nice idea, Marigold. Perhaps first you could
guide me to a clothier's for a purchase I want to make, and
after that we can go someplace for dinner."

" 'At's the style, duckie! Wait 'ere one shake of a nanny-
goat's tail while I go an' get dressed pretty. . . . "

iv

With no trouble they found a clothier who kept late hours,
and Paul bought a suit of somber dark broadcloth off the
rack. Then, hailing a two-wheeler, they went to Paddington
Station, where Paul said he wanted to check train schedules.
Marigold waited in the carriage while he went into the
station and purchased a second-class ticket to Southampton
on the London & Southwestern, leaving at six the next
morning.

Afterward they were soon clattering through a maze of cobbly streets and bestrewn alleys cloaked in mephitic glooms, and punctuated at each corner by asthmatically spluttering gas jets. Marigold directed the driver to an unprepossessing café, over the doorway of which hung a blue lantern glowing like an evil eye.

Inside the atmosphere churned with rough and sinister-looking customers and odors. The dirt of many years, tobacco smoke, whiskey, beer, frying fish and sweaty flesh allied themselves in one grand assault against the nostrils. All made weird by the pallid bluish lighting.

"It's run by a Chinky, an' the food is like nothin' yer ever et before. 'At's why I brought yer 'ere."

Paul grinned his appreciation, beginning to enjoy himself. Marigold was neatly dressed in a long dark skirt and white frilly blouse, cut daringly low, showing the tops of snowy-white breasts. The baggy old working dress she had worn at the hotel had concealed a nicely shaped, lissom young body. He guessed she was no more than seventeen, although her eyes had the wisdom of ages.

"I think we should have a bottle of wine," he suggested after they were seated at a small corner table. "Along with our dinner, of course."

"'At's the style, duckie. Live 'er up, I always say, 'cos we're a long time dead."

They were served by a scrofulous-looking waiter with brawny tattooed arms and an aura of sweatiness. He quickly brought the wine, which quickly went to Paul's head. So much that he was not too aware, nor too caring, about the food, which in a vague way he knew involved rice, fish, dried sharks' fins, rare pickled eggs twenty years old, bitter melons, lychee fruits and other items he would never remember. The wine had an exotic taste and was much stronger than any wine he had ever known. Furthermore, Marigold had taken it on herself to order another bottle. She seemed unaffected by it. At one point a drunken sailor came close to the table and leered down at her. Her voice jabbed out at him like a whetted knife:

"Get orf wiv yer, old cock! Beat it or I'll sick the coppers on yer!"

The man beat it, crestfallen.

"I don't take no kibosh from nobody, mind yer," Marigold said proudly.

Somewhat later they were back at the hotel and he was

unlocking the door of his room. By this time his head had cleared and he well knew what he was doing.

Hardly were they inside the room, still dark except for stray fragments of light slivering in from the street, when he turned to take her in his arms. Her arms came around him at once in a starved kind of way and she returned his kisses impetuously, greedily. After a few moments she drew away.

" 'Old it 'alf a jiff, duckie, till I get me duds off. . . . "

V

On the narrow bed their naked bodies lay interlocked. He was showering her with kisses, on her lips, cheeks, neck, down to her breasts . . .

"Easy there, duckie," she said, gently pushing his head away. "I don't go fer any a that Frenchy stuff. . . . "

Her words jarred him only briefly, because it wasn't Marigold the chambermaid who had set his blood storming, but Woman. He was so starved, so starved—he had been so long without a woman's love—and the supple young body of soft warm curves was so delicious to hold, to fondle. He wanted to gobble her up in his arms.

Her hands had found his hardened organ. "Oh Gawd—" she said in an awestruck whisper. "Oh my Gawd!"

Eager as he was, with the blood thundering in his head, he was in no hurry. He wanted to savor every moment of the excruciating joy of unfolding the mysteries of her body.

"Whatcher waitin' fer, duckie?"

At his entry, she let out a gasp and soon began rhythmic, almost mechanical, responses to his thrusts. All too soon the unbearably pleasant sensations began rising toward a climax. Her fingernails were clutching into his back. A shuddering started up his spine and then the long-pent-up ejaculate spasmodically found its release, merged with her murmurings of pleasure.

For a while they lay armlocked, relaxed. She began singing in a pretty little voice:

> "Roll me over
> In the clover,
> An' les' 'ave a go a' it agin. . . ."

Her playful fingers brought his organ again to instant

hardness, and he rolled back into the willing cradle of her spread thighs.

This time she bounced around under him joyfully, more uninhibited, and as his joyance stretched out, all the tensions of the past weeks seemed to drain away into a blissful timelessness. . . .

Afterward he lay utterly relaxed, with Marigold cuddled against him like a contented kitten, and soon fell into deep sweet sleep. From somewhere in the distance a big clock was sending twelve crashing notes through the night. . . .

vi

He awoke suddenly with the notes of the clock still reverberating in his ears and saw gray dawn streaming through the window. After five notes, the clock was silent. Five o'clock! And the train left at six!

He rolled out of bed, only then remembering the girl, who was nowhere in sight. Perhaps, he thought, she had gone to the water closet down the hall. A terrible thought seized him and he leaped across to where his jacket hung over the back of a chair. Reaching to an inside pocket, he was flooded with relief at the feel of the wallet—a feeling that swiftly changed to panic as his fingers detected that the leather thong around it was undone.

With a sinking heart he took it out—yes, its fatness was gone—and opened it.

All that remained was a single note and the ticket to Southampton. At least she had been considerate enough to leave him that.

In a spate of fury he gathered all his things together and left the hotel. Reporting the robber to the police who were looking for him was impossible, as was the folly of trying to track Marigold down. He could prove nothing.

All he could do was kick himself for being the biggest fool on earth. Because of his stupidity he had lost the bulk of the money that good old Alex had gone to so much trouble to get for him. All for a roll in the clover, pleasurable as it was.

But recriminations were also a waste of time. He had barely more than thirty pounds left with which to escape from England and find passage to America.

All that was left to him was hope that he might obtain the position as ship's physician. It was his last chance.

THREE: The Clytemnestra

CAPTAIN Caleb Cunningham, of the H.M.S. *Clytemnestra*, was in an evil temper. At dinner the first night out in a February gale that was roiling the Channel, he confided to Paul that he didn't like it. Didn't like it at all, this damned business of making a special, unscheduled stop at Le Havre.

"Damned greedy shipowners," he grouched. "Kowtowing and kissing arse for a few extra pounds! Thinking nothing of my schedule or the comfort of my passengers. What do they care? Sitting on their fat arses in the comfort of an office and counting their sorrows. Well now, I am a fair man and I will admit they do have sorrows. The Collins line is slitting our throat with a dull knife, and the Admiralty might commandeer the old *Cly* any day now to carry troops and supplies to the Crimea. All right, that's as bad as damn-all, but I've my ship and passengers to worry about. They come first with me, always have, and damned if I'm not going to be heard from in this matter."

Paul nodded and tried to look properly sympathetic. Which wasn't too hard, as he was still elated at having obtained the position of ship's physician only that morning, and with surprisingly little difficulty. His old Certificate of Medicine from Iowa, granted by the local preceptors after two years of apprenticeship with Jere and attendance at a few medical lectures, had been enough to satisfy the captain. He surmised that the shipping company was in dire need of a doctor and couldn't afford to be choosy.

After settling into his modest cabin, he had explored the infirmary, seeking—and finding—the mercury preparation he would need in case Marigold had given him the pox. He took some comfort in the belief that she was not a professional doxie and was probably free of disease, but for the next week or so he would be sweating it out until he was sure.

Now, at dinner at the captain's table as he listened to the loquacious master of the ship, he was content enough with the relief of having at least escaped from England, and with a job that somewhat blunted the bitterness of having been robbed. The other two at the table—First Officer McKeon and Chief Engineer Slattery—occupied themselves mostly with eating and nodding. They were evidently accustomed to the captain's domination of table talk.

Cunningham fixed Paul with piercing, ice-blue eyes. He was a thin, weathered man in his fifties with graying side-whiskers and mustache. Paul had judged him to be of a splenetic temperament on the basis of his harsh, gruff questions during the interview, and he trimmed his sails accordingly.

"It was bad luck," said the captain. "Cursed bad luck. An hour earlier and we would have been away. Damned inefficient stewards never do anything properly."

Paul nodded agreement, not having the faintest idea of what the damned stewards had done improperly, meanwhile clinging to his chair as the dining saloon—all plum-colored plush, thick Turkish rugs and coruscating chandeliers—tilted to leeward, hovered a moment at a down-sloped angle, then swung back to starboard. Shakers, vinegar cruets and assorted bottles slid down to be caught by the fiddle. Gimbaled lamps, unaffected by the plunging ship, shed a steady soft glow of yellow light. There were but a scant dozen people at the other tables. Since leaving the shelter of Southampton Water, the sea had become increasingly rough. All afternoon Paul had been kept busy dispensing digestive powders to the first- and second-class passengers—none to steerage—and he now reminded himself that soon he must get back to the infirmary and mix a new batch against the morrow. Luckily, he was not himself affected by *mal de mer*.

McKeon and Slattery got up to go about their duties. In departing, Slattery gave Paul a sly wink, as if to impart the sympathetic message that the new man always caught the guff.

The captain stared over his wine at Paul. "I doubt you understand why I'm so damned angry. So I will inform you, Dr. Abbott."

He held out a hand and began to count off on his fingers, as though making separate indictments.

"In my normal manner of sailing I could have left Southampton and made some westing behind the Isle of Wight. Which would afford some protection from the blow, you understand. Not that it is all that much of a gale, but confounded uncomfortable for those not accustomed to weather."

The ship rolled and creaked alarmingly to port, and there was a sudden increase in vibration. Even in his vast ignorance of such matters, Paul surmised that one of the great side paddles was out of water and racing without restraint. It might not be much of a blow to the captain, he conceded—a mere teacup of wind—but it was more than enough for himself. He would never be a seaman, nor did he desire to be.

"As it is," Cunningham went on querulously, "I must cross the broad reach to Havre—exactly the widest spot in the Channel, sir. The damned worst and widest, and this the poorest time of the year."

Paul, thinking of his infirmary and the batch of digestives to be mixed—not that they were of much avail to the afflicted—entertained the notion of rudely breaking off the conversation by pleading duty, then thought better of it. The matter was not all that urgent. Most of his patients—some fifty-seven of them—were gagging and puking in their cabins, wishing for death and too ill to summon him in any case.

The captain slopped more wine into his glass, spilling a bit as the ship pitched, her bow smacking the sea with a resounding hollow sound before going into a long shallow roll.

"Damned telegraph can be a curse, you know," he grumbled. "Can fetch a man up short. Upset all his plans at the last minute. The message came over the cable from Calais. Dover sends it on to Southampton. Delivered to me at dockside half an hour before I should have sailed—and would have, too, were it not for those damned dunderhead stewards—and once it's in my hand and signed for, then I'm buggered. No way out of it. I'm under orders to cross the confounded Channel in this damned brew-up and fetch the Frenchies aboard."

"Frenchies, sir?"

The captain nodded and drank more wine. "Four of them —three women and a man. Not real Frenchies, as I take it. From New Orleans, what they call Creoles. To be treated with all courtesy and every consideration. Oh, the message was explicit enough about that—London itself got onto the Southampton office to see to it."

Paul's interest was whetted. He had never been to New Orleans, had not in fact been farther south than St. Louis, but he had heard of Creoles. His imagination had been stirred by tales of the Sugar Coast and the fabulous city on the Delta.

"They must be very important people, sir. And very

wealthy, to have the ship make a special out-of-the-way stop
for them."

Cunningham scowled. "Damned if I know how important
they are, but you're right about the money. They must be
rolling in brass and ready to spend it, else the company
wouldn't be so anxious to kiss their arses. The Creoles have
taken the Victoria suite, which otherwise would have gone
empty this voyage, at twenty pounds a day."

Cunningham broke off his carping and gave Paul a stabbing, thoughtful look. "How do you find matters in the
infirmary?"

"Well enough equipped, sir. A bit small, but adequate. The
other man—a Dr. Palmer, I think?—seems to have left
matters well in hand. The place is tidy enough and I've
begun to catch on to his system of storing."

"Did they tell you anything at the office about Palmer?"
the captain asked wryly.

"Only that he'd been taken ill and couldn't make the
voyage."

The captain snorted. "Palmer's an old man—too old for
his work, and a drunk in the bargain. I told them that time
and again, but they never listened—not until this last time,
as I have it, when he ended up in a hospital. So that's why
you're here."

Rising from the table, he added, "It's an ill wind, eh?
Well, Dr. Abbott, I'll leave you to your duties for now.
Which shouldn't be too onerous now that you've dosed them
for the pukes—and a lot of good that will do. Good night,
sir."

ii

Alone at the table, Paul glanced about the saloon and saw
there was still a single diner here and there, and at the far
end of the long room a family of four—obviously a momma
and papa and two small boys. The *Clytemnestra* seemed to
be rolling and pitching with more violence than before, and
though Paul was no longer bothered by the wild movements,
he would have begun worrying whether the ship could hold
up under such severe battering had it not been for a re-
assuring talk earlier with Slattery, the chief engineer. An
outgoing, friendly chap with a rubicund nose bespeaking a
fondness for drink, Slattery was much in love with his
engines, seizing every opportunity to speak of them. Paul

had heard more of shell boilers, inverted beams and side-lever engines than he really cared to know. He had no mechanical turn of mind.

Both Slattery and McKeon had assured him at the beginning of dinner—before the captain arrived to take over the conversation—that a little blow like this was nothing to the *Clytemnestra*. She was very new, iron-hulled and of three thousand tons displacement. A veritable floating palace, three hundred and eighty feet from bow to stern, with two red-and-black funnels—like plump tall hats—and a full set of sails for her three masts. She boasted the latest Napier engines, and a high bridge linked her two huge, embossed paddle boxes.

Slattery then had explained why the *Cly* was making the extended and unusual voyage to New Orleans.

"It's the bloody war. The Admiralty has been snatching up every bottom in sight for the Crimea. For troops and horses. They've commandeered near all of Cunard and now they're looking about again. The company figures to keep the *Cly* at sea as long as possible and cheer for the war to end. Might happen, too. I read we been giving the Russkies bloody what-for."

There came a tap on his shoulder.

"Excuse me, sir, but you seem to be as alone as I am. And with a long face in the bargain. Would you be caring for a hand or two of cards in the smoking lounge?"

Startled, Paul turned and stared up at the speaker, who had flaming red hair and sidewhiskers. He was plainly drunk, though he managed to stand well enough and go easily with the roll of the ship. He smiled at Paul.

"My name is Quinn, sir. Michael Quinn. Mike to my friends—of whom I trust you will account yourself one, at least for the duration of this pesty voyage. I am a lone man, sir, and likely to remain so unless I can find a companion. Would you be caring for a drink perhaps? At my expense?"

Paul had no desire to appear surly, and indeed there was an air of bonhomie about the fellow that forestalled curtness. Irish, Paul guessed, at least a touch of it, with the façade of a gentleman and an educated man. So instead of a brusque word and an abrupt departure, he smiled and indicated an adjacent chair.

"Sit down, Mr. Quinn. My name is Paul Abbott. I'm the ship's physician, for this voyage at least, and I'm not a drinking man." He smiled again to take the edge off his words, and added, "Not in the way I take you to be."

Quinn laughed and sank into the chair. He returned Paul's stare with eyes of clear cold blue, only slightly reddened by the liquor he had so obviously consumed and in stark contrast to his red hair and rosy complexion.

"Damme, you've diagnosed me rightly enough, Doc. I've had a fill of the gin and whiskey tonight, and no doubt will be the worse for it tomorrow. I'll be in your cubby for a draught in the morning, you can bank on it. But how about it? If you won't drink with me, how about a hand or two of cards? Whist, nap or trump, swabbers? We can make do with just the two of us, y'know. Play dummy or solo."

When Paul shook his head, Quinn sighed heavily and gazed at the empty wine bottle.

"Damme, but 'tis a dull ship, I will vow to that, and on the first day out. There's naught aboard but family men with their good wives watching every penny, or old men who all look like undertakers, or old ladies who would screech at the sight of a playing card."

He sighed again and held up the empty bottle. "And now it appears the wine has run out."

"If I were you, Mr. Quinn, I would not add wine to whiskey."

"Well now, Doc, at least the advice is free. I don't suppose you'll be sending me a bill for what I already know, will you now? Not that knowing and doing are the same thing, mind you. Not at all, they aren't. But I am grateful for your thought."

Chuckling, he beckoned to the steward and ordered a fresh bottle of whiskey, saying to Paul, "I shall take your advice and restrict myself to the good Irish drink. You're sure now that you won't join me?"

"Thanks just the same, but I have work I should be doing."

"Work is it? Surely not sawing off arms and legs at this hour?"

Paul grinned. "Nothing so drastic. I have powders to mix for draughts in the morning—for stomachs such as yours will be."

Quinn nodded wryly. "Right enough. I may be along. But it's a usual thing with me, a bad stomach in the morning. As a rule, a glass of water with a dollop of brandy does me well enough."

Then, persisting, he added, "If dummy whist doesn't tempt you, how about some poker? Do you know the American game?"

Although not a gambler, Paul had been taught the rudiments of poker by Jere. His foster father, when riding his medical circuit, always packed a deck of worn cards in his bag.

"I know a straight from a flush," he said, smiling, "and I am an American."

Michael Quinn struck his forehead with the heel of his palm. "Of course! It's blind I am—or deaf, rather. Or too drunk to know American speech when I hear it. I should have tumbled."

He added shrewdly, "But you've been away for a long time—that I would wager on. There's a bit of Scots in your tone."

Paul explained briefly how this came to be, but at the same time he was examining Quinn with a more discriminating eye. Alert observation, as old Professor Guthrie had drummed into him, was the forte of any good diagnostician.

"Observe your patient—*really* look. You must see beyond the surface, under it. His occupation, habits, his whole mode of life—they will all leave signs which can be read if you're astute enough. There are many times when a patient will not or cannot tell you things you must know for a proper diagnosis. In such cases you must find out for yourself."

Quinn appeared to be about thirty. Tall, over six feet, with a sturdy physique just beginning to go to fat. There was a blurring of chin into throat and a bit too much belly beneath the double-buttoned weskit. Alcoholic fat. Paul had learned much about alcoholism from Jere.

Otherwise, Quinn was well featured and clean-shaven, except for the sidewhiskers, with a firm mouth and chin. The nose was big, with a slightly flattened bridge, as though from a blow long ago, but all in all it was a handsome face. Still, there was a certain shiftiness around the eyes, which Paul for the moment discounted as a purely subjective reaction. It was hardly following scientific principles to judge a person too speedily.

Although he was well turned out, the checked pantaloons and jacket suggested that Mike Quinn was indeed a raffish character. The weskit had faked gold coins for buttons, his linen was not precisely immaculate, and his stock was plain maroon worn with a high cut-throat collar. It was not any one of these items but rather the sum total that led to Paul's appraisal that the man was a gambler, a drifter and a gentleman of fortune.

Not unaware of this scrutiny, Quinn gave Paul back stare for stare with an amused grin.

"I hope that we're going to be friends, Doc. I'm going all the way to New Orleans, and as I made clear, it looks like a dull and profitless voyage."

Paul laughed. "I'm sure, if only from circumstances, we'll be seeing quite a bit of each other." Quinn's assumption of easy familiarity was not much to Paul's taste, but he held to the man's credit his frank admission that he was after profit. There was even—though for the life of him he could not put his finger on it—something likable about the man.

The steward came with the whiskey and Paul used the interruption as an excuse to leave. Rising, he said, "Good night, Mr. Quinn. I hope you will *not* require one of my medicaments in the morning."

Quinn smiled and raised a hand on which flashed a showy ring. "Good night, Doc. And don't forget—my friends call me Mike. As for the draught, if past experience is any teacher, I'll be calling on you in the morning."

iii

Paul's modest cabin and the adjacent infirmary were well to the stern. Here the first-class passengers were as far removed as possible from the vibration and commotion of the giant paddles. Descending to B deck, Paul made his way aft, clinging to the handrails as the corridor lurched and rolled. There were no steam heaters in the corridor, and by the time he reached his cabin, his hands were numbed. He decided to let the digestive powders wait until morning and go straight to bed.

Locking the cabin door, he undressed rapidly and pulled on one of his new nightshirts—more largess from Alex. Outside, the waves roared and the wind wailed, and the locked porthole glass was constantly streaming water from the gale-whipped seas. Even here at the stern, the steady flailing of paddle wheels and juddering of motor transmitted their vibrations in peculiar humming rhythm through the cabin. After a time he found it not unpleasant, and soon drifted into sleep.

FOUR: The Creoles

PAUL awoke early, suddenly aware that the ship was in relatively quiet water. The engines had been rung down and speed had lessened. Peering through the single porthole, he saw lights moving past, then realized it was only the ship moving, not the lights. They were getting into Havre.

After washing and dressing, he had a pot of coffee brought to the infirmary by a steward and set about crushing and mixing his peptic powders. Above the workbench was a calendar advertising a Paris medical-supply house, portraying a smiling *demimondaine* in an enormous hat and scanty frock and displaying a daring eyeful of shapely calf. With a wry grin, remembering Marigold, he took a pencil and crossed off the days up to the present—the ninth of February.

Twelve days since the hanging of McIlwain. Twelve days on the run.

With the powders mixed, and since it was too early to go about his rounds, he adjusted the swinging oil lamp and began taking inventory of the stock.

A quick scan of the bottles, flagons, jars and flasks indicated that the *Cly*'s pharmacy was fairly up to date. All the old standbys were there: camphor, senna, nux vomica, sal volatile, both ether and chloroform, quinine, calomel and colocynth and the like. There was a goodly supply of vinegar and brown paper for superficial bruises and plenty of muslin, linen and sticking plaster for more serious injuries. On another shelf were burners, phials, retorts and some fine glass-stoppered flasks indicating that Dr. Palmer might have done some experimentation before being overtaken by alcohol. Beneath the bench was a small keg of ipecac roots which needed pulverizing and preparation. He took a few from the keg to smell and feel, judging them to be of Cartagena origin—*Cephaelis acuminate*.

He tossed the roots back with a laugh. The last thing needed aboard the *Cly* this morning was an emetic.

ii

Under a leaden dawn blurred with thick mist, three steam tugs poked and prodded and pulled at the majestic *Clytemnestra* to usher her to the quay. Two of the tugs were sidewheelers, one a sternwheeler, and mingled with all their fussing and splashing about could be heard spates of excited French. Now and then McKeon and the captain bellowed through their trumpets as the thick hawsers came thumping aboard. At last the big ship, her engines dead, began to glide toward her slip.

Paul turned away from the porthole in the infirmary where he had been watching, deciding to go on deck and watch the Creoles come aboard. He had completed his rounds, finding nothing among the passengers other than a few minor ailments, easily disposed of. The infirmary had been scrupulously scrubbed and the stock rearranged, and was now in shipshape order. There was little else to do with his time. Besides, he had never seen a Creole, let alone a person rich enough to alter the schedule of a giant shipping line, and he was curious to get a look at them.

Donning his new hat and throwing Alex's greatcoat over his shoulders like a cape, he went topside. A new shouting and a great tweeting of bosun's whistles had arisen as the *Cly* was nudged into her slip. Almost at once the gangway was set into place and from the bridge McKeon was trumpeting, *"Vite, vite!"* at a line of porters starting to bring luggage aboard. His bad French in a Scot's accent appeared in no way to energize the porters. Paul could sympathize with them. He had never seen such piles of rich-looking luggage: immense boxes, trunks, valises, portmanteaus and hat cases. The rich did not travel light.

Climbing on one of the great paddle boxes, which was cleated with a small roped-in space at the top, Paul surveyed the scene. Lanterns and gaslight illuminated the murky dawn, and patches of mist lay over the harbor. It had rained during the night, as was evident from the pools and puddles that spotted the cobbled quay. The steam tugs were standing by, chuffing back and forth, and the huge ropes attached to the *Cly* had not been made fast to the quay bollards but were simply belayed, with deck hands standing by to cast them free at a command. Plainly, Captain Cunningham did not intend to tarry. They awaited only the new passengers.

iii

There was a clatter of hooves on cobbles as a barouche came
wheeling down the quay, the shoes and rims striking an occasional spark in the dull morning light. The folding top
was up, shielding the passengers from Paul's view. On impulse, he left the paddlebox observatory and went down to
stand near the gangway. Here, more sheltered from a stiffening westerly breeze, he watched the new passengers debouch
from the carriage and come aboard.

First to come up the gangway was a Negress, a lithe young
woman with a skin like a coffee bean, what he could see of it
beneath a veil and saucy hat. Her gloved hands were thrust
into a tiny muff of black fur. She stepped to one side and
waited.

Paul's interest, at once piqued by the black woman—was
she a Creole?—shifted to the three persons now ascending
the gangway. Nothing had been said of an invalid, but the
tall man being assisted up the incline by two women most
certainly was one. An irritable one. It was plain from his
expression and the angry tone of his muttered words that he
hated the assistance from the women even as he was forced
to accept it. He was richly dressed in gray and wore his
greatcoat, like Paul, in cloak fashion over his shoulders. For
this there was a reason—his right arm was in a sling and
beneath his jacket showed a bulge of bandages.

Both women were white, and heavily cloaked against the
weather. They wore bonnets, one plain, the other trimmed
with a fluted band and a spray of ostrich feathers. Doubtless
the latest Parisian creation. The one with the fancy bonnet
was veiled, and being entirely solicitous of the man, did not
glance at others around her.

The other woman looked Paul's way for an instant. Her
wide-set eyes, in a strong and attractive face, were a deep
brown. Her steady gaze, as it swept over those watching
their arrival, was cool and inquiring.

On impulse, Paul stepped forward and raised his hat.
"May I be of some assistance to you, ma'am?"

Her eyes stabbed at him for a moment, and her rather full
lips quirked in the faintest suggestion of a smile. For a
fleeting moment she seemed to be studying him. Then she
shook her head and looked away.

"I think not, sir. We can manage quite—"

She was interrupted by a soft sweet voice with the faintest

slur of accent. "If you could direct us to the Victoria suite, sir, it would be most helpful.".

Before he could answer, the purser and Captain Cunningham—the latter trying to hide his anger at the inconvenience caused by these high-paying guests—bustled forward with a retinue of stewards to attend to the situation. Excluded for the moment, Paul took occasion to study the male passenger.

Standing at the end of the gangway, one hand on the ship's rail for support, the man showed a singular lack of interest in the proceedings. Paul guessed why—the man was very ill. He should be in bed at the earliest possible moment and under treatment for whatever his indisposition might be, instead of standing about on an exposed deck getting thoroughly chilled.

A capricious harbor breeze at that moment did a sudden turnabout, swirling inboard, and Paul caught a whiff of something putrid—the deadly odor of gangrene. There was no mistaking it. He'd been in too many surgical wards, had smelled too much pus and sloughing dead flesh to be in error. The man's bandages were saturated with such exudations.

Paul moved a few steps closer for a better view of the man's face, which only confirmed his first diagnosis. The man's eyes were bright with fever. What would normally have been a sallow—and Paul would have bet, malarial—complexion was flushed with red. As he drew nearer, the sweetish-sour stink of pus was more apparent.

The sick man, who seemed to be in his early thirties, came out of his pain reverie as he became aware of Paul's scrutiny. Stiffening his posture, he pulled his shoulders back and scowled at Paul.

"And what the hell are you staring at, sir?" His voice had the same fluid slur of speech as the veiled woman's.

Paul bowed slightly. He knew that this one would be a difficult patient. "I am the ship's physician, sir. My name is Abbott. Paul Abbott. At your service, sir."

Then, because he hadn't liked the man's arrogance—a touchiness only worsened by his recent misadventures—he added, "You're going to need my services, sir—take my professional word for it. And the sooner the better. I can smell gangrene on you at this moment."

The tall man glared back at him. "Gangrene, eh? I had hoped never to hear that word."

"You're hearing it now, sir. I would like to look at that arm as soon as possible."

The man's mouth twisted into a half-laugh, half-sneer. "Why not? What harm can one more butcher do? I've had the arm looked at and bungled about and probed into as if it were a practice leg of mutton. By all means, sir, come and do your damnedest."

Paul nodded. "I'll be there shortly."

He stepped back then as the purser and Captain Cunningham—the latter nearly as hypocritically obsequious as the former—escorted the party aft to the Victoria suite.

Already thinking in terms of amputation—he would guess at a disarticulation near the shoulder—Paul lingered at the rail to watch the ship get underway again. Not a moment had been wasted. The quay, some of the lights still burning in the mist, receded as the tugs hauled away the *Cly*'s bow, then raced around with an impudent snorting and chuffing of engines to her stern to push. Soon they would be at sea again in the Channel, and though the gale had blown itself out there would still be rough water. He had never operated in a rolling, pitching room. It would require restraining straps, that was certain, not so much to hobble the patient's struggles as to keep him on the table.

Returning to the infirmary, he found Mike Quinn, the gambler, waiting outside puffy-eyed and sick-looking.

"Morning, Doc, though I can't say there's anything good about it. I'll be having that draught after all, lacking a hair of the beast."

Following Paul in, Quinn glanced around hopefully. "You'd not be having a dram or two? I woke up this black morning with an empty bottle."

Paul shook his head. "I'm not running a bar."

He mixed a draught of magnesia and seltzer, and picking up the speaking tube, ordered ice brought. While they waited for it he fashioned a bag of muslin.

Quinn, after some belching and curious glances around the infirmary, said, "So the Creoles got aboard? I hear they're rich as sin. I wonder now, are they card players?"

Paul grinned, at the same time wondering why he liked the rascal.

"You're not as close to death as you feared," he said. "Nor as sick—not if you can be thinking about a new easy mark to cheat."

Quinn bridled with offense. "Who says I cheat?"

Paul waved a hand. "I'm sorry. It was a poor joke. Let it go."

Michael Quinn smiled and shrugged his thick shoulders. "To be honest, my friend, I seldom cheat, only because I seldom have to. The pure fact of it is—and no blarney—I am better at cards than most people. I win without cheating. It's only when I run into another professional, or a man with a real stunner run of luck, that I might try a trick or two."

The steward arrived with a bucket of ice. As Paul filled the muslin bag as an ice cap for the man, he said, "I'm glad you told me. Remind me never to play with you—should I ever get that crazy."

Quinn slapped his shoulders. "No fear. I never cheat with friends. But about those Creoles—do you think a man would stand a chance of profit? A straight game, of course. Four of them, I hear. Three women and a man. Now there's a whist table, and—"

Paul shut him off by plopping the ice bag on his head and pushed him out the door. "Best forget it. The man is very ill, and the three women are obviously ladies. I doubt they'd be interested in playing whist with you, Mike. Or anything else. Now, if you'll excuse me . . ."

Holding the ice cap on his head, Mike bowed.

"Yes, your worship. This is one Irishman who can take a hint. I am gone. Mayhap I will see you later in the saloon or lounge."

After Quinn left, Paul pulled the long narrow operating table away from the wall and fell to scrubbing it with a solution of carbolic. There was no slightest question in his mind that an amputation would have to be done, but only that it might be too late. Blood poisoning might already have set in.

In that case, there would be a burial at sea.

Or perhaps not, since there was a plentiful store of ice aboard, and the Creoles were rich enough to afford it. It was February in the North Atlantic, and with the ice to help, quite possibly the corpse could be preserved for the ten days of the voyage.

He washed his hands carefully, then rolled down and fastened his cuffs. By this time the ship was again feeling the Channel weather and rolling a bit. The oil lamp hung steady in its compensating gimbal over the operating table.

Next, he opened his surgical bag and began to select the instruments he would need and one by one cleansed them with the carbolic solution.

His array of instruments was sparse. He had three bone saws, several large and small forceps, a pair of iridectomy scissors, some small knives of his own devising and four scalpels of various sizes. The scalpels were wooden-handled with cross-scoring to ensure a firm grip. He took special care to scrub the riveting, where bits of flesh and blood had a tendency to adhere.

For diagnostic purposes he had a percussion hammer and a stethoscope of the trumpet type. He had read of George Camman's invention, the binaural stethoscope with ear tubes, but had never seen one and could do without. He had an unusual knack for auscultation, having opened hundreds of corpses after the fact and found to be proved right in his diagnosis fully eighty percent of the time. Nor did he have a pulse watch, or even a watch at all—it having long ago gone to the pawnbrokers—and no minute glass. No matter, for he had long been expert at timing a minute.

He glanced at the flasks of ether and chloroform on the shelf. The Creole gentleman, if it came to amputation, was going to be one of the lucky ones.

Finished with the cleaning, he went over to the voice tube, and after a delay spoke to the purser. A Mr. Perry, as he recalled.

The purser sounded irascible. "Yes? Yes? *Who?* Oh yes, Doctor, what is it you want?"

Although the purser's office was just above the infirmary, Paul had to shout over the tube. "An invalid's wheelchair, Mr. Perry—do we have one aboard?"

"What—what's that? . . . Oh, a chair, you say . . . an invalid's chair. Should be one right there in the infirmary, Doctor."

"There is none here."

"You're sure?"

"I'm sure, dammit! I am not blind, Mr. Perry."

After a series of unintelligible sounds, which Paul took to be cursing, the purser allowed that the chair might have been put into a storeroom. "I'll send someone to look at once. Has there been an accident, Doctor?"

Paul assured him that there had not, and directed that the wheelchair be sent to the Victoria suite.

iv

Taking with him the medical kit, he left to visit his new patient.

He was admitted by the Negress, who though dressed as finely as the two white ladies, he now presumed to be a maid. She didn't look well and during his entry she gave him a piteous look of entreaty as she dipped in slight courtesy, placing a hand on her stomach.

Paul smiled. "I'll give you something presently. Where is the gentleman?"

She pointed toward a door, which at that moment opened. The unveiled woman, to whom he had first addressed himself on deck, came into the room. Through the opened door behind her he saw the man in bed and the other woman—now without her hat or veil—seated beside him holding his hand. A book opened to a page lay on the bed between them.

The deep brown eyes appraised him steadily as she came forward and held out her hand—a mannish gesture to which he was not accustomed.

"I am Fern Venable—companion and private secretary to Miss Sylphide Beauvais. You are Dr. Abbott?"

He nodded as he took her hand. Her palm was cool and dry, and he thought her fingers clung to his a bit longer than might have been expected. She was of moderate figure, though rather full-bosomed, and it struck him that she surely wasn't wearing a corset—a camisole perhaps, or not even that, for her breasts moved freely beneath her dress.

Releasing his hand, she looked at the Negress. "Mr. Pierre is burning with fever, Aurora. Will you fill a jug with the coldest water you can find and take it at once."

"There's plenty of ice aboard," said Paul. "All you need do is summon a steward. Now, Miss Venable, if I may see the patient. His name is—?"

"Pierre Gayarre of New Orleans. You have not heard of him?" Again the dark brown eyes probed into him, and again he had the sense that her examination was for some particular reason. It was disconcerting.

"I'm afraid I have not had that honor. Should I have heard of Mr. Gayarre?"

Miss Venable's full, and, Paul thought, rather voluptuous lips parted to show dazzling white teeth. She shrugged. Her full breasts moved beneath her dress.

"He is very wealthy," she said, *sotto voce*. "One of the richest men in the South. Most men are alert to such things. . . ."

She stepped aside to permit him passage to the bedroom.

As he entered, the other woman rose from beside the bed.

She was slimmer of figure than Fern Venable, he noted, and tightly corseted. Her loose and flowing gown was of a rich brocade with a flounced bodice and a high tight neck caught with a cameo pin. He was a bit surprised, because he had vaguely imagined all Creoles to be dark-haired, to find that she was a blonde. Though not an ordinary blonde. Caught in masses atop her head and well pinned back, her hair was a rich coppery gold, which intensified the depth of her dark-blue eyes. Sylphide Beauvais—though he could not know it at the time—was that not altogether rare phenomenon, a blond Creole.

She made no move to shake hands as had the Venable woman—he had the impression that such a familiarity would never occur to her—nor did she speak, but stood gazing at him from great blue eyes alongside a pert and patrician nose. Her lips were less full than Miss Venable's, but delicately shaped, as was her smallish, determined chin.

Bowing slightly, Paul placed his bag on the bed. "I would like to be alone with the patient, ma'am."

The blue eyes blinked and she compressed her mouth in a tight line of anger. For the first time she appeared to acknowledge his presence—unflatteringly. She glanced at his medical bag, her expression making her distaste obvious. To the man on the bed she said, "Pierre, darling—wouldn't you prefer that I remain with you?"

The man held up a gaunt left hand. "Do as the good doctor asks, Syl. And don't worry. I think I can hold my own with a ship's sawbones. You might tell Aurora to hurry with the cold water. I'm dying of thirst."

She left the room quietly, closing the door behind her. Paul picked up the man's left hand and took the pulse. As he expected, it was rapid and thready.

The patient regarded him with eyes that were jet black and sparked with a touch of scorn. "What happened to your watch, Doctor?"

"I left it for repair in a shop in Southampton. It wasn't ready in time. I had to sail without it." Putting the hand down, Paul drew back the bedclothes. "Now let's have a look. . . ."

Pierre Gayarre, who had been struggling to sit up from stacked pillows, now fell back and said, "By all means. As I told you before, do your worst. I hardly see how you can maltreat me more than your colleagues in France have already done."

"Can you raise your right arm at all?"

"Not a damned inch."

"Are you in much pain?"

"Most damnable pain, sir."

There was a knock at the door and the Negress entered with a jug of water. "Dad ice no come," she said.

Paul took the jug and poured a glass of water, handing it to the patient with two morphine pills. Then he set about cutting off the arm of the nightshirt, which was of fine silk. The bandages beneath were soaked with pus and the smell of primary gangrene was fetid.

"I make it a point to be truthful with my patients, Mr. Gayarre," he said while scissoring the bandages away. "When they're up to the truth, that is—which I deem you to be."

Gayarre scowled. "What is that supposed to mean?"

"There's every chance that you are going to lose this arm."

The man regarded him with absolute hate, and Paul, still scissoring away, only smiled while taking full measure of his patient's physiognomy.

It was a long and narrow head, a dolichocephalic type with a cephalic index definitely below eighty—a common enough European type. The hair was of darkest black and worn a bit longer than the current fashion. The face was also long and bladelike, the nose aquiline, the mouth wide and thin-lipped. The complexion was without doubt of a malarial hue. There was a thin mustache and not much in the way of sidewhiskers. It could be, Paul decided, a pleasant enough face when not contorted with pain, anger and disgust.

With the last of the pus-saturated bandages cut away, Paul looked at the bared arm with dismay. It was worse than he had expected. From elbow to shoulder it was half again its normal size, the flesh swollen and tight and darkened by rubic colorations, with purplish-blue and yellow predominating. The stink of it filled the bedroom.

"One hell of a goddam sight, is it not, *m'sieur*? And cursed bad luck, too. My dueling arm, for your information, so there can be no question—no question at all—that it must be saved. Understand that clearly, Doctor."

"We'll see as to that. . . ." Paul rearranged an oil lamp on a bedside taboret and bent for a closer look under the better light. The entrance wound was just above the elbow, an ugly purplish-black hole, and the festering flesh around it was beginning to crack and slough. Gently he picked up the arm in both hands, extended it and tried both elbow and shoulder for articulation. Gayarre winced and stifled a moan, but apparently there was no breakage.

Again he examined the wound, which was the size of a penny, with a raw and ragged edging. It exuded a thickish green-yellow pus. He wondered if the man realized how close he was to death.

He lowered the arm. "How did you come by this?"

Gayarre, whose strong white teeth had been biting his lower lip to ease the pain, grimaced. "The fellow shot me, dammit. A fair enough exchange, I suppose, since I killed him—but damned bad luck all the same. His shot came late —a reflex it must have been—and struck me just after I had fired."

"A duel?"

"What else, my good doctor? I'm not in the habit of shooting men—or of being shot at—as a matter of daily routine."

Damned fool, thought Paul—risking his life on the chance spin of a bullet!

However, this was none of his affair. Taking a small knife from his bag, he leaned over the arm.

"Be prepared for a bit of pain, Mr. Gayarre."

"As I told you, do your damnedest. The dueling surgeon botched it, and later the French quack botched it again. For your information, Doctor, a part of the bullet is still in there. The last butcher probed and probed, near killing me in the process, and never did get it all."

Paul scraped with the knife. Gayarre cursed. He scraped again, making a little trough in the flesh about an eighth of inch deep and of a pale-gray color. Slough. Grainy and weeping, with the typical smell of rot.

He showed Gayarre a fragment of flesh adhering to the knife. "You seem to be an outspoken man, Mr. Gayarre, and so I must be. Gangrene has set in and is now in an advanced state. I see nothing for it but to take off the arm."

"No!"

Paul stared grimly at the man. "I would give that answer more thought if I were you. You're feverish, Mr. Gayarre, and not thinking too clearly. Try to comprehend exactly what I'm saying—if the arm doesn't come off, you're going to die."

Gayarre lay back on the pillows, breathing hard, face flushed, his too-bright eyes staring back in defiance. After a moment, he said, "Are there any other doctors aboard this ship?"

"No." Paul had indeed scanned the passenger list, hoping to find a colleague.

"Then your opinion must be final? You, sir, are the resident god?"

"I hadn't thought of myself that way, but I suppose that in this instance it comes to that."

Gayarre was silent for a moment, studying Paul. Pale drops of sweat dotted his forehead and cheeks.

"But you can't take off the arm without my permission."

"Of course not. It's your arm, sir—and your life. Which you'll certainly lose unless you let me amputate—and may lose in any case. I can offer you no guarantees, sir."

Gayarre managed a smile. "It sounds, Doctor, like a case of damned if I do and damned if I don't."

Paul was studying the arm again. All his instincts, training, and experience told him that amputation was the only chance.

"The wound is old and rotten," he said. "It's been badly treated—worsened instead of bettered—and the bungled probing certainly didn't help. How long has it been since you sustained this?"

"Three days. Three days ago I killed the miserable foulmouthed bastard in the Tuileries and have been on the run since. He was the son of a crony of the Emperor, as it turned out. I didn't know—not that it would have mattered if I had. We were given three days to leave France, and had it not been for Eugenie—"

Paul held up a hand. "There's no need, nor the time, for your personal history of the wound, sir. We must get on with it."

Gayarre scowled. "It has just come to me, sir Doctor, why I dislike you so much. It's not just because you are—like most doctors—a charlatan and a quack. You are also a Yankee. By God, sir, a damned Yankee! It just dawned on me. I've just placed you, for which I am a slow fool. I took you to be an Englishman, or a Scot."

Paul took no umbrage; he had dealt with far worse patients. This was fever talking. Fever, fear and near hysteria. Men wouldn't admit to hysteria, but it was as prevalent in them as in females.

"It doesn't matter a damned whit, sir, if I'm a damned Yankee or not. Now speaking as frankly as I may—do we or do we not take off the arm? Or do you prefer lying here in agony to die of blood poisoning and slow rot? It's not a pleasant death, let me assure you. I've seen it often and I know. But if you insist, if you persist in being a pig-headed fool, then I'll just have to leave you to it."

Somebody tapped on the door and opened it a bit. It was Fern Venable. "The wheeled chair is here, Doctor."

"Thank you, Miss Venable." Closing the door, he turned back to the bed.

"The chair is here to convey you to the infirmary, sir. Do we need it? What is your final decision?"

Gayarre glared at him. "I refuse. I will not lose my arm. I will submit to anything else; I will endure any treatment you propose—but no amputation."

"That is final?"

"Absolutely final."

Nodding, Paul picked up the arm again and extended it, bringing another groan from Gayarre. Silently Paul studied the limb from a new and different aspect. It was a very slim chance, but since the man refused amputation he must still do his best. With barely any hope for success. He continued to survey the arm, not simply as an arm but as bone, humerus, a shaft and two extremities. He looked below the putrescent flesh and saw the greater and lesser tuberosities, the bicipital groove, the long tendon of biceps muscle and the anterior circumflex artery. For that would be the problem—to excise the rotted flesh, clear away the gangrene without slashing an artery, and leaving as much healthy tissue, muscle and tendon as possible.

He shook his head, not at all sanguine. This was the first operation he had ever faced that he didn't really want to do.

Gayarre saw the shake of Paul's head. "What is it, man?"

"All I can do is try a radical debridement. That means carving away all that rotted flesh as deep and far as it goes."

"Then, for Christ's sake, do it! Do it and leave me my arm. You should have told me that first instead of all this wasted talk about cutting the whole arm off."

"Once again, Mr. Gayarre, I want you to be sure of what you'll be in for. The chances are very long against the operation succeeding. I may not be able to cut out all the gangrene, if it's extended too far. And if I do succeed in saving the arm, there won't be much of it left. Understand that, sir. I will have to remove a mass of muscle and tissue. You won't have an arm left in the sense that you had it before—and you certainly won't get any use from it. Do you understand that?"

A curious change came over Gayarre, a sense of complete

calm. In a temperate voice, with a sad smile, he said, "I understand, Doctor, so let's get on with it. . . . And if you'll accept my apologies for bad manners, I would be pleased. I'm a fool and an inexcusable boor when I'm in pain. And"—his thin mouth quirked wryly—"when the hell is scared out of me. So do what you must, and I'll suffer it. But I must have your word as a professional man and a gentleman that you will not cut off the arm."

Paul smiled. "The word of a Yankee?"

"I'm sorry for that, sir. I told you I am a damned fool. I have the honor of knowing many Yankee gentlemen."

"Then you have my word, sir. I won't take off your arm. If you die, as you probably will, it will be with two arms. Or at least one and what is left of the other."

"Will there be ether or chloroform? Or do you intend to fill me with whiskey and give me a bullet to bite on?"

"You'll feel nothing. There will be a deal of pain afterward, I assure you of that. I can give you morphine for it."

"One more thing, Doctor . . . please call the ladies into the room—and the nigger, too. I want them to hear our agreement."

"As you wish, sir." Opening the door, Paul summoned the three women into the bedroom. By this time the *Cly* was well into the Channel and the waves were beginning to run large again. The bed tilted and yawed as they gathered about it, clinging to whatever support could be found. The book the Beauvais woman had been reading fell to the floor. Paul bent to retrieve it, noting that it was Stendhal's *Armance*. He had always read as much as he could, going beyond medical matters, but was not familiar with Stendhal. He put the book on a stand.

The Negress turned away from the bed and went to one of the two chairs in the finely appointed room and flounced into it, pulling her gown down over high-buttoned shoes. Her dark eyes stared defiantly at Paul.

"Dad ice not come still," she said.

Pierre Gayarre raised his good hand. "Syl, Fern"— Gayarre glanced over at the black girl—"and you, Aurora. Hear this. The good doctor is going to perform an operation on my arm. He has promised not to take it off. I wanted all of you to hear this in witness. This is so, Dr. Abbott?"

Paul nodded curtly. "True. I have promised. Now, if you think you can trust me to keep that promise, let's get on with it."

Gayarre sighed. "I am ready whenever you are, Doctor."

Sylphide Beauvais spoke up: "What can we do to help?"

"I would like a new nightshirt put on Mr. Gayarre, with the right sleeve cut off at the shoulder. Then see to it that he is well bundled against drafts and chill. After that, have him wheeled to the infirmary.

"I'll send along two men to assist," he added. "One of you may accompany him if you wish, but only one, and you must have a freshly made bed for him when he returns. I must stress, ladies, that Mr. Gayarre is going to need a great deal of care. I will do what I can, of course, but I cannot be in attendance all the time. I'm afraid that you must look forward to some long hours of nursing."

Gayarre smiled. "And I will be a terrible patient, dear cousin." He looked fondly at Sylphide Beauvais. Gravely, she reached down and took his hand.

So that was the relationship, Paul thought. Cousins. Beyond that he had not yet made heads nor tails of this menage.

"Yes, Pierre," said Fern Venable. "You'll surely be that. Until now you've merely been impossible. After the operation we can expect you to be atrocious." She looked at Paul.

"I would like to help, Doctor, to be of any assistance I may. I'm not afraid of blood or illness."

Paul studied her. She looked the type who would have steady nerves, not too squeamish. He certainly could use an aide. He was extremely fast with a scalpel, and once into an operation could not tend to other matters. The swifter the surgeon, the less the patient's agony.

Before he could answer, Sylphide Beauvais said, "I too wish to help, Doctor. I'll do anything."

Brave enough words, he thought, but she'd turned a shade whiter as she spoke. He glanced at the pile of pus-covered bandages beside the bed. Not this lady, he told himself; she would faint on him.

He nodded at Fern. "Very well, Miss Venable. I will welcome your assistance." And to Sylphide Beauvais, "Miss Beauvais, I shall depend on you to oversee the nursing when the patient returns."

Putting his things into his bag, Paul left the room. Sylphide Beauvais followed, and somewhat to his surprise put a small and very well-tended hand on his arm.

"Tell me the truth, Doctor. There is much danger, is it not true? Is Pierre going to die?"

He could almost feel her nearness. The scent of delicate

fragrance from some doubtless expensive perfume mingled with the sense of her exquisite femininity made him a bit giddy. The huge blue eyes were moist. A tear slid down one cheek.

Paul had an impulse to give comfort by lying, a thing he would never before have considered doing with either patients or kin. But this was his first experience with the rich, and she was so beautiful. It might be somehow to his advantage to administer a dose of soothing, falsely hopeful words. But he couldn't bring himself to do it; it was not in his nature to hide a blunt truth when it was something that had to be faced.

"What I propose to do, Miss—you are a miss, aren't you?"

"Yes. I'm not married."

"It is very dangerous, and I don't think he will survive it. If you have any influence with him, Miss Beauvais, I urge you to try to get him to change his mind and let me take off the arm. Even then I can't promise that he'll live, but his chances will be vastly better—a hundred times better."

She dabbed at her eyes with a tiny handkerchief. "He won't change his mind, Doctor. I know my cousin too well for that."

Sylphide Beauvais was now regarding him with an odd intentness. The delicate beauty of her thin lips was suddenly marred by a bitter twist at the corners.

"It was a duel, you know. Pierre fought a man over me—because of some remark of no possible consequence to me. And now this! It was so foolish, so terribly foolish."

From the intensity of her words, he saw that she meant it. Plainly she had some brains as well as wealth and beauty. How, he wondered, could such a lovely creature ever occasion an insult coarse enough to warrant a duel to the death?

Tipping his hat, he started out.

"My sentiments exactly, Miss Beauvais," he said over his shoulder, "except for calling it merely foolish. The word should be stupid."

FIVE: The Operation

THE *Clytemnestra* was running into heavy weather again. The wind, which had been out of the north, had backed to the west and was kicking up a heavy swell. It moaned dirge-like in the rigging. The great paddleboxes caught the seas, causing the ship to heel and yaw, with at times a greater lurch that scattered deck furniture and set her plates to complaining.

Paul, returning to the infirmary, had to brace himself against the hatchway for a few moments to recover his balance. He swore softly. How in Christ's name could he operate amid all these plunging movements?

Worsening the dismal situation was the abrasive confrontation he had just had with Captain Cunningham, whom he had felt obliged to advise about the impending operation on his most valued passenger.

"Are you utterly daft, man?" the captain had exploded. "He's an important man! I don't want his blood and death on my ship. I forbid it!"

"But he's sure to die without an operation, sir, and probably even the best I can do can't save him, but he deserves that chance."

"Let the poor bastard die in New York. Surely you can keep him alive that long."

"If he'd let me take his arm off, I might manage it. For that matter, if I can keep him alive until New York, he'll be making a recovery. It's the next day or two that's crucial."

Cunningham cursed. "Damn and blast the luck! This has been an ill-fated matter from the very first. Damn all telegraphs!"

Then turning away with a snort, as if to end the conversation, he had added, "All right, operate if you must—but don't let him die on my ship, Dr. Abbott. The owners won't like it and I won't like it. Give the line a bad name. That's an order, sir!"

Now, as he pushed into the infirmary, Paul was feeling the clutch of fear in his guts. Neither the captain nor Pierre Gayarre knew the full truth of what he faced.

For once suppuration and gangrene had set in—the scourges of all surgical wards—death could be expected to follow as surely as the final step to the gallows. Few nonmedical people were aware that most operations, no matter who performed them, were fatal. The world's best hospitals all stank of gangrene and death. Suppuration following even the simple amputation of a finger often proved fatal.

Jere wouldn't have attempted a radical debridement after gangrene had set in. Nor would Paul's favorite professor, the great James Syme, rated as the best surgeon in the world. Both would have insisted on full amputation, or simply have let the patient die.

Nor would Paul have considered such a rash procedure had it not been for his friendship with Joe Lister and the theories that the two had discussed so often. . . .

He had met the brilliant young Lister during his first year in Edinburgh. Only a couple of years older than Paul, Lister had already won attention with his papers published in medical journals and at the time was supernumerary clerk to Professor Syme. A year later he was appointed resident house surgeon, the following year to positions as lecturer on surgery at the College of Physicians and Assistant Surgeon to the Royal Infirmary.

Following a particularly harrowing session in the wet room where Paul had served as the prosector to do dissections for one of Syme's anatomic demonstrations, Paul had been surprised and flattered by Lister's invitation to join him for a glass of ale at the Boar's Head.

That first talk was to change his entire outlook on the profession he had chosen.

"Paul," Lister told him over their ales, "I've observed you at work on patients both dead and alive, and I swear I've never seen better scalpel work in my life. How did you get so adroit with the knife?"

Paul told briefly of his background, the hunting and trapping of wild animals since childhood and the hunting-knife dexterity that came from skinning and cutting them up for food. Embarrassment kept him from telling of the crude surgery he had practiced on human beings under Jere's tutelage.

Lister laughed. "That may explain it. I am skilled with the knife, too, but I could never hope to match your dazzling speed. Be that as it may, the point I wish to bring up is what a shameful waste our surgical skills really are. . . ."

"I'm afraid I don't understand, sir."

His dark eyes burning with a strange intensity, Lister said: "Paul, are you aware of how many surgical cases die?"

"The proportion is high, I know that."

"As high as ninety percent in most hospitals—and surgical skill, or lack of it, has little to do with the mortality rate. The patients of crude butchers stand almost as much chance of survival, slim as it is, as a patient operated on by Syme himself."

"At least the skilled surgeon causes less pain to the patient."

Lister gave a bitter laugh. "What is pain to a patient who will soon die anyway? The blunt truth is that many cases would stand a better chance of recovery without any 'skilled' surgery interfering with nature's normal healing processes. In my judgment, when we physicians win our Certificates in Surgery, what we are actually acquiring is *jus impune necandi*."

Noting Paul's perplexed expression, he added, "Translated that means, 'the right to kill unpunished.' "

"That's a damned harsh indictment of our profession, Joe."

"But unfortunately, only too true. While it is also true that a few of our colleagues suffer under the impotence and helplessness of our surgical activities, racked with doubts as to whether our efforts are not pernicious, most of them accept the death of patients entrusted to them with equanimity, not to say indifference. They regard the slaughter of humans as a farmer regards hail, drought or the failure of crops."

"But what else can we do? Give up? Let the patients die without even trying?" Paul was a bit angered at the seeming cynicism. "Am I wasting my time training for a profession that's little better than a license to rob and kill the sick, as you seem to think it?"

"Damme, Paul, you know it isn't that! We will always need the finest surgeons we can turn out. But that isn't enough— something is missing, something we're not doing right . . . and we've *got* to find out what it is." Lister had begun softly beating a clenched fist against the table for emphasis. "I must confess that I shall never be free of an oppressive sense of guilt over the patients that I and other surgeons have killed— and will keep on killing—until we can put an end to pyemia, erysipelas, puerperal fever, suppuration and hospital gangrene. It is what I have dedicated my life to solving—and solve it I will!"

Paul expressed his doubts. "How can you expect in one lifetime to solve problems that have baffled doctors for ages?"

"Very few have ever even bothered to think about such problems, Paul. Unfortunately, our profession attracts many more who seek to advance their personal fortunes than it does those seeking to advance the profession. How many, for example, have ever troubled themselves to seek the reasons why a broken bone heals easily enough, even though tissues have been squashed and an effusion of blood has resulted, as long as the skin remains unbroken—whereas a similar fracture, if the fragments of bone only slightly pierce the skin, begins suppuration and usually proves fatal? In short, why does a closed wound usually heal and an open one invariably suppurate?"

"I have been taught that it is the air that causes suppuration."

"And you accept that as truth?"

"Have I the right to question professors who are famous the world over for their medical knowledge?"

"Yes, Paul, it is your right, nay, your *duty*, to question any teachings not supported with absolute scientific proof! Our profession shames itself by the tenacity with which it clings to time-honored beliefs, its slowness to change. The role of air in suppuration is not yet known. I am myself convinced that it is not the air that brings infection to an open wound, but something *in* the air. It is not a new idea. The theory that innumerable small invisible animalculae infest the air and scatter disease was first advanced hundreds of years ago by Varro, then by Kircher and Leeuwenhoek, and today we have Bassi—an old man close to death—with his parasitic theory of infection. But none of it is enough. We still know virtually nothing about wound sepsis and how to prevent it—and until we do, our surgical patients will continue to die. . . ."

It was not until nearly a year later that Lister made his first breakthrough. He had visited France to meet a chemist beginning to be known for his work in the new field of bacteriology, Louis Pasteur. Lister was jubilant.

"I think I've found some of the answers," he told Paul. "Pasteur's work on putrefaction and fermentation points the way. He has demonstrated that an infusion, when boiled in a flask which is left open, will putrefy, whereas if the neck of the flask is drawn out to a fine point, the solution will remain pure because the air will not drop the dusts and germs that it carries at the opening of the neck. What does that suggest to you, Paul?"

"That if we can keep air and the germs it carries from an open wound, it will not putrefy."

"Precisely! But that's still not enough. The bacteria are everywhere. On our hands, everything we touch, on our operating tools. How do we keep all these germs from reaching the wound?"

"Destroy them," said Paul.

"There you have touched the crux of the problem. We can easily enough protect a wound from germs in the air, but how do we destroy those that have already reached the wound and started sepsis? What is the antisepsis? Pasteur's experimentations have shown that wound sepsis and fermentation are virtually the same thing—you have noted the repulsive stench that accompanies both processes?—but his methods of control stop short of the ends we seek. In the case of lactic and alcoholic fermentation, he has found that the alien organisms causing it can be destroyed by heating the milk, wine or beer for a few moments at a temperature of fifty to sixty degrees Centigrade, but certainly we cannot apply that to humans and cure them by burning or cooking them to death!"

"I have read," said Paul, "of Semmelweis's insistence that the hands of nurses and doctors must be carefully washed and the patient's room cleaned with calcium chloride."

"I know of that," said Lister. "I also know that the poor man has been so fought and persecuted by all the great physicians of Vienna that he has been driven into an insane asylum, where he is at this moment. You see, my friend, the thorny road that must be traveled by all medical pioneers who would presume to bring change to our moss-grown traditions! Yes, I have already tried the chloride solution, as well as alcohol and tincture of iodine, but they are only slightly effective. A much stronger antiseptic is needed."

Paul sipped thoughtfully at his ale. "You want a strong antiseptic, Joe? Why not try carbolic acid? The city is presently using it to good effect to disinfect and kill the stink of the sewage drains. If it will kill sewage entozoa it should kill any kinds of sepsis germs."

Lister stared at Paul for a full half-minute as if transfixed. Suddenly he smote a hand on the table.

"By God, Paul—that's an inspiration! Of course carbolic is so corrosive it can burn a hole through you, but it's only a matter of experimentation to determine the amount of dilution necessary. Come, let us go. . . ." Hastily rising, Lister threw money on the table to cover the drinks. "I can hardly wait to begin experiments. . . ."

Imbued with enthusiasm, without saying anything to the proctors or professors, Paul had tried a few experiments of his own with a carbolic solution. Two were dismal failures, but one, he still believed, was a success. The patient had lost a leg under a dray, and under Paul's treatment the stump had healed cleanly, with a minimum of pus and sloughing. Though he could not prove it, he believed it was because he had kept the stump bandaged with cloths immersed in the carbolic solution.

He began washing his instruments with greater care than ever before, using hospital soap, water and his ever-present carbolic solution. His colleagues had scoffed and laughed at him for doing this. It was, as any damned fool would know, the pus particles in the air that infected new wounds, they maintained. The stench of pus was everywhere in any surgical ward. And pus was necessary for the proper healing of wounds—they even called it "laudable pus."

Perhaps they were right and Lister was daft; there was no proof one way or the other. Paul pursued his experimental method in search of proof.

ii

In the lavish Victoria suite, Pierre Gayarre lay back against the pillows trying to mask his pain with a smile.

"*L'homme sérieux*, that one," he said in reference to Paul Abbott. "He didn't laugh at my little jokes, and I couldn't bully him. But enough of this frivolity." He turned to Syl. "Fetch me pen and paper, Syl. My will is made and all is in good order, but I must add a codicil. If anything . . . if the worst should happen, you must give it to Etienne, who will see that old LeBarone gets it."

Sylphide put a hand to her mouth. "My dearest cousin! Pierre, don't speak of—"

"Nonsense, Syl—" He reached for her hand and squeezed it. "I can't tell you to be a man about this matter, but I can tell you to be the brave woman I know you to be. People do die, Syl—even Gayarres, even sinners like me—but though I may be a sinner, I am not a fool. It's no great matter. I merely wish to assign my guardianship of you to Etienne. He will see to your affairs, my dear, as well or even better than I ever did. Now get the paper and pen and you can all bear witness. Hurry—I want to be ready when the men come for me. . . ."

iii

Fern Venable listened to the others with mixed feelings. She agreed with Pierre's comment about the doctor. Abbott was certainly *réfléchi*, of a serious turn of mind—a sobersides, her father would have said.

Indeed, if Paul Abbott was the same man she thought him

to be—and how could he not be with the same name, the
same description?—then he had a great deal to be dour and
sober about.

Her knowledge burdened her with a question she was still
struggling to answer. Could she allow a fugitive from justice,
a man wanted by the Edinburgh police for questioning in a
matter of murder and body-stealing, to operate on Pierre?

Quite by accident she had come across the news item just
before boarding the ship. The substance of the news article
had been of macabre interest. Fern loved to read chilling
Gothic romances, and the mere mention of body-snatching
had caught her eye at once. After reading it, she'd tossed the
paper in a wastebasket and forgotten it.

Until, after boarding the ship, she heard the name of Dr.
Paul Abbott.

Why hadn't she told others what she knew—that Abbott
was a criminal wanted by the police? It was still not too
late. . . .

Pierre's voice, a bit sharp, brought her out of her introspec-
tive mood:

"Fern—your signature on this, if you please."

Almost mechanically, without bothering to read the document, she went over and signed. There was a loud knocking
on the outer door.

Pierre laughed grimly. "That will be the messengers from
Charon. Let them in, Aurora." By now he had been fitted
into a fresh nightshirt and was smoking a cigar.

Aurora opened the door and two burly stewards came in
with the invalid's chair. As Pierre was lifted into it, Sylphide
began to weep.

Tears didn't become Syl, thought Fern with a touch of
venom, for long ago she had admitted to herself her envy
of Sylphide's beauty.

Getting into her cloak—not fur-lined like Syl's, but warm
enough—she followed the stewards pushing the wheelchair
down a corridor and through a door to the open deck. Pierre
was well bundled in blankets and smoking a cigar. Fern overheard him remark to the stewards that he was enjoying the
cigar, as it might be his last.

The winds shrieked down, slapped at them. The high,
plunging waves, toothed with white, smashed against the
gunnels. Lines had been rigged from one companionway to
another, and with their aid the stewards started maneuvering
the chair across the chilly, spume-swept deck.

"Gets any rougher, sir," said one of them, "we'll have to forget the paddles and lay on sail."

Pierre didn't answer. Lying back in the chair, he kept puffing at his cigar, emitting plumes of smoke that were instantly whipped away into the gale.

Following, bent into the wind, Fern tried to sort out her various reasons for keeping silent about the doctor. Why had she decided impulsively to help the fugitive? Was it her Abolitionist instinct?

iv

First Officer McKeon met them at the far companionway and supervised the descent of the wheelchair to the corridor leading to the infirmary. As the chair was being pushed through the door of the infirmary, Dr. Abbott nodded to McKeon, then to Fern—ignoring Pierre as if he were no longer a person but merely an object of medical interest.

"Put him on the table," he told McKeon. "Have the men stand by outside with the chair."

Turning, he faced Fern with his inscrutable face and smoky eyes. "You're quite sure you want to do this? It's going to be bloody and messy, and I have no patience with weaklings."

"I can do it," she said with a touch of anger. "I'm not a weakling."

"And you must follow orders—exactly and without hesitation or question. Can you do that?"

Her cocoa eyes flared at him. Male arrogance!

"I'll do exactly as you say."

"Good. Now go over in that corner and stand out of the way until I'm ready for you. . . ."

Fuming inwardly, Fern did as he told her. Nothing could raise her hackles faster than being given blunt, imperious orders by a man. She recognized, of course, the need for discipline in the operating room, but it seemed that Abbott was only too ready to play God.

She watched Paul as he strode over and rudely plucked the cigar out of Pierre's mouth, tossing it into an iron bucket. The momentary expression on Pierre's arrogant face, with the still-opened mouth, was ludicrous. The trivial act in that instant had brought home to him for the first time the enormous reversal of roles, from that of lord and master to the humble one of being completely at the mercy of another man.

Her heart went out to Pierre. He had not yet uttered a word since being wheeled into the infirmary. She saw him glance at the array of glinting surgical tools on a stand beside the operating table. His face was pale and beaded with trickling sweat. He was a brave man—she supposed it took a great deal of courage to face a man with a pistol—but this was another matter. The scalpels looked evil and cruel.

Paul set about strapping Pierre's legs and left arm to the table, so positioning him on the India-rubber sheet that his right arm lay outstretched, palm up. After the patient was fully pinioned, the doctor looked down at him for a moment. He brushed the sweaty hair back from Pierre's forehead.

"You have thought this matter over thoroughly, Mr. Gayarre? I can have the arm off in five minutes, and the putrefaction with it." He picked up a scalpel and touched it lightly to Pierre's shoulder. "We are still in time for that—just in time. I can even leave you with a bit of stump."

Pierre flinched from the touch of scalpel and glared up at him. "No, damn you! Either save my arm or let me die."

Paul turned away, and taking a leather apron from a wall hook, handed it to Fern. Her nose crinkled in distaste as she saw it was caked with what she was sure was dried blood. Paul noted her expression of disgust.

"The previous surgeon was not as finicky a man as I am," he said. "Put it on and then wash your hands carefully in that basin."

The odor rising from the basin had a sharp tang that made Fern's eyes smart. Her hands burned when she immersed them. She made a small sound of surprise.

"It's only a carbolic solution," Paul said. "When you've finished, take the lantern on the bench and stand near the operating table so that the light can be directed on Mr. Gayarre's arm."

Finished, she took the lantern. Meanwhile Paul had placed an iron bucket of carbolic and a sponge beside the table, and near it an empty bucket for the debrided flesh and tissue. Beneath them the deck rolled, slopping the solution in the bucket back and forth.

Caught up in the impending drama of life and death, Fern watched in fascination as Paul swiftly fashioned a cone of muslin inside another cone of old newspapers. Then he took a flask from a shelf, and sprinkled some of the contents on the muslin. She recognized the sweetish, astringent fumes of chloroform.

He glanced at her. "Stand closer with that lantern—but don't inhale too deeply."

Pierre's dark eyes glinted in the light. He was sweating more profusely. Droplets of moisture shone even in the hairs of his beard. He closed his eyes as Paul clamped the cone over his nose.

"Breathe deeply. Don't struggle against it."

Paul alternately held the cone of muslin over Gayarre's nose, removed it while he thumbed back the patient's eyelids for a look, then replaced the cone. From time to time he sprinkled more chloroform onto the muslin. After a minute or two he pressed the point of a scalpel into Gayarre's neck. There was no flinching, no response. Paul waited another half-minute before handing her the cone.

"Put that within easy reach. If I ask for it, I'll want it fast."

Swiftly he put a tourniquet around the arm at the shoulder, using a stout cord with wooden handles at each end. After twisting it to the proper tension for checking the flow of blood, he bade her move closer and hold it just as he had it.

"Loosen it just a bit only when I tell you—not before."

For a moment he held a long shining scalpel balanced in his hand while looking down at the outstretched arm. The purplish-yellow-black limb, by now swollen nearly double, exuded stink and pus from the bullet and probe wound and from where he had earlier sloughed away the leaking crust. With the scalpel he lightly traced the operating area from armpit to the elbow, bringing a thin line of blood.

"We're in a bit of luck. Most of the important arteries and veins and nerves run through the armpit. The gangrene is not so bad on the inside of the arm."

Then with movements so fast and sure that she could hardly follow them, he made a lateral and then a transverse incision, still cutting lightly but deeply enough to bring blood, pus and some light-colored exudates welling out. He reached swiftly for the sponge and wiped the mess away, dropped the sponge back in the bucket and went back to cutting.

Fern knew nothing about surgery, but she knew skill and deftness when she saw it. His grip on the scalpel, his fingers parting and holding apart the severed flesh, the astonishing speed with which he worked—all this impressed her.

Only once during the operation did he pause to look squarely at her tense, pale face.

"Are you all right?"

"I'm fine."

Now as he continued working, he began to talk, as though delivering a lecture but appearing to be talking more to himself than to her.

"Not too long ago they would have tried cautery on an arm like this—not only killing the patient, just as I am likely to do, but causing him much unnecessary pain."

Turning the arm, he incised again and again, then picking up the scissors, began to snip rapidly. He found half a bullet and, lifting it out with forceps, dropped it into the bucket with a clang.

"My incompetent colleague!" he said angrily.

He continued cutting away bits and strips of near-deliquescent tissue, tossing them into the iron bucket. Now and then he lifted the arm from the wrist to survey it from different angles for a moment before putting it down gently to snip and cut some more.

"Lucky again," he went on. "The groove is deeper than most. I've not had to touch the muscule-spiral. No cause for cheers, though. He'll have a dead arm—if we get a miracle. Do you believe in miracles, Miss Venable?"

He didn't expect an answer and got none.

"Loosen the tourniquet just a trifle, if you please."

Blood welled up along the arm. He sponged it up and down with the carbolic and nodded to Fern. "Tighten it again."

Tossing the sponge back, he bent over Gayarre and again thumbed back the eyelids and listened to his breathing.

"Now we've got to be on the watch for Cheyne's syndrome. Do you happen to know, Miss Venable, if he's ever had any symptoms of heart or lung disease?"

She was still marveling at him and aware that she was liking him more and more—perhaps far too much—but still she gave way to the perverseness she felt toward all dominant males.

"Shouldn't you have asked those questions before?"

He slashed her with a cold glance. "I observed him well enough, Miss Venable. My opinion is that he's had no difficulty with his heart or lungs. I only wanted the confirmation of an opinion from someone who has lived close to him. In any case it makes no difference. Mr. Gayarre was determined to take this risk."

From that point he ignored her, only giving curt orders

when necessary, which she obeyed instantly. There was no Cheyne's syndrome, no stoppage or fluctuations of breathing. He stitched in six ligatures, leaving the ends long and protruding, and began to bandage the arm in carbolic-soaked muslin.

She noted how gentle he was with the bandaging; it was a strange contrast of tenderness after the savagery of the scalpel and scissors. When he had finished with the bandaging, he was dripping sweat.

On impulse she picked up a fragment of muslin and wiped his brow. Their eyes met and held for a moment. "Thank you," he said.

Another subtle change was taking place in Fern. Until then her attention had been held by his amazing surgical skill, admiring his sureness of movements and obvious concern for the patient. But quite suddenly she became again aware of him as a man, the nearness of the hard angularity of his tall, lanky body, the invisible force of his maleness. Her reactions now had nothing to do with his medical abilities, or his character; it was purely a physical thing. She saw his hand slide over his shoulder while removing his surgical apron and imagined those long and slender skilled fingers sliding down her shoulder, fondling, arousing, removing her garments. She felt her heart beginning to pound with excitement. . . .

Realizing then that the heat of her body had risen to her cheeks and he would be sure to notice, she looked down quickly at the small gold locket pinned to her bosom. Only ten minutes had passed!

"Are you feeling all right, Miss Venable?" He was staring at her.

"Oh, I feel perfectly fine, Doctor."

"If you feel you're coming down with a fever later, let me know right away. . . . Meanwhile, our patient is showing signs of life." Indeed, Gayarre was stirring on the table, breathing deeply and trying to say something. Paul loosened the straps and began fashioning a sling.

"Call the stewards in," he went on. "I want Mr. Gayarre back in bed before he comes completely awake. Make sure you have a basin handy beside the bed. He's going to be very sick. And in great pain at first. I'll give you some morphine pills for the pain and prescribe how they shall be taken."

"You're not coming with him?"

"I have other duties, Miss Venable," he said a trifle

harshly. "I realize Mr. Gayarre is very rich and very important, but I am a physician to all on this ship."

The rough side of him again. She wondered about it, the bitterness she sometimes sensed in him, his chip-on-the-shoulder attitude at times. She guessed it was because he'd had a difficult life. Her theory accorded in a vague way with his appearance; she supposed doctors didn't make much money, but still he didn't look genteel-poor. Of course he was young—she guessed at twenty-six to thirty—and he appeared a bit gaunt and underfed. His clothes were too obviously cheap and off the peg.

About his face she could not quite decide. It was not exactly handsome, yet not unhandsome. It might be the gauntness of cheeks and his dour manner that baffled her. But he was clean-shaven, which she liked in a man—whiskers tickled and occasionally smelled bad—and his chin was firm, his brow high, the eyes wide-set, and she had not as yet noticed any really annoying mannerisms.

It came to Fern that she was surveying him now with entirely different eyes—seeing him as a possible bed partner. Intriguing, but ridiculous. Even if he shared her interest, there would be no time or opportunity.

Unless she created one. . . .

v

After Fern and the stewards were gone with Gayarre in the wheelchair, Paul set about cleaning up. The slops would go through the porthole into the sea, after which he would wash himself thoroughly, inspecting his hands and forearms minutely for nicks and cuts. More than one surgeon had died from an infection received in the operating room.

First Officer McKeon pushed through the door.

"How did it go, Doctor? Is moneybags going to make it?"

Paul frowned at him a moment. "It's a roll of the dice."

McKeon shook his head. "Meaning no offense, Doctor— I'm sure you did your best—but I wouldn't give tuppence to be in your shoes if the man dies. The Old Man and the owners will want a scapegoat. And they have ways, sir, they have ways. . . ."

"If the captain has such a personal interest in the matter," Paul said curtly, "tell him to start praying."

McKeon gave a sour look and departed.

Paul continued with the cleaning job, both angered and

depressed. He'd done all that was humanly possible; few surgeons, if any, could have done any better. But failure would brand him as no better than a butcher.

And failure was the more likely outcome. Gayarre would soon be beset with fever, and already his body was in the grip of the trauma that always follows such radical operations. The trauma was the big unknown factor, an unpredictable equation of the physical constitution that had baffled physicians for ages. Only God could say whether Gayarre would survive the odds against him.

As he washed, he pushed such depressive speculations out of his head. There were pleasanter matters to consider.

He found himself thinking about Fern Venable.

BOOK TWO

The Slaveholders

ONE: Zambullah

THEY came upriver by night in the pinnace. Arabs, Spaniards, Danes, black Moors and a few Englishmen with faces burned red from rum and sun. A motley crew heavily armed with muskets, pistols, iron maces, clubs and nets. They were also equipped with loads of shackles and chains.

Luck was with them. There was just enough moon. The breeze was favorable, saving the need for oars and kedging. The light sailing ship skimmed up the Congo with barely a ripple. They reached the village, had it surrounded and torched before the confused and terrified blacks who came spilling out into the blinding red glare of crackling flames knew what it was all about.

The old and useless ones were swiftly destroyed with mace or bullet; the strong or young were herded aside to have iron rings clamped around their necks and strung on a long chain. With only one did they have any trouble, a huge man who fought with the fury of a cornered lion, and as a result two of the slave hunters got their heads bashed in by one of their own clubs in the hands of the black man, who had wrenched it away. The two weren't of much account, and Smythe, the factor who had accompanied them, didn't grieve overmuch.

"Don't kill that nigger, and don't cripple him!" he bawled at the men with clubs and nets who were finally subduing the black giant. "Put him to sleep and double-iron him, and get him back to the barracoon separate from the others. He'll fetch a price, that one will, and God help the fool that buys him."

ii

At dinner that night with his assistant, Smythe enlarged on the subject. "It pleasures me, now and again, to sell a rogue nigger like that one. Like selling a bad horse to someone you hate."

The assistant looked puzzled. "I don't quite understand, sir. The nigger will be sold in Cuba, or New Orleans, wherever. I mean, how can you know who's going to buy him?"

"Of course I won't know personal, you fool. But *someone* will buy him, you can bet your liver on that. The traders will lie about it, and he *looks* like he'd make a good plantation nigger. And so someone is going to get stuck—one of them rich la-de-da fat-arsed planters—and I only wish I could be there to see when that big nigger bastard breaks out again. Sure to kill somebody."

"*If* we ever get him back," Tyson said mournfully. "If we bump into another man-of-war, or the Portuguese, even *we'll* be lucky to make it back, unless it's in irons. I wasn't advised, sir, that slaving was to be so full of risks."

The factor drank his rum and stared his disapproval. He didn't like young Tyson, hadn't from the beginning. The boy thought he was too good for slaving. Had his nose so high it was practically out of joint. And the spine of a cur. Still shaking in his boots because just off Liberia they'd been over-hauled by the steamer H.M.S. *Viper*, a British man-of-war on antislaving patrol. To be sure, their own ship, the *Betsy Ann*, didn't have a lily-white reputation, but proof was another matter. They'd been hard put to keep from laughing in the *Viper* commander's face when he found they were under

American registry with proper clearance papers and only carrying a couple of Spanish "traders" with their stock of goods to trade for palm oil.

There was some danger, of course. Under British and American law, slavetrading was considered the same as piracy. Had been since 1808. Called for capital punishment, though Symthe had never known it to happen. Then there were the damned Portuguese, who had lately developed a nasty habit of sending slavers to their penal colonies. Yes, it was no business for the yellowbellies, but a man expected that if he wanted to get rich.

"With enough brains to cover a pinhead," he told Tyson, "you'd grasp it's only thanks to risks that you'll be profiting five times over more'n you're worth."

Tyson, who came from good if penniless people, didn't need to be reminded of the money. The lure of the golden reward at the end of the voyage was all that sustained him. For that he could endure the harsh insults and crudeness of the factor, whom he had long thought was around the bend anyway. The Gold Coast, African heat, sun and filth along with drink, disease and black women had softened Smythe's brain. Such was his opinion, but he kept it to himself. In any case he was disillusioned with the slave business. Niggers were harder to come by each passing day, while the risks increased. Who could tell when they just might have the bad luck to run afoul of a U.S. man-of-war with a Yankee commander? His days were filled with fears of yellow fever, malaria and strange, deadly African ailments that had killed many a slaver, and his nights with nightmares of the gallows. Tyson felt like a man holding his breath while they were anchored at the mouth of the Congo getting "slaved," unable to breathe until they would be again at sea.

iii

While the *Betsy Ann* was loading, feeding, oiling and ironing the blacks as they were transferred from the barracoons to the slave decks, the giant black man went berserk again. He managed to swing his heavy chains—near a hundred pounds of iron—against the head of one of the crew. He didn't kill the man, at least not immediately, but cracked his head so badly that he had to be left behind.

Mr. Elias Hogg, who owned the *Betsy Ann* and was this

voyage aboard her as supercargo, did not like the matter and complained bitterly to the commission merchant.

"Slaving," he expostulated, "is chancy enough without niggers like that. Dammit, Mr. Symthe, I believe you have done me."

Smythe was curt. "You bought the niggers sight unseen, Mr. Hogg, and lucky to get them at that. As you well know, niggers are hard to come by these days. But for the wars inland, we shouldn't have these. And at two hundred dollars a head, they're a bargain from heaven. Look at the children. And half of those black sluts are pregnant. The issue is free, sir, thrown in for nothing."

"Ha! Half the babies will feed the sharks, and you know it. They don't stand up to the voyage. Do you take me to be a greenhorn, sir?"

Smythe switched to jocular tactics. "It might do a good turn and calm the big nigger at the same time if he's allowed to amuse himself with the young wenches—a few different ones each day, you understand. Then even if you lose a few babies, you could be certain of a full crop of swelling slut bellies soon enough. What better stud could you ever find for the breeding stock?"

Hogg puffed out with righteous indignation. "Sin and blasphemy! I'll have you know, sir, that I am a God-abiding man and I will not have such shameless devil's mischief afoot on my ship. Keep him securely chained, Mr. Smythe."

"It was but a jest, Mr. Hogg. Truth of the matter is that I was about to suggest that you keep him caged. I have old iron and wood, if you've none. You are welcome to it. Build him a cage and keep him separate, for if he can't get at whites, he'll kill blacks. Put the cage on deck where the crew can keep an eye on him. And stop your moaning, sir—he'll fetch a thousand to fifteen hundred in the States. Being, of course, if the jobber shows him properly and lies a bit."

"On deck you say? Exposed to the weather where he's like to catch a pneumonia and die?"

The commission merchant chuckled. "That one! No fear. You couldn't kill him with a double-shotted cannon."

iv

So they built a special cage on deck for the man called Zambullah. It was of wood and iron, and in addition they weighted him with chains and shackles. The cage was above the forepeak near a grating that sealed off the hatch to the slave deck, and through it he could hear and smell his fellow captives as they wailed and cried out and implored gods which he knew would never help them.

At first there was rage. Rage and fear and stunned bewilderment. As the days passed and the children began to die and be tossed overboard, the rage of most of them turned more to grief and apathy. There were some five hundred of them cramped together in a space little better than a " 'tween-decks" meant for half their number, and so ill fed, so whipped and sick and hopeless that rage had fled. When the crew hosed them down once a day with icy seawater, most of them did not so much as turn their heads.

But Zambullah kept his rage. He preserved it carefully, hoarded it, concealed it deep within his huge black frame and waited.

In the roughest and coldest weather a tarpaulin was thrown over the cage. At times, when the skies cleared, some of the sailors would gather to stare at him through the bars. They were awed by the physique, the sheer bulk and shining muscle of him. The cage was six feet high and he could not stand erect. They made a game of guessing his weight, in pounds and stone, and the best consensus was two hundred and forty. They were ten pounds shy.

One of the bolder and more stupid of the crew once took to teasing the caged slave with a belaying pin. Zambullah had the pin before the man knew what was happening and broke his wrist with one blow. He might have pulled the fellow's arm off by sheer brute strength had not his companions dragged him free. The sailor with the smashed wrist, which was set by a mate and would forever protrude at an awkward angle, got no sympathy.

"Leave that nigger alone," the second mate warned him, "or by God I'll put you in there with him for his dinner."

Zambullah was fed twice a day instead of once. He watched all that happened with dark, expressionless, half-hooded eyes. He kept his muscles supple by crawling and squatting and scampering around the cage. He crouched impassively while they hosed him down each day with cold seawater. His food was poked into the cage with a long stick, as was a jar of oil that he might anoint himself. Always he excreted in the same corner of the cage, and it was hosed away each day.

And he hated. Hated and thought. Thinking back, working it all out in detail, coming to understand it. Gradually he got his hate under control, hiding it deep within him, making hate a part of the essence of himself. Nurtured, cozened it. For instinct told him that so long as his hate remained strong he was still a man. No matter the chains and manacles—they couldn't fetter the inner part of him, the part where hate burned.

No one tried to take the belaying pin away from him. He beat it on the iron bars until he had splinters for chewing sticks. He would crouch and chew and watch them. There were times when the crew, or even the officers, would throw the tarp over the cage just to get away from the feel of his eyes on them.

Worst of all, at first, was the white smell. It was everywhere. Even when they fumigated his cage it did not vanish, was in fact worse because they had come so near. For the first day or two the white stink sickened him. Then, gradually, he became accustomed to it.

He understood not a little of what they said around him. He had a smattering of Gold Coast English picked up from his visits to the factory and from his wife, Tembah, and his father-in-law, Apuk. It was Apuk who had sold him. He had schemed and conspired against him. Against Zambullah, the slayer of leopards.

That was what his name meant: Zambullah—slayer of leopards. It was why he wore leopard skin, headpiece and girdle, and why his spear was the longest, the sharpest-honed, among all the Ebo.

Sometimes during the first long nights, when the brig raced and racked under full sail in dirty weather—speed was important because each day blacks died and profits dwindled—he would remember his last hunt. Disdaining the white man's guns, though he knew how to use them, he would find a leopard in a tree and begin to taunt him. His last leopard had been the biggest he had ever killed.

There were other leopard hunters, of course, but none as mighty as he. Few with his courage and patience. He would find his leopard and begin to taunt him. Then to speak kindly to him, to cajole him. Then once more to taunt him. From boredom and disinterest the leopard quickly came to anger. Eyes glaring, tail lashing, spitting and snarling, his brother the leopard—all leopards were his brothers—would prepare to spring.

Zambullah would wait, kneeling, below the tree with his lance firmly butted in the earth and between his hip and elbow. When the leopard sprang, Zambullah impaled him, falling away skillfully from the flailing claws. Not always. He had scars.

When he could no longer make himself dream of leopards, he thought of the ignominy of his capture. They had caught him sleeping, and thrown rope nets over him and struck him on the head with an iron bar. He had not come to his senses until he was in the barracoon. They had not yet double-ironed him, and one of his chains had a weak link. He strained it apart and killed two whites by dashing their heads against the logs of the stockade. There was no way out, the main gate being closed, but he wrenched the framing away from the gun port and was almost free when they came at him again with clubs and more nets and an iron mace.

He should have known, and been more wary, of the schemings of his father-in-law, Apuk. There had been jealousy there, and dislike and fear and hate, but Zambullah had not heeded it enough. He knew this, now that it was too late. He did not blame Tembah, his wife and the daughter of Apuk. Tembah was a woman and of no account in these matters and had not known how Apuk schemed.

But Tembah was his woman nonetheless, the comeliest of all the women of the Ebo, and one who knew well how to pleasure him and satisfy his hungers. That he had been unable to protect her was part of the sick fury that gnawed at him. She had run, terrified, toward the jungle when the white men came upriver by night in the pinnace, and from her screams he knew that she too had been captured.

He had looked for her among the chained slaves, listened for her voice, but it was no use. He wondered and worried ceaselessly about what had happened to her.

And on some nights, thinking of her, his hunger was so great that heat came to his loins and soft moans to his lips, and his great body squirmed from the desire for her soft blackness in his arms and her ways of bringing him peace. . . .

v

On the third day out, as the *Betsy Ann* made her westing, bent to the winds and slapping on every stitch her two masts would take, the dirging in the slave decks became almost continuous. From his cage Zambullah listened and watched them bring up the dead and hurl them to the sharks. First the children, as ever, and then the mothers who went insane and would not eat and tried to kill themselves. Many of them went over the side while still alive. An insane slave could not be sold, at least not by traders of good repute, and the cost of food was saved.

Mr. Hogg, already prophesying ruin from the voyage—the officers and crew knew he lied and was only trying to hedge against their wages—came often to stare at the cage and the huge, naked black man. Zambullah would at times ignore him, at times would stare back, unblinking. Hogg remembered something that Smythe had said:

"The big one has got royal blood in him. The son of a bloody king, or prince, or some such." He had sniggered in his near-toothless way. "You see how well I serve you, my friend. Selling you royal niggers."

Watching the big black, Hogg would think: Smythe was probably right about that. He has got royal blood. He'll never make a plantation hand, not in a thousand years. He'll kill someone. But that's their worry, not mine.

Again and again his glance would go back to the half-hooded eyes staring at him. They were both chilling and hypnotic. Hogg, who had hunted much, was reminded of a crocodile.

"I would give a silver penny," he told an officer, "to know what the fellow's thinking."

The officer laughed. "Nothing, most likely, sir. Niggers can't think. Not in the ordinary way of thought, not as we think of it."

"I wonder . . . " said Hogg, and added, "I will tell you one thing plain—I wish I'd never seen him, never let myself be gammoned by Smythe into taking him. That nigger is a curse on this ship. Look how many we've lost already."

The officer, not being of a superstitious nature, stared at the humming rigging and was silent. A nigger was a nigger. This bastard was just meaner and bigger than any he had ever seen before.

By late afternoon of that same day, Hogg's foreboding of trouble seemed to materialize when the H.M.S. *Tigris* hove in sight, perhaps alerted by the *Viper* to keep an eye on the *Betsy Ann* or perhaps even at that distance alerted by the festering stench that usually betrayed the presence of closely packed human cargo.

Hastily the *Betsy Ann* went into the ruse they were prepared for. The two Spanish "traders" took over temporarily as captain and mate and hoisted Spanish colors while the American officers went into hiding. They had a bogus set of

Spanish papers to show any boarding party—which would put them outside the jurisdiction of British or American law—but they had no intention of risking it if not necessary.

The *Tigris*, finding her warning shots ignored, opened fire in earnest at long range. But her gunnery was not all it might have been, and the *Betsy Ann* was a Baltimore-built clipper of a design renowned for speed. Thanks to her breeding and a lucky wind, she soon showed her heels to the puffing little English teakettle.

Through it all Zambullah made no sound or indication in any way that he knew or cared what was happening.

His whole existence had been reduced to watching and waiting. And hating.

TWO: The Immigrants

IT'S one of the new screws," said Mr. McKeon, who had a pair of binoculars trained on a ship astern and about a half-mile to port. "I take her to be the *Perseus*." He handed the glasses to Paul. "Do you not make her so, Doctor?"

Paul, who had been strolling on the deck with Syl and Fern until they were invited to visit the bridge by First Officer McKeon, took the glasses. A week had passed since the operation on Pierre Gayarre—a week of almost constant vigil at the patient's bedside battling postoperative fever. In desperation he had filched an idea from a long-ago medical tome, a procedure he would not have dared try except as a last resort, and packed Gayarre in ice. The fever had ebbed quickly, whether from the ice or from the patient's tremendous will to live, Paul didn't know. But Pierre was beginning to mend, and today both Syl and Fern had insisted that Paul take a rest from his medical ordeal and promenade with them on the deck, since the day was fair and clear, though cold.

It was indeed the *Perseus*, a long, slim, graceful craft without the awkward paddleboxes of the *Clytemnestra*.

"She's a beautiful, clean-looking ship," said Paul, handing the glasses to the ladies.

McKeon laughed. "Not so clean inside, I warrant. She's an immigrant."

At their questioning looks, he explained, "She carries immigrants only. Packed in like cattle, thirteen to the dozen, at thirty dollars a head. For that matter, we usually carry some ourselves in our steerage."

"You have immigrants in your steerage?" said Paul. "What if some of them fall ill?"

McKeon gave him a strange look. "Steerage is not entitled to medical attention. Under no conditions are you to go there."

The *Perseus,* meanwhile, was gaining steadily. Syl and Fern were taking turns observing it with the glasses. The bridge telegraph whistled, and McKeon winked at Paul as he picked up the tube.

"That will be the Old Man. He doesn't like to be passed at sea."

McKeon listened to the tube, nodding. After saying "Yes sir" and "Of course, sir," he hung up the tube and turned to Paul with a grin. "My orders are not to be passed by any dirty immigrant."

The bridge was enclosed in glass, which protected it from the smoke, cinders and hot ash pouring from the *Cly*'s stacks. Looking out at the greasy smoke trailing back like an elongated flag, Paul said, "Any danger she will blow her boilers?"

"Not much. More likely that the Old Man will blow his stack. He hates screw craft. He sees them as putting the paddlers out of business."

Paul shrugged. "Progress is inevitable, Mr. McKeon."

"Not to the captain. He's too old a dog to change tricks. But he has the right of it in this—come twenty years, there won't be a paddler left on the high seas."

McKeon picked up another tube and gave orders to the engine room. The volume of smoke pouring from the stacks soon increased. Deck chairs were hastily deserted as back drafts caught the smoke and whirled it about. Some of the hot cinders struck and smoldered.

Fern handed the glasses to Paul. "They're going to pass us, it looks like." Their fingers brushed as he took the binoculars, and at the same time she gave him the same calm, intent scrutiny he'd received from her frequently over the past few days. He sensed that her attitude was one of unspoken invitation, of waiting for him to make some overt move. Or was it all his imagination?

By this time the *Perseus* had drawn abreast of the *Cly-*

temnestra, and Captain Cunningham, still fumbling with a collar button, appeared on the bridge. Nodding politely to Paul and the two women, he shouldered past McKeon and began bellowing orders into the engine-room tube to pile on more coal.

There was no noticeable increase in speed. Instead, the screw steamer, her stern kicking up a boiling wake, began passing and moving ahead.

Fern and Syl were using the glasses again. Paul, who had excellent eyesight, did not need the glasses to see quite clearly the crowded immigrants aboard the *Perseus.* Most of the men and women packed to the rails were yelling and gesticulating at the *Cly.* Some waved, some screamed or shouted as if in hope of being heard, and then Paul became aware that many were making obscene gestures. One man in particular, a huge bearded fellow, thrust out his two fists and made masturbatory signals.

McKeon, who had also seen, reached quickly to take the glasses from Syl. "Excuse me, miss. I'll need those for a moment."

Syl was crimson. Not looking at the men, she caught at Fern's arm. "I think we'd better go."

Fern had also seen, and now gave Paul a sly, stabbing glance. Her lips quirked with a brief smile before she left the bridge with Syl.

The captain made a snorting sound of disgust. "Scum, that's what they are! All Europe is cleaning out their criminals, paupers, misfits, the insane and the rest of the dregs. Shipping them to the States. With that element pouring in every day, Dr. Abbott, I'd be curious to know what your great new America is going to be like a hundred years from now."

"Perhaps it's just as well," said Paul, "that neither of us will be around to find out."

As the captain went back to bellowing orders into his tubes, McKeon nudged Paul, who was watching the women headed down the deck.

"I believe, Doctor, that the Venable woman has the eye for you. Speaking plainly, if a man had the time and wit to seek it, I would say there's cranny there to be had."

Paul nodded coldly, tipped his hat and left the bridge without replying. Perhaps it was hypocritical of him, he thought, but he did not like to hear lewd thoughts put into speech, particularly in regard to one he knew and respected.

Thoughtfully he returned to the infirmary.

ii

That evening when Paul went to check Gayarre's progress he was admitted as usual by Aurora.

"Good evening, Aurora," he said, smiling. "How's your tummy feeling?"

The black girl gave a little moan and rubbed her stomach. "It bad again, Marse Abbott. Kin I hab mo' dad sweet *remède?* Dad do real good fo' my belly."

Paul had originally given her the usual peptic powders, which Aurora claimed didn't help, whereupon he'd administered a nostrum of ammonia and barley water, which she objected to bitterly because of the taste. Then to quiet her constant complaining he'd made the mistake of giving her laudanum—a tincture of opium—in a menstruum of alcohol and syrup, with strict orders that it was to last three days. Aurora loved it so much she finished it all within a couple of hours, which left her floating in dreamy euphoria.

By this time Paul had recognized her for the skilled little actress she was.

"I'm sorry, Aurora, but that kind of medicine is habit-forming and too much of it will only make you sicker than you were before. I'll have to give you one of the other medicaments."

"Nemmine dad odder stuff!" she said hastily. "I rudder be sick." Giving him a look of distrust and dislike, she flounced away.

Syl appeared and greeted him warmly, but Fern, beside her, barely nodded. She had definitely cooled. Again Paul was struck with the difference between the two: Syl with her breathtaking beauty, her princesslike charm, appealing to the purest, most romantic side of a man's nature; and Fern, apparently the more intelligent of the two, yet somehow like a bitch in heat stirring the lowest element in a man: his lust.

"Ah, our good doctor," said Syl, taking him by the hand and leading him toward the patient's bedroom. "Pierre is beginning to act like his old self—too much so, I fear. He's smoking cigars endlessly and clamoring to get out of bed. It has been all I can do to keep him resting. Perhaps you can dissuade him from straining himself."

Pierre waved his cigar jauntily as Paul opened the door. "*Entrez,* my friend, and pay not a particle of notice to what Syl said—I heard every word. My dear cousin does not understand the need of a man to be active. I propose that we all go to the salon together for dinner—as a celebration. And I must insist that you join us, Paul."

Surveying his spry, cigar-smoking patient, Paul again found it hard to believe. Never had he seen such a remarkable recovery. He no longer doubted that the theories he had borrowed from Lister—who in turn took his reasoning from Pasteur's studies of fermentation and putrefaction—had much to do with it. About Pasteur's microbes Paul knew next to nothing, but certainly *something* contaminated wounds and made them putrescent, and plainly this *something* was defeated by Lister's aseptic approach. In Gayarre's case there had been very little of what other doctors mistakenly called "laudable" pus, no signs of secondary hemorrhage when the long ligatures sloughed off, and his fever had long since lifted. Of course Pierre's right arm, in a sling and still swathed in carbolic-soaked dressings, would never again look like an arm—it resembled more a skinned and scarred red stick. But the salient fact was that he still had the arm—and his life.

"You do not answer me," said Pierre as Paul set about changing the bandages. "I have invited you to dinner."

"I am afraid, sir—"

"Not 'sir,' Paul! I wish you to call me Pierre. In the brief time we have known you, you have managed not only to save my life but to enchant my two favorite women. We must forget formalities."

"You flatter me, uh, Pierre, but what I was about to say is that I do not advise that you leave the suite as yet. In fact I forbid it. The arm is knitting nicely, but we can't risk a setback."

"Comment! You're telling *me*, Pierre, what I cannot do! I think those who say all surgeons are at the bottom pure sadists must be right, but haven't you punished me enough? Who knows better than I do how I feel?"

"If you wish to ignore my advice, I won't be responsible for consequences."

"All right," Pierre said grumpily, "I will obey—but only until we reach New York. Then if you instruct me not to go ashore, I shall find another doctor more agreeable to my temperament."

"That is your privilege."

Pierre laughed. "Can you not see I am only joking, my friend? I am not quite so stupid as I seem. In Paris I procured some medical reading matter concerning wounds, and

I am well aware that what you have done, overcoming the gangrene, is a miracle. I confess frankly that when I was wheeled to the infirmary I fully expected to die, and I intend just as fully to see that you are properly rewarded."

"Seeing you recover is reward enough."

"We'll discuss that later, Paul. But for the moment. . . Since I am denied an evening out, would you permit me to indulge in a mere token of a celebration? Perhaps, say, a bit of brandy?"

"I have no objection to moderate drinking."

Pierre raised his voice. "Aurora! Bring me one of the special bottles from France. And two glasses."

Aurora soon appeared with a bottle and two brandy glasses on a tray. Skillfully she opened the bottle with a silver corkpuller and poured the pale-amber liquor into the glasses.

"The cognac," Pierre said as Paul was handed his glass, "is from Napoleon's own cellars, a gift from my friend Gena."

Raising his glass, Pierre continued: "I would like to propose a toast to Eugenia Maria de Montijo de Guzmán, daughter of my dear friend the Conde de Teba of Granada, for she too had a great part in saving my life. Had it not been for Gena's influence and help, I would still be detained in France by my enemies and at this moment be either dead or dying. So here is to the health, happiness and long life of the most beautiful woman in the world—Gena, better known as Eugenie, the Empress of France. . . . "

Paul savored every drop of the rare liquor as it slid down his throat, fully appreciative of the fact that it was doubtless the only chance he would ever get to taste Napoleonic brandy, let alone to drink to the woman acknowledged as the greatest beauty of her time.

iii

Neither Fern nor Syl were in sight when Paul left Pierre's room; Aurora was stationed near the door as if eager to see him depart.

"Good night, Aurora," he said as she opened the door for him.

"G'night Marse *Docteur*," she said sullenly.

On deck the bitter chill of a stiff wind knifed at him, but for once he didn't mind. The pleasant warmth of Napoleonic cognac was rising to his head. What a shame, he thought, that he had missed a chance to talk to Fern.

He started down the deck, braced to the wind and roll of ship, and then—exactly as if it had been planned for him (and perhaps it had been?)—he saw her strolling near one of the paddleboxes.

It was the perfect time, he decided, to find which way the wind blew. He walked close and stopped directly in her path.

"Fern—"

She looked up at him, her rosy-cheeked face registering surprise. She wore a plum-colored bonnet ruffled with white and tied under her chin with a yellow bow and a long plum coat over a pale-green dress that was whipping about her ankles in the blustery air. "Yes, Doctor—?"

"Could we find a place out of the wind and talk for a few moments?"

"If you wish."

They found a relatively calm cubby back near the taffrail.

"What is it you wished to speak about, Doctor?"

His courage was fast draining away, and he blurted out the first thing that came to mind:

"About Aurora—she seems not to like me. Have I offended her?"

"Not at all. She likes you very much. You're the great Yankeedoc who saved Marse Pierre."

"She looks at me as if she distrusts and resents me."

"It should be understandable if she's a bit ambivalent—I mean both likes and dislikes you at the same time—because after all, in her eyes you're still a Kaintuck. Slaves as a rule don't like Yankees. They're taught not to. They're afraid to."

"Then she *is* a slave. I was wondering about that. . . . "

"Does it shock you to know she's a slave, Doctor?"

"Yesterday you were calling me Paul. Why this sudden formality?"

"All right . . . Paul. But you haven't answered my question."

"About Aurora being a slave? No, why should I be shocked? From what I've seen she's a happy, saucy, well-treated girl, almost like one of the family. She's dressed just as richly as Syl and better off in most ways than many white girls. What's so bad about that?"

"Don't you understand? Aurora is *owned* by another person. She belongs to Syl. If Syl were not a kind person, she could dress Aurora in rags, beat her at will and order her to do any degrading thing she cared to. Aurora would have to submit and obey her owner's every whim."

Alarmed by the intensity of her words—an argument with Fern was certainly the last thing he wanted—Paul tried to make light of it. "For that matter, aren't all women, white or black, in a sense owned by someone—first the father, then a husband? He might treat her with kindness, or brutality—there's plenty of that—but that seems to be a woman's fate, and there's little she can do about it."

He was unprepared for the chill, clipped words of her response. "I don't take you to be the kind of man who would beat his wife, Doctor, but your attitude indicates that you take it as a matter of course that women should be subjugated!"

"But I didn't mean that at all, Fern! Frankly, I've never had occasion to give any thought to the matter."

"As you've never given any thought to slavery! I doubt that you're even aware of the Black Code, as it applies in Louisiana, which gives any white man or white woman—no matter how low or degraded—police powers over Aurora or any other black. *Any* white has the power of life and death over any black. Is that not something, Dr. Abbott, that you should start thinking about?"

He was astonished by her vehemence, the fiery look of her cocoa eyes. How had he blundered into derailment from his original, romantic intentions?

"I confess my ignorance about slavery, except to know that it exists. I have been away from the States for four years, and saw none of it before that time. My only first-hand knowledge of slavery is what I've seen of Aurora living with Syl and Pierre. They seem nice enough."

Fern gripped his arm as if to shake it. There was nothing at all intimate or sexual in the gesture.

"Forget Aurora! She's an exception. Syl and Pierre, with Pierre's cousin Etienne, own nearly a thousand slaves between them. Nice as Syl and Pierre may be, as slaveholders go, they *own* all those lives that labor for them. Is that just?"

He didn't like the trend of conversation. The issue of slavery had transformed her into an entirely different person. Doubtless she was an Abolitionist, and a fanatic one at that.

"It doesn't make sense," he said, "hearing you talk this

way while at the same time you're traveling, on intimate terms, with slaveholders."

At once she drew back. "I'm sorry. I let my feelings fog my judgment. Syl and Pierre are dear friends, and I beg of you as a favor that you make no mention of this talk to anyone."

Without waiting for an answer, she turned and hurried away.

Disgruntled, cursing himself for a fool, a coward and a clumsy bumpkin who would never learn the art of pleasant light talk with women other than cheap bar trollops, he turned and headed toward the salon. In his present mood, another drink was in order.

In the smoking lounge he spotted Mike Quinn seated alone at a table and on impulse, for want of something better to do—*faute de mieux,* as Syl would have said—went over to join him. Tonight almost any company would be welcome.

iv

"Bejabers, it's too long I've been without the companionship of the leddies—God bless 'em," said Mike, raising his glass. "It's miserable I am with 'em and more miserable without 'em, so it's a sad fool I am to be alone on this fancy, paddlin' cigar box without one of 'em along to help enjoy my misery, mutual-like."

Paul nodded sympathetically. For the past half-hour he had been a captive listener to the verbal ramblings of the big Irishman. He had rashly ordered a bottle of whiskey, from which Mike was partaking freely. The gambler was now pouring more from the half-finished bottle.

"I must warn you, Mike, that your heavy drinking will sooner or later wreck your liver."

"Shure, an' I'll fret about that when the day comes. I'll not be afther borrowing trouble, there being enough of it ready to hand."

Mike had lapsed into a loose brogue as he drank but could still, if he wished to make the effort, speak somewhat like an educated gentleman, which he claimed to be. His family was well off, he said, and he had been ejected from the University of Dublin because of being plagued with too much "divilment." Thereafter for a number of years he had dabbled in divers kinds of employment, but mostly occupied himself with the ladies and the sporting crowd and learning the art of dodging creditors. In the judgment of good and sober folks, he admitted, he was something of a scoundrel and a rogue. Which had its good effects, for his father had committed himself to paying him a small monthly dole in exchange for getting out of the country and staying out, which was necessary in any case to stay out of gaol.

"Ah yes, 'tis a mere pittance I am allowed," he went on. "Not a tuppence will the old man begrudge me for drink—and him a rich son of Erin! As a consequence, here am I, poor as a sod of smoldery coal, seeking adventure and fortune in America. I had hopes of remedying my condition aboard the *Cly*, until Cunningham—a hard, unrelenting man is the captain—advised me no playing for high stakes would be allowed, or it would be the irons for me."

"You should have no trouble repairing your finances in the States. Jobs are plentiful there."

"I was nivver a man to sweat his duds for a pot of porridge. Ah, 'tis a cruel thing when the divil drives. I've always had a mind to be a man of substance, and I have schemes. . . . I had a letter from my dear sister a year or so ago—she was not encouraging, you'll mind, but kinship is thicker than drink amongst the children of Erin. She and my brother-in-law live in New Orleans, where there are many of our blood. Some are doing well and some are working on the levees, and of less account than the niggers. That, you understand, is because the slaves cost dear to purchase and the Irish, free and penniless, are scarce worth a farthing.

"Be that as it may, I have heard wondrous tales of the river steamboats. There's a fortune to be made there. All I need do is touch off my brother-in-law for some starter money. Mary was always a good lass and is that fond of me. It's through her that I will be getting William's ear—and into his purse."

Paul regarded him with a frown. "I take it that you intend to make a living gambling on the boats. If so, you're an amateur fool. That's dangerous stuff."

Mike laughed. "A fool I may be, but no amateur. It's a slick one I am, no blarney about that—sometimes too slick for my own good. I admit, but as to danger—" he tapped his right sleeve below the elbow. "I've one of the new derringers and know how to use it."

"You carry a pistol!"

"Just to get the feel of it. It's not charged, you'll know. I practice with it in my cabin."

"And do you also practice cheating card tricks?"

Quinn slapped a hand on the table. "Take care with your words, friend! A man must practice to keep his fingers supple, but as I told you, I only cheat when I must, or when luck runs bad against me."

Paul, who had been smoking a cigar—Pierre had given him a box—dropped the butt into a spittoon and was silent. A man who admitted he cheated even some of the time was something new in his experience.

"I know you spent a deal of time in Scotland," Mike went on, "and some of the Scots' dour humor seems to have stuck to you. Your face is as long as the ship herself, and your disposition no better. What I think you're the worse for needing, me lad, is a visit to the girls. We'll soon be laying over in New York and I have heard the bordellos there are prime. And since you saved the Frenchy's arm, for which he will no doubt reward you handsomely . . . which brings up a point. I was wondering—"

Paul shook his head with great firmness. "No money, Mike. Let us have that straight here and now and for all time. I will not lend you money."

For a moment Quinn looked crestfallen, then waved it away with a grin. "No matter then, though it *was* the quiddity of the thing. At least you'll be one friend I'll not owe. I had only hoped—"

He broke off.

A scream, sharp as a razor, had pierced through the deep thumping of motors and rhythmic churning of paddle wheels. It was followed by a brief series of frantic cries that suddenly sliced off into silence.

"Those cries came from a woman—"

Quinn shrugged his burly shoulders. " 'Tis but a family quarrel, I would venture. Or mayhap a flirting wench getting her proper comeuppance from some hellfire buck. Steerage passengers, you understand, aren't overburdened with delicacy of breeding or manners."

Paul stood up. "In any case, I'm going down to check. . . . "

"Now you're showing no sinse at all!" Mike blazed at him. "You'll get no thanks but a kick in the arse if you go down in that stinking pesthole against ship's rules."

Quinn was probably right, Paul thought as he started away. The scattering of other passengers in the lounge who had briefly stopped talking at the first sound of screams had already forgotten it, and a tired buzz of conversation again filled the salon.

But the cries still echoed in his head. His doctor's ears had heard them not as cries of anger or hurt from superficial blows, but something deeper than pain—something he had heard in operating rooms, though he could not recall when or in what circumstances—something laden with special poignance, the final cries of the helpless and the hopeless. . . .

v

He had almost reached the hatchway leading down to the steerage when he became aware that Quinn was striding along close behind him. Was it just Irish curiosity, or some quixotic impulse to help?

As he started down he saw the portly second mate, Bleekins, standing a few feet to one side staring at him in surprise. "Doctor Abbott," he called roughly, "you're not supposed to go down there, you know! Captain's orders."

"I'll explain to the captain later," said Paul, continuing down.

Entering steerage, he almost recoiled from the fetid stench of the hot, humid air that roiled out. The hold was a gloomy, largish cubicle evilly lit by oil lamps and crammed along both walls with rough bunks, one on top of the other, each with a lumpy pallet of straw. Most of the bunks and much of the floor space teemed with people, some of them half nude, either crouching or lying in the bunks or lounging on the floor amid an indescribable debris of broken utensils, rotting scraps of food, soiled clothing and other garbage. The odious smells of human defecations, urine and crowded, unwashed bodies mingled with oily exhaust from the adjacent engine room, from which came a steady, throbbing racket like a brutal counterpoint to a continual din of coughing, quarreling, groaning of the sick, and crying babies. Even the workhouses and jails filled with insane or dying paupers and criminals that Paul had seen were hardly worse.

Quinn snorted in disgust. "B'jabers, the stink is too loud entirely. If pigs smelled but half as bad, I would forswear pork for the rest of me life."

Several girls untidily garbed in soiled dresses had started weaving toward them through the massed humanity on the floor. Their ages could have ranged anywhere from twelve to twenty, but all wore the same bold, inviting smile.

"Ah, sich foine gintlemin!" cooed one of them. "A shilling apiece is all I be—"

She was roughly elbowed aside and propelled backward by a larger girl, not unattractive except for a few purplish, petechial eruptures disfiguring her face. "She ain't for the swanks," she advised them. "It'd be enough to make a bug sorry to be masheeshin' around in the same bunk with the likes of 'er. Me own bunk is back in a corner where it be dark an' cozy-like. A shilling an' a 'arf fer the both of yus. Which of yer cocks want ter 'ave at it first?"

Paul shouldered past her and moments later heard the two whores engaged in a screeching, catlike brawl somewhere behind him.

The origin of the screams was a young woman lying on her back on one of the bottom bunks with a clustering of idly curious, bored spectators watching her. Her head was turned sideways, her eyes closed, and she was whimpering softly. Her ragged dress had been rolled up above her hips and from between her limply spread legs was seeping blood. A young man, probably her husband, sat on the floor beside the bunk and was muttering, "Oh my Gawd," over and over again. Nearby, seated on a pile of blankets and bloody undergarments, was an old crone, probably past fifty, her wrinkled face smug with the kind of exultant solemnity that some oldsters feel when they see someone much younger close to death.

"I done me best, sweetie," she was saying, "but there's no 'elp to give ye. The wee one's twisted in there all sideways an' nothin' I bin doin' will straighten 'er out. . . . "

Paul pushed the old woman aside. "Stand back, please. I'm a doctor." He kneeled beside the girl.

The trouble was obvious: a cross-birth in the second stage of expulsion of the fetus. A blanket beneath the girl showed that the amnion had ruptured, spilling out its water along with bloodied bits of the placenta from the crude bungling of the apparent midwife. That is what must have triggered off the piercing cries—the pain caused by those clumsy old fingers inside her plus the sudden and certain knowledge of the mother, perhaps instinctive, that her pregnancy had turned to disaster.

Paul turned and looked up at Mike. "Get back to my cabin and bring my bag—the one that's already packed and sitting on the bench. And tell the steward to get some hot water down here fast—plenty of it."

"I much doubt that the steward will be of a mind to give any hot water for steerage, m'lad—but you'll be swimming in plenty of it when the captain hears of this."

"To hell with your doubts! Just get the bag and the water. Bribe or threaten if you have to—tell the steward he'll be held personally responsible for a death on the ship if he doesn't comply."

The big Irishman strode away purposefully.

Examining the girl more closely, Paul wondered if there was a chance. The girl's pelvis was too narrow, underdeveloped. She looked scarcely fifteen, and malnourished. Even with a normal birth, the fetus would have difficulty passing through the bony girdle of her pelvis to the vagina. A breech birth—the feet of the baby emerging first instead of the head—would have been enough of a crisis, but in this case, the most dangerous of all malpresentations in which the child lies across the womb and pelvis, the chances of saving the baby and the mother were slim under the best of conditions.

"If yer a doctor," said the crone, "whatcher waitin' fer? Git yer hand in there an' start yankin'."

Paul ignored her. The midwife would not know about forceps, of course, and in fact the majority of deliveries, even by doctors, were still accomplished without them. Fortunately, Professor Syme had insisted that forceps must be included among the instruments owned by every student.

He swiftly considered his options: the obstructed birth had to be premature—the very positioning of the child would have stimulated the womb into premature contractions in futile efforts to expel the child. By now the womb was doubtless too exhausted to contract anymore. It could even rupture. Still it would be necessary to make an attempt by hand manipulations and forceps to straighten the position of the fetus enough to permit passage to the vagina, at the same time trying to avoid strangulation of the baby from the umbilical cord and hoping that the mother still had enough energy left for a few more contractions to help expel it. A last resort would be surgical intervention with the added danger of shock and internal bleeding. In either case there was sure to be postpartum hemorrhage, and worse—infection from the torn placenta, abrasions and large raw interior surface of the uterus exposed to the muddling unwashed hands of the midwife. Followed by puerperal fever and septicemia with all the poisons invading the bloodstream, bringing certain death.

Mike Quinn returned, carrying Paul's bag. With him was a plainly annoyed steward's assistant balancing in one hand a large bowl and in the other a big pitcher, both steaming with hot water. Following close behind was First Officer McKeon, his face dark with repressed fury.

"The captain sends his orders, Dr. Abbott," he said tightly, "that as soon as you've finished here, he'll be expecting you without fail in his office. . . . "

vi

The blue eyes were bleak and the stubby little black pipe in his mouth emitted boiling little puffs of smoke at steady intervals. Otherwise Captain Cunningham appeared in full control of his temper as he leaned back in an ancient swivel chair in his crowded little office amidships and stared at Paul. When he removed his pipe to speak, his voice was mild:

"Are the mother and newborn going to make it?"

"It's a long chance. The baby is none too vigorous, and premature, and will need a deal of special attention." Like the captain, Paul was making a studied effort to conceal his seething emotions. "And the mother's in bad shape. . . . "

Which was an understatement. It was close to a miracle that he had even managed to force passage of the fetus through the underdeveloped pelvis, during which phase the infant's head had been considerably pressed upon, so distorting the shape of the soft-boned head that it would be unlikely ever to regain its normal contour. Unlikely even to survive for long—and if it did, with a high probability of a damaged brain. He would have preferred surgical removal, but under the filthy conditions of steerage and the mother's depleted reserves of energy and resistance it would have been a virtual death sentence.

For her he had the barest of hopes. The expected hemorrhage had been halted by brutally grasping the abdominal muscles and compressing the womb along with applications of scalding water to the vulva, later administering a hot vaginal douche of weak carbolic solution. But there was no way he could prevent the numerous lacerations within the womb and birth canal from infecting.

The captain leaned sideways to expectorate with neat accuracy into a heavy brass spittoon.

"Do you not recall, Doctor, that you were advised that steerage is not entitled to medical attention and that you were instructed to stay away from there?"

"That is true, sir, but I feel it is my duty to give all medical help within my power to anyone in need of it."

"Your duty—?" The captain's eyebrows arched in mock wonder. "To some higher law than mine perhaps? I was under the impression that I and I alone command this ship."

"That is my understanding too, sir. It is also my understanding that the captain of a ship is responsible for the health and safety of *all* passengers aboard."

Cunningham's face reddened. "I'll thank you, Doctor, not to be telling me the ins and outs of maritime law! I've lived with it—mostly under it—for most of my life. My steerage conforms strictly to the regulations. The ones we carry there know in advance they're not to get medical treatment—nor food either, except what they bring with them. We furnish water rations and passage only. It is written into the agreement and signed before a single blasted one of the buggers is allowed aboard."

"Still, I should think it would be an embarrassment for you to know that the inhuman conditions in steerage exist on the same ship that also provides comforts and luxury for the rich passengers such as Mr. Gayarre."

Paul's brief overall inspection of steerage before leaving had appalled him. Some of the immigrants were weak with ship's fever, a kind of typhus resulting from the lice infesting the straw pallets. Others, hearing he was a doctor, had complained of swollen necks, an ailment common to unclean ships known as "rotten throat." One man had terrible cramps and vomited frequently on the deck near his bunk, where it remained as a yellowish festering mess to add to the stench of the garbage-strewn floor.

"Inhuman conditions, ye say!" snapped the captain. "With that I can agree—but it's only the likes of the ones there who make it so. Steerage is fumigated and scrubbed down as clean as it will ever be after each voyage. If they wish to live like animals not caring or too lazy to clean their own quarters, they deserve nothing better."

Like animals, yes, Paul thought. It could hardly be otherwise, confined as they were in crowded quarters breathing unclean, oxygen-depleted air, forbidden to go on deck, malnourished from trying to exist on such fare as moldy potatoes, musty peas, watery barley soup, hard bread and meat beginning to rot after a few days in the hot, humid temperature. And only one toilet for fifty of both sexes. Some couldn't wait and went where they could. There was utterly no privacy for dressing or undressing. It was no wonder that many of them sank to an animal-like state of physical lassitude and moral laxity. He had caught a shocking glimpse of a boy and girl, no more than eight or nine years of age, copulating in a far corner and surrounded by a group of giggling or jeering kids of various ages, some making coarse sexual motions of their own, but none of the apathetic adults seemed to notice or care. . . .

"In any case," the captain went on, "they're all unloading in New York two days from now and we'll be well rid of them, so there's no need to harp on the subject. I'm a fair man, and this one time I'm willing to overlook your infraction of the rules—it being in the nature of an emergency, as you saw it. But that's the end of it, Dr. Abbott. You are forbidden to ever again set foot in steerage."

For a moment Paul remembered the helpless, anguished look on the young mother's face and a kind of rage kindled in him.

"Under the circumstances, sir, I am afraid I must respectfully decline to obey. The mother and her infant are my patients, and though I have little hope of saving them, I must still do my best."

Cunningham's mouth sagged open in astonishment.

"I also request," Paul continued, "that you send some of your crew to steerage to scrub and slush down the floor to prevent the spread of disease."

"My God, man, you must be daft!" the captain finally exploded. "And deaf as well! Ye heard not what I just told you?"

"But I'm only trying to tell you—"

"Enough!" The captain rose to his feet quivering with rage. "I'm of a mind to clap you in irons this instant"—his expression changed to a sly, savage grin—"and on arrival in New York, turn you over to the police. . . . "

A chill stabbed through Paul. Could the captain possibly know of his past? Telegraphic messages, insofar as he knew, could not yet reach across oceans. Cyrus Field's much-talked-about project of laying a telegraph cable across the bottom of the Atlantic was barely started, and in any case the captain was not yet in contact with New York.

"Of what concern would my breach of ship discipline be to the New York police?"

With a tight little smile Cunningham sank back into his chair and took a puff from his pipe. "Think back, Dr. Abbott. Do ye not recall any reason why you should not be anxious to have anything to do with the police?"

Paul clung to his bluff. "Could you be more specific, sir?"

"It just happened that a message arrived by telegraph in my office at Glasgow just before we sailed. After you made application, I was certain it applied to you."

The cold sensation in Paul's stomach grew worse. "Then why did you sign me on?"

The captain allowed himself another smile. "Because I was ready to sail, sir. On the morrow. Of all things in the world I can least tolerate, it is delay. And there were no other applicants, for as you understand, the pay is low and no competent doctor would sign on—unless he had some personal reason, such as you had. . . . "

"Then you've known all along!"

Cunningham nodded, puffing contentedly on the pipe. "I've told no one else. Even the telegraph was destroyed. I got what I wanted. A doctor to fill the position as required by law, and I sailed on schedule." He frowned. "And would be in New York by now except for those blistering Frenchies!"

Then he grinned again, triumphantly. "So what have you got to say now, Dr. Abbott?"

Paul took a deep breath. "My demands are the same, sir."

"Ye're mad!" In a resurge of rage the captain flung his pipe against the floor, which snapped the stem off and sent the bowl rolling a few feet over the floor. "Completely out of your senses!"

"The port authorities wouldn't think so, sir, if they come aboard and find there's danger of an epidemic spreading through the ship!"

Cunningham ceased all movements as if suddenly turned to stone. "What's that ye say! *Epidemic?*"

"That's what I've been trying to tell you, sir." Actually, Paul's words had been inspired by desperation only minutes ago. He had suddenly remembered the man with violent cramps and vomiting. The symptoms could be those of one of the rare and deadly dysenteries from India or Africa, or even the dread killer cholera. In either case the disease could spread rapidly, kill within hours, or at best, a few days. There was no way of being certain until the first death occurred.

Briefly Paul explained this to the frozen-faced captain, adding, "If I even hinted at such suspicions to the port officials, they would impound the *Cly* at once. The ship would be quarantined for days or weeks, possibly for months—"

"So now it's blackmail ye have in mind—threatening to spread lies about diseases in steerage to save your own neck!"

"But if they're not lies, sir, you're the one who would be held criminally responsible for failing to heed my warning and take steps to protect the health of other passengers on the ship."

Cunningham stared at him with absolute hate. Paul knew that the captain was only too aware that he had only to breathe the word "cholera" to the port inspectors and they would at once quarantine the ship without further inspection. Too little was known about the disease. Many doctors had died in hopeless efforts to help cholera victims, and there were few who cared to risk their lives by venturing into possibly contaminated areas. It was certain to be a long delayed process before a quarantined ship was properly inspected.

"I could clap you in irons and keep your lying tongue from ever speaking to the inspectors."

"That would be a mistake, sir. You well know that the inspector will want to speak to the ship's physician to get a clean bill of health—it is illegal for you to be without one. Even if you turned me over to the police, I couldn't be removed from the ship—nor could any other person aboard go ashore—until such time as the quarantine would be lifted. In any case, I am only wanted for questioning in a matter of which I am innocent—there is utterly no proof of any charges against me—and I much doubt that New York police will cooperate to the extent and great expense of shipping me back to Scotland on unsupported charges." Paul only wished he could believe his own bluff.

The captain reached inside his desk and took out another pipe, almost a replica of the one that had broken. He tamped it carefully with tobacco, then leaned toward a lamp with the pipe bowl upside down over the glass chimney and puffed until it ignited. He faced Paul, glaring.

"All right, I will accede to your demands—on the condition of your complete silence."

Paul considered for a moment.

"I will also require more medical supplies for the infirmary."

"Draw me up a list of your needs and I shall see that they are provided while we lay over in New York."

"Then I agree."

The captain smiled sarcastically. "You have no choice, do you, Doctor? Are you perchance a poker player?"

"I've played a bit."

"So I thought. So I wish you to keep in mind that I still hold the trump cards. In short, I shall not embarrass you by putting you in irons, or speak to anyone about your past as long as you don't abuse the privilege—but that does not extend to allowing you shore leave in either New York or New Orleans. . . . "

"You intend to hold me as a prisoner!"

"Do you think I would allow a competent doctor to jump ship?"

Paul's heart sank as he contemplated the sea voyage back to the hostile shores he thought he had escaped for good.

THREE: New York, 1855

NEW York was digging out from under a blizzard when the *Clytemnestra* glided majestically into harbor, pushed, hauled and guided by several steam tugs with armored prows. Other tugs bustled around clearing channels amid the chunks of floating ice that clogged the East River. Boats tooted and whistled; steam jetted and hissed; in the distance were myriad dockside and city noises that merged like a giant beehive into a vaguely threatening discord of sound. It was bitterly cold, and a down-pressing ceiling of bleak dark clouds trapped the coal smoke spewing from endless chimneys, stinging nostrils with each breath and smudging the snow.

Leaning against a railing, Paul watched morosely. Even the awesome cityscape of seemingly endless and astonishingly tall buildings failed to lift his mood—which was rooted in the events of the last two days. . . .

True to his word, the captain had ordered resentful crewmen down to clean up steerage and had allowed Paul full freedom to administer medical treatment to the immigrants. Some he had helped greatly, but with the serious cases he had failed abysmally. The man with cramps and vomiting had died two nights ago, the suddenness of it indicating cholera, although it could have been one of the strange and rare fluxes which within hours could deplete a body of all its life-supporting fluids. His vast ignorance about so many killing diseases galled Paul into a seething sense of frustration. The best he had been able to do was enforce complete isolation of the dying man, destruction of the straw pallet and all the man's belongings after his death and a thorough scrubbing of the area with a chloride solution. He could only hope the disease, whatever it was, had not yet infected others; if it had, in the case of cholera, it could spread among the rest like wildfire.

The corpse had been wrapped in canvas and stealthily slipped overboard during the night by two crewmen sworn to secrecy, to avoid panic.

The mother and her newborn infant had fared no better. Both had died last night.

The two sailors assigned to the burials had been almost cheerful about it. "It's the best record yet," said one. "Some trips we lose more than a dozen of 'em."

Paul felt a tap on his shoulder, and turning saw the steward's assistant.

"Mr. Gayarre would like to see you in his suite, Doctor."

ii

Pierre was in his room, out of bed and fully dressed, his arm in a sling.

"Ah, come in, Paul," he said with a wave of his hand. "As you can see, I am preparing to go ashore but felt it my duty as a good patient to inform the doctor." His smile had a look of mischievous guilt.

Obviously Pierre was enormously improved, but Paul felt obliged to make a token protest. "I had hoped to keep you in bed until at least after we had left New York."

"Another four days? Impossible! I wouldn't miss a chance

to see New York again if my life depended on it. So I have devised a grand plan that will solve everything. In short, I am taking my doctor with me. You can watch over me like a hawk, or a mother hen—whichever you prefer—and share the pleasures while I indulge my love of the theater, the excellent restaurants and other entertainments. Syl and Fern, of course, will be with us some of the time—when they're not shopping and doing their best to make a pauper of me. How does that strike you?"

Paul would have loved nothing more than to tour the fabled Big City, but the captain's dire threat still dominated his thoughts. He shook his head.

"I'm afraid I'll be too busy for that, Pierre."

Pierre frowned his surprise. "But my friend, I have already taken the liberty of reserving a suite for you at Meyer's Hotel, where we'll all be staying. I shall be greatly disappointed, as will Syl and Fern, if you fail to join us."

"I thank you kindly for your generous intentions, but my place is here. There are other passengers needing attention, and new ones will be coming aboard. The line isn't paying me for a pleasure jaunt." With an inner wince he remembered that he wasn't going to be paid a cent.

"Let's get matters straight, my good doctor. We are friends. Ours is no longer just a professional relationship. You have done much for me. . . . " With an obvious effort he raised his right arm a bit in the sling and wiggled his fingers. "You see? I can even move my fingers. For this—for the arm, for my life—I will always be in your debt. When I went into your infirmary my life was not worth a pistareen. Yet here I am having to argue with a friend to accept a bit of the reward he has earned."

"But as I said, sir—"

"Goddammit, Paul, the truth is that you come damn near to insulting me by your attitude! I swear to it, if you call me 'sir' once again I shall take it as an insult and call you out." He shot out his left arm and pointed a finger like a pistol at Paul.

"I couldn't hit a barn with my left hand," he went on. "So you would kill me and have that on your conscience. Then my cousin Etienne would have to call you out in revenge, and he's a terrible marksman. You see?—there would be no end to it."

Paul laughed. If Pierre and Syl were at all representative

of Creoles, they were a most charming, likable and hospitable people.

"Much as I would like to see New York—"

"Perhaps the right inducement would change your mind." Pierre gave him a sly smile. "Fern is going uptown to visit Mr. Latting's Observatory on 42nd Street and the museums and other points of interest. Why don't you accompany her? I know she would enjoy it. . . . "

"But as I've said—"

"Or perhaps your needs are of a less aesthetic nature. . . . I have friends in the city—some damned Yankees I made acquaintance with at Harvard—and they will know a delightful assortment of ladies—of the kind who will have many ways of making your evening most enjoyable."

"Even with such enticement," Paul said, smiling, "I must again refuse."

Pierre flipped his hand in disgust. "A damned stiff-necked Yankee! So prim and moral! Dammit, sir, you'll never make a Creole."

"I don't aspire to be one, Pierre. I'm aware of my limitations."

"If you insist on missing Meyer's chef and Jenny Lind, not to mention beautiful female companionship, it's your loss, my friend, and a foolish one, but what can I do?"

"You can take care. Too much excitement and rich food could bring the fever back. After all we've been through, it would be a pity to lose you now."

"Damned sad-faced doctors—you're all alike! It's always you can't do this and mustn't do that. There's only one way to get a smile out of the medical profession—that's when money is involved. Now, as to your fee . . . "

Out of sheer pigheadedness, Paul said, "The treatment was in the line of duty. You owe me nothing."

Pierre's dark eyes flashed. "I'm losing patience with you, my friend! Are you trying to tell me that you don't want money, that you don't need money?"

Paul was already regretting his remark. He was still a pauper—with the certitude that the captain had no intention of paying him at the end of the voyage. Quickly, he backtracked:

"I must admit I could use the money. If you insist, I'll accept whatever fee you feel is right to offer."

"That's better. The thing is, you'll have to wait a bit for it. I don't have the cash on hand. I will cash a draft at my New

York bank and pay you when I return to the ship. Is that suitable?"

"Whatever is most convenient for you is entirely suitable."

Pierre gave him another sly smile. "Of course, if you decide to slip ashore anyway, and need a bit of money for enjoying yourself . . . "

"No. My Yankee head won't budge on that matter."

Gayarre flourished a hand at him in dismissal. "Get out, you damn sobersides! There's no hope for you! I beg of you to end your voyage here. Don't come on to New Orleans—you'll spoil our lovely city. All its pleasures will be wasted on you. Good day, my friend."

He waved gaily as Paul bowed slightly and left the bedroom.

In the sitting room just outside he found Fern in front of a large French mirror fussing with a ribbon in her hair. She was dressed to go out in a full sweeping skirt of teal-blue hard-finished serge and close-fitting jacket with tailored lapels of the same material, relieved only by a froth of ruffled blouse at her throat. She turned, her brown eyes bright and a smile on her lips.

"We haven't seen much of you on the deck lately, Paul."

"The weather has not been suitable for promenading."

"Paul—" She came closer and touched his arm with a hand. "I know I should apologize. . . . "

"For what?"

She hesitated. Then in a lowered voice, "Could we go outside for a few moments and talk? Syl and Aurora are still busy packing to go ashore, and this may be the only chance for a few words alone."

"Of course." He followed her out, puzzled.

In the corridor she turned and looked up at him. "Paul, I'm sorry for my abruptness in our last talk . . . about the slavery question, I mean. It was entirely unthinking and rude of me."

"There's no need for apology. I took no offense."

"The fact is we scarcely know each other, I mean *really* know one another's personality and thinking. If we did, I think we would find much to agree about—and that's something I hope soon to remedy. . . . "

"I am in full accord with that hope."

"I am well acquainted with New York and if it wouldn't bore you too much, I would enjoy showing you around."

"That's very kind of you, and it certainly wouldn't bore me, but—"

"And our generous Pierre told me he has reserved a suite for you at Meyer's. He has also reserved a suite for me as well. . . . "

Again she put a hand on his arm and smiled up at him. Her face seemed a bit flushed, her eyes shone. In some intangible way she exuded a kind of femaleness that stirred his blood.

"Such an arrangement," she went on, "would provide opportunities . . . to talk more freely. . . . "

Her hand was still on his arm and she had moved imperceptibly closer. There was no mistaking, no mistaking at all this time. . . . He felt an involuntary tightening in his crotch.

"Fern . . . I can't tell you how much I regret . . . What I mean, it will be impossible to accept your invitation. There are compelling personal reasons why I must stay aboard."

Her hand slipped away from his arm and she stared up at him for a few moments, no longer smiling.

"I think I understand."

"But you don't! If I could only explain . . . "

"There's no need even to try, Paul." She turned and rapidly walked away.

Glumly, Paul turned and headed back to his lonely cabin.

iii

In her sumptuous suite at Meyer's Hotel, Fern Venable luxuriated in the big copper tub. She stroked her arms and torso with soap, and bending down lifted one leg and then the other and lathered them. She felt oddly irritable. Part of it, she knew, was fear; she'd lived with fear for years, trying to ignore it, concealing it, often wondering how long she could endure it. Ironically it had not been so bad in New Orleans, in the very stronghold of danger. But here in New York—abolitionist territory—she felt nervous and insecure. Perhaps because here there were copperheads planted everywhere—spies who pretended to be antislavery but were really in sympathy with the South. One of your best friends could be one and you would never know. Copperheads kept close contact with Southern friends and would be quick to report about an abolitionist living in the South. Fern knew that if she were ever so reported it would be the end—probably the end of her life, or at least the ignominy of being tarred and feathered and the end of her role as a conductor in the Underground Railroad.

The trip to England and Europe had been a blessed respite —a Grand Tour, combining Pierre's business transactions with an attempt to cure Syl's melancholy following the death of young Nicholas Landau. Syl seemed to be getting over it, but did one ever get over the loss of one they loved and intended to marry?

Mixed with her sympathy for Syl was always that element of jealousy because of the galling knowledge that Syl's beauty so far outshone her own moderate attractions. Of late that jealousy had sharpened by noting the way Syl sometimes looked at Paul. In her own delicate, subtle way Syl was already exerting her powers over Paul. Was that why the man had rebuffed her? Fern felt heat rise to her face at the memory of how she had exposed her feelings. . . .

Angrily she began sloshing warm water over her body, but the sybaritic sensation did nothing to abate her tensions. She knew why; or more correctly, her body knew. It always knew first and then let her know. The beginning signs were when she became more fidgety than usual. She had flashes of heat and a prickling sensation in her breasts and lower parts. Worst of all it seemed to intensify all her little irritations, worries and fear—that constant fear she fought so hard to repress—until all her apprehensions and physical yearnings grew and swelled in her together almost to the point of hysteria. Then her body begged for relief.

Which only a man could provide.

Her thoughts returned angrily to Paul Abbott. She wondered if his refusal of her tacit invitation was from fear of getting emotionally involved. Doubtless, like most men, he would prefer to sneak away to some bordello and pay some slut to relieve his tensions. For men it was so easy! What an irony it was that she had to depend on men—her natural enemies—for the relief she needed. Being a sensual woman, she had tried alternatives—even a couple of times with other women—which she had found deeply lacking, perhaps because her needs were somehow tied up with that eternal struggle against men. She had to meet them on the battlefield of the bedroom and defeat them to gain relief. Then and then only would ensue that blessed time of calm and freedom from tensions.

Aurora came in as Fern was toweling herself.

"You wearin' your best underwear tonight, Miz Fern?"

Fern shrugged. It would be a waste, but why not? "Yes."

"The batiste with the lace? You sure?"

"I'm sure. And my black silk. And the black silk stockings. And my highest shoes. The streets will be full of slush and if I can't get a hansom I may have to walk."

The black girl left the room and returned minutes later with an armful of petticoats, a camisole and knee-length pantalets, all of fine white batiste laced with blue ribbon.

Fern grimaced at the petticoats. They were just another of the many inequities from which women needed to be emancipated. Anyone's health was bound to suffer from such imprisonment in all the layers that most women wore—the flannel petticoat, the under-petticoat, the petticoat wadded to the knees, the white starched petticoat, then the two muslin petticoats, and at length the dress—all hung suffocatingly from a wasp waist.

However, she thought realistically, the three petticoats that she would submit to wearing tonight might prove to be very welcome in the bitter wintry weather outside.

Aurora piled the undergarments neatly on a chair, then held up a bandeau of white cambric.

"You wear dis tonight?"

Fern shook her head negatively.

Aurora giggled, displaying fine white teeth. "You de limit, Miz Fern! Showin' yourself so—dem titties of yourn wobblin' 'round like dat. Mens'll think you's a bad woman, law dey will!"

They had been through this kind of badinage many times before. Most of their talk, even down on the plantation, was deliberately superficial. Their understanding, always meticulously observed, was never to discuss secret matters except in secret places. Meyer's Hotel didn't qualify. Who knew what ears in the hotel might be eavesdropping?

Aurora tossed the bandeau aside with feigned disapproval. "An' I don' reckon no corset neither?"

"You know I can't abide corsets. They hurt my tummy."

"Dey hold it in good, too."

Fern surveyed her flat stomach. "Mine doesn't need holding in."

Aurora giggled again. "But up above whar de men like it, maybe dat do."

"Enough of this nonsense, Aurora! Check and see if

Pierre and Syl are in the hotel. What time is it getting to be?"

"Don' know. I go see. . . . "

After a while she was back. "It quarter pas' four an' Marse Pierre still on de boat, I reckon. Miss Syl, she be gone shoppin' two hours now. She like· to buy out de stores. You g'wine to a meetin' tonight?"

Even though she supposed there was no danger—the chambermaid had gone—Fern shook her head warningly. The discipline of secrecy and continuous vigilance must never for a moment relax. One mistake could be her last.

Making no answer, she drew on the pantalets and tightened the drawstring, surveying her waist with satisfaction. Not as tiny as Syl's, but small enough. She remembered Paul's hands, so capable, skillful and swift, and wondered if they could span her waist, then angrily thrust thoughts of him aside. He was too insistently on her mind. She knew it couldn't be love, but she didn't want any kind of close involvement with a man—it was too dangerous. For what she wanted, it could be almost any personable man.

iv

The Astor House was the city's class establishment. Its grand lobby was floored with marble, mostly covered with rich oriental rugs and enlivened here and there with large potted green plants of exotic origin. It boasted two of the first steam-operated elevators—open platforms enclosed with ornate iron grillwork—manufactured by Elisha Graves Otis.

Deciding not to wait for one of the slow-moving elevators, Fern worked her way among the expensively garbed guests to the main staircase and started up. It was fortuitous, she reflected, that Pierre was so enchanted with the chef at Meyer's. Most rich Creoles patronized the Astor House during their jaunts to New York, but Pierre deemed Meyer's to be superior. It might have been awkward indeed if he had preferred the Astor. . . .

After mounting three flights of stairs, she trudged down a corridor and gently rapped with the polished bronze door knocker.

The woman who opened the door after a brief wait had a pleasant but rather sharp face around which her hair, slightly graying, fell in fashionable ringlets. The hazel eyes were wide-set and penetrating, the nose aquiline, the mouth a bit

wide and set in a determined way as if she were not a woman
to be trifled with. She regarded Fern with expressionless
hauteur for a moment before recognition suddenly transformed her face with an astonished but cordial smile.

"My gracious, if it isn't Fern Venable! Do come in, dear.
. . . " Taking Fern's hand, she drew her into a pleasant
sitting room furnished comfortably with fine pieces of furniture. A cheery coal fire glowed in a marble fireplace.

"You look positively frozen," she continued. "Come sit
by the fire and warm yourself while you tell me what brings
you here. It's such a pleasant surprise after all these years.
How long *has* it been?"

"About four years, I believe. It was in New Haven—the
time you spoke at the Congregational church."

"Oh yes, I recall—in '51," said Harriet Beecher Stowe as
she pulled chairs close to the fire. Turning, she clasped
Fern's shoulders and looked her up and down affectionately,
then leaned and kissed her cheek. "And before that you were
in Cincinnati. All that seems so long ago. So much has happened—so much water, you might say, has flowed down the
Ohio since then. But tell me, dear child, how in the world did
you know I was staying at the Astor?"

"I read many periodicals and I came across the information in one of the articles about you. You've become very
famous, you know, since the days when I was one of your
students, Mrs. Stowe."

The older woman made a deprecating gesture. "Please,
Fern—not 'Mrs. Stowe'! You're no longer back in one of my
classes at the seminary. You must call me Harriet."

Fern smiled her pleasure. She felt happy and secure here
in the presence of this great woman, who had done more to
shape her girlhood ideals than her own mother. Her Southern-
thinned blood, which had seemed close to sludge, was beginning to flow normally again from the fireplace warmth.
"And how is your sister, Catherine?"

Harriet laughed. "Still fit as a fiddle, as you can well
imagine."

Her reference to her older sister's good health was a
tribute to Catherine's zeal for exercise. Catherine Beecher
had won modest fame of her own as the founder of several
seminaries and female institutes. One of her firmest beliefs
was that girls should be prepared for intramural activities,
just as boys were. To that end she strongly advocated
physical exercise, even coining an impressive new name

from the Greeks, "calisthenics"—never dreaming that one day the name would become a household word. Harriet, before winning success as a writer, had taught in her sister's Cincinnati school, and that is where Fern, as one of the students, had met both women.

"And I trust Mr. Stowe is in good health?" Fern said politely.

"Very healthy, very happy, and very busy. We've been at the seminary in Andover for over three years now, and Calvin wouldn't leave for anything in the world. Teaching is Calvin's first love, you know, and he's very understanding about my maintaining residence at the Astor House."

"Are you here most of the time?"

"Gracious no! I spend most of the time at Andover with Calvin. I'm happiest there, but it's a convenience to have a place here because of the frequent need to see my publishers, give talks, gad about and that sort of thing. And I can afford it. My writing earns surprisingly well."

It had not always been so, Fern remembered. Mrs. Stowe had given birth to six children (one had died in Cincinnati), and her early teaching income combined with her husband's had hardly been sufficient—partly because both Calvin and Harriet were remarkably unbusinesslike and overly generous. They had been in sore financial straits until Harriet's first published novel, *Uncle Tom's Cabin*, brought her fame and fortune virtually overnight. Fern had read and reread the book a dozen times, cherishing every page of it—not only because of its great antislavery impact but because it had been written by a woman. Harriet Beecher Stowe had proved that a woman could hold her own in the male world of publishing, and not merely by writing silly romances.

"If it's not too presumptuous to ask, Harriet, what are you writing now?"

Harriet waved at a pile of manuscript on the desk.

"I'm starting a book most difficult to get into, and with an impossible title: *Dred; A Tale of the Dismal Swamp*. The editors of *National Era*, who plan to serialize it, don't much like the title. Still, they haven't been able to come up with a better one. . . . But shame on me! All I've been doing is telling about my affairs, and I'm dying to hear about yours."

"Affairs?" said Fern, unable to resist an occasional play on words. "Unfortunately, I've had none recently. My life has been entirely too dull and blameless."

Harriet laughed. "Certainly it can't be from a lack of ardent young men! Have you met none that interest you?"

Fern thought of Paul and wondered, with annoyance, if he had really stayed on board the *Cly* or had by now ventured ashore to visit some bordello.

"I've met one who attracts me greatly," she said, "and at times I sense he's attracted to me. At other times he seems cold and aloof, and he's always a bit on the dour side. I must confess he's a type of man I don't understand."

"Tell me, dear, does he wear a beard?"

"No, he's quite clean-shaven," Fern said, surprised.

"Good! 'Whiskerandos' is what I call men who follow the fashion of beards and mustaches, and they're not to be trusted. In my opinion persons who hide their faces behind a mask of this sort cannot be supposed to possess clear consciences, for honesty and fair dealing have no motives for such concealment."

Amused, Fern said, "I do hope your rule doesn't apply to your own husband, since the last time I saw him I clearly recall he was wearing a beard."

"Not at all," Harriet said blithely. "The dear man has an uncanny knack for being the exception to all my rules. Besides, Calvin's most valiant efforts to nourish his wispy facial hairs into vigorous growth have never been effective enough to conceal any secrets from me."

Both women laughed.

"But seriously, Fern . . . and please don't take this amiss . . . your militant attitude toward men in general could possibly discourage the very kind of men you might find most admirable."

"I don't think I understand."

"Since your student days, dear, until your more recent activities as an abolitionist I've known you as a courageous activist, quite ready to resort to bold and dangerous means to achieve your ends as swiftly as possible. Weak men may give way to you, but strong men—the only kind you can admire—will resist."

"I refuse to apologize for what I'm trying to achieve, or excuse those who resist it. I'm only fighting for what is *right*—equality for women, for slaves, for any oppressed people—and I couldn't possibly admire any man who is too blind, selfish or ignorant to see that these are noble causes!"

"But you must remember that concessions you may hope to win for any of your causes must first be made by men, who control everything. And men, proud and stubborn creatures that they are, are never disposed to make concessions to firebrands."

"Men have had thousands of years to grant the freedoms which in all justice should have been accorded from the beginning of time," Fern said bitterly, "and so women— and all slaves—have no choice but to take forceful action."

"I don't disagree with the ends you desire, Fern. As you must know, I am deeply involved in the women's suffrage movement—my writings and lectures attest to that. Sara Hale and I and many others work constantly to free women from their roles as voiceless household drudges and open doors for them into fields of advanced education long denied to us, such as medicine and the sciences. One of our successes is the Female Medical School of Philadelphia, which has since graduated Elizabeth Blackwell, the first woman in the United States to receive a degree in medicine. And as you surely know, I am wholeheartedly in favor of freeing the slaves, and I attend many abolitionist meetings—I am going to one tonight, as a matter of fact—but I have not joined the abolitionist movement because I believe their methods are too extreme."

Fern was astonished. Previously she had assumed that the great and talented woman who had written *Uncle Tom's Cabin* would of course be a fervid abolitionist.

"If you criticize abolitionist methods," she said, "what methods *would* you endorse?"

Harriet smiled. "The tools of psychology will win anything desired from men—whether it be love or new freedoms."

"Can you give me an example?" Fern challenged.

"I'll give you two. When Sara Hale—who edits *Godey's Lady's Book,* as I'm sure you know—was campaigning for funds for the female medical college, she knew the money had to come from men. Consequently, her editorials and other writings were full of admiration of the wonderful talents of power and usefulness that God has entrusted to men. She praised men's mechanical ingenuity which discovers natural laws of science and applies these to marvelous new inventions and told of how much they have done in the world in the last century—"

"But isn't that a dishonest, hypocritical way to go about it?"

"How so? Extolling men's virtues is neither dishonest nor hypocritical. Be that as it may, after such praise Sara's male

readers, swelling with pride and magnanimity, little suspected that they were about to be induced to share one of their centuries-old privileges. Very persuasively, Sara went on to point out what a vastly more interesting companion and helpmeet a wife would make if she were intelligent enough to understand and talk sympathetically with her husband after a day's work. In this light men saw that they stood to gain more from the education of women than women themselves did, and they could not justify opposing it. As a result, the fund-raising campaign was spectacularly successful."

The example was irritating to Fern. Such results were achieved not on the basis of a woman's inherent worth but smacked too much of feminine wiles. It was how a Syl would get her way, how women of all time had been forced to degrade themselves by stroking male conceits to win small favors. But out of courtesy to the older woman, Fern held her silence.

"My second example," Harriet went on, "is my own *Uncle Tom's Cabin;* it angered and shamed and forced perceptions of facts concerning human slavery that many unwilling eyes did not wish to perceive."

"No one admires your novel more than I do, Harriet. Without doubt it has done more for the antislavery cause than all our other efforts put together. Still, slaveholders are no more disposed to free their slaves now than they ever were. Books will never change them. They must be *compelled* to end slavery!"

Mrs. Stowe shook her head sadly. "A confrontation between a hardheaded Yankee and an equally hardheaded Southerner over an issue on which neither will yield can only lead to one thing: a fight."

"If nothing but fighting will settle the matter, then the sooner the better!"

Harriet threw up her hands in dismay. "Fern, you can't mean that! Such passions fanned to white heat on both sides could mean the most dreadful sort of internal strife—a holocaust of death and destruction that could wreck our great young country. One evil should not be used to stamp out another evil."

"There may be no other way—"

"But there is—by our writings and lectures, by working toward the legislation of just laws, by appeals to those oft-hidden decencies to be found in nearly all human hearts, and eventually, by full and just compensation to all slaveholders who voluntarily free their slaves."

"I fear that would take until doomsday, Harriet, and for a slave in chains that's much too long to wait. I, for one, intend to pursue my present activities more vigorously than ever. I've managed to help over a hundred slaves escape to freedom and hope soon to increase that figure to thousands."

The older woman looked surprised. "I was under the impression that fewer and fewer slaves are escaping via the Underground Railroad, because of sterner vigilance in the South."

"We are constantly changing our methods. At the moment I am working on plans to open larger new escape routes via coastal steamers."

"Dear child, do you realize the increasing dangers to your life by getting so involved while you're living right in the heart of the Slaveocracy itself?"

"Indeed I do! I can't forget it for a moment."

Worry grew heavy on Harriet's face. "You're in it so deep, Fern, and the longer you're in it the more dangerous it will become. I wonder if perhaps you shouldn't consider that you've done your share—more than your share—and come back North before it's too late. . . ."

"Never! I'm situated in a safe place, and with all the knowledge of waystations, conductors and the secret Southern abolitionists hidden away in my head—no one could replace me without months of training. I'll stick it out. I must."

"Your situation may not be as safe as you think, child. Already the pseudonym you have chosen to work under— Nora Starr—has become legendary. Rarely have I attended an abolitionist meeting without hearing tales of the thrilling escapes that Nora Starr brought off with success. I have no doubt the slaveholders would pay handsomely to know the true identity of their most daring adversary."

Sometimes Fern regretted having chosen an alias as a cover for her abolitionist work, or at least one of such obvious significance. "Nora Starr" was too patently derived from "North Star"—that signpost in the sky that guided escaping slaves at night. From earliest childhood every Southern black person became familiar with that star as the only guidance to be trusted. She had picked the name one evening after hearing an elderly slave explain it to his grandchild:

"Chile, you see dat lil dipper up dere—you jus' watch whar de lip of it point. . . . It go 'roun' n' 'roun', de dipper do, an' it jus' keep pointin' smack at de Nor' Star like at de hub of a wheel. Someday yo' gwine follow dat Nor' Star long 'nough an' it lead you straight to whar freedom is. . . ."

"I think my secret is safe enough," Fern said. "Aside from you, Harriet, only a handful of our top abolitionists, such as William Lloyd Garrison, Suzy Grinnell, Sam May, Levi Coffin and a few others, know that Fern Venable and Nora Starr are one and the same person."

"They're all trustworthy enough, surely," said Harriet with a relieved expression. "Which reminds me—" She broke off as a handsome Thomas clock on the mantel began chiming six.

"Gracious, it's later than I realized! In a little while I must be leaving for a private meeting at a home in Washington Square. What I was about to say, Fern, is that some of the eminent individuals you just mentioned are quite likely to be there, as this is supposed to be a very special abolitionist meeting. Henry Raymond, editor of *The New York Daily Times,* will be there. He's most influential and gives a lot of space to the cause. Why don't you have a bit of dinner with me, my dear, and then accompany me to the meeting?"

"I'd be delighted. I've read many of Mr. Raymond's editorials and would like to meet him."

Mrs. Stowe clapped her hands. "Good! Then it's settled. I'm sure you will enjoy the evening."

v

They went by streetcar. Fern had suggested a cab, but Harriet demurred:

"No. I make it a point to use the public transportation whenever possible. It's not the money, of course. You may think me an old humbug, my dear, but I feel a bit guilty about being so well off when there is so much terrible poverty all about us, especially in New York. It's nonsense, I know, and you may laugh at me, but I don't allow myself the ostentation of carriages except when I must."

Fern shrugged to herself. Living the luxe life with the Gayarres had spoiled her. She personally didn't enjoy streetcars—the floor of this one was strewn with dirty straw and it stank from smoking oil lanterns—but Harriet was entitled to her quirks.

At Washington Square they left the car. The square had been swept and shoveled to some degree, and laborers working by lantern and gaslight were still at it. Harriet's destination was a small neat house of Federal design and ablaze with light. The entry walk from the street had been cleared of snow into smoke-darkened heaps on either side. A number of carriages, some of them handsome equipages, stood at the curb. Blanketed horses wearing feed bags stood waiting, now and then clomping restlessly on the cobbles, seemingly impervious to the sleet and snow that melted and steamed as it struck their broad moist backs.

Harriet lifted a brass knocker shaped like a unicorn and thunked it against the heavy door. After a minute or two of waiting beneath the ornate fan light, they were admitted by a maid wearing a black dress, white lace cap and frilled white apron. Their wraps were taken and they were ushered into a crowded library. Most of those present were in formal dress. Apparently they had arrived at a special moment, for as they entered the room was being hushed by a bald gentleman who was waving a telegraphic form above his head. Meanwhile Fern and Mrs. Stowe had just been greeted by their hostess, Mrs. Rhinelander, who now whispered:

"That gentleman is Mr. Raymond, the editor. His newspaper has just sent along a telegram which I fear is dreadful news."

With quiet achieved, Mr. Raymond began reading from the yellow slip of paper:

"Grieved to inform that Mr. William Buckner died of mob injuries on February sixteenth. Signed, Harris Sloane."

There ensued a minor tumult among the assemblage: gasps, sighs, whispered ejaculations from the gentlemen, moans from the ladies.

Again Mr. Raymond gesticulated for silence.

"I did not myself," he said solemnly, "have the honor of Mr. Buckner's acquaintance. I don't suppose that many of us present tonight did have that honor. Suffice to say that he was a worker for our sacred cause, that he has given his life in that cause. I now have two proposals for you ladies and gentlemen. One is that this sad affair may open your hearts and your purses wider than before, and I propose a minute of silence in the memory of Mr. William Buckner. . . ."

During the hush, broken only by a few coughs and snifflings, Fern became aware of the eyes of a young man boldly surveying her, almost inch by inch. She knew the look, and it didn't make her particularly uncomfortable. She knew he was seeing beneath her gown, judging her limbs and breasts and perhaps sketching a mental picture of her nakedness. She well knew this type of man who made a game of playing with every young and comely woman he saw. She deliberately met his glance with a cold and distant stare fully as bold as his own, which after a moment caused him to look away.

Later, as Fern and Harriet were being served punch and cake, their hostess confided, "My husband knew poor Mr. Buckner slightly. He was very active for the cause." Her haughty glance shifted to Fern. "Do you understand my meaning, my dear?—the UGRR?"

"It sounds terribly mysterious," Fern said innocently, amused at the thought of how little this pampered Mrs. Rhinelander in her rich little house on Washington Square really knew about the Underground Railroad. It was, by necessity, composed of so many separate, secret organizations—each with its own nuclei, its own chains of command—that even Fern had never heard of the recently deceased Mr. Buckner.

"I refer to the Underground Railway, of course." Then, lowering her voice and glancing around as if suspecting copperheads behind the arras, their hostess continued: "It's so extremely secret that even I was not told the name of the Southern city in which this terrible event occurred. Under the circumstances, Mr. Rhinelander doesn't think it wise to speak too openly of these matters. Nonetheless I have come by some of the particulars—most horrifying!"

She sighed and went on: "The poor gentleman was caught while endeavoring to assist some poor Negroes to escape bondage. He was at first only tarred and feathered, I understand, and then chased from town by a mob. Barbaric enough, one would think—but at least he still had his life. It was later that a band of toughs set upon him and beat him to death. I suppose none of them will be properly brought to justice."

Fern felt suddenly chilled. All her fears came swooping back. She had an obsessive desire for the temporary forgetfulness, the surcease of a man's embrace.

As they were led about the crowded room to be introduced —for the hostess was vain about the famous Harriet Beecher Stowe's presence—Fern tried to shake off her mood of foreboding. There was an aura of falsity in the gathering that was spoiling her evening as well as her sense of purpose.

At times like these she wondered whether it was all worth it. It would be so much easier to quit her position and remain in New York to lead a simple life devoted primarily to her own selfish interests. As she was introduced around to people whose names she never quite caught, she barely listened to the polite interchange of conversation. Her introduction to Mr. Raymond, the esteemed editor of the *New York Daily Times,* who was most gracious, lightened her mood a bit and she became attentive. After a few moments of chatting he turned to a young man standing beside him.

"And this is Jaspar Bledsoe," said Raymond. "He is one of our reporters and will do a story of this meeting for the society page." With a nod and a wink at the young man, he added, "You must be sure to spell the young lady's name correctly, Jaspar, and no excuses—this time you won't be allowed to blame the printers. Those poor devils take enough blame as it is."

Fern stared coldly at Jaspar Bledsoe—the same young man who earlier had studied her so boldly. He obviously considered himself quite a dandy with the ladies, for his dark muttonchops were meticulously trimmed, his beard gleaming with bear's grease, and his red lips quirked in an arrogant smile of male superiority. She could see him preening before a mirror while fitting into his frilled white shirt and silk waistcoat, from the tail pocket of which protruded a fine embroidered handkerchief. He affected the English style and wore an oversized E.D. necktie instead of the more conservative black cravat.

He bowed and smiled—rather an oily smile, Fern thought —and took out a notebook and pencil.

"Miss Fern Venable—it is 'Miss,' is it not? You are unmarried?"

Apprehension touched Fern. Pierre read the *Times*. It would never do to have her name appear as one in attendance at an abolitionist meeting.

"Oh no—" she said quickly. "I don't want my name in the paper! For personal reasons. . . ."

Jaspar Bledsoe's eyebrows arched. "Personal? Something to do, I suppose, with an affair of the heart?"

"The word *personal*," Fern said coldly, "means just that."

Bledsoe chuckled. "In certain circles it is not so easy to escape publicity, Miss Venable. Two days ago I already knew of your pending arrival from France in the company of Mr. Pierre Gayarre and Miss Sylphide Beauvais. . . ."

"But how—"

"This is the age of speed, Miss Venable. The new steam packets are now crossing the ocean in only nine days—and they all carry news dispatches from our correspondents abroad."

It took but a moment to grasp the unintended import of Bledsoe's words, and then her mood soared.

That had to be why Paul Abbott had not accepted Pierre's or her own invitation to join them at Meyer's Hotel! Paul must have known or feared just such an eventuality—swift steam packets bearing news to the New York Police Department that he was a wanted man suspected of grave-robbing and murder. He had been unable, of course, to explain his true motives, that he dared not go ashore and risk seizure by the police.

"Ah, you're smiling now, Miss Venable! That's much better. . . ."

She looked at him, her smile suspended. The crowd had thinned, and Mrs. Stowe and Mr. Raymond were conversing a bit apart, perhaps purposely leaving her alone with the unprepossessing young man. Why she so intuitively disliked him she didn't know. The fact that newspaper people were reputed to be drunks and roisterers did not too much matter—although surely a society reporter and personal assistant to Mr. Raymond could not be in that category— nor were his bold eyes undressing her anything new. She had an urge to be unbearably rude and walk away and leave him standing there, but repressed it out of deference to Harriet.

"It's just my usual social smile," she said. "Nothing personal about it."

Moments later she wished she'd followed the urge to walk away. . . .

A hearty voice rang out and another smiling, bewhiskered young gentleman approached.

"As I live and breathe—" he exclaimed in delight. "Nora Starr! What a surprise and honor to have you with us tonight, Nora."

Jason Moore was her prime Northern contact—one of the few living souls aside from Harriet Stowe who knew her pseudonym.

How could he have so blundered?

She looked back at him coldly and distantly. "I don't know

who *you* are, sir, but you certainly have me mistaken for someone else."

Jason Moore reddened, suddenly aware of his mistake. He was holding a brandy glass, and she saw now that he was a bit tipsy.

"Uh . . . I'm very sorry, Miss. I see my mistake now . . . a trick of the lighting. From a certain angle there's a slight similarity, but I see now that you're not at all like Nora Starr. . . ." Still mumbling apologies, he gave a little bow and hurried away.

Jaspar Bledsoe was studying her shrewdly. "Nora Starr? The name does become you, Miss—it is Venable, is it not?"

"I thought I made that plain enough, Mr. Bledsoe. Also that I do not desire to have my name in the paper."

He pocketed his notebook and pencil. "Never fear, Miss Venable. I really wasn't querying you in connection with the paper, but for reasons of my own. . . ." He stepped close and touched her arm. "While you're visiting the city, I should very much like permission to call on you."

"I'm afraid that won't be possible. I have already made all my plans for the brief time I shall be here."

"Seeing the sights, perhaps? I could show you around to many interesting places." His lips twisted into something more of a smirk than a smile as he added, "And how exciting it would be if I were to discover that you really *are* Nora Starr."

"Don't you ever give up, Mr. Bledsoe?"

Coiling a finger in his abundant muttonchop whiskers, he bowed. "I hope you do not find me too forward, Miss Venable."

Summoning her coldest smile, Fern said, "I do not find you anything at all, Mr. Bledsoe. Good night."

Turning away, she went to rejoin Harriet.

vi

When the gentle tapping came at the door, he thought at first it was just one of the myriad harbor sounds seemingly brought close by some trick of acoustics. But after a pause the tapping came again, with more urgency.

"Paul—?" The feminine voice was barely audible.

Rolling out of bed, still clothed except for his shoes, he went to the door and pulled it open.

Fern rushed in.

"Close the door quickly and lock it!" she said breathlessly. "I don't think I was seen coming aboard, and I'd rather not risk anyone finding me here."

Paul closed the door and latched it. Turning, he looked at her in astonishment. She was removing her cloak, which she flung over a chair with her fur muff.

"This is a most pleasant surprise, Fern, but I thought you were spending the night ashore."

She looked at him as she loosened the ties of her bonnet. Her brown eyes, aglow in a rosy-cheeked face, had a bit more of that vaguely oriental upslant that came with certain of her smiles. Her parted lips looked moist and fuller. Dropping the bonnet on the chair, she fluffed hands through her luxuriant chestnut hair.

"I intended to—until I realized *why* you couldn't join me at Meyer's Hotel. Then, being an activist accustomed to taking calculated risks—and acting on intuition—I decided to join you instead."

Totally thrown off balance by this unexpected twist of events, Paul floundered for words. "Uh . . . I'm delighted, of course." He felt like an oaf, all clumsiness and bad manners, lacking all courage to speak or act as most men would in the same situation. He indicated a chair. "Have a seat."

"I'd rather not sit, Paul. . . ." Her low voice seemed to have a richer vibrance. "And I would like it if you would extinguish the lamp. . . ."

Paul's head was suddenly afire with excitement. The impossible had happened. He had fantasized about her frequently, had erotic thoughts about her. And now, here she had come breezing out of the night into the privacy of his room, bold as any hussy could be. . . .

Quickly he put out the gas lamp on the wall and, turning, almost stumbled over her in the darkness trying to reach her. Then, regaining his balance, he encircled her with his arms and they were kissing feverishly.

"I knew the barrier between us had to be torn away quickly," she whispered. "And I knew I had to take the initiative—if I waited for you, the voyage would be over and it would be too late."

"And I thought that there was a stone wall that had to be demolished. It turned out to be only gossamer."

As they started kissing again they began abandoning their clothes. Clumsily he did his best to help her. My God—all those petticoats! Pantalettes! All sorts of invisible obstructions

crinkling and rustling as they slid down around her feet. . . .
Eventually everything was on the floor, including her high
shoes and even the silk stockings and garters and all of his
own things. By now his eyes were a bit adjusted to the dark,
helped by a muffled gleam of moonlight through the porthole, and he saw her nakedness. Embracing her, he guided
her toward the bunk, and they fell in it together.

And now he began to devour her, lips and hands feasting
on the silken smoothness of torso, breasts, thighs, drinking
her in with grateful murmurs. Her soft warmth, the clean
odor of her hair and provocative scent of perfumes, was
intoxicating, a reality alive and responsive in his arms that
exceeded even his fantasies. And this was only the beginning,
the promise; the fulfillment was yet to come. He would be
slow and careful with her, he decided, restrain himself until
he was sure she was ready. This was too beautiful to spoil.

But the next moment, as one of his hands slid down her
burning flesh, he found her to be slippery and open, and he
did not wait. Up and over, between her legs, and his hardness
plunged into her. She gasped, falling at once into his pattern
of movement, her intense excitement translated into clutching, kissing, writhing and straining, biting him and uttering
a series of wordless little cries. He had a strange sensation
of being above it all, viewing them both from a distance and
thinking, with wonder, that this was the first time he had
ever truly known a woman. Those brief sordid couplings he
had known with squaws and frontier tarts, the few times
with more respectable ones who yielded only with shame
and near-motionless bodies, and even the lively bout with
Marigold were but weak travesties of this.

Her small cries sounded almost tormented now, her face
was wet with tears, and she was showering him with kisses
as wildly, joyfully, he drove his being into her with low,
hoarse outcries of his own finally welling out.

"Oh Paul . . . oh my God . . . Paul. . . ."

vii

They had a second time. This time was slower, longer and
in many ways more pleasurable, because with their first
importunate hungers satisfied they took more time for ex-
plorations of the flesh, savoring each new sensual delight to
the fullest. Fern introduced variety into their kissing—prolonged sweet kisses with her mouth opened and her tongue
caressing his. It was something he had only heard about,

something supposed to be practiced only by immoral French women. At another point she shocked him with something even more depraved: slipping down and taking his semi-tumescent penis in her mouth and laving his glans with her tongue until the organ grew so rigid with unbearable sensory tensions that he could barely wait for release again within her. He was in control now and was able to continue until her moans ceased and her breathing went gasping and ragged and, with her legs locked around his buttocks, he felt her final tremors beginning. And then the explosive climax. . . .

Afterward they lay close, sweating, unwilling to move apart, and he thought briefly of Syl—almost immediately feeling shamed for thinking of her in context with the abandoned carnality just enjoyed. As a doctor and from the purely medical viewpoint he knew the sex had been more than good, a magnificent example of bodies and glandular functions performing at their peak. Never before had his own body reached such sexual heights. Yet . . .

In his wildest dreams he could not imagine Syl acting with such unrestrained sexuality. His lifetime of thinking about women—absorbed into his very emotional fabric, as un-thinkingly as a sponge, from the society he had grown up in—placed them roughly in two categories: the pure heroine type he hoped someday to marry, and the "bad" ones.

According to such an attitude, Fern was one of the "bad" ones. At best a mixture of the two, but certainly not a lady. It was confusing.

She wriggled away from him. "I must wash."

"There's only cold water, since we can hardly ring the steward to bring hot."

"It doesn't matter."

"The pitcher and basin and towels are on the stand. Can you find your way in the darkness?" He didn't volunteer to relight the whale-oil lamp. Perhaps she wouldn't mind performing her lavage in his view—she was a strange one indeed —but he knew most women would consider that particular procedure too indelicate for male eyes.

She laughed, as if reading his mind. "Where are the matches? I can light the lamp, and you can look in the other direction if you like."

He rolled out of the bunk and found the cardboard box of Allin's Bright Devil big phosphorus matches and lit the lamp, then returned to the bunk, discreetly managing not to look in her direction.

After a while she returned, shivering a little, and cuddled up beside him.

"You are thinking terrible things about me?" she said.

"Why should I?"

"You know what I mean. . . . Men don't think women should be immodest, or have the same sexual appetites that they have. Unmarried females are expected to be virgins. Like Syl. She's twenty-three now and still a virgin, and will be until the day she marries."

That bit of information filled him with happiness—followed by a sense of shame. Shame for thinking of Syl as on a higher level than Fern—Fern, who had just given him the most joyous, exalting sexual experience of his life. But he could not change his feelings. He cherished the purity of Syl, and was unreasonably pleased to know she was still an unplucked virgin.

"It would be most ungrateful of me to think the worse of you for not being a virgin," he said with a devilish grin, "since at the moment I feel so much the better for it."

"Do you also feel it has changed everything between us?"

"And has it not?"

She traced a finger over his chest. "No. Not in the way I suspect you may think. I must make it clear that I am not in love with you, Paul, and I don't want you to be in love with me. I am a woman with physical needs just as strong as yours. You have for the moment satisfied them, and that's all there is to it. Nothing more. If you can understand that, Paul, and accept it—*really* accept it—matters will go well between us. We can have beautiful times together."

Paul was taken aback. From the vast welter of his misinformation and ignorance about women, he had taken it for granted that Fern would automatically be in love with him and perhaps become a problem. He was as yet uncertain of his feelings for her. He knew he was fond of her, certainly found her physically exciting, but his concept of love was still anchored in that mysterious, magical alchemy of feeling that Syl had wrought upon him.

"You're the damnedest, strangest woman I've ever met!"

"Stranger than you think. . . . Right now I have an urge to do something very wicked."

"I thought I had just fulfilled you."

"Something more wicked than that. Right now I would like a cigar."

He had heard about Creole ladies sometimes smoking

cigars, but Fern seemed bent on proving she was no lady. On the other hand, he was no gentleman. He tried to be droll:

"Don't you know that smoking is injurious to your lungs?"

"No more for women than it is for men. I've seen you smoke cigars."

"It's a matter of custom. Cigar smoking is a masculine habit. To give a reverse example, how would you like it if I took to wearing perfume and hoop skirts?"

She giggled. "Try it and see if I care."

"But that's the point—I wouldn't try to emasculate myself by aping a woman. If in your eagerness to share all male rights you must also take over male habits, you will only defeminize yourself."

She raised up and gave him a fast little kiss, then twisted around so that her breasts were close to his face. "Do these seem unfeminine?"

"Your body is surely feminine, but I'm not so sure of your thinking. . . ." He kissed one of the nipples and at the same instant, somewhat to his own surprise, felt a sudden new surge of arousal.

Her alert eyes had noticed, and a hand drifted down to caress the stiffening organ. She sighed. "I am beginning to think, Dr. Abbott, that you are among those unfortunate freaks collected by Mr. Barnum. Do you realize that this is the third—"

"I realize. I have been long without women."

"There were no women in Scotland?"

Her words jolted him, and his thoughts flashed back to something she had said when arriving . . . about realizing why he couldn't join her at Meyer's Hotel.

"How did you know I was in Scotland?"

She hesitated. "You told me. At least you told me you had studied in Edinburgh—"

"You're lying, Fern. I have a near-perfect memory, and I told you no such thing."

"All right, Paul. . . . I was only trying to save you embarrassment. . . ." She then proceeded to relate everything she'd read in the French newspapers about him before the ship had sailed.

Paul swore softly, remembering the sly, weasel-faced news writer, Robert MacCampbell, who had been paid so handsomely by Alex Ushant for advice and help—then immediately afterward had betrayed their trust by selling "inside" stories to the news syndicates. The syndicated dispatches would probably have reached New York before now.

"So you assumed that my reason for not going ashore was fear of arrest?" he said.

"Are there any other reasons?"

Briefly he considered revealing the dilemma he was in with Captain Cunningham, but saw no benefit to be derived. A hunted man develops caution.

"I would say that's quite sufficient reason," he said sourly. "But tell me, Fern, do you believe the facts of the story?"

"In the light of how I've come to know you, I refuse to believe you've done anything as terrible as the article said—yet the fact remains that you *are* running away."

"But only because of false charges! I am guilty only of stupidity." He then told her the whole dismal story, from the moment of his first blunder of bad judgment to the step-by-step deepening of his involvement until Alex had brought in the newswriter, followed by his making a run for it.

"I'm glad you told me the whole story, Paul, and I know you're telling the truth—but others may not be so easily convinced. . . ." She gave him a teasing smile. "Do you realize, sir, that my knowledge gives me the upper hand? You are now completely in my power."

He smiled wryly. "You are to hold me in thrall? To service you when you feel the need?"

"No. That would be an insult to my female conceit. I have other plans. . . . But to put them into action requires a revelation on my part. It just so happens, Paul, that my situation is no better—perhaps far worse—than yours."

"You too have been accused of bodysnatching?" he said, grinning. "Aside from mine, I mean."

"That was not amusing, sir!"

He moved his head around to kiss her other nipple. "By way of apology . . ."

"Don't distract me, Doctor. . . . As I was about to say, since you've told me your story, I shall go against my better judgment and make it a fair exchange by telling you some of my dark secrets. . . ."

There was an undercurrent of bitterness in her voice as she sketched out the story of her involvement in the Underground Railroad, telling of the burning anger first ignited in her when as a child in Cincinnati she had witnessed the brutal whipping of a slave escapee who had just swam the Ohio River—only to be caught by a Southern bounty hunter who was there on the shore of freedom waiting for him. Her fiery attachment to the cause of equal freedoms for all humans, regardless of sex or race, had been fanned higher and higher by heavy reading of liberal publications and the teachings of crusaders, and now she was helping slaves escape, and in it very deeply. . . .

"So you see, Paul, all you would have to do is breathe a word of this to Pierre or Syl and I would be finished. I've exposed myself to you, but it makes things fair. Now we're both in each other's power. It can be a bond between us."

Paul, for all his unthinking scorn of abolitionists, had been impressed by Fern's story.

"Our situations are far from alike, Fern. You've *chosen* the dangerous path you're following, which takes courage. I'm not at all brave. I am only running with my tail between my legs because I have no choice."

"You *are* brave, Paul! I saw you undertake an impossible operation. You could easily have refused to attempt it or have insisted on an amputation, and no one would have blamed you. Not even Pierre."

Paul, embarrassed, sought to change the subject. "What are those 'other plans' you hinted at?"

"I won't beat about the bush. I am in great need of new communication channels. A doctor's office in the South would be a great help."

"No, Fern—absolutely not! I refuse to get involved. I have a big enough fight on my hands as it is."

She looked momentarily disappointed, then laughed. "And I refuse to take no for an answer. But we can argue that at a more appropriate time. . . ." Sinuously she turned and snuggled against him, her lips seeking his mouth while an experienced hand trailed with butterfly lightness down to his male organ, which again surged with instant arousal.

"What about that cigar you wanted?"

"That can wait, too," she said.

FOUR: Day of the Porpoises

ON a bitterly cold, gloomy afternoon the *Clytemnestra*, outward bound, churned uneasily through a veil of sleeting snow that was falling on New York Bay. Paul, leaning against the taffrail, peered through the whitish murk until the shadowy skyline of the city had completely vanished astern, merging into the universal canopy of a snow-swirling world. Over the Narrows and on the rolling dark seas beyond, night was already falling.

Whither now, he wondered? To New Orleans and freedom, or to the gaol? A return to England could mean the noose. Perhaps he had erred in not attempting to jump ship in New York.

The first gong rang for dinner and he went back to his cabin to get ready.

At dinner he ate alone. Mike Quinn, the gambler, did not appear; perhaps was resting in his cabin after the carouse in New York. The new passengers looked uncomfortable, as if expecting soon to require his services. He visited Gayarre's suite later and found his arm still healing nicely, but Pierre's countenance was gloomy.

"Paul, I have a matter to discuss with you in confidence. Would you oblige me by closing the door?"

Paul closed the bedroom door and Pierre motioned him to be seated.

"First let me explain, Paul, that during my trip abroad I purchased a great quantity of expensive machinery for the cane-sugar refinery that Etienne and I are building. On visiting my New York bank I found that my account was overdrawn. It is but a trivial matter, and of course they honored the drafts I had already written. I telegraphed to Etienne to send on a bank draft, but it did not arrive before we sailed. For that reason I cannot give you the fee I had promised to pay you in New York, but be assured it will be paid promptly after our arrival in New Orleans."

Paul made a deprecatory gesture. "It matters not, Pierre. Since I expected no fee, your generosity needs no timetable."

"The sum I have in mind is one thousand dollars. Is that satisfactory?"

Paul was stunned. A thousand dollars! In his wildest dreams he had never thought to see a thousand dollars in one lump sum. Why, some of the professors in Edinburgh at the Royal College didn't make so much as eight hundred dollars a year. He would be a rich man!

He was about to demur with a polite protestation that he couldn't possibly accept such a sum—no operation was worth that much—then choked back the words. The money could assure the beginning of his medical career, with all the equipment, books and medications he had dreamed about!

If he could ever get ashore to collect it.

"The fee is more than generous and I will accept it most gratefully."

Pierre smiled. "I didn't think you were a fool, so that encourages me to get on to another matter. . . . There were letters waiting for me in New York informing me of an outbreak of smallpox at the plantations. Etienne is much concerned. Slaves, you will understand, are our most valuable properties. Without them we would be paupers. Therefore I am proposing that you return with me and accept a position as our plantation doctor."

The thought of becoming a salaried plantation doctor immediately after landing was a dazzling prospect—except for the serious obstacle that blocked him from accepting.

"Your proposition interests me very much, Pierre, and I will surely consider it, but at the moment I cannot make a firm decision."

Pierre's expression cooled. "The salary would be, I think, most fair."

"That I do not doubt, but—"

"How soon can I expect your decision?"

"The moment I debark in New Orleans. Will that be soon enough?"

Pierre nodded in agreement.

ii

The following several days were everything a voyager could wish for. Out of the soundings into blue water, the swells flattened. The moderated weather grew warmer with each passing day, and the skies grew remarkably clear, magnificently star-spangled at night and of clearest pale blue during the days, with only a gradual building of clouds along the horizon that melted aside before each morning's spectacular rise of the sun from the ocean.

Paul's duties were light. The common ailment of seasickness was absent. He spent more time strolling the decks and often encountered Fern and Syl out for a promenade. Since that night in his cabin, Fern's manner toward him was most casual, almost cool. He wondered whether he had unknowingly offended her in some way or if she were merely taking great care to keep Syl and Pierre from suspecting their closeness. Syl's manner, on the other hand, although demure and modest, was always cordial, and she insisted that he join them on their walks.

One bright forenoon the ladies were intrigued by a large school of porpoises playing about the ship like romping schoolboys. They kept following the *Cly* in this playful manner for an hour or two and then departed, steering a course to the southwest.

"That means a storm coming," said McKeon. "It'll blow from the same direction the porpoises are headed. Right now I'm steering a course, latitude 34° 30'—headed right into it. By evening we'll be in a gale." He turned to Paul. "And tomorrow you're going to be a busy man, Doctor. Most of the passengers will be down seasick, mark my words. . . ."

"I can't believe it," said Syl with a gay laugh. "There's not a cloud in the sky."

"Nevertheless, Miss Beauvais, you'd do well to batten your valuables down tight tonight."

Soon after, the First Officer excused himself to return to his duties. Fern and Syl decided to sit and read for awhile in their deck chairs. Paul returned to the infirmary and began grinding his powders for *mal de mer* on the hunch that McKeon might be right.

iii

By late afternoon, Paul was beginning to have great respect for McKeon's sea-savvy. A sudden quietude seemed to fall like a mantle over the seas, accompanied by a weird darkening of the skies. The still air was heavy with a strange palpitance that could almost be felt. Out of curiosity and a vague concern for the ladies he went on deck.

Their deck chairs were abandoned, but in one of them was a book, inadvertently left behind. Paul picked it up and saw that it was *Armance*, by Stendhal—the same book that Syl had dropped on the first day he had met her.

He took the book back to his cabin, intending to return it during his evening check of Pierre. Since Syl had been reading—or rereading—it he could not resist opening it to see what her literary taste might be. It was in French, which he could not read, but in the front a handwritten inscription drew his eyes:

For my dearest Syl—
Would that I had the courage to tell you vis-à-vis. But even
had I the courage, my boundless love for you would in itself
be an impediment to my poor efforts to properly explain, in
a manner fit for your chaste ears, a matter of such delicacy.
. . . So I beg of you to read this novel and from it gain the
understanding of that which I dare not express. . . .

Paul clapped the book shut, shamed. It was as if he had
peered into a stranger's heart. The unsigned inscription had
doubtless been written by Syl's now deceased fiancé for her
eyes alone.

A charcoal sky had brought premature twilight and the
seas were churning into foam-crested hills and valleys pushed
by moaning winds when Paul went to the Victoria suite.
Aurora admitted him as usual. Since neither Syl nor Fern
were in view, he was about to hand the book to the black
girl to return to Syl, but a roar of anger stayed his hand.

"One moment, Doctor—! Give me that book!"

He turned and in astonishment saw Pierre, his face livid,
striding toward him. Pierre snatched the book from his hand.

"Where did you get this book?" he demanded.

"I happened to see it in the deck chair where Syl had
been sitting and took this occasion to return it."

Pierre's dark eyes bored into him. "Have you read it?"

"I have not, sir. I cannot read French."

"But did you not open it?"

For Paul, even polite lies came hard, but he did not wish
to increase Pierre's high dudgeon, for whatever the puzzling
reasons.

"Pierre," he said gently, "I have no interest or concern
with what may be contained in the book. I merely found
it, quite by accident, and am now returning it. Nothing more.
I see no reason for your upset."

Pierre took a deep breath and visibly relaxed. His features
began to resume a semblance of his usual affability.

"My deepest apologies, Paul. . . . I cannot explain what
came over me. Mayhap I have been worrying too much about
the problems that will face me on my return to the plantation. It could be an effect of the weather. . . ." His glance
dropped in embarrassment.

"I shall have to ask you to excuse me for now, Paul. I feel
no need of medical attention tonight, but only to be left
alone."

"But Pierre—"

"No, Paul. Go. Please."

With a brief bow, Paul turned and left.

Outside, the weather was rapidly becoming worse. The sou'wester had caught them on their beam, and the *Clytemnestra* was alternately pointing her bow at the bed of the ocean and lifting it toward the hidden stars. Seen from above, Paul thought, there might be something magnificent in the way the giant waves reared and combed and fell seething across the deck, but for him it was a frightening experience as he sloshed across the slippery planking, shoes and trouser legs soaked and staggering for balance.

In his cabin, Paul puzzled over Pierre's reaction. Obviously the novel *Armance* and the inscription inside had great and disturbing significance for him. Was he in love with Syl? It was easy enough to believe that a man as young and vital as Pierre could lose his head over a girl as charming and beautiful as Syl—but being cousins, such a romantic relationship would be considered as incest in many societies. Was it also forbidden among the Creoles?

For the first time in his life, Paul felt a gnawing sense of jealousy—something he knew he had no right to feel. He had utterly no claim on Syl. Scarcely knew her. Indeed, the idea that she could ever be interested in a rough clod of an impoverished doctor was preposterous. Nor was the enigma of Pierre's reaction any of his concern. In any case, the mystery was apparently locked away in the pages of *Armance*, and it was just as well that he couldn't read French. . . .

iv

The wind had increased to gale violence. Every bolt and bulkhead seemed to be creaking and straining to the breaking point as the floundering vessel hung suspended at the peak of mountains of water before plunging downward again. Through the porthole—scarcely two inches of glass that separated him from the maelstrom of wind and sea—Paul had a weird view of the unstable world outside. There seemed no ordained place for the water. One minute the surface of the sea dropped below sight, and the next it had risen far above his head. The submerged view gave the sensation of being in a submarine, especially when fish swam against the glass. With the storm came thunder and lightning and such a heavy downpouring of rain that it seemed the heavens had cracked open. Knowing it was impossible to sleep, Paul lay on his bunk, legs bent and propped to keep from rolling out, and attempted to read under the wildly flouncing rays of the wall lantern. So loud were the groanings and creakings of the ship and the raging elements outside that he was scarcely aware of the knocking on the door until it grew urgent.

When he opened the door and she rushed in, her clothing was as sopped as if she'd been swimming in them.

"My God, Fern, you shouldn't have risked your life coming here in such a storm—you could have been washed overboard!"

"Don't talk now—just help me get these damn soaked things off. . . ."

With his help she began tugging off the clinging layers of garments, but even before they were finished she began tearing away at his shirt and trousers.

When they were both stripped naked, her arms encircled him almost savagely and her wet hot body crushed against him while her fiery lips found his. She seemed in fever. They swayed on the heaving flood kissing for a few moments before he tried to guide her to the bunk, but fiercely she resisted, pulling him off balance.

"I don't want to wait, Paul! *Now* . . ."

They fell armlocked and sprawling and almost at once her legs spread and wrapped around his thighs as if trying to encompass him while one of her hands was feverishly reaching for his suddenly jutting penis. A sudden lurching roll of the ship sent them both sliding over the floor, still clinging together, and during the brief pause before the vessel swung back to right itself he succeeded in penetrating her. Scarcely had he begun his rhythmic plunging when with a quick, twisting movement of her own, aided by the yawing of the ship, she rolled over until she was above but still coupled to him. And now the fervid abandon of her passion pumping against him had all the wild and raw fury of the elements outside.

Though the sensations were pleasant, the reversed positions were not entirely to Paul's liking, and he sought to roll her back. She at once made it apparent that her intention, most decidedly, was to remain atop, and she balked his every move to regain the dominant position. She was determined and remarkably strong and used spread-eagled arms and legs to keep him pinned down, all the while driving her crotch down against him.

For a while it became a three-way battle; the two of them against the violent yawing, pitching and lurchings of the ship and each of them against the thrusting furies of the other. Finally Paul reared up with his mid-section, his back and pelvis arching like an uncoiling spring in the way a wild bronco tries to unseat its rider. For a moment, still locked to his organ, her legs dangled helplessly above the floor before he twisted away, dislodging her. Before she could recover any leverage or balance, he had rolled her over and was jammed into her, back in the rider's seat.

"Oh damn damn *damn* you, Paul!" She hissed and fought as furiously as a puma while at the same time her nails raked blood down his back and buttocks in her clutching efforts to devour all of him within her being. Outside the seas raged and the waves crashed and both of them reached the cotidal moment at the same instant, as if flung there by the storm.

v

They lay limp and lax in the bunk, where Paul had carried her. Fern burrowed her head against his neck. "Are you angry, Paul?"

"At what?" he said, surprised.

"At me for being . . . so aggressive."

"You provided me with much pleasure." He grinned and added, "But it's fortunate that I am quite strong and in good physical condition. Do you often get so combative in love-making?"

"Violent storms bring out something in my nature . . . something I can't understand or change. Most of the time I am full of fears, insecure, emotionally tense. Storms, the smell of danger, seem to make the pressures so unbearable that I must seek release in a way that . . . I mean, it's as though I must conquer in sex in order to conquer my fears, and if I can't conquer, at least fight until all the emotional pressures are drained away, and then I am at peace. . . ."

Outside, the turbulence of the storm continued unabated; the bunk tilted and heaved, swaying their bodies with the rhythm of the elements.

"Are you at peace now?" he said.

"Very relaxed, very content."

"Would you like to sleep?"

"No. There's too little time, and we have much to talk about."

"About what?"

"Your future, for one thing, Paul. Pierre has told me he offered you a position as plantation physician, but that you didn't accept."

"Nor did I turn it down. I told him I would give him my decision on arriving in New Orleans."

"But why wait, Paul? Pierre is a very sensitive man and I think he was offended. He needs good medical help for the slaves, and I know he would pay you handsomely. You would also be furnished with a private residence on the plantation —not large but very comfortable—"

"As well as most convenient and pleasurable," Paul interrupted with a laugh, wishing to evade the subject. "Especially during the storm seasons. . . . "

"Fine surgeon or not," she said tartly, "you're certainly not a gentleman! And you're talking like a fool. Have you forgotten that you're a wanted man and notices about you may be posted in the Southern police stations? Working for Pierre in the privacy of a large plantation, you would be safe. Only a fool would hesitate for a moment about grasping such an opportunity."

Paul sighed. The time for truth had come.

"Fern, it happens that you're not the only one on this ship who knows the police of Scotland are looking for me. Captain Cunningham got a telegraphic message before we sailed, and though he's told no one else as yet, it's a sword he's holding over my head as a means of getting my services without payment, and he also plans to take me back to England—in chains if necessary—in hopes of collecting a reward. I couldn't tell Pierre this, but the fact is I never expect to see your charming city of New Orleans."

"Oh no, Paul. . . ." Fern grasped him to her, putting her face against his chest. After a while she said intensely:

"Now it's equal for both of us . . . a sword is hanging over both our heads. But I'll find a way to help you—if you help me—and we'll win out together. . . ."

FIVE: Slavers' Nest

ZAMBULLAH lay on the cage floor, scorning the stiff straw pallet which along with a filthy blanket had been shoved into the cage from an opening in the top. The concern of his white captors had not been for his comfort but solely to ward off sickness from their most valuable nigger. At times during the worst of the Atlantic storms Zambullah had used them for warmth, but only when violent winds and slashing rains tore aside the canvas covering of the cage and deck-flung waves sloshed over its floor. It was not the vermin crawling in the bedding that bothered him; it was the discomfort of the softness and the white man's stink that he found intolerable. Myriads of tiny crawling things had always been a part of his existence but were of no bother to black skin as they were to white. Nor had they ever invaded the thatched mud hut in which he and Tembah had lived. Tembah had put layers of cattle dung over the floor, packed it down with patient beating of her hands to make the surface hard and smooth, then polished it to a gleaming brownish-black by days of circular movements with the palms of both hands until it felt pleasant under bare feet and made the hut fragrant with its smell. Insects avoided cattle-dung floors. The whites, who were not as clean, did not know these things.

Tembah so filled his thoughts that he had stopped dreaming of leopards. Being deprived of the pleasures she offered and with no outlet for his surging energies had bottled up his manhood juices until the yearning for her was constant anguish. He knew that she must be somewhere among the five hundred slaves packed in the hold of the ship, and once he thought he had heard her plaintive cry, but it was so submerged amid the continuous dirge of fear and lamentations that he couldn't be sure. Whenever they brought up a body to toss overboard—almost daily, sometimes several times a day—he strained with a terrible dread to see the face. As some burials were at night, he could not know if she still lived or had fed the sharks.

Also burning inside was always that other thing. Hate. He tried to hide it when faces peered in at him, but not always. One bewhiskered face, not young, he knew to be of great importance because of the fine clean clothes, a golden chain across the fat soft belly and the respect shown the man by all others. They addressed him as "Mister Hogg," and Zambullah stored the name carefully in his memory. It gave focus for his hate; it helped to palliate his frustrations by dreaming of the pleasure of slicing a knife deeply across that plump belly and watching the blood and guts gush out thickly. Hogg stared in at him frequently, and sometimes Zambullah stared back while hate welled up to flood against his teeth in a sour bile and brought guttural sounds to his throat until the man backed away hastily. It pleasured Zambullah to know that the important white man was cowardly and afraid.

ii

Elias Hogg, after backing away from the cage imprisoning the black man, scuttled away out of sight but soon paused to rest against the gunwale just abaft of the larboard forechains. He was trembling, breathing raggedly, and his heart pounded, bringing the usual pain in the upper part of his chest. May the Lord forgive and protect me, he appealed silently, for I have looked into the face of the devil.

The face of the devil was black.

What it was that drew him back day after day to peer into the nigger's face he could scarcely fathom. It was hypnotic, irresistible, akin to the fascination that the timid get from gazing upon safely caged ferocious animals. But for Hogg it had much more—the pull of evil against which throughout his churchy life he had fought so vigorously.

For Hogg was a very religious man, and like so many who make an ostentatious show of their love of God for the betterment of their own bankbooks, Hogg was not without an array of private superstitions and biased opinions quite in contradiction to Biblical teachings. When at home, he gave his tithe to the church (cheating considerably but reckoning that it hardly mattered since the Creator had no need of worldly wealth), and he prayed every morning and night as insurance against his profits, devoutly believing that a grateful God would look after his interests to the exclusion of his enemies and victims.

And had he not prospered? Once he had thought that one million dollars would more than fulfill his fondest dreams, but having already achieved that—all from slaving —and most of it so soundly invested that he could live in luxury for the rest of his life on interest alone—his greed for ever more wealth had become a consuming passion.

Leaning against the gunwale, he looked aimlessly at the rhythmic monotony of greenish-blue waves as the *Betsy Ann* slipped through the water, leaving in its wake a gentle hissing stream that would have lulled the senses of most, but in Hogg's case did just the reverse. They had crossed the Atlantic and were now in Caribbean waters, which should have been cause for relaxing, but instead Hogg was in the grip of inward tensions born of a sense of approaching end and climax that could sweep away all the profits of this voyage.

Money at sea is money halfway lost. Not worth a farthing until the vessel's tied in and the cargo unloaded.

Several times during the terrible Atlantic storms he had feared it was the end. A judgment onto him? *Vengeance is mine, saith the Lord.* But for what? He had prayed mightily during the big blows, reminding God of His duty to His devout servant. And the storms had passed. The Lord had been good to him.

Still, the prescience of evil lingered. *Thy sin will find ye out. . . .*

There was no doubt in his mind now that the nigger was evil. The devil incarnate. From the beginning he had known he was a curse on the ship. Look at what had happened— seventy-nine niggers already gone overboard, from disease and insanity—a loss of near $100,000 they would have fetched in the Cuban and American markets.

And now this. . . . For days the winds had been fickle. He looked up at the sails, bellied out loose and heavy as ill-hung curtains. They were nearing Cuba and at any moment might encounter a British man-of-war or one from the fleet of the Viceroyalty of New Spain. With a decent wind the *Betsy Ann* could outrun most steam-driven craft, but in this lazy breeze she could easily be overtaken.

A year ago it wouldn't have mattered, but this year of 1855 was bringing new tribulations to the slave trade. General José de la Concha, who for the past decade had ruled the "Pearl of the Antilles," as Cuba called herself, had permitted slaving, being a large slaveholder himself. But this year Isabella II, who sat on the Spanish throne in Madrid, had dispatched General Juan M. Penzuela to replace Concha as the new Captain-General. Penzuela, a liberal and an abolitionist, had at once banned the illegal slave traffic and even talked of soon liberating all unregistered slaves. To worsen matters, Britain, pushing Spain to honor an 1817 treaty to abolish the slave trade, had won permission to station a commission in Havana to free all slaves imported in violation of the treaty.

Which wouldn't diminish the slave traffic one whit. The new laws only meant that more caution must be exercised.

Instead of unloading slaves on the mainland, they were now being diverted to the "slavers' nests" in the archipelagoes, that scattering of islands off the Cuban coast. From these nests it was relatively easy and safe to ferry small boatloads of slaves to the mainland via one of the numerous, remote bottlenecked harbors to be readily purchased and absorbed by the large sugar-cane plantations. With the same ease, many of them would be shipped the short distance to New Orleans, purported to be "legal" slaves from Cuba for sale in the United States.

"Mr. Hogg, sir . . . "

Hogg swung around, startled from his gloomy reveries. The swarthy face of Captain Ignacio Perez regarded him solemnly. "Yes?"

"Smoke on the horizon to the northwest, sir. Approaching. With your permission I shall change course to southeast. I don't think we've been seen, but it could be a man-o'-war and—"

"Yes, yes," Hogg said hastily. "By all means. And another thing—" His eyes drifted to the cage holding the big black man. "Get that cage down in the hold out of sight. A man with a spyglass on a passing vessel might see it and have his suspicions aroused."

"But sir, if we keep it covered with canvas—"

"No, no—" Hogg's voice was edged with hysteria. He had a compelling new sense of the terrible evil seeping from that cage, the smell of it spreading across the waves to draw other evil. "Get that nigger down in the slavehold!"

"Yes, sir. At once, Mr. Hogg."

                                iii

Down in the slavehold, Luis Labat looked contemptuously at the two rough-looking men approaching. One was short and chunky, but muscular enough. His name was Jed Dort. The other, Milo McNeely, was tall and sinewy with a tobacco-stained yellowish beard. Labat could count on this pair to the minute. As soon as they were off duty, they came hustling down with their balls afire and cocks half out. . . .

"*Cuanto*, Luis?" said Dort, the chunky one. "How much today?"

Labat turned and let his glance run sourly over the hundreds of naked sweating black bodies, so close-packed that many had to sleep in half-sitting positions or curled to fit into whatever available space. The festering stench from defecations and all those unwashed bodies, intensified by tropical heat and the lack of ventilation, would have sickened most, but Labat hardly noticed. As the slave overseer on many a voyage he was so blunted to noxious odors that he could have eaten his lunch in a *pissoir*. Yet Labat had his own kind of fastidiousness; why any man would pay good money to hump over the belly of one of these filthy black *putas* was beyond his comprehension. The thought filled him with squeamish distaste. His own preference was for boys.

"I asked how much?" Dort repeated with angry impatience.

Labat slashed him with a scornful glance. He had no need to hurry his answer. He was in that enviable position of having a commodity to sell that others must have. For these two, wenches were like a drug they couldn't go long without, and Labat adjusted his prices accordingly. Moreover, he was proudly aware of his authority. He stood over six feet, all solid bone and rippling muscles, as was clear enough to see with every movement beneath the sleeveless, sweat-soaked jerkin he wore. His swarthy face in itself was intimidating, relieved here and there with white scar slashes from previous knife fights, and one dark eye had a way of rolling fiercely over the one he was speaking to while the other, being of blue glass—a replacement of one lost in a fight—stared fixedly. Too, his black mustache drooped like the long pointed fins of some devilish kind of fish, and his stringy black hair was tied down tightly at the nape of his neck.

"The price is five pesetas each," said Labat.

Dort clapped a hand to the side of his head. "Five hundred centimos! Yesterday it was three pesetas. When we left Africa it was only fifty centimos."

"So?" Labat shrugged. "Tomorrow it may be ten pesetas each."

Dort and McNeely went away a few feet to confer, but soon returned. "We'll pay the five, Luis—but that's for both of us because we'll both use the same wench."

Labat took some dried tobacco leaves from a pocket, folded them carefully in his mouth and began chewing, saying nothing. It was the best answer. He knew the value of his merchandise. Indeed, the extra profits from each voyage were making him rich. Nearly every member of the crew visited the slavehold at various hours of the night and day and always ended up paying the fee he had set for that particular day. Labat's skill with a knife was too well known for argument.

"All right, you cutthroat robber, we'll both pay five pesetas."

They always selected the same one—the wench who had cried out so piercingly in fright the first time they had handled her and fought like a tigress—but after that she had been submissive. Labat unlocked her and they began leading her toward the pallet.

She had, Labat noted, begun casting apprehensive glances toward the cage holding the huge nigger that had been lowered into the hold earlier, and she was holding back, struggling weakly.

When they flung her satiny black body on the pallet, she whimpered like a dog about to be beaten by its master, knowing it was inevitable, making only a token show of resistance.

Dort unbuckled his belt, unbuttoned his trousers and let them drop down to his hairy calves. His thick stubby penis jutted out stiffly.

The girl's beautiful mahogany face convulsed with terror and she made a feeble effort to rise, but the other man, accustomed to this, at once hunkered down behind her head and quickly pinioned her back with his large toil-hardened hands biting into her shoulders. By this time Dort had kneeled, forcibly wedging her legs apart. He was emitting little grunts, sweating profusely, and his porcine little blue eyes glistened with a kind of madness as they focused on that one spot—the end-all of everything in his circumscribed life—nestled in fur between her thighs. He positioned himself closer. His hips jerked.

As he penetrated, she shrieked.

Labat was missing out on the entertainment because his attention had already been diverted by the unusual commotion coming from the cage. There was a furious shaking and rattling, and before his unbelieving eyes one of the steel bars came loose, bent out. Another . . .

Then came the most unearthly sound Labat had ever heard, a wild jungle roar that made his blood run cold. . . .

iv

The sound, like the roar of a leopard, shocked Elias Hogg to a standstill.

He had been out taking his constitutional in the pleasant tropical twilight, having just dined amply, and reflecting that all was going well since the threat of smoke on the horizon had vanished.

But now the bellows of animal rage erupting from the slavehold, mingled with shouts and howls of pain, sent chills up his spine, started his heart thudding. *The black devil has broken out, gone berserk. . . .*

He turned to call for help, though none of the crew was in sight. At that same moment he was distracted by a dark form emerging from the hatchway. The iron grating usually nailed over the opening had earlier that day been loosened and pulled aside to allow passage of the cage to the slavehold, so there was nothing to block the naked black girl who came rushing out. Clumsily he flung out his arms to halt her.

"Stop, stop—I am ordering you to—!"

Sidestepping him, she darted toward the railing and moments later vanished overboard into the swirling waters.

Hogg sagged against the railing, an arm flailing for support. One of the comeliest wenches . . . would fetch as much as two thousand . . .

Where was everybody? He tried again to call but couldn't summon enough breath. His heart was *lunk-a-lunking* in his ears and it was all he could do to suck in a little air through the squeezing pain in his chest. *God, help thy servant!* As from a far distance he was aware of the furor below, the meaty thumps of iron against flesh, screams of sheer terror. . . .

Labat the overseer appeared in the hatchway. He was dragging one leg, hopping along frantically on the other. Blood streamed from his forehead, was running into his one good eye, dribbling into his open mouth, which was shouting wildly:

"Ahoy mates! Gun this beast down—he's kilt two of us a'ready!"

The black man, who was close behind, paused for a moment in the hatchway opening while his burning eyes swiveled between Labat and Hogg. Then he bounded forward with the sinuous grace of a panther.

Oh God, God, thy servant implores—!

The prayer died silently in Hogg's throat as those great hands clamped around his neck. *Vengeance is mine, saith the Lord. . . .* He floated upward, his neck snapping with a single jerk before his body went flying, its legs still jerking in final reflexes, far overboard.

Moments later the aroused crew went at the black man like a pack of dogs, overwhelming and beating him into insensibility with clubs and belaying pins.

"Just be careful you don't kill the bastard!" howled the captain. "That's our most valuable nigger!"

Had Hogg been alive to know, it might have gratified him to note that they were taking all due steps to protect his slave property.

BOOK THREE

Creole Country

ONE: Balize

THE anchor dropped into the water with a loud splash and rattle. The ship blew off steam and let out a little more chain. Then followed several short blasts from the boat whistle and the *Clytemnestra* lay at anchor, rocking in nine fathoms of sullen swift current at the mouth of the Mississippi.

At the larboard railing, Paul stared through the cloud-dulled atmosphere in dismay. The forenoon sun was still obscured in a gray sky and streamers of mist hovered over the murky waters, but he could still see land clearly enough about a mile away. He had expected white beaches, blue waters and lush masses of exotic green palms. Instead he saw only a low swampy coastline, seemingly of black mud, fringed with an indifferent growth of weeds, scrub brush and low willows. Beyond was an assemblage of mean wooden buildings among which rose two framed towers that he assumed were lookout stations.

Noticing Chief Engineer Slattery sauntering past, Paul pointed at the dismal view. "Are those habitations the outskirts of New Orleans?"

Slattery guffawed. "What you're looking at, Doctor, are the abodes of sin. That's Balize—it's a Creole word meanin' 'buoy,' or 'beacon.' Our pilot will be coming from there, when he gets around to it. New Orleans's still a hundred ten miles up the river."

"Why do you call them the 'abodes of sin'?"

"Except for the pilots and custom officers, nobody lives there but smugglers, pirates, all sorts of riff-raff, and of course the kind of women they fancy. It's a dangerous place. I'd sooner bed down with rattlesnakes than set foot on that island."

"It's just an island? I assumed it was part of the mainland."

"No. It's one of them islands you see all around that gets started first with a log sticking in the mud, then grows to a sand bar and keeps building up with weeds and trees and so on. But now they say Balize is sinkin,' or gettin' washed to sea, whatever. In another ten or twenty years it could be gone, or the bayou will fill in, and then they'll have to move the pilot station up closer to the head of the passes."

"How soon will a pilot be out to guide us in?"

"Could be by noon, could be midnight." Slattery chuckled. "Depends on how much carousing they did last night."

"If they're really that inefficient, I'm surprised they haven't been fired."

"Hah! You expect efficiency from the government? I got an old copy of the *Commercial Review,* saved it special because it's got a legislative report made several years ago of how bad the situation is at Balize, and nothing's been done about it yet. Loan it to you if you're interested."

"Please don't bother."

"No bother at all," Slattery said airily, and ambled off.

Paul stared glumly at the dreary waterscape. The only items of interest were the schooner *Abigail* outward bound, a brig at anchor, a bomb ketch and several smaller vessels moving about. Slattery's description of Balize had only depressed him.

Even more depressing was the knowledge that he would

never get to see New Orleans except, at best, through a porthole window. . . .

The steward's assistant approached.

"Mr. Gayarre wishes to see you, Doctor. . . ."

ii

One arm in a fresh white sling, the slender fingers of his other hand holding a cigar from which he had been puffing with nervous gusto, Pierre paced back and forth in the study of the Victoria suite. Today his trim figure was garbed in a beige linen suit that was a shade lighter than the sun-bronzed coloration of his skin from a lifetime under southern suns. His shirt was of pale-olive silk, his stock a delicate magenta, and he wore highly polished brown boots. In every way he looked like a Creole dandy, a gallant—except for the peregrine quality of his profile, the hawkish nose, eyes as piercing and cold as black ice. He paused to frown at Paul.

"The story that Fern has told me about you clarifies many things, Paul. . . . "

"I only regret," Paul said stiffly, "that Fern took the liberty of telling you of my personal matters without consulting me."

"I beg you not to condemn Fern for what may appear to be a breach of confidence. She did it solely for your own good. Would you have told me had she not?"

"No."

"I don't understand you, Paul. Are we not friends?"

"I am honored to think that, but I still wouldn't presume to burden you with my problems."

"You would prefer being taken back against your will to England—possibly to the gallows?"

"Need I answer that?"

"Then answer this: would you accept my offer of employment if you were free to do so?"

"Gladly and most gratefully. It could perform wonders in easing the difficulties of my career, but since I have no choice in the matter, I can only give you my thanks for what might have been. At least you know now why I can't accept."

Pierre smote his good hand against the back of a nearby chair in a gesture of annoyance.

"Paul, I am beginning to think you are a fool in all matters except those of surgical and medical concern! You know nothing of the world—you are a veritable babe in the woods. Have you never heard of the power structure, the social fabric that holds the world together? Do you imagine for one moment that I, Pierre Gayarre, do not have access to that power structure—indeed, am not a part of it? I am a close friend of Jean de Baptiste Castillon, the French consul. I am on equally familiar terms with Baron le Pontalba and Pierre Caron de Beaumarchais, just to mention a few. These are among the men who rule New Orleans, which is to say all of Louisiana. We're almost back in my country, my friend, where I have powerful allies and where enemies dare not provoke me."

"That may be true, sir—"

Again Pierre smote a hand against the chair. "I told you many times—not sir! My friends call me *Pierre*."

Paul smiled. "I promise not to forget again, Pierre, though I doubt there'll be much opportunity to prove it. Perhaps you don't know the stubborn character of the English. Captain Cunningham is a splendid example of that trait. If he's determined to take me back to England, neither reason nor bribes will deter him. No matter how powerful you and your friends may be, you cannot flout English law on English property—as this ship happens to be."

Pierre laughed. "Excuse my laughing at your naiveté, but you don't understand how many ways there are of circumventing unyielding obstacles such as our hardnosed captain. For example, we are now at the mouth of the Mississippi, where this English ship, by American law, must cast anchor and await the pilot. He will come aboard with a naval officer to check the ship's papers before giving the necessary clearance, without which the ship cannot proceed to New Orleans. I will be watching, and when the pilot boat arrives I shall have a few words with the officer. . . . " Pierre waved his hand airily. "So your problem will be solved, my friend. As to the means, I do not yet know how it will be handled, but never fear. A way will be found."

Paul could not help laughing at Pierre's ebullient optimism, but he did not really believe that even Pierre with all his influence could budge the captain.

"You must be in very dire need of a doctor," he joked, "to speak of going to such trouble."

"You are correct," Pierre said soberly. "My slaves are my fortune. I couldn't replace my trained ones for an average of fifteen hundred dollars apiece. So for each of them you can save from the smallpox epidemic, I'm that much more indebted to you."

"If I ever make it ashore I'll save as many as possible, but nothing I can do would ever be sufficient payment for my freedom."

Pierre waved his hand impatiently. "Go now, Paul. I must be alone to do some careful thinking on this matter—perhaps more for the sake of my fortune than for your freedom. . . . "

iii

Any small hopes that Paul might have had that the captain's determination to keep him prisoner might soften were soon dispelled. Returning to his quarters, he found the ship's carpenter, a competent-looking man of middle age, at work fitting a new lock on the cabin door.

"What's this for?" said Paul, indicating the new lock.

The carpenter shrugged. "It's not for me to question the captain's orders, Doctor."

"Where are the keys?"

"You'll have to see the captain about 'em, sir. He's the one who give me the lock to install."

Paul found Captain Cunningham in his small office amidships.

"Sir, is it your intention to keep me locked in my cabin?"

"Waal . . . " The captain, seated at his paper-littered desk, took his stubby little black pipe from his mouth and expelled a thoughtful puff of blue smoke. "Answer to that is yes and no. . . . From dawn till dusk ye'll be free to move about the ship. Nights your door will be locked. If you're not in your quarters by darkfall, ye'll be placed under arrest. We'll soon be in port and I've advised certain of my men that under no circumstances are you to be allowed to leave the ship without my express permission. Is that clear, Dr. Abbott?"

"It's clear enough," Paul said bitterly, "that you're bent on taking me back to England in hopes of collecting a reward as well as availing yourself of my medical services without paying me."

The captain let out a few more puffs of smoke. "On that matter I've given much thought. . . . You've performed your duties well and at the end of the voyage ye'll be paid every cent of the salary. There's no reason why the line should not pay for services rendered, and ye'll need the money to hire a barrister for your defense in the higher courts. If there's any reward, it will be turned over to the Seafarers' Fund. I would want no part of it."

Paul smiled sourly. "I do not, of course, expect your actions to be as noble as your words."

Cunningham, misunderstanding, said sharply, "If you doubt my word, Mr. Gayarre could attest otherwise. Just this morning he visited me and dropped enough of a hint, mind ye, that he knew of your trouble and would pay handsomely if I blinded myself to the law. I made it plain that money could not swerve me from my bounden duty. Being close to retirement, comfortably enough fixed for money, I do not wish my ending years clouded with the knowledge that at this point in life my sober and seasoned judgment failed to uphold English law. Good day, Dr. Abbott."

Paul left, surprised that Pierre had approached the captain on his behalf. It was to be expected, of course. A sophisticated man like Pierre would have first tried the easiest way, knowing that money unlocks many doors.

iv

From the taffrail Paul watched the pilot boat arrive. Two men came aboard. One was a customs-house officer wearing the insignia of a captain and the other a naval officer of lesser rank. Both appeared unduly florid of face, particularly of nose, and from the excessive loud cordiality with which they greeted Captain Cunningham it was plain that they had come well fortified with liquid stimulants for their arduous work. Which was soon accomplished. The handshakings and courtesy-talk consumed at least five minutes, but when the ship manifests and other papers were produced they required but a cursory glance and a few scrawled signatures to complete the task. As they bid their goodbyes and were about to leave, a commanding voice rang out:

"Captain Drake—!"

Both officers turned toward the voice, as did Paul. Pierre, with Syl on his good arm, was approaching.

"Ah, Mr. Gayarre! What a surprise and honor." The senior officer walked toward Pierre with new dignity, hand outstretched. The other officer followed. Both had straightened their shoulders, seemed considerably sobered.

"I regret that I cannot return your handshake," said Pierre with a wry smile. "As you can see, my right arm . . . "

Suddenly embarrassed at eavesdropping, Paul withdrew until he was out of earshot. He looked back briefly to see Pierre going through the introduction of Syl, the low bowing and expansive smiles. Then obviously Pierre was inviting them back to his suite, for soon the four of them started away in that direction.

Dejected, Paul went back to his cabin. The glimpse of Syl—a glorious vision in a pale-lavender gown, her coppery-gold hair cascading in the breeze around her smiling face—had filled him with wistful pain. He was sure that he would never get to know her. The talk with the captain had convinced him that Pierre could do nothing that would help him now.

In his cabin, left unlocked because of his lack of a key, he found an opened copy of De Bow's *Commercial Review* lying face down on his small table. Slattery had been faithful to his word. Picking it up, he glanced at the title of an article that had been pencil-marked: "Reprint of a Legislative Report on the Infamies of Balize." He threw it down in disgust. Depressing reading matter he did not need.

He lay on the bunk and tried to look at his situation objectively. What were his options for escape? All he could think of was jumping overboard and swimming to shore, but he doubted he could swim a whole mile. Besides, these tropical waters probably teemed with sharks.

Hours passed before the knock came. He bounded up and opened the door. Fern came in and, ignoring him, went directly to the porthole window.

"What's this all about, Fern?"

"I'm just checking to see if you can squeeze those broad shoulders of yours through the porthole."

"You mean I've got to make a swim for it?"

"Let's hope not. Sometime during the night—probably close to dawn—a boat with muffled oars will arrive. Pierre has drawn a sketch of the ship pinpointing the location of your cabin, which will help them guide the boat, but it's bound to be very foggy, so I have brought a little lantern which you are to light shortly after midnight and hang in the porthole window as a beacon. There'll be several men in the boat who will help lower your bags and you into the boat."

Paul's first surge of elation quickly subsided. The escape plan had all the sound of some childish adventure.

"And I am to be totally dependent on the two alcohol-fogged pilot officers I saw talking to Pierre as to whether this plan is ever put into action?"

"Tipplers or not, Pierre seems to have remarkable faith in them. And before I forget it, here's something else. . . . " She opened her purse and extracted an envelope. "One hundred dollars. It's the best Pierre can do until he's back at the plantation, but it should be sufficient for all your necessaries."

Paul accepted the money gratefully.

"Your instructions are to go directly to the Pontalba Apartments, which are facing the Place d'Armes—that's the public square, so you'll have no trouble finding it. Pierre maintains a suite there for business purposes. In the envelope with the money you will find a note addressed to the concierge authorizing you to have full access and use of the apartment—that's in case Pierre has not yet arrived, but quite likely he'll get there first."

"If I am to leave tonight, why should Pierre be 'quite likely' to get there before I do?"

"Because you'll be going by a more circuitous route in a small sailing craft. And you may be delayed for a while at Balize while they make preparations for the trip."

"Balize!"

"Yes. That's the pilot station. You see, this whole thing is a quasi-official affair. A matter of closed eyes on the part of the authorities involved because . . . well, because Pierre is *Pierre*."

She smiled and impulsively put out her arms and drew his head down and kissed him on the lips.

"I'm not *in* love with you, Paul, but you know I love you very dearly. I was hoping to spend some of the night with you, but I know of the curfew imposed on you—the captain made the error of telling Pierre about it this morning, which is why this plan was devised. So now I must leave. It will soon be dark and it would never do if I were locked in here with you."

She kissed him again and left.

v

Soon after Fern's departure, Paul heard a key turning in the lock. The captain was proving true to his word.

With hours yet to kill—assuming the boozing pilot-station

officers had not already forgotten Pierre's "plan"—he picked up the *Commercial Review* left by Slattery, and adjusting the light over the bunk, lay down to skim through the article on Balize:

. . . your Committee has been informed by witnesses of unblemished character that Balize is a scene of barbarous strife and drunken debauch and that the pilot service is negligently performed, and more especially are the persons engaged in it, as a body, a desperate, worthless, reckless class of men.

Located on the margin of the Mississippi, Balize is a mere mud bank whose natural loathsomeness is made more intolerable by the beastly scenes enacted there. Riots and brawls are daily exhibitions, and low revelry and debauches the pastimes of the night. It is a dangerous place to visit; the savageness of man invests the desolation of nature with appalling attributes. The land itself is but a recent acquisition from the ocean wrenched thence by the great father of rivers. All around is a prairie overgrown with the rank luxuriance of the tropics; the waters of the Gulf in daily tides cover the face of the earth for many miles; there is not a tree, nor a mound, nor a monument of any sort, unless placed there by the hand of man, to relieve a monotony that oppresses the beholder. This dreary and inhospitable vision is the first that greets the stranger approaching the shores from seaward; and it is appalling to reflect that the characters of the people who dwell there, and hold appointments from the State, are yet more savage than the scene that surrounds them. . . .

Paul threw the publication down, disgruntled. So that was his next destination!

Shortly before midnight he lit the small lantern brought by Fern and hung it in the porthole window. Then he lay down again and tried to relax his taut nerves to endure the long wait. . . .

vi

Despite his best intentions he dozed, but so lightly that when the smooth sonance of the Mississippi waters rushing into the sea was subtly altered by the soft, gurgling *plup, plup* of muffled oars he came instantly awake. Hurrying to the porthole, he peered out. The fog was so thick that at first he could see nothing. He unhooked the lantern and waved it vigorously, and soon through the luminous vapor a vague outline of a small skiff appeared. As it neared he saw that it contained five men. One was standing with an arm raised in signal as the boat drifted closer, finally to bump gently against the *Cly* directly beneath Paul's window.

His two medical bags were the first objects thrust through the porthole and dropped—to be skillfully caught by the man below. Then followed the heavier portmanteau of clothes and books. Finally Paul stuck his feet through and by dint of much twisting and straining managed to get positioned hanging by the hands from the porthole, his legs dangling eight or ten feet above the boat. He let go.

The drop, short as it was and somewhat cushioned by the attempts of two men to catch him, sent a jolt of pain up his spine from a crashing impact that sent his two would-be helpers sprawling as he landed half on his buttocks and side. The boat rocked perilously. Clambering up, one of the men held a finger to his lips for silence while others were already shoving the boat away from the *Clytemnestra*. In a few moments the skiff drifted into the fast current and was rapidly carried away from the sidewheeler. Soon four men were back plying the oars while the fifth sat at the stern wielding the rudder. No one had spoken or appeared to pay any further attention to Paul, who sat near the prow amid his baggage.

The wide muddy river slipped past, making gurgling rushing noises in its haste to unite with the sea. The fog, so thick that Paul was already drenched to the skin, was odorous with the stench of river muck, salt and fish. The *Clytemnestra* was completely obscured from sight.

One of the rowers, a burly, black-bearded man wearing a seaman's cap and a red-and-white-striped tight shirt, finally twisted his head toward the man at the stern and broke the silence: "Hey, you froggy whoremaster back there—you asleep again? Heave to the port! Git us outta this zig-zagging current afore we git carried off to Cuba!"

"You don' like eet, you bastard son of cockroach, you jump out an' walk, yes? *Oui!*"

The others joined in the bantering, throwing insults back and forth as they rowed. The boat skimmed easily over the muddy water, which was growing calmer and shallower, as indicated by a few water reeds thrusting up here and there. After a while the boat nosed into a narrow bayou of quiet black water choked on both sides with large rotting trees and floating logs. The banks were fringed with scrubby willow growth and occasional palmetto brakes.

For another five minutes the boat slipped along through a labyrinth of bayous, the men guiding it by some sense of direction that was a complete mystery to Paul. To him all the twists and converging channels of bayou streams looked alike. From the thick waterweeds all around came the thousand-voiced barking *ker-chunk* of bullfrogs, punctuated occasionally by the hoarse grunting of sluggish alligators. A night bird screeched at them.

Finally the skiff pulled in at a small dock constructed of warped, weather-grayed boards and rotting log pilings. The man at the rudder advanced along the gunwale, nimbly stepped up on the dock and at once made it apparent who was boss.

"You, D'abbadie and Clum, take care of boat and oars. Pujo carry small luggages, Manuel *la otra maleta*. Pronto, or a kick in ze ass. *El equipajé al cuarto*."

As the men fell to their assigned duties without protest, the leader turned to Paul, who had just clambered up on the dock, and thrust out a browned, hairy hand. "Me Jean-Baptiste. *Et vous?*"

"Paul Abbott," said Paul grasping the hand. It was his first clear look at the man, who was large and strong-featured, probably a mixture of French and Spanish, and perhaps some Negro. Over his black hair, which was drawn tight down to the back of his neck and held with a red ribbon, was wound a black silken scarf like a turban, knotted at one side. Around his waist was a scarlet sash, and his feet were thrust into thonged sandals. In contrast to his great vitality there was something decidedly feminine about him, an impression heightened by a large gold earring, the size of a shilling, suspended from his left ear and the unexpected slim softness of the hand Paul had just shaken.

"You *medico? Docteur?*"

"Yes."

"Ah, Balize geeve you plan-ty beezness." He clapped Paul on the shoulder and swung away. "Come . . . *Allons!*"

vii

Madame Charbaud's place was plainly the class establish-ment of Balize, certainly by far the largest and most brilliantly lighted among the cluster of low, mean buildings. From within came the sounds of music and revelry.

Entering, Paul's first impression was that of a frontier saloon or bordello . . . with a difference. . . .

The largish smoke-filled room was crowded with tables around which sat men and girls drinking and laughing, and along one wall was the usual long mahogany bar, also thronged with customers. The men, on the whole roughly dressed and unsavory to look at, were mostly white or swarthy-skinned with a scattering of blacks who mingled freely among them, but none of the girls—all astonishingly young and attractive—were white. They ranged in colorings from palest tan to black and wore virtually transparent organdy dresses of various bright hues which hung to their ankles, yet were slit at the sides to reveal much nakedness of limb, and more shocking to Paul, were cut so low that their bosoms were proudly and unashamedly displayed. Some of them had smeared their arms, shoulders and breasts with a whitish powder, doubtless to enhance their powers of coquetry.

Jean-Baptiste laughed. "Ah, you feel *le frisson*, eh? Would *le docteur* like a little company—something pale-brown from Santo Domingo? The Creole girls from Domingo are famous for just the right *mélange* of Spanish nobility, Caribbean curves and African passion. . . . *Quien sabe?*"

"No thank you. Not at the moment. I—"

"Ah! *Je comprends*. A drink first." And taking Paul by the arm, Jean-Baptiste herded him to the bar, firmly elbowing aside other customers who, after one glance at Paul's guide, made no protest. A bartender was summoned and given orders in a rapid-fire mixture of French and Spanish.

"I have ordered brandy of the finest for you," he told Paul. "Compliments of Madame Charbaud, *la maitresse*, who will be here to greet you shortly. As for me, *mon ami*, I must leave you, as I have other matters on my mind. . . . "

From somewhere, guitars accompanied by the beat of a drum and the percussion of maracas thrummed out a soft and sensuous rhythm. A number of couples began dancing, clinging close. One of the girls pressed a hand against her partner's crotch, making gentle movements. In a few moments Paul saw Jean-Baptiste move onto the floor, leading by the hand a slim Negro boy of perhaps fifteen wearing a silken white shirt and tight black pants. His face was lightly coated with white powder, his lips painted crimson. The two began dancing close, with sinuous grace.

Paul turned away, thoroughly mystified. He knew that trappers and other frontier types of men sometimes danced together after long months without seeing a woman, but when finally they did see one again they went near wild with excitement. Why should Jean-Baptiste, with all these seductive girls around, so obviously prefer a boy? And a strange one at that. Paul had heard about sexual perversions from snickering hearsay only. The medical books he was familiar with made no mention of such things, and it was beyond his comprehension.

His brandy arrived. He took a big gulp, feeling better as the amber liquid burned its way down his throat.

The music was rising louder and faster. A blast from a wind instrument joined in, followed by the tinkling of a marimba. But now drums were taking the lead, submerging the rest of the music in wild booming rhythm. Then came a barbaric female cry and Paul turned again.

A coal-black Negress had risen from a table and was stripping off her dress. When naked except for a brief skirt of fringed tassels hung from a string around her hips, she moved sensuously over the floor. Short curling hair clung in tight ringlets to her head, and large golden earrings glistened against the curve of satiny black neck. Carmine rouge had been applied to her lush lips and the nipples of her full breasts. The other dancers moved back to watch as she started dancing alone to the beat of the drums. Her projecting buttocks swayed and rolled; her belly undulated; the short skirt flared outward, revealingly, with every sudden twist of pliant torso.

As her movements grew faster, encouraged by calls and clapping, several other girls ranging in color from pale golden to sable brown sprang up one by one to join her. Unfastening their dresses at the neck, they made no further effort to remove them except by the wanton twistings and undulations of their supple torsos, causing the garments to slide away teasingly, revealing more and more naked flesh until they reached the floor, to be kicked aside. The audience roared approval.

And now another girl appeared, slipping among the nude dancers to begin spinning on her toes and whirling like a dervish. She wore a gaily colored bandana around her hair and a silken blouse and skirt, and to Paul's surprise her skin

was white. Her large, luminous eyes darted about coquet-
tishly. Then with arms upraised, her delicate young body
began twisting, whirling and writhing in seductive contortions.
Her loose blouse was open at the throat, showing a long,
narrow cleft of ivory flesh. She danced faster and faster,
arms quivering, hips vibrating, ripples gliding down her limbs
to her toes.

The music grew wilder. The wail of a horn merged with
the twanging guitars, rattling maracas and frenzied staccato
of drums.

All eyes were focused on the girl, waiting . . . for what?

Suddenly she stopped, throwing her head back until her
spine was arched seemingly to the breaking point. Her
shoulders jerked, the blouse fell away, and her tautly stretched
young breasts popped fully into view, nipples pointed at the
ceiling.

"Ah! *Encore! Répétez!*" howled the audience.

Tossing her blouse aside and letting her skirt slide off—
now completely naked—she continued her mad gyrations.
But now the other girls, not to be outdone, had become a
savage symphony of flashing limbs. The swirling bodies
seemed scarcely connected to their legs. Upraised arms
writhed, fingers twitched with aphrodisiac motions. Torsos
rippled snakelike, spread legs vibrated, and hips churned
with erotic jerkings to a crashing fusillade of drums.

Paul had a sense of slipping into the madness, becoming
a part of it. The savage jungle rhythm, the unbridled vitality
of seductive females incited into paroxysms of sensuality was
hideous, fascinating, compelling. Tension grew and swelled
in the room. All eyes blazed with desire. Trickles of sweat
started down Paul's back; his pulse throbbed in his ears. All
of those smiling blood-red lips and shining eyes seemed meant
for him.

Fiercer and wilder grew the music. The atmosphere was
heavy with a sense of explosive forces breaking loose, out
of control and about to rip away the last restraints of primal
passions. The rapt watchers were leaning forward, lips drawn
back in lascivious grins. Paul could hear the breath of a
man near him hissing in and out through clenched teeth.

Lust was out in the open, explicit in the dripping bodies
of the girls, in their ecstatic faces in their final convulsions
of sexuality as the music rose to a demented crescendo before
slicing off into utter silence.

"Ah, bravo! Bravo!" roared the audience.

A bearded white giant leaped up and caught the coal-black jungle queen. She yielded readily, kissing him as they embraced while one hand snaked down and ripped at the fastenings of his trousers. Clinging together, the two pushed through an open archway into a dimly lit adjoining room.

Couples who had been embracing, some beginning to disrobe each other at the tables, also rose and pushed their way toward the archway.

Meanwhile the other nude dancers had been darting about, giggling flirtatiously before allowing themselves to be captured by the eager male arms of their choice. All except one . . .

The fiery young white minx had been nimbly evading two scrambling would-be lovers, laughing at their clumsiness, and now the two were engaged in a snarling, jealous scuffle. After a moment of joyously watching the battle for her favors, she turned and looked directly at Paul.

Reaching up, she deftly undid her colorful bandana and a mass of dark hair tumbled down around her face in wild disarray. Her luminous eyes brimmed with excitement and passion. The soft red lips parted to show a perfect display of gleaming white teeth.

Paul smiled back, entranced by the unusual beauty of the oval face with its high-jutting cheekbones and mocking smile —a face betraying an untamed, even cruel trait in her nature. Or was it merely the mischievous expression of a high-spirited young flirt? The large eyes directed at him were almost black with golden flecks and had a slight but piquant upslant.

What kind of blood coursed through the veins of this sensuously shaped nubile she-devil? Was she descended from some savage, swaggering pirate captain? Was there a mingling of Spanish nobility in her bloodline? Or French? Whatever it was had created an exotic blend of the rarest kind of beauty that could have turned the heads and hearts of the rich and mighty the world over—and yet here she was like a rare blossom soon to fade in the bestial atmosphere of this sordid pleasure house hidden away on an island of mud.

She stepped closer, raising her arms toward him, her smile openly inviting. A fierce shudder passed through Paul and all his will power, all semblance of self-control melted away. Hypnotically, he started toward her. . . .

A scream of agony broke the spell.

Paul's gaze jerked toward the sound and he saw that one of the two who had been fighting for the girl—a swarthy, bearded man—was staggering drunkenly, eyes eloquent with disbelief as the fingers of both hands fumbled for the handle of a knife embedded deeply in his chest. The girl too had turned. Her lips parted in an expression of dismay as her dark, shining eyes watched the man slowly collapse to the floor.

Springing forward, Paul knelt beside the man. He reached for the knife handle.

"Leave 'im be!" bellowed the other fighter, a stocky muscular man with sparse hair plastered over his dome like a black satin skull-cap.

"I'm a doctor, and this man needs help."

"Shit on what he needs! I say leave 'im be, or I'll—" From somewhere beneath his shirt he yanked out a pistol, pointed it.

Ignoring the gun, Paul turned back to the victim. Even the lowest kind of skunk wouldn't shoot another man in the back—certainly not with others watching. Gripping the handle of the knife, he worked it out, which brought a new welling of blood. Instantly he knew that nothing in the world could save the man now. The deep stab was high on the left side, opposite the fourth dorsal vertebra, and the copious bleeding indicated that the left subclavian artery had been cut. There was no possible way the man could be saved from exsanguinating hemorrhage and quick death.

Crack!

At the sound of the gunshot, Paul whirled, expecting the impact of a bullet. Instead, he saw the man with the gun crumpling to his knees. A little black hole in the side of his temple was beginning to dribble a dark rivulet of blood as he slumped forward on his face.

The girl, who had been watching with dismay and growing horror on her face, was now staring with fright at a point beyond Paul, whence came a shrieking, furious feminine voice.

"Micaela—you shameless hussy! You tease and stir the *canaille* and now you see what happens? All because of you! Go to your quarters. *Va-t'en!* Quick before I lose my temper!"

Hands over her face, weeping copiously, the naked girl fled. Paul rose from his kneeling position beside the stabbed man as the angry woman, still holding a small pearl-handled gun in one hand, approached.

"Is he dead?" she asked in a voice that was now soft and cultured.

"Yes."

The beauty and aristocratic bearing of the woman had taken Paul by surprise. He guessed that she must be about thirty-five but exceedingly well preserved, with an appearance of being much younger because of the artful use of makeup. She had a flawless creamy golden skin, blue-black eyes with a faintly Negroid look and beautifully arranged hair the color of polished teak. The neckline of her chartreuse satin gown plunged low in front, showing the bold curves of her bosom, and clung tight down to her hips before swelling out into a voluminous skirt that reached to her ankles. Bending, she hauled the skirt up knee-high and returned the small gun to a holster strapped to her right calf, then straightened and smiled at Paul.

"You are Dr. Abbott?"

"Yes, ma'am."

"I am Olymphe Charbaud, the *maitresse* here." With a charming smile she held out a jewel-studded hand in a graceful manner that permitted no recourse for Paul but to take it lightly in one hand while he bent and kissed it. "Welcome to Balize, Doctor."

"I am very happy to be here, ma'am."

"I most regret that the shooting was necessary," she said with great dignity, "but you must understand that I run here a very respectable place. I do not allow such ruffian behavior. But enough of that. . . . You are wearied from your journey, *non?*"

"Not at all." He smiled. "All the work of rowing me here was done by others."

"Work!" She frowned. "The lazy dogs here do not know the meaning of work. Which reminds me . . . you must excuse me for a moment while I handle a small matter. . . . "

Turning, she cupped delicate hands on either side of her carmined lips and called out with all the strident vitality of a foghorn: "Jean-Baptiste! Pujo! Come at once and drag away these miserable scum. Take them out and feed them to the alligators!"

Smiling at Paul, she resumed her soft, well-bred manner of speech. "Come with me, Dr. Abbott. We shall go where it is quiet and private to talk. . . . "

viii

Madame Charbaud's quarters on the upper floor were sumptuous. The large living room was decorated for the most part in cool white, jungle greens and gold, and was tastefully furnished with chairs and sofas of hand-carved mahogany with rich brocaded upholstering, a few marble tables and a luxurious rug of Oriental design. On the walls were a number of fine paintings and a colossal French mirror in a rococo golden frame.

Before leading Paul upstairs, she had given orders to the bartender to have champagne sent up. It arrived now as they were seating themselves, carried by a pretty black girl. To Paul's surprise the bottle was in a silver bucket encased in ice and even the hollow-stemmed glasses were frosted from chilling. Obviously Madame Charbaud was accustomed to luxuries.

"Open the bottle and pour the champagne, Justine, and then you may leave," she told the girl, and to Paul: "I must apologize that the champagne is only of the 1851 vintage. Until some of my indolent men, *les fainéants paresseux,* go out and sack another ship it is the best I have to offer. . . . "

"You have, uh . . . , pirates working for you?"

"Not pirates, *non!* They are privateers who plunder the ships only of unfriendly nations, though sometimes mistakes are made. . . . " She shrugged. "Nor do all of them work for me. I provide safe refuge, food and entertainment to any who—like me—have been excluded from the society of respectable people. In exchange I receive a percentage of all their profits. They pay extra for food, drink and entertainment. When their money is used up, they are not allowed to stay."

"Do you require permission of the pilot station officials to carry on your business here?"

"It is not for the pilot officials to give permission; it is *I,* Olymphe Charbaud, who permit *them* to stay. If they were of a different mind I would have them replaced. Even though I am excluded from New Orleans, I have high connections. But *j'en ai assez,* enough of that. . . . "

Justine finished pouring the champagne and handed each a glass, then departed. Olymphe raised her glass. "Will you join me in a toast, *monsieur?"*

"With pleasure."

"Balize is sinking back into the sea—in a few more years it will be gone. But when I was driven from New Orleans society it was kind to me. It has made my fortune. I wish us to drink to Balize—may it long be remembered as a home for free spirits scorned by the rest of the world!"

She tilted her glass, as did Paul, and they drank in unison.

"And now you will please tell me how you, a Yankee, came to be so close a friend to Pierre Gayarre, whose father was my dear friend."

"It came of no great matter," he said. "I performed an operation on Pierre, for which he feels grateful."

"You are fortunate to have such a friend. Except as a favor to Pierre, I would not trouble myself to help a Yankee."

"I am very grateful and indebted for your help, ma'am."

She gave him a shrewd smile. "Are you of a mind to repay the favor?"

"Anything within my power."

"*Bon!* We shall discuss it later. First I must explain other matters so you will understand. . . . You see, I am of that special class in Louisiana society known as *gens de couleur,* the offspring of illicit unions between white masters and female slaves. My mother was a mulatto, very beautiful, and my father a prosperous white businessman. I myself am a quadroon—one-quarter Negro. The Code Noir prohibits *gens de couleur* from marrying either black slaves or whites. Therefore the only hope of improving our station in life—if we are attractive enough to men—is to find a rich white 'protector' to care for us."

She paused to sip at her champagne. "Do I bore you, Doctor?"

"Not at all. I find it very fascinating."

"*Alors* . . . So I found a protector—I had many to choose from—and he built me a fine little house with slaves for my servants. André was very wealthy, and a kind man. He supplied me liberally with costly clothes and money, and I loved him deeply. I would yet today be living there very happily except for an unfortunate occurrence. I was insulted by one of his acquaintances—another important man—and my protector, André, did the only thing a gentleman could do and challenged him to a duel. Instead of a duel it was murder. André's pistol misfired, due to a defective cap in the charge. His opponent took advantage of this and shot my protector without giving him a fair opportunity to begin the duel again with a proper bullet. I am sure it had been arranged that way—a plot to kill André, because the other man was a business competitor who wanted him out of the way."

Madame Charbaud sat up straighter, looking proud. Her eyes misted. "Then I did the only thing I could do for the man I had loved. André had given me this pistol you have seen and trained me to shoot. I went to the house of the murderer and killed him with one shot. He was a very influential man and I was forced to flee with my small daughter, or I would have been imprisoned.

"I came here because the law does not look this far. I had enough money to start a business supplying men who do not love the law with the kind of entertainment they desire. I have profited, but my daughter has suffered from our exile. Had her father, André, lived he would have assured her of the finest white girl's education and perhaps eventually acknowledged her as his daughter. His untimely death came before he had made the financial arrangements he intended. I myself tutored my daughter so that she can speak excellent French and good enough English and has been taught almost as much as any proper young white lady—as well as perhaps too many of the sterner realities about life and men that respectable young ladies shouldn't know. . . . "

Madame Charbaud made an expression of disgust.

"You have seen the terrible influences here! My daughter is now seventeen—a virgin, of course—I have guarded her virginity well and taught her how to preserve it until the day she wins the love of some wealthy Creole gentleman. This is no place for her, and I cannot allow her to remain any longer. She needs surroundings of culture and the company of well-bred people. Therefore I have arranged to send her to be tutored by a most distinguished lady of my acquaintance who resides in New Orleans and is in the business of schooling inexperienced girls in all the arts of proper behavior required in high Creole society."

She raised her champagne glass, and noting it was empty held it out with an imperious gesture. "Please, *monsieur* . . . "

Paul complied and took the opportunity to refill his own glass.

"The favor I am asking of you . . . It is something I cannot trouble Pierre with—it could be an embarrassment to him, and he does not even know I have a daughter. I wish you to escort her to New Orleans and see that she is safely delivered to the home of Madame Silkwood."

Paul's eyebrows shot up. "But ma'am—I am a complete stranger to you and your daughter is so—"

"My daughter is quite capable of taking care of herself, *monsieur*. I can entrust her to your company because you are a friend of Pierre's. And because any fool would know that with my connections, swift and terrible punishment would be the certain fate of any who treated her improperly."

Paul took a gulp of champagne. "I will be most happy to escort your daughter to New Orleans. But by what conveyance? And when do we start?"

"The conveyance will be taken care of by Jean-Baptiste. You will rest here today and start at sundown. Now I shall bring my daughter here so that she can be told. *Excusez-moi pour un moment. . . .*"

She left the room and after a while returned accompanied by a slender girl wearing a turquoise silk gown with long sleeves and a low-scooped bodice that fitted snugly around her waist before swirling out in glistening folds over her petticoat. Her dark hair was pulled back sleekly and tied with a ribbon, the rest of it cascading down her back.

Paul stared at her in wonderment. Where had he seen her before?

"Dr. Abbott, may I present to you my daughter, Micaela Delacroix."

Micaela! Of course! The naked white minx who had outdanced the others.

Paul bowed. "I am honored to meet you, Miss—"

"Delacroix," said Madame Charbaud. "You see, I have chosen another name for her—otherwise, my enemies in New Orleans might seek to do her harm."

Micaela curtsied, demure in manner, eyes downcast. "It is my pleasure, Dr. Abbott."

Madame Charbaud smiled archly. "You show surprise, Doctor. Is it because of her white skin?"

"Well, frankly, I had expected—"

"Of course, that her Negro blood would be obvious. But you must understand that she is an octoroon—only one-eighth black. She could pass for white anywhere—anywhere but in New Orleans."

Meanwhile, Micaela had raised her eyes and, out of her mother's view, gave Paul a big flirty wink.

TWO: New Orleans, 1855

THEY left Balize in the evening. Night was fastest and safest for sailing up the river, explained Jean-Baptiste, who would captain the small sailing craft—a fore-and-aft-rigged ketch

with a small cabin to provide shelter and privacy for Micaela
—because then the water would be three feet higher, due to
the tides. By morning it would drop again, but then they
would have daylight to aid them through the twists and
turns and over the shallows. With fair winds and luck they
would reach New Orleans the following evening.

Micaela soon retired to her tiny cabin, and Paul, bone-
tired, found space forward beneath the jib where he could
roll up in a blanket. Despite the hard surface he fell almost
at once into deep sleep—to awaken, it seemed, only minutes
later and discover to his astonishment that early dawn had
arrived.

A luminous fog obscured the world. It was so thick that
Paul found his hair and blanket as wet as from a moderate
rain—doubtless the cause of his awakening—and he wondered how anyone could guide the boat through such murk.
Two of the four-man crew were on duty. Paul looked for
Jean-Baptiste and saw that he was slumbering only a few
feet away in a tumble of blankets in embrace with his *ami de
coeur*, the slim young black boy.

For most of the morning the going was slow. Although the
breeze was favorable, the water had fallen during the night,
exposing many mud banks, and a man had to be posted in
the prow with a pole to take frequent depth soundings. They
passed a number of small islands covered with willows, ash,
persimmons and other trees, most of them still in their
winter leafless state. Here and there they passed clusters
of palmettos entwined with lush, looping vines and scatterings
of wild yellow asters in full bloom. Often they came suddenly
around a bend to startle a deer, raccoon, hare or other wild
animal.

Several times the boat grounded, making it necessary for
a few men to go ashore—Paul always volunteering with
them—and with a long rope haul the boat into deeper waters.
The men took advantage of these delays for their morning
ablutions, making do with screening trees and broad green
leaves for their excremental functions, afterward washing in
the brown river water. Jean-Baptiste confided to Paul that
Mademoiselle Micaela had fresh water and bath facilities in
her tiny cabin that flushed waste into the river.

On one such occasion Jean-Baptiste took a gun and shot
down a beautiful white crane, which his black lover, whose
name was Faustin, promptly cleaned and made ready for
cooking. Paul found him to be a cheerful young fellow as

well as a wondrous cook. Over a small coal stove on aft
deck he prepared a forenoon feast of broiled crane, fried
eggs, sausages and coffee, along with fresh fruit. The savory
odors brought Micaela out of her cabin. She was dressed
simply in a long dark skirt and light cotton blouse, her hair
tied back primly at her neck. Her manner was demure and
quiet, though she ate as zestfully as the men. Immediately
after eating she returned to her quarters to protect her skin,
for now the sun was blazing down with tropical virulence.

By midday the river had grown to nearly a mile wide with
a margin of reeds on both sides, and under a good breeze
the boat skimmed along at surprising speed. The first houses
began to appear, the homes of rice planters on the lower
stretches of the river.

It was late afternoon when the sloping fields of cane of the
first sugar plantation appeared. It had two grand houses of
two stories each, of brick with a portico on the front and an
extensive assemblage of low but large buildings nearby which
were the sugar works. Orange trees grew around each house,
and beyond were strings of mean little shacks for housing
the slaves. A number of the black men were grouped close
to the river repairing the levee under the direction of an
overseer with a long whip in his hand.

Paul's interest in the riverscape flagged. The sun blazing
down from a cloudless sky was becoming intolerable, sapping
all his energy, mental and physical. It seemed not to bother
the others, but he was perspiring freely even though he had
removed his jacket. So this was Louisiana climate!

He was relieved when twilight came and Jean-Baptiste
announced that soon they would be in New Orleans.

ii

New Orleans in early darkness with its flaring street gas
lamps and handsome buildings alight was a most imposing
sight, but more amazing to Paul were sounds stranger than
anything he had ever heard anywhere. Even before they tied
in among the queer-looking fishing boats at the market his
ears were smitten with a loud, rapid, incessant gabble of
tongues of all the tones that were ever heard at Babel. It was
more to be compared, he thought, to the myriad noises that
issue from an extensive marsh—the residence of a million or
two frogs, from bullfrogs to whistlers—than to anything else.
It proceeded from the market place itself and the adjacent

levee, on which numerous people strolled for the cool of the evening breeze.

Jean-Baptiste and his men carried Micaela's and Paul's bags up the wooden flight of steps to the top of the levee opposite to the center of the public square. A man was dispatched to fetch a carriage, which soon arrived, and the luggage was quickly stowed in the vehicle.

With a somber expression Jean-Baptiste embraced Micaela, kissing her on both cheeks.

"Micaela, *cherie, ma pauvrette,*" he lamented, "from now on you must be a lady. *Hélas!*" Tears trickled down her cheeks. He kissed her again, patting her on the back in a comforting way. He swung toward Paul:

"And you, *mon ami, à bientot. . . .*"

Paul put out a hand to shake, but Jean-Baptiste embraced him instead, kissing both his cheeks as thoroughly as he had Micaela's. Then after a final wave he and his crew strode off without a backward glance.

Paul helped Micaela into the carriage, which was really more of a dray, an open boxlike conveyance with two enormous wheels, rough board seats for the passengers and an elevated one in front for the driver. Micaela seemed not to mind. Eyes bright with girlish curiosity, she was avidly drinking in the sights of her first visit to a city. Paul, too, was intrigued.

Along the top of the levee—a level bank of earth about fifty feet wide—were numerous strollers or idlers as far as the eye could reach in either direction. They ranged from white men and women to all hues of brown; all classes of faces from stern Yankees to grisly and lean Spaniards, filthy half-naked Indians, black folks, mulattoes and quadroons—these latter with hair curly, straight or frizzled, the mulatresses with brilliant turbans and gowns of the most flaring yellow or scarlet. Outdoing them were the professional gamblers with flowered waistcoats and enormous diamond rings, escorting women of easy virtue more gaudily dressed than their darker sisters.

Adding to the carnival atmosphere were the endless rows of market stalls or tables—sometimes only a piece of canvas or a parcel of palmetto leaves on the ground—all lighted by oil lanterns suspended from poles and displaying a multitude of wares as diverse as the faces of the buyers. Wild ducks, oysters, poultry, fish, bananas, heaps of oranges, sugar cane, potatoes, green ears of corn, apples, carrots, eggs, trinkets, tinware, dry goods, wretched-looking chunks of beef and other meats, even a bookseller with piles of old and new volumes. Most of the noisiness emanated from this huge market area, where all the buyers and sellers appeared to be straining their voices in several languages to exceed each other in loudness.

"Where to, *m'sieur?*" said the driver, a mulatto.

Paul looked at Micaela. "What is Madame Silkwood's address?"

Reluctantly Micaela withdrew her fascinated gaze from a stall exhibiting racks of glittering cheap jewelry and strings of beads.

"I don't wish yet to go to Madame Silkwood's. First I must go to a hotel where I can bathe and dress properly to meet her."

Nonplussed, Paul feebly tried to remonstrate, but Micaela was adamant.

"If you refuse to take me, I shall go by myself to a hotel!"

Unworldly as he was, Paul knew that for a single young lady to register into a hotel in a large city at night—or at any time for that matter—was dangerous as well as improper. He thought of taking her to Pierre's apartment, but flinched at the thought of what Pierre would think, since surely the concierge would tell him. He turned to the driver:

"Do you know of a hotel that is, uh . . . not too expensive?"

"Tremoulet's," the driver said at once. "I take you there. . . ."

iii

The room clerk was a bald little man with a series of double chins, a pale round face and little black button eyes expressive of weary cynicism. He stood behind the desk in his shirtsleeves, his glance darting between Micaela to Paul as she spoke in rapid French. Previously she had persuaded Paul that she must do the talking, since the Creole patois was the language most commonly spoken in New Orleans and if the police were looking for Paul they would question the hotels about any man who spoke like a Yankee. That possibility had occurred to Paul, as the *Clytemnestra* might well have arrived ahead of them and an irate Captain Cunningham would surely alert the police. Micaela was to ask for two rooms, one for herself and one for her English guardian. Fending about for an assumed name to use, Paul had decided on that of his old Scottish friend, Alex Ushant.

With a shrug that seemed to indicate disbelief but disinterest, the clerk shoved out a registry book, quill pen and bottle of ink.

"The rate will be two dollars daily. You may pay when you leave. The boys will accompany you with your bags."

Micaela had snatched up the pen and after signing, quickly took Paul by the arm to lead him away.

"But—"

Her warning glance stopped him, and after she had led him out of earshot she explained in a whisper: "I feared the ship captain might give the police a sample of your handwriting to compare with the hotel registry, so I told the clerk that you had damaged your wrist in a fight and were unable to sign."

Paul wanted to laugh. She certainly had a young girl's fanciful imagination!

The two "boys" carrying their bags—elderly Negroes with frizzy gray hair—led them up three flights of stairs and down a dark corridor. One produced a large key on an iron ring, unlocked a door and beckoned them to enter. Micaela stepped inside and turning, signaled for Paul to follow.

"No," he said. "I think it better if I go to my own room for now, and I'll see you in the morning."

"But there is only one room! You must come in and I will explain later. . . . "

Puzzled and angry, Paul entered. All the bags had been brought in, and the porters waited expectantly. Paul found a few small coins to give them, and after they left he looked at Micaela with an accusing frown. "Now what's this all about?"

Her large eyes widened with innocent hurt. "But you must understand I am protecting you! The story you wished me to tell, that you who are a man and me a woman—plainly not related—wished separate rooms . . . in New Orleans there is *nobody* who would believe such craziness!"

"Then what *did* you tell the clerk?"

"That we were just married, *naturellement*. It matters not if he doesn't believe it, as it is more to be expected that we would desire one room. It is less suspicious. Also it saves you the extra expense of another room."

Paul felt another urge to laugh. The devious little minx! Then, glancing around the fairly commodious room and noting there was only one bed, he felt less inclined for levity.

"We'll have to have another bed sent up."

"*Pourquoi?* The bed is quite large enough for both of us."

"But you're just a child—and I must say, a damned precocious one!"

Her eyes sparkled knowingly. "The way you looked at me when I danced . . . you did not then think me so much the child, *non?*"

"I didn't know then that you are only seventeen—and a virgin at that!"

"But that can be taken care of—so simply. . . . "

"I am neither practiced nor interested in the art of seducing virgins."

"*Alors*, it is *I* who shall seduce *you!* Maman has told me everything about men, how to please them . . . and I have seen much. I am sure I could make it *very* interesting. . . . "

"Now listen to me, Micaela! I have an obligation to your mother—"

"Poof! About some things Maman is so old-fashioned!"

"She's still your mother, and you promised her you would save your virginity for the man you will someday . . . uh, who is to be your protector."

"*Non, non*—! Maman talked much, very sternly. But I did not *promesse*. It is for *me* to decide to what man I first give myself, just as Maman herself picked her first lover when even younger than I am. And I have chosen you, *monsieur le Docteur*. . . . "

"Flattered as I am—" Paul's blood was seething with an excitement that filled him with terrible feelings of guilt—"I simply cannot . . . be your first lover. I am the type of man plagued with a conscience—"

"Conscience!" Her voice was filled with scorn. "It is but a word used in fairy tales for children."

Paul let out a small groan. "I wish it were . . . but in any case I have already decided."

She looked at him incredulously, then laughed. "Hah! Then I say to you, *poof!* You are not romantic." She tossed her head with a saucy air of insouciance and, turning away, wandered over to the doorless opening of what Paul assumed was the bathroom, for through the opening a portion of a big iron tub on the floor was visible.

"I think now I take my bath," she said and began unfastening her blouse. "You will please pull the bellcord by the door for service, and instruct the *serviteur* to send up *much* hot water for the unhappy *mademoiselle* who must console herself without a lover. . . . "

iv

Paul slept badly.

A black chambermaid had brought up two buckets of water, one steaming hot. Then amid much splashing and snatches of song, Micaela bathed by ladling water over her head with a tin dipper, as Paul noted when once his vagrant gaze was drawn through the doorless opening at her soapy nakedness.

For himself Paul had ordered cold water—the colder the better—but it had been only tepid, of little value in cooling his blood.

He had also ordered an extra sheet and a blanket.

Micaela, wearing a flimsy, diaphanous silken nightgown, stared in wonder as he folded the blanket into a makeshift mattress on the floor and proceeded to make his bed.

"Tell me, *Docteur*—are all Yankees crazy like you?"

"Shut up and let me sleep! Trying to deliver you to the young ladies' school, virginally intact, is the hardest chore I've ever undertaken!"

Wrapping himself in the sheet, he attempted to sleep. Meanwhile Micaela jounced around a bit on the bed with little squeals of joy before snuggling down, making little cooing sounds of comfort and soon drifting off into the deep sweet sleep of the innocent.

Paul's sleep was fitful and riotous with forbidden dreams.

v

Morning brought an unsettling surprise. . . .

They had just descended the stairway to the hotel lobby, where Micaela, clinging to Paul's arm, immediately became the cynosure of admiring eyes. She had transformed again to a demure young lady, most elegantly turned out in a cool organdy dress of pale cream sprigged with tiny violets. Her hair was arranged high on her head with ringlets that fell around her face and down her neck. Her dark eyes were bright as jewels, and she seemed to glow with health and a fresh young innocence as delicate as the subtle fragrance she wore.

The lobby was already bustling with life. Cigar-smoking men chatted, strode about or lounged in chairs reading newspapers. As Paul and Micaela started across toward the dining room, one of the seated men, flamboyantly garbed in a checked suit and flowered waistcoat, abruptly dropped his paper and stood up, his eyes bugging out at them.

Mike Quinn!

There was no choice but to brave it out, Paul decided as the gambler strode toward them, a wide grin now on his face and his eyes goggling at Micaela.

"Well strike me for a poddle swaddy, if it isn't my old friend—!"

Paul's warning glance cut off the words, but Mike still approached with outstretched hand, which Paul accepted reluctantly for a brief handshake.

"I have been hoping to find you, my elusive friend," said Mike, "for I have important news—" His gaze returned to Micaela. "But rude it would be of me to continue without first the pleasure of meeting your enchanting companion. . . . "

With ill grace Paul made the introductions.

"Ah . . . " Mike breathed as he bowed low and kissed her hand. "I shall treasure this moment to my dying day."

"And now if you'll excuse us, Mike . . . "

"Before you hear my news? Which concerns a certain captain who has been madder than a fighting cock with singed tail feathers since you flew the coop without—" He glanced at Micaela, then back at Paul. "Or would you prefer that I speak to you alone on so personal a matter?"

"You can speak freely in front of her," Paul said impatiently. "Get on with it."

"The *Cly* tied in only this morning, you understand, and I had it direct from Slattery that the Captain went ashore early to file a report on you with the authorities, and—" He broke off suddenly and his eyes slid sideways toward the hotel desk. Moving closer he went on in a lowered voice:

"I would swear that those two men talking to the clerk are from the police. . . . "

Paul looked at the two, who were in earnest conversation with the desk clerk. One was a ruddy-faced, burly fellow wearing a gray beaver and a hound's-tooth tweed suit. The other was slim and sallow-complected, clad in black broadcloth and none-too-clean frilled linen. The sharp look on his face was reminiscent of the weasel-featured newswriter, MacCampbell.

"What makes you think they are from the police?"

"It's a smell I have developed from much experience with the breed, and a man in your situation cannot be too cautious, my friend. My advice is to take the young lady into the dining room and wait for me. I will go to the desk on pretense of purchasing one of the papers and perchance I can overhear what it's all about. . . . "

Micaela tugged at his arm. "Mr. Quinn is right. Come."

Paul went into the dining room with her, laden with new worries. Could he trust the big Irishman? If the men really were plainclothes police and Mike thought a reward might be collected, wouldn't he be tempted to turn him in?

They took a remote corner table and ordered coffee. Scarcely had the black waitress left than they saw Mike striding in. He looked distraught.

"It's as I feared," he said hurriedly, taking out a handkerchief to mop delicately at his handsome big face. "I heard particular mention of two black medical bags the doctor would be carrying, and the clerk was saying his recollection was hazy—he was not wanting trouble, you understand—but if the officers wished to check for themselves he would be only too happy to provide them with a house key."

Paul groaned. "And did he give them a key?"

"That I did not wait to see. There's not a second to waste, but I have a plan. . . . First, you must get out of here, fast. Find another place to stay for a day or two. Leave me the key to your room, and if the police come to question me, I am quick with the words. Obviously our descriptions differ greatly but I have answers for everything. As for Miss Delacroix, it will be safer for her as well as you if she stays with me."

"Like hell she will!" Paul burst out. "Micaela is under my protection. She stays with me."

"Are you insinuating that I would offer harm to this lovely lass?" Mike blazed back at him. "Let me tell you, friend, that though I love women, wine and gold, I love honor and virtue more. For such a heavenly creature I would fight to my death to protect."

"Gentlemen, please—" Micaela cut in. "We must make haste. Maman has told me that Madame Silkwood, to whose home I am going, has great influence with the top police officials. Paul will take me there and he will be safe."

"That's where I intend to take you," said Paul, "but first we must get our bags."

"It's too late for you to go back to your room," said Mike. "But have no fear. I promise to save all the luggage. All I need is the key to your room."

With misgivings, Paul gave him the room key.

"And there's one other small matter," said Mike in an aside to Paul. "I am temporarily embarrassed for funds. I shall need a quid or two for the room and services, and then the carriage for delivering the baggage to Madame Silkwood's—"

"Not there—bring everything to the Pontalba Apartments. I'll be staying there in Mr. Gayarre's apartment."

Mike's eyes widened in surprise. "As you wish, my lucky friend. It comes to me now how you managed to gammon that shrewd old devil Cunningham. But back to the business at hand. Twenty-five American dollars should do me nicely. . . . "

Sourly, Paul counted out the money.

vi

Madame Betsy Silkwood's home on Dauphine Street was a three-storied structure of pale-coral-tinted stucco with a red tiled roof and upper balconies featuring black iron grillwork. Many of the rooms facing the street had large French glass doors but were hidden from the street by lush tropical trees and a high fence.

Micaela, accustomed only to the rough dwellings of Balize, was ecstatic. "Ah! Never have I seen such a *grande maison!*"

When the haughty black maid who opened the door asked them for their *carte de présentation*, Micaela handed the Negress an envelope. "This is a note from my *maman*, who was a dear friend of Madame Silkwood's."

In a more friendly tone the maid bid them to enter, leading them from the *porte-cochère* into the drawing room. "Please be so kin' to wait here till I have deliver your message."

Waiting, Paul felt uncomfortably overwhelmed by the elegance of his surroundings: the silken brocaded drapes, fine carved furniture, rich paintings. He was acutely aware of how out of place he was in his rumpled cheap suit and soiled linen. A ripple of music drew his attention through an archway into an adjoining room where several expensively gowned young ladies of astonishing beauty were grouped around a pianoforte. They began singing in joyous, birdlike voices.

How would Micaela, reared in the debauched atmosphere of Balize, take to all this ladylike refinement, he wondered.

Madame's appearance was signaled by a rustling of taffeta and a swirling of skirt that brought Paul hastily to his feet to behold a most queenlike lady. Diamonds sparkled from her ears, neck, wrists and fingers and she was gowned in silver gray—matching the color of her smoothly coiffured hair— with a low-scooped, snug-fitting bodice that accented the fullness of her bosom and a surprisingly slender waist for one of her years. He judged her to be about fifty. Once she must have been a great beauty, and she was still a very handsome woman.

"Ah, so you are Olymphe's daughter! You are so beautiful, *cherie!*" Rushing forward, the older woman embraced Micaela, kissing her on both cheeks. "How happy I am that Olymphe has sent you to join our family of young ladies! Had I known she had so lovely a daughter I would long ago have insisted that you come for a visit."

"You are very kind, Madame," said Micaela, making a little curtsy.

"And you, Dr. Abbott—" Madame Silkwood had turned toward him with a haughty grandeur that made him wonder if she expected him to kneel. "I am always pleased to meet any friend of Olymphe's." She extended her hand.

Paul took the hand and touched his lips to her fingers. "I am also pleased to meet you, ma'am."

Her blasé eyes flicked over him from head to foot, making their instant assessment, and though her manner was still gracious Paul knew that he had been dismissed from any further interest on her part.

"And will you do us the honor of remaining to dine with us?"

"I appreciate the invitation, ma'am, but there are other matters I must attend to that cannot wait. Now that Miss Delacroix is safely in your care, I regret that I must take my leave."

"I am so sorry," she murmured, but appeared relieved. "Perhaps another time . . . "

"Yes, you must come again soon to visit me," said

Micaela, and rushed up to throw her arms around him.
"And this is so you will not forget. . . . "

Drawing his head down, she kissed him fervently on the
lips.

"Micaela—!" Betsy Silkwood's tone was like the snap of a
whip. "Such unseemly lack of decorum with gentlemen is
not permitted in my house!"

With a tiny smile on her lips, Micaela backed away and
hung her head in feigned shame.

"Come, Dr. Abbott," said Madame, "I will guide you to
the door. . . . "

Outside on the red brick *porte-cochère* the gracious manner vanished and the handsome face turned hard as graven
granite.

"I wish to make one thing very clear, Doctor Abbott.
Visits from you to see Micaela will not be welcome. She is
destined only for a gentleman of wealth and high station."

With a brief bow, Paul turned and strode away, angry and
disgusted. And depressed.

vii

Pierre Gayarre, his right arm in a black silk sling against
a pale-gray suit, greeted Paul with a wide smile.

"I was beginning to worry about you, my friend," he said.
"By my reckoning you should have arrived yesterday."

Paul had just arrived at the Pontalba Apartments, having
walked the short distance from Silkwood's.

"My boat was very late, so I thought it better to stay
last night at a commercial hotel before coming here."

"From the deep sunburn on your face, I infer it was an
open boat that brought you. It becomes you. Your shipboard pallor gave you a look of illness. Our Southern suns
will be good for you."

Paul grinned wryly. "If I can take the heat. Yesterday
almost did me in."

"Yesterday was unseasonably warm, not usual for early
March. Generally our Creole springs are superb from January
until June—when the rains come. But come, let me show
you around. . . ."

The rooms were immense, the ceilings very high, as were
the French windows which opened like doors onto an iron-
grilled balcony. There was a salon, study, large dining room,
several bedrooms and an expansive kitchen area that sepa-

rated the main part of the apartment from the servants' quarters. Pierre's cultured taste was reflected in the large oil paintings, book-lined walls and figurines and the general elegance of the furnishings.

"I find it most agreeable and beautiful," said Paul.

"It has been designed in the Renaissance tradition. These apartments were built only a few years ago by the Baroness Pontalba, who commissioned the architect James Gallier, Sr., to draw up the blueprints. They are the first apartments ever to be built in the United States. For me it is a great convenience to maintain quarters in town for business and social purposes. I predict that someday such apartments will be widespread. But I talk too much. . . . I'm sure you're anxious to get settled here. By the way, where is your baggage?"

Paul told the story—omitting mention of Micaela—of the two detectives spotted by the gambler Mike Quinn at the hotel, which had forced him to leave without returning to his room, but that Quinn had promised to get the bags and bring them here.

Pierre's eyebrows arched. "Do you really take the word of such a raffish character, a professional gambler?"

"There would be no reason for him to keep my clothes, since they wouldn't fit, and he would have no use for my medical items."

"Did you give him any money?"

Shamefaced, Paul admitted that he had.

Pierre burst into laughter. "Paul, I am continually amazed at your naiveté! Your trust in your fellow man is phenomenal! But no matter—such things can be replaced, and in any event you will need new clothing for the Grand Bal Paré tomorrow night at the St. Charles. The ladies deserve a bit of entertainment after putting up with my bad temper for so long, and since we shall be in town for only a few days it will be their last chance for some time. I shall take you to my tailor today and have you outfitted properly."

"But such an extravangance at this time, I cannot—"

"Never fear—I shall deduct the cost from the salary you are to be paid, a subject we can discuss later."

"That is very considerate of you, but since I'm not the type to attend balls, I will hardly need a fancy outfit."

"Working for me you will at times require more appropriate suits than dark broadcloth. As for attending the ball, Syl specifically ordered me to invite you. The fact is, with my arm in a sling I have no desire to dance, and Etienne is a most abominable dancer, so we are dependent on you to keep the ladies entertained."

Paul, whose knowledge of dancing was almost nil, suddenly felt trapped. "But—"

Pierre waved him to silence. "It is settled! We'll go to the tailors at once—and also stop off at the Banque des Citoyens to open an account for you and deposit the remaining nine hundred dollars of the thousand I promised you."

viii

The trip to the bank and the tailor took up the rest of the morning. Never would Paul have dreamed of buying so many and such fine articles of clothing, but Pierre insisted. In addition to the formal attire for the ball he was fitted for a linen hot-weather suit, and Pierre selected for him a whole array of shirts, boots, stocks and other items of wardrobe, to be delivered the next day.

"Now I think it's time for lunch at Antoine's," said Pierre. "It's an unpretentious place but the cuisine is superb."

Riding in Pierre's gleaming black calèche, Paul was beginning to feel a bit like a prince in some fairy tale, a virtual Cinderboy touched by Pierre's magic wand. True to Pierre's boast about Creole springs, today the temperature was perfect. There was a pleasant breeze and a splendid sun washed down over the exotic beauty of the town: the endless balconies with their ornate black-iron grillwork, white and yellow lime-washed walls stained to rainbow colors by wind and rain, the red brick *porte-cochères*, great bolted doors opening into mysterious inner courts where flamboyants bloomed around ancient magnolia trees; and nearby, always, the sense if not the view of the swirly dark waters of the great Mississippi. All of it laden with a languorous atmosphere of adventure and romance.

"It is a most beautiful town, Pierre."

Pierre beamed. "Wherever you find Creoles, you will find beauty. My greatest pride is my heritage. Creoles are unique, like none other in the world."

"I must confess that I'm still not sure what a Creole really is."

"Mayhap it would be better if you didn't know," Pierre said with a laugh. "But with you I shall be honest. I regret that I must inform you that our first settlers, who came in 1718, were French-Canadians. The very scum and refuse of Canada, ruffians who had cheated the gibbet of its due, vagabonds with no regard for government, law or religion, graceless profligates so steeped in vice that they preferred Indian wenches to French women. When later in the century new immigrants came over from France it was impossible to prevent those with Indian blood from intermarrying with the new French arrivals."

"Then Creoles have Indian blood?"

"Only the oldest families—you could term it as but a dash of alien spice to improve the stew. The headier spice came when in 1766 Louisiana was taken over by the Spanish occupation, followed by a heavy migration of Spanish people and much intermarriage between the French and the Spaniards. In 1803 Louisiana was transferred back to France, and Napoleon soon after, quite foolishly, sold the whole Louisiana territory to the Americans for a paltry fifteen million dollars. So you see, that leaves most of us as a mix of French and Spanish blood—predominantly French—and in some a touch of Indian."

"Is there not also in some cases," Paul asked in all innocence, "a touch of Negro blood?"

Pierre's face reddened. "Never! Never a drop of black blood in any Creole!"

Paul was taken aback by the passionate denial. "I'm sorry if I gave offense. I didn't know it was of any great importance."

Pierre managed a sour smile. "I'll admit—it is commonly enough known—that many a Creole has been responsible for begetting mulattos, but *never* are they acknowledged, *never* is there a marriage. It would be unthinkable! The Creole blood must be kept pure."

Paul couldn't help smiling to himself at the contradiction.

"At the risk of offending you again, I am curious to know if your exclusion of intermarriage with other races includes white Americans from the North."

Pierre's lips tightened. "You have touched one of my sensitive spots. The Anglo-Americans moving into New Orleans are greatly increasing in numbers and power. The Creoles do not like it. As a general rule we do not sell them property near our homes, or invite them to our social functions. No true Creole would marry an Anglo-American."

"What is it you have against them?"

"They are aggressive, overbearing, crass-mannered, with

little or no sensitivity for the finer things. They understand nothing about honor, or being a gentleman. They are ruining the charm of our city by bringing in vulgar architecture, ugly as fortresses. Yet they are growing so much in power that they now dominate the City Council, and as an example of what I mean, they have generated considerable sentiment to change the name of our public square, the Place d'Armes, to Jackson Square. Already some of them are calling it that—riding roughshod over all our cherished antiquity to immortalize a hero of the moment. I understand that a statue of Jackson is to be installed next year, and after that the new name will be official. It is a great shame. I fear greatly for the future of New Orleans."

"I didn't realize there was such a deep antipathy toward Yankees," Paul said a bit stiffly.

"I can only be honest, my friend. I can truly say that you and Fern are the only Anglo-Americans for whom I feel any affection."

Pierre's charming smile was impossible to resist. "I hope that you never have cause to feel that I've let you down, Pierre."

"If I've misjudged you, I would lose all faith in human nature. . . ."

ix

Antoine's was an unadorned restaurant, and the table to which they were immediately ushered by the very attentive Antoine himself—a courtly gentleman obviously well acquainted with and very respectful of Pierre—was simple enough, with plain family tableware and linen.

"An *apéritif*, gentlemen, while you select from the menu?"

"Yes, bring my usual, Antoine." Pierre looked at Paul. "And you, Paul?"

Paul embarrassed by his ignorance, said, "I'll have the same."

"*Oui, messieurs*." Antoine left and Pierre glanced through the menu.

"Since you are not familiar with Creole cuisine, I shall make suggestions. . . . I would recommend beginning with Aubergines sur Canapés, which are of eggplant, or perhaps Escargots aux Champignons—mushrooms stuffed with snails. For the *entrée* there is Boeuf Périgord, beef in aspic, or a *rémoulade* of shrimp, very popular here, or Rôti de Chevreuil, venison—"

"I am already bewildered," Paul interrupted. "I will trust to your judgment to select for me."

Pierre laughed, signaled a waiter and placed their order.

The *apéritifs*, in long thin-stemmed glasses, arrived. Paul found the strange, exotic taste agreeable on his tongue. He was about to take another sip when a glimpse of two new customers just entering made him pause. One was a burly chap in a hound's-tooth tweed suit and the other slim and sallow, clad in black broadcloth.

The plainclothes police who were asking about him at the hotel! Were they following him?

Startled, Paul put his glass down so hurriedly that he spilled a few drops.

"What is the trouble, Paul? Do you dislike the taste so much?"

In a low voice Paul told his friend about the newcomers.

Turning casually, Pierre glanced at the two, who were now headed in the direction of their table. Pierre chuckled.

"They are friends of mine, Paul. I will introduce you. . . . "

Before Paul could object, Pierre rose and greeted the two men, who returned the greeting enthusiastically as they shook hands. Turning back to Paul, he introduced them as a Mr. Jeffers and Mr. Schwartz, sugar brokers from the North.

After they were gone, Pierre laughed uproariously. "So you see, my credulous *Docteur*, you have been flim-flammed! The word of your gambling friend isn't worth a pistareen."

Paul ate his excellent lunch glumly, inwardly furious at the perfidy of Mike Quinn.

"And now," said Pierre when lunch was finished and both men had lighted cigars, "on to more serious matters . . . the smallpox outbreak. . . ." He paused to puff gently on his cigar, a troubled look on his face.

"Under Etienne's directions, all of my sick slaves were separated from the healthy ones and locked in the 'pesthouse,' a shed we keep for that purpose. As of Etienne's last visit to the plantation two days ago, eight of them had died. Nevertheless, it was hoped that the outbreak had been nipped in the bud, but such is not the case. It appears to be spreading again among the healthy slaves."

"Didn't Etienne go for a doctor when the disease was first discovered?"

Pierre spoke with a bitter twist on his lips: "He went to

all the best physicians in town, but not a one of them cared to expose himself to smallpox to save black lives."

"But surely they all know of the cowpox vaccine which has been proved highly effective against smallpox."

"Who knows? Is anything more carefully concealed than a doctor's ignorance? Be that as it may, what thoughts do you have for attacking the problem, Paul?"

"We must get a supply of the vaccine quickly—in a city this size it should be available. Then get to the plantation as soon as possible and begin the inoculations."

"Unfortunately we cannot leave until the day after tomorrow, because of urgent business matters Etienne and I must conclude with the bank. In the meantime you can visit our apothecary shop, where doctors go for their supplies. Before we leave, I'll give you the address and a note to the proprietor, who is reputed to be a fine chemist. Order the vaccine and all of your medical needments on my account, to be delivered by steamer to the plantation at the earliest date."

X

Tureaud's Apothecary was murky in gloom, because of thick shades drawn against the afternoon sun, and the torpid air was heavy with an unpleasant mingling of chemical and moldering odors as Paul walked in. The shop was somewhat narrow, but its several aisles extended far back and were lined on either side with tables piled high with a curious assortment of medicaments, and from the ceiling hung scraggly bunches of dried herbs, roots, flowers, leaves, berries, barks and other relics of plant life entirely strange to Paul.

Before he had a chance to examine any of them, a smallish man materialized out of the shadows in the rear. He moved forward to stand behind a counter and lean on propped arms with the barest suggestion of a merchant's mandatory smile on his round little face, which was distinguished mostly by a trim little mustache—all the more notable because he was almost entirely bald—and a pince-nez perched on his nose.

"Monsieur?"

"My name is Paul Abbott. I am Pierre Gayarre's new plantation physician and I have been directed here to inquire about some medical supplies I shall be needing."

"Ah yes, *Docteur*, and what are the medicaments you have in mind?"

"I am presently in need of the cowpox vaccine. I will need a large supply of it." .

"We have but a moderate supply on hand. However, I have heard of a smallpox outbreak among the slaves up the river, so I ordered a larger quantity by wire and it will be arriving on the next packet from New York."

"The outbreak you speak of is on Pierre Gayarre's plantation. I wish to order all of your present supply of vaccine for immediate delivery to the plantation, and also the entire shipment of vaccine that will be arriving from New York, to be delivered at the earliest possible moment. I shall be inoculating not only the Gayarre slaves, but also those on the plantations of Mr. Etienne Troyonne and Miss Beauvais—I understand the total to be about a thousand slaves. If there is any vaccine left over, I shall vaccinate the slaves of any neighboring plantation owners who desire it."

"I will follow your instructions, *Docteur*. Is there anything else?"

Paul handed him a list of other medicaments that he had prepared. The chemist perused it quickly, then raised his eyebrows.

"Carbolic acid? But it is not an apothecary item. However, I think I could obtain it locally, from commercial sources."

"Please do. It is very important for my purposes."

Business matters finished, Paul turned and glanced around the shop.

"I am curious, Mr. Tureaud, as to the other medications you have here." He waved a hand in the direction of the rows of dried plants hanging from the ceiling.

"They are therapeutic plants collected by agents of mine."

"Do the New Orleans doctors purchase such therapeutic plants from you?"

Tureaud's laugh was scornful. "The *docteurs*, no. Many of these plants are not even known by name to the white race. Since you are obviously new to our area, I should explain to you that many of my customers are colored—free, but still members of the black race, and only the blacks know the medicinal powers these plants possess. They come here to get cures they cannot get from white doctors."

Meanwhile Paul had noticed a large box on a nearby table with a label scrawled on it: *Animaux Mortes*. Curious, he lifted the lid—and abruptly dropped it again. The stench that wafted up was sickening. The box was filled with dried little mice, rats, bats and small birds.

"Are these also medications?"

"They are fetishes."

Paul began to smile, then stopped at Tureaud's sudden frown.

"You are scornful. That is because, as I can tell from your accent, that you are from the North. If you live here long enough and have the eyes and intelligence to interpret what you see, you will someday learn to believe in the healing powers of certain dead animals."

"Are you telling me that *you* believe these rotting vermin have curative powers?" Paul asked in astonishment.

"Doubtless you do not believe in magic, *Docteur*. I myself have always kept an open mind, but once I too sneered at magic as being only hocus-pocus. Now I am no longer in doubt. I have seen too much. I have seen the fantastic cures made by voodoo medicine women after white doctors could do nothing."

"Voodoo? That's nothing but a superstition of ignorant minds."

Tureaud smiled thinly. "How would you know, *Docteur*? You have lived on this earth perhaps twenty-five years. You must realize that curative magic is just as old—perhaps much older—than our white man's medicine. It has been fostered and developed through the ages for a very good reason. In the case of the black man, it is the one great reality of his life; it has taught him how to protect himself against the terrible dangers that face him daily."

"Yet you still handle modern medications such as the smallpox vaccine," Paul protested. "Don't you believe the findings of modern science are superior to *this*—?" His hands indicated the boxes and their weird contents.

"Some of it, yes. Much of it, no. Plainly I don't sneer at the modern advances of science, nor do I think you should sneer at the age-old truths of other races. Since the beginning of the world, man—white as well as the black—has created his own gods of good and evil, lightness and dark, and so forth, basing his beliefs on observations of cause and effect in nature. He has seen how thunder and lightning storms can destroy his home, how earthquakes can demolish a whole village. He knew such things could not happen by themselves. He began to fear his own insignificance, and was thus forced to create his gods. Whenever new problems arose, new gods were created to solve them. This firm belief in his god is half the answer to his cures."

Tureaud paused to breathe deeply a few times, obviously quite emotional about his beliefs.

"Have our white Christians not followed the same reasoning?" he went on. "Their own version of it? Are their own gods any more reasonable? Do they offer better cures? I suggest, Dr. Abbott, that you do not laugh at the black man's cures, which in some instances are better than yours. As to why this is so, I can only suggest that perhaps it is because the black race is far closer to the earth than the white race, and for this reason the black man is able to believe without having to ask the logic of it. By giving himself to nature, he is less harmed by it."

Much impressed by the man's sincerity and the intensity of his little philosophical discourse, Paul said, "I see you have great understanding of the black man, and that I have much to learn."

Monsieur Tureaud smiled. "I have the advantage, of course, of being one-quarter black. It is no secret—everyone who deals with me knows it. I had a fair white man's education and possess a creditable library—but I have also benefited much from the teachings of my black forebears."

Masking his surprise, Paul said, "Perhaps someday you would help educate me a bit about some of the curative plants you have here."

At once the chemist's eyes lidded over, an unconscious signal that he was not about to impart, willingly, any of his hard-earned medical lore.

"If you come to me for advice as to the proper cure for a specific ailment, *Docteur*, I shall advise you to the best of my ability."

Then with a little nod of dismissal he indicated that he had nothing further to say.

THREE: Le Grand Bal Paré

WITH astonishment Paul surveyed the distinguished gentleman who stared back at him through gray eyes from within the frame of a large French mirror. Did he really know this man? To be sure, the face was familiar, though more neatly shaved, the hair more meticulously trimmed—thanks to a visit to an excellent barber earlier—and the skin of a better color than he had seen in years. But the effect was that of a stranger.

Even the burgundy-colored frock coat, cut to fit his wide shoulders, added a dash of *élan,* tapering in to his narrow hips and the pearl-gray trousers, which fit closely and smoothly all the way down to the shining congress boots. Beneath the coat was a tiny-figured white waistcoat, and beneath that a frilled shirt of incredible whiteness. It had taken considerable fiddling around with the black silk tie to manage the long bow to suit him, but now that was done, and he hadn't forgotten the simple gold studs and cuff links. However, there still seemed a final touch missing. After a few moments he remembered, and taking a fine embroidered silk handkerchief from the miscellany of cartons on a dresser stuffed it into the tail pocket of his coat.

Ah! If Jeremiah could only see him now! He had never seen poor Jere dressed in anything better than his worn black jacket and breeches.

Which reminded him. He had a letter to write. That afternoon he had obtained a bank draft drawn on his new account and made out to Jere in the amount of two hundred dollars. He had considered sending a like amount to Alex Ushant in Scotland as a first installment in repayment of his loan, but recalled that Alex had warned him not to write for at least a year to avoid being traced by the police.

Seated at Pierre's elegant desk in the study, he hastily scrawled out a letter to Jere, explaining that unforeseen circumstances would prevent his return to Council Bluffs for a few more months, perhaps longer, but that he would write again soon at greater length and expected that he would also be able to enclose additional money.

After sealing the letter, he felt saddened, heavy with guilt feelings. Poor Jere had long been looking forward to his foster son's return, fully expecting him to join in his humble, ill-paying medical practice. Paul had never been able to summon the courage to write and tell Jere that he could never return to frontier doctoring. The truth would break Jere's heart.

His brooding was interrupted by the door knocker. Doubtless it would be Pierre come to pick him up. At the restaurant Pierre had advised him that he and the ladies would be staying at Etienne's townhouse, as it was more commodious and well staffed with servants. "You will use my Pontalba apartment as your own," he had said, handing the key over to Paul.

Paul went to the door. It was the concierge.

"Monsieur Troyonne's chaise is outside waiting for you, sir. . . ."

ii

Pierre waited until Paul was seated in the gleaming black four-wheeled carriage before introducing him to the man who sat in the back seat with Syl.

"Paul, this is my cousin Etienne Troyonne, of whom I have spoken so often. Etienne, Dr. Abbott. . . ."

Clasping the man's hand as the two murmured perfunctory amenities, Paul was surprised at its slimness, but the return pressure was firm enough. At the same time Etienne's burning dark eyes under heavy black brows, which had a slightly satanic upward twist toward the temples, were boring into him with what Paul thought to be suspicion or dislike. His equally black hair was worn a bit longer than the current style and curled at the ends, giving him somewhat the look of an artist or poet—an impression enhanced by his slender, almost delicate build and finely chiseled features of an unusual pallor that suggested he might be phthistic. It would not have surprised Paul to see the man spit blood. The cut of his clothes was faultless and he wore them with ease and grace, but nothing about him gave the appearance of a popinjay. He looked to be a few years older than Pierre, perhaps thirty-four.

"I have heard marvelous things about you, Doctor," he said in a surprisingly deep but soft voice. "If your medical talents are but half Pierre's estimate of them, I shall be seeking you for advice."

"I shall be only too happy to give it, sir."

Syl spoke up. "I refuse to let you gentlemen discuss medical matters on the way to the ball. Talk of something pleasant."

"There's no need to talk at all, Syl," said Pierre with a laugh. "We can just sit and enjoy looking at you. . . ."

In truth she was ravishing tonight, in a gown of such extremely low décolletage that Paul was almost uncomfortably aware of the round curve of her breasts and ivory gleam of her bare shoulders. The gown matched the bluish-green of her eyes. At least he supposed it to be of a pale turquoise color until the carriage passed one of the flaring gas street lights, which made the shimmering material magically change into other flashing, iridescent colors that continued to fluctuate like nothing he had ever seen before until the light was behind.

"But it is not fair," she said, "that Fern could not be present tonight to get her share of the flattery," and to Paul, "Unfortunately Fern had a prior social commitment elsewhere and was unable to join us. You shall have to put up only with me."

Pierre smiled at her. "That, my dear, is a blatant begging for more compliments. Haven't you already had enough for tonight to satisfy you?"

"Not yet from Paul," she said archly.

Paul laughed. "I'm not practiced at compliments. Even if I were, I could not possibly find the words to describe how beautiful, how enchanting—"

Pierre burst into laughter. "Paul—you must forgive my amusement, but from a dour Yankee doctor it was so unexpected, and so well said. I could not do better. There is hope yet that we can teach you to be a Creole."

But Etienne, Paul noted, was scowling at his boots.

iii

Seated in the ballroom, Paul dutifully scanned the beautifully engraved program that had been handed to him:

St. Charles Ballroom
On Friday the 19th instant (for the benefit of Charity Hospital)
A Grand Ball (Grand Bal Paré)
To be preceded by a Grand Concert, Vocal & Instrumental, Distribution:
1. *An Overture—full orchestra.*
2. *A Sonata & Rondo for the Forte Piano executed by Miss Ursula Labat.*
3. *A Duet "The charm of voice" sung by Madam Labat & Mr. Rochefort.*
4. *An air of Mozart variated by Ries, executed on—*

Paul fidgeted uneasily in his seat and let the program, half unread, fall to his lap. The majestic overture with the full orchestra had thrilled him. Even the sonata and rondo on the forte piano had charmed him. But now the pretty soprano warblings of Madam Labat—which seemed strangely at variance with the mellifluous bass of Mr. Rochefort—were failing to sustain his interest. It was from his own lack of refinement, he realized, and there was still more to endure. . . .

Syl leaned close to whisper past her ivory fan into his ear: "Try to relax. It will soon be over. . . ."

Paul grinned his appreciation at her, and making a determined effort, kept a pasted smile on his lips for the duration of the program, which ended with bows, curtsies and polite applause.

While the black servants were clearing away chairs, the orchestra struck up a new lively tune and a few couples began to dance. Syl and Etienne were among them. Watching them glide among the others with such smoothness and grace, Paul felt a twinge of envy mingled with regret that he had never learned anything about dancing except the rough frontier jigging and hopping around to a fiddle and banjo.

Pierre had excused himself to speak to old friends, and Paul, left alone, had a chance to look about more carefully. Never had he seen so many beautiful female faces below the age of twenty-five collected together in one room. Some of them were in face and figure perfect; the great majority were far above the merely agreeable; all were alluring. He was soon able to distinguish between the American and Creole ladies. The Americans had rosy cheeks from rouge, but the Anglican slang of "painted French woman" certainly didn't apply to the French and Creoles here; all of them, like Syl, had healthy fair skin, but the cheeks were the same color as the forehead. No powder or rouge was used, or if so, it was not noticeable.

Such modesty in facial makeup did not apply to the Creole feminine dress, however. Whereas the American women had succumbed to the stiff fashions of Victoria, the Creole ladies followed the daring new styles of Empress Engenie. Their loose gowns flowed and swirled and melted against soft limbs as they danced, and milky-white breasts were all but exposed by low-scooped necklines.

Their dancing was another notable distinction. The Creole ladies whirled about with perfect grace and a kind of abandon that Paul had heard was to be expected of French women; in the case of the men the manner of dancing was what Lord Chesterfield would have called "too good for gentlemen." By comparison the dancing of the Americans was stiff and markedly deficient.

"Paul, why haven't you asked me for a dance?"

He turned to see Syl smiling at him, her eyes shining like sapphires. The music had stopped. Etienne was standing nearby with a brooding frown on his face.

"I must confess I don't know how to dance."

"I will teach you. I have requested of the orchestra a medley of waltzes, which I love. With a waltz it is not necessary to dance. You can walk to the rhythm until you get the feel of it. . . ."

Pierre reappeared with Etienne beside him. "Syl, Paul . . ." he said with an apologetic smile. "As you know, I am not of a mood to dance tonight because of my arm, and Etienne is feeling a trifle indisposed, so we beg of you to excuse us for a while. We wish to go over to the Salle d'Orleans for a game or two of cards. . . ."

Somewhat coolly, Syl nodded acquiescence.

After they were gone, Paul said, "You are offended?"

"It is so transparent!" she said hotly. "The Salle d'Orleans has gaming rooms on the ground floor—as a pretext for men to go there. Their main reason is that one floor above is the ballroom where are held the notorious quadroon balls."

"Balls for colored people?"

"*Non!* Although the balls are held by free women of color, they are blatantly for the purpose only of attracting rich white gentlemen, who go there to pick concubines. It is well known that the quadroon balls are preferred by Creole men to their own balls with white women."

"But surely you don't suspect Pierre of—"

"What you do not understand is that it is customary for young Creole gentlemen to keep a quadroon concubine—even when they marry, they continue to keep her in high style and lavish her with gifts. It is not advertised, but white women know it and have no choice but to accept it. It does not mean that we like it. . . . Even Pierre's father—such a dear, sweet man—"

She broke off as the music started, slipping a hand under his arm. "Come," she ordered.

He began clumsily, trying to watch the others to see how it was done.

"It is easy," she said. "Like this . . . *one*, two, three, *one*, two, three . . . Walk the rhythm until—ah, now you are getting it! So fast! You lied to me. You *do* have rhythm. Soon you will be an excellent dancer."

"I doubt it. I'm only trying my damnedest to please so beautiful a teacher."

"Take care! As Pierre warned, if you say too many nice things, you're in danger of becoming a Creole."

"Well, there's no danger of me ever becoming a Creole. I'm too clumsy, too raw."

"But no," she protested. "You're just *different*."

"I didn't realize *how* different until I became aware of how many eyes were watching—a bit shocked—when I arrived with you and Pierre, and then of course there's Etienne's attitude. . . ."

"Etienne? You must get used to his strange moods. He blows from hot to cold all the time, plunges from happiness to despair from one minute to the next. You never know what to expect. Tonight he is suddenly in a bad mood—for no reason at all! When he is like that, nobody can help him. He prefers to drink instead, and sometimes it makes him nasty. . . ."

"Perhaps he is jealous?"

"Jealous? You must be joking! He is my cousin. Nothing more. Protective maybe, but not jealous."

"Maybe he just resents me because I'm not Creole."

"I don't think he resents you—although it is true he doesn't like Americans."

"But Creoles are American citizens just as I am."

"We are Creoles first and Americans second."

"That, of course, implies that Creoles are superior."

"Creoles *are* superior—in the ways that are important to us."

"Aren't you speaking merely of your own culture—of manners, of appearances? Beneath the surface aren't people pretty much the same?"

"Perhaps. But the 'appearances,' as you call them, are everything. All our lives we are trained to our code of behavior. What we do behind closed doors may be another matter—but even behind closed doors our standards are never violated by the Creoles."

"I am afraid," Paul said sadly, "that it would take another lifetime for me to know what it's like to be a Creole."

Syl laughed. "In your case, there's no need. It is expected that you do not know, so you will be forgiven much—by friends like Pierre and me. But I must warn you, do not expect too much hospitality from Etienne and others who don't know you. Perhaps nowhere other than in *haute* Paris are the social circles tighter and more impenetrable than in our Creole world in New Orleans. You would not even tonight be dancing with me except that Pierre is so fond of you."

The music swung into another waltz, and Syl gave a little exclamation of pleasure.

"Oh, that is one of the new waltzes of Johann Strauss, the Younger! During our Grand Tour we stopped in Vienna, and I met Johann Strauss at a ball, where he led his own orchestra and played some of his own waltzes. How excited I was when he danced with me! His music is becoming the rage of Europe, even more popular than his father's. And he is still young, only thirty. I was so flattered when he told me if he ever visited New Orleans he would write for me a waltz about our *Grand* Mississippi."

Feeling another twinge of irrational jealousy, Paul said, "Since you apparently met so many famous people over there, did you also have the good fortune to meet in Germany Rudolf Kölliker, or in Paris, August Nélaton?"

She looked puzzled. "The names are not familiar, but then I met so many. . . . Do they also write songs?"

"No. Kölliker happens to be the greatest biologist and anatomist of modern times—certainly as eminent in the medical field as Johann Strauss is in music—and Nélaton, who is surgeon to Napoleon, has produced some of the most advanced volumes on the art of surgery ever written."

"Oh, if medicine is their profession, then I would not have remembered the names, even if I had met them," she said lightly. "I am very healthy. You will please forgive me for saying this, *Docteur,* but I think medicine is something too morbid to be concerned with unless it is necessary, only if one gets sick. . . . "

Her words were deflating, and he could not help thinking that her values were really quite superficial. Yet at the same time he knew it didn't matter. She was so beautiful! Among all the lovely females at the ball, none was so breathtaking. Just to be near her, to touch her, dance with the movements of their two bodies merged in mutual rhythm, made him a bit giddy. What ecstasy it would be to clasp her tight and kiss her! For such a privilege—for even the remote dream of it—he could forgive her anything. Still, he was vaguely depressed.

"It is plain, then, that you don't think very highly of my profession."

"Oh, but you misunderstand! I think it is a most respectable profession, and requires great intelligence. However, it seems such a shame that it is so ill paid. With the same intelligence applied elsewhere—perhaps in business—you could become rich."

"Is being rich that important?"

"Of course. Without much money, how else could one have a fine home, fine clothes, travel where one pleases? Would you not like to be rich?"

"Very much."

"Then let Pierre help you. There are fortunes to be made in cotton, sugar, tobacco and such things."

"It's not what I want. Much as I would like a lot of money, there are other things more important to me. . . . "

"Like what?"

"Saving lives, for one thing."

"Saving lives, yes—it is very noble, like the priesthood— but why not let others who perhaps don't care much about money save lives or become priests? You could spend the rest of your days saving other lives—but how much of a life would you have?"

"It could be a very exciting life, Syl. I don't mean just saving the lives of a few of my patients—I'm talking about making discoveries on the frontiers of medicine that could save untold thousands of lives."

"I don't understand."

"There are leaders in medicine—men like Lister and Pasteur, whose names will some day become very famous— who are doing what I can only dream of doing. Research. So many people die every day from diseases we don't understand. Only from dedicated research can we ever hope to find the cures to such diseases."

"If what those men are doing means so much to you, why don't you too do what you call 'research'?"

He smiled sadly. "The equipment for such research—a good microscope, the laboratory instruments, chemicals and so forth—is very costly."

"So you see? It is as I told you—without money you can do little. . . ."

iv

There had been a brief intermission following the waltzes, and now the orchestra struck up a fast, stirring rhythm. Syl clapped her hands in delight. "Ah! A *paso doble*!"

Paul looked at the dancers returning to the floor in dismay. All began whirling and gliding with incredibly fast movements to the lively music. Syl watched with glowing, eager eyes, and from the way her shoulders moved unconsciously to the cadence it was plain that she would love to be among the swirling dancers. But such skilled movements would require much practice and perhaps an inborn talent for it. Paul knew if he attempted it he would only make an ass of himself. If only Etienne would return so she would not have to be disappointed!

"Mademoiselle Beauvais . . ." A most elegantly dressed gentleman was making a sweeping bow before Syl. His shirt studs were sparkling diamonds, as were his cuff links, and another flashed on a finger. "I see you are not dancing. Would you do me the honor of giving me this dance?"

"I am sorry, Monsieur Jacquard," Syl said politely, unsmiling, "but I am feeling indisposed at the moment and do not care to dance."

"Perhaps the next dance then?"

"No. Not the next time either."

"But I wish very much to dance with you." Jacquard's tone carried an undercurrent of anger. "One time at least this evening. Surely you cannot deny me such a simple request?"

Noting the flush that tinged Syl's face, Paul stepped forward. "The lady has already answered your question, sir. Obviously Miss Beauvais does not wish to dance with you."

The man's glance slashed over Paul like an invisible razor, and Paul felt a tingling premonition of danger race down his spine—reminiscent of a time long ago when he had caught a live timber wolf in a deadfall. Indeed, for all his faultless clothing and silken-smooth manner, Jacquard exuded a sense of raw ruthless power and even had a bit of the look of a wolf. He was a big man, fully as tall as Paul, with a swarthy skin and a mass of glossy black hair that tumbled to his massive shoulders in an uncurried way as if no comb could tame it. The yellowish-brown eyes had the stabbing alertness of a stalking carnivore, and his strong white teeth gleamed in a smile that seemed more of a snarl. He had a pencil-thin mustache, a hawkish nose and a long powerful jaw ridged with muscles that tautened as he spoke:

"*Monsieur*, your interference is presumptuous. Mademoiselle Beauvais is quite capable of answering my questions directly to me."

Paul stared back into the burning, hostile eyes. "Miss

Beauvais is in my company, sir, and since she has made her attitude clear, I must ask you to leave."

Jacquard's chest heaved from the violent emotions boiling inside. "Your implication, *monsieur*, that my presence is in any way molesting *mademoiselle* can only be taken as an insult—"

"*Messieurs—!*" Syl moved between the two men. "I demand that both of you end this embarrassment at once!"

Jacquard inclined his head in a brief bow to her, then turned back to Paul.

"I will look forward to discussing this matter with you at another time and under more favorable circumstances. . . . " After another little bow he strode away.

Syl's fingers were trembling as she touched Paul's arm. "I was so frightened."

"There was nothing to fear."

"Leon Jacquard is a very dangerous man, hot-tempered and vengeful toward those who scorn him. His reputation with women is scandalous. He has had many duels because of women, and all decent women avoid him. He is said to provoke fights over women just for an excuse to kill his rivals. It frightens me that he keeps trying to force his attentions on me, although he knows I do not welcome them."

"So that's why you wouldn't dance with him!"

"More than that. I can't stand his rude, overbearing ways. Like so many of the *nouveaux riches*, he pushes in where he is not wanted. Nowhere in proper Creole society is he accepted. Nobody knows how he made his wealth, and there are suspicions about his background. He is from Santo Domingo, and it is rumored that he killed and stole and—"

Her expression changed suddenly from anger to alarm as she looked past his shoulder. "Pierre and Etienne are back, but something terrible has happened. . . . I can tell by the looks on their faces. . . ."

v

The ride home from the ball was dismal. Etienne sat in one corner of the rear seat, withdrawn into his own brooding thoughts. Pierre was equally unwilling to talk, but Syl was insistent.

"You say Etienne is involved in a duel. Why? What happened?"

Pierre almost snapped at her. "Does it matter why? There

were words . . . and I was unable to accept the other man's cartel because of this damnable arm. Etienne had no choice but to accept it for me."

Syl moaned, holding her head in her hands. "A duel—all because some stupid words were spoken! Who is the other man?"

"Domergue."

"*Mon Dieu*! They say Adrien Domergue is one of the best shots in New Orleans. He will kill you for sure, Etienne!"

"Come now, Syl," Pierre said placatingly. "Etienne's an excellent marksman, too. They'll be quite evenly matched. In any event the die is cast and the damage cannot be undone."

Paul, listening to the senselessness of it all, cut in harshly:

"You say the damage cannot be undone, Pierre. I say the real damage is not yet done and should be prevented. In my opinion only idiots would sanction a duel for any reason! Do you think that dueling proves you're not a coward? What it really reveals is another kind of cowardice—the fear that if you don't go along with this ridiculous custom somebody will *think* you're coward. I submit that it would take greater bravery to ignore the whole affair."

Even Syl was staring at Paul, shocked, in the deep silence that followed.

"I shall forgive your unseemly outburst," Pierre said after a few moments, forcing a tolerant smile, "because of your ignorance of our ways. A man's honor is at stake here."

"Honor?" Paul flared back. "And so is a man's life at stake! Is not a life of greater importance?"

"Of the two," Pierre said coldly, "honor is the greater. Cowards deserve to die."

"But what of human intelligence, reason? Brutes in the jungle fight, but cannot civilized man use his superior brain to resolve differences? Could not Etienne and Domergue meet privately when they have cooled off and discuss it logically like men of culture and enlightenment and settle the matter with words only?"

"You fail to understand," said Etienne, "that once a physical blow has been struck there can be no attempt at reconciliation."

"Apparently nothing can dissuade you from going through with this ridiculous performance of pride, so I'll say no more."

Pierre's words were iced. "I shall be Etienne's second and

had wished you to be the attending physician, but if you prefer to refuse, let me know at once and I'll make arrangements with another doctor."

"My personal beliefs about dueling in no way affect my medical capabilities. I would agree to be the attending physician except that since I have lost my bags, I lack the surgical instruments and medicaments."

"That will be no problem. I can easily borrow the necessary equipment from one of my doctor acquaintances. If you are agreed, Etienne and I will pick you up just before dawn tomorrow."

"I'll be waiting."

FOUR: The Duel

A light rain fell during the night, and Paul, sleepless, listened to the random patter against the roof and windows and could not help thinking that in some societies human lives were held in no higher esteem, nor had any more control over their destinies, than the falling drops of rain. Sometimes it seemed an immense waste of medical talents to expend them on a human race so seemingly bent on self-destruction.

He rose while it was still dark, prepared coffee and a light breakfast, and was outside waiting when the Troyonne carriage appeared through the early morning murk.

The greetings were brief. After informing Paul that he had procured the necessary medical items, Pierre resumed the discussion he had been having with Etienne concerning the duel. As Paul was to learn later, the two had been up half the night in preparation. Being the challenged party, Etienne had the privilege of choosing the weapons, and had chosen a brace of Pierre's long-barreled dueling pistols. Most of the time had been spent going over the procedures. Dueling protocol was as formal as a high church service, and strict adherence to proper behavior as established by precedence was mandatory.

Paul, glumly looking out of a carriage window, saw that between the scattered clouds were still a few pale stars. The fine drizzle had ceased, but a gray sky threatened still more to come—the eternal darkness of death.

"Hurry!" Pierre called to the driver. "We don't want to be late."

The driver flicked his whip. The horses threw their weight into their collars and the carriage moved forward with an increased whirring of wheels through the wet dirt.

Soon the coach reached the end of Metarie road and Les Trois Capelines, the traditional dueling grounds, were in sight. . . .

ii

Domergue's carriage had already arrived, and at the dueling site—a little glade about a hundred yards from the road— haze-muffled figures awaited them. Debouching, they strode in silence through wet grass, getting their shoes soaked. Except for the distant, plaintive call of a mourning dove, muffled in the thick moist air, the whole world under the leaden morning sky seemed oddly silent, suspended of all life.

Paul stood back while Pierre and Etienne went forward to confront Domergue and his second and exchange any last-minute requests or instructions. A third man whom Paul assumed to be the other party's physician stood in the background watching.

With great care each man examined the pistols until satisfied that everything was in order. Each had agreed upon twenty paces, after which the two contestants were to turn and bow briefly before raising their pistols to the sky. On signal they would lower the pistols and fire within a time limit of five seconds. The necessity of shooting quickly was balanced against accuracy, the need to hit the other man in a vital spot before he had a chance to aim properly. Cool nerves, speed and skill were all-important.

With both adversaries agreed on the arrangements, Pierre and Domergue's second now moved off a few feet, carrying the pistols, to confer on matters of protocol having to do only with their functions as seconds.

For the first time Paul got a glimpse of the other man's face.

Leon Jacquard!

With the final agreement reached, Pierre and Jacquard returned and released the loaded pistols to the principals.

"When I give the signal," Pierre announced, "you will both

walk your twenty paces and turn. . . ." He raised his left arm.

Moments later the arm dropped and both men began an unhurried walk in opposite directions. It was not necessary to count, as the positions had already been paced off and marked, nor was speed necessary at this point, since neither could shoot before a final signal had been given.

On their firing lines both duelists turned and bowed briefly, then raised their pistols high in the air.

"Gentlemen," said Pierre, "are you both ready?"

"Ready" answered both men at the same moment.

Pierre began the slow count to three with the measured cadence of a metronome, followed by:

"Fire!"

Paul, held to the scene almost as intently as if he himself held one of the pistols, watched both arms fall to firing position and was torn with suspense at the silence. It could have been no more than one or two seconds, but it seemed like several agonizing, wasted minutes before the first gun roared and a puff of red exploded from Etienne's weapon.

Almost simultaneously another burst of fire from the muzzle of Domergue's pistol blended in with a scream of pain.

The smoke still drifting from his pistol, Domergue sagged to his knees. One hand was frantically fingering at his breast as if trying to stop the blood that quickly stained his fingers, seeped down his waistcoat. The gun slipped from his other hand as he collapsed slowly forward on his face on the grass. Etienne was still standing.

The other physician and Jacquard rushed forward to kneel beside the fallen man. Since Etienne appeared to be unscathed, Paul started toward them too, with the thought of offering assistance. The physician was feeling for the pulse with one hand while rolling back an eyelid with the other. Paul took one look at the utter laxness that no living being can feign and knew that the other doctor's ritual check for vital signs was unnecessary.

"He's dead," the man said quietly.

Jacquard let out a low moan of anguish, and then rising to his feet with one hand over his eyes began to sob.

"How can it be?" he cried out brokenly. " I can't believe it! My best friend . . ."

Mingled with Paul's sympathy was disgust.

"When two grown men insist on playing childish games

with loaded weapons," he said curtly, "what can you expect?"
He heard Pierre calling:

"Paul—come quickly—!"

As he turned to go, Jacquard's hand gripped his arm and
spun him around. "You have insulted the honor of my dead
friend! I demand an apology—"

"I offer no apology for saying what I think."

The blunt words only incensed the overwrought man even
more. "I will avenge the dishonored memory of my friend!"
he almost screamed at Paul. "I will have satisfaction!"

"Isn't that satisfaction enough for you!" Paul said, pointing
at the corpse. "How many deaths does it take?"

"Jac, Jac—" The other physician caught at Jacquard's
arm, which had been drawn back to strike at Paul, and drew
him away. "You must calm down. . . . Apparently Monsieur
Troyonne has been hit after all, and you cannot obstruct a
doctor in the performance of his duty. . . . "

iii

Paul quickly cut away the clothing and examined Etienne's
wound. The bullet had entered the upper left side of the
abdominal cavity at the seventh rib—less than four inches
from the heart. Both men, excellent marksmen, had apparently
aimed for that vital organ, but Etienne, by firing a fraction of a second sooner, had succeeded in hitting the mark
and by so doing spoiled the other's aim enough to save his
life.

There was only a moderate oozing of blood, indicating that
at least the bullet had not severed an artery, although it
could have pierced the left lobe of the liver, unless deflected
by the rib. Carefully, Paul rolled Etienne over on the blanket
where he had been placed and cut away the back portion of
shirt. There was no evidence of the bullet having passed
through; it could well be lodged in rib bone, or have been
deflected elsewhere. Finding it might be a problem, and
extracting it even worse.

Rolling his patient back to his former position, he sponged
the wound with alcohol—how he missed his carbolic solution!
—and began applying a compress. Etienne had not made a
sound, although the pain must have been great.

"I am curious," Paul said to the tight-lipped man. "Why
didn't you make an outcry, or in some way let us know right
away that you were wounded?"

"I could not give Domergue the satisfaction of knowing that he had hit me before he died."

Pierre laughed. "Etienne is a proud one. It took a great effort of will for him to remain erect for so long. But tell me, why are you bandaging him before removing the bullet? It does not appear to be a very serious wound."

"The bullet could be lodged near the heart, close to the large arteries. I would not attempt it here on the ground. We must get him to a hospital. . . . "

FIVE: Jus Impune Necandi— "The Right to Kill Unpunished"

KNOCKING roused Paul from deep sleep.

Opening his eyes resentfully, he glanced at the wall clock and saw with surprise that it was already two-thirty in the afternoon. Pierre was coming to pick him up at three to visit Etienne in the Charity Hospital.

The knocking was louder, more insistent. Rolling off the bed, he headed for the door, rubbing sleep out of his eyes. Except for his shoes he was still fully dressed, having flung himself on the bed in exhaustion after returning from the hospital that morning.

Extraction of the bullet had been nerve-wracking. It had indeed been deflected by the seventh rib, coming to rest in a ligament barely an inch from the inferior vena cava artery. He had spent nearly a half-hour of slow, meticulous probing with scalpel and forceps to remove the bullet—only too aware that one slightest slip of the razor-sharp scalpel into the big artery could have started the blood gushing out, quickly leading to death. He had been drenched with sweat, more from tension than the heat, when finally he called for compresses and bandages.

Not having carbolic, he made do with a chloride solution that the nurse had managed to find for him. It was used by the hospital workers as a floor-cleansing agent, and the nurse —an elderly woman in the flowing robes of a nun—was plainly appalled at Paul's use of it for saturating the compresses.

Reaching the apartment door, he flung it open—and at once started to slam it shut again in the grinning face of the man outside.

"Hold it, my friend—!" said Mike Quinn, throwing the weight of his burly shoulders against the door and forcing his way in.

"Mike, I don't want to see you or—" Then he noticed the two familiar medical bags the gambler was carrying.

" 'Tis a foine greeting to be giving a friend who went to such great trouble and risk to save your royal doctorship from the toils of the police," Mike said huffily, placing the bags on the floor while his eyes roved admiringly around the big lavish apartment.

Paul smiled sarcastically. "And I suppose after taking such a great risk—as well as bilking me out of twenty-five dollars —you went all over town trying to sell the luggage. I'll wager you couldn't find a pawnshop willing to accept stolen goods, so now you're here in hopes of getting more money. Where is my portmanteau, by the way, and Miss Delacroix's luggage?"

The gambler drew himself up to his fullest height.

"I will forgive you, Paul, on the score that you are sadly lacking in charity and understanding of your fellow man. Your portmanteau and the young lady's luggage are downstairs in the safe custody of the gentleman who manages these apartments. That you would suspect me of stealing from one I considered my friend, or from such a heavenly creature as Miss Delacroix, is a foul blow to one who deserves better. As for the money I borrowed—"

In a lofty manner Quinn produced a fat wallet from which he extracted twenty-five dollars and handed it over.

Paul took the money, slightly mollified. "Why did it take you so long to bring my things?"

Mike spread his hands in a gesture of innocence. "I happened into a little game with a few other gentlemen at the hotel. Luck, you'll agree, cannot be planned or foreseen, but it must be seized upon when it comes. I fell into a winning streak that went on for two days, until"—he made a grimace of offended pride—"the hotel manager requested that I depart the premises, as it was rumored, most unfairly, that I was by way of cheating a bit at cards. Does that satisfy your suspicions, Sir Doctor?"

"Not quite. The men you pointed out as police asking questions about me turned out to be only cotton and sugar brokers. Why did you lie to me?"

Mike sighed and put on a contrite grin. "Begad, and there you have me dead to rights! I confess, it's an errant liar I was, but my reasoning was pure as the new-driven snow."

"A lie is a lie, no matter how you twist your reasoning to justify it!"

"When the devil drives, a man canna always follow the path of angels." The gambler paused to give Paul a sly grin. "As you yourself well know, the need sometimes arises to invent a tale or two. . . . "

"*Touché.*" Paul grinned wryly. "But it's still not the same thing. My case was that of an innocent man trying to escape a trap."

"And you think mine any different? Let me tell you, my friend, if being bereft of cash is a crime, then it was the lowest criminal I was. And in a trap. Not a tuppence did I have left in my duds. My one small trunk containing all my worldly possessions was being held on the *Cly* as security for a small loan I had from Slattery. Even a room was denied me at the hotel, except for cash in advance, because I was without luggage. Then bejabbers and holy Moses, like a vision from heaven my eyes were smote with the welcome sight of you in the company of an angel and I knew luck was smiling at this poor sod who could afford not a thimbleful of Irish cheer to warm his gob. A small amount was all I needed to get started again while luck was with me, but it being my best judgment that my parsimonious Yankee friend would not be quick with the helping hand, I had to fall back on my wits to save my mutton."

His grin broadened. "And that's the how and why of it, Paul. I came to America to make my fortune and with your unwitting help have made a tidy little start. I am not one to forget my friends and I wish to express it in practical terms—"

With a lordly mien, he again took out his wallet and thumbed through the fat sheaf of bills inside. "If you are in need of a bit of extra cash, I would like to share some of my luck with you. . . . "

"No, Mike," Paul said, surprised and considerably softened by the unexpected generosity, "I too have had some good fortune and am not in need of more, but I thank you kindly for the offer."

Making a fine show of disappointment, the gambler replaced his wallet. "Your refusal makes it more difficult for me to bring up the favor I was about to ask of you. . . . "

"And what is the favor?"

"There's another side to the coins that jingle in my pocket. The hotel has barred me from staying there, and I have yet to find suitable lodging for the night." Mike's glance roved longingly around the luxurious apartment. "So I am asking if you will allow me the use of a spare bed here for only as long as—"

"No, Mike, no!" So that was the real motivation behind Mike's seeming generosity! "This apartment belong to Mr. Gayarre and I have no right to extend its use to others."

Mike looked crestfallen. "But only for the night. Surely it could do no harm."

"I'm sorry, Mike, but—" He broke off at the sound of discreet knocking.

This time it was Pierre's black driver.

"Miché Doc, suh, Massa Gayarre he a-waitin' fo' you in de carriage. . . . "

"Tell him I'll be right down."

Quickly Paul prepared to leave, first rinsing his face with tepid water and running a comb through his dark hair to bring it into some semblance of order. Mike was still there when he returned to the living room to pick up his medical bags. The gambler was the picture of abysmal dejection.

"Oh hell, Mike," he said in exasperation. "You can stay— but just for tonight!"

ii

Charity Hospital was an impressive three-storied building on Tulane Avenue built of bricks ranging in shade from the palest rose to deepest red. It was set back from the avenue on a raised part of the landscape pleasantly shaded by towering oleander trees, palms and other tropical types.

Inside was not so pleasant.

Entering, Paul's nostrils were again assailed, as they had been that morning, by a familiar odor—the bestial stench of sickness and suppuration that permeated the hospital. His mind's eye automatically envisioned the suffering faces that filled the wards.

When in his lord-of-the-manor style Pierre made his identity known to the nun at the admissions desk, she made haste to fetch the hospital director.

Dr. Emil Burrelle was a most affable gentleman with a coif of silvery hair and chin beard of the same distinctive hue, and he wore a gold-rimmed monocle attached to a black silken ribbon.

"A pleasure indeed, Monsieur Gayarre," he said, inclining his head in a bow. "The head nurse has informed me of the tragic mishap to Monsieur Troyonne, and I assure you that all the resources of this institution will be used to the fullest effect to hasten Monsieur Troyonne's recovery. I have instructed our head surgeon, Dr. Claude Landau, to devote all his energies to that end."

"There will be no need of Dr. Landau," said Pierre, "since Monsieur Troyonne will be attended by his own private physician, Dr. Paul Abbott, who accompanies me—" And turning, he made the introduction.

"Ah yes . . . " said Burrelle softly, but with eyes suddenly gone icy and probing into Paul as they shook hands. "And where have you practiced, *Docteur*?"

"I have only just arrived in New Orleans and have not yet established a practice."

"You are accredited, of course? Since there are so many doctors around without even a medical diploma, you must understand that to maintain our high standards we find it necessary to inquire into the credentials of any private physician permitted to attend his patients in our facility."

At Paul's momentary hesitation, Pierre cut in with a touch of indignation. "Dr. Abbott has trained in the finest medical academies in Edinburgh. I vouch for it that his credentials are the best."

"Ah yes," said the director with an instant change of attitude, all smiles again. "What could be better? If you have no objection, I should like to accompany you while you attend Monsieur Troyonne."

Etienne, at first glance, appeared to be coming along nicely. At least his face had been freshly washed and glowed with a pinkish flush that could have passed for health on any but one of his normal pallor. The bed, too, had been freshly made and the sheets folded back neatly. He responded to their greetings wearily.

Paul stepped forward and drew down the sheet to examine the wound and at once felt a surge of anger. His bandages had been removed and the wound stuffed with the commonly used swabs made of lint. Since the days of the French Revolution such swabs had acquired a romantic aura for use on wounds, originating as they did during wartime when women sat around tables by candlelight plucking threads from old scraps of linen while their men were away fighting. The threads were collected into piles, thrust into sacks and dispatched to the wounded at the front. Hospitals abroad and in America still used these unwashed threads, cleverly twisting them into swabs of various sizes and shapes to be used as ready-made compresses over bleeding wounds or suppurating sores. In most hospitals, doctors thought nothing of rinsing a used swab in a pan of water and using it over and over again on other patients.

"But he wasn't to be touched until I changed the bandages myself!" Paul said angrily. "Who authorized this?"

The nun chattered a few sentences in French, looking to the hospital director for support.

"We only use the sound and proven medical procedures in this hospital," he explained politely. "We are aware that there are some misguided doctors who are willing to endanger the lives of patients with wild new theories, but here the traditional methods are meticulously followed."

"But Mr. Troyonne was brought in only this morning and already he's flushed with fever. The wound has begun to suppurate. That would not have happened if someone had not changed the dressing."

Burrelle raised his eyebrows, smiling tolerantly. "You are a young man with perhaps too little clinical experience. Never have I known a wound of that sort—even an operation so small as removal of a finger—not to have caused fever and suppuration within hours, or certainly within one day's time. What else would you expect?"

Paul knew it was useless to argue. Pasteur's pioneering work on sepsis and fermentation, proving that bacteria existed in the air and would infect any break in the skin, was yet known to only a handful of researchers such as Lister. Lister's own theories on the destruction of such infectious germs, insofar as Paul knew, were not as yet on record in medical journals for others to read. Even when all their theories were someday proved beyond doubt and known worldwide, the traditional resistance of the medical fraternity to new ideas and procedures was so adamant that more than likely another generation would pass before they were generally accepted.

Meanwhile the death rate from wounds and operations in hospitals, even in the medical centers of Edinburgh and Glasgow, averaged eighty percent, and he was sure it was no better here. Once an operation was finished, the surgeon and nurse merely washed the blood from their hands and considered their work was done. The patient was sent back to the ward and was thereafter on his own. By evening he was sure to run a high temperature, usually up to 103. The following day profuse suppuration would begin—yellow and green pus forming with the blood that was continuing to seep out. But this was considered a natural healing process. Instead of bemoaning the loss of eighty percent of their hapless victims, surgeons were proud of achieving the high ten to twenty percent of successes. As some critics said, a man on the operating table was in far greater danger than a soldier in the thickest hail of bullets.

Only too aware of the futility of argument, Paul said, "Since Mr. Troyonne is my patient, I shall change the dressings in accordance with my own procedure. I request that the nurses be instructed that they are not to be changed without my permission."

Dr. Burrelle agreed amiably and transmitted the instructions in French to the nurse, whose face turned tight-lipped and sullen at having her own pet procedures countermanded. Then with a chuckle the director turned to Paul.

"The nurse doesn't understand a word of English, so I will explain that the hospital is run by the nuns. They even resent the doctors. The sisters' main concern is to see that the face of the patient shines with cleanliness in the eyes of God, and that he constantly says his prayers so that he can die as a pious Christian."

Meanwhile Paul had opened his bags and removed some of the instruments and medications. The director watched with interest as Paul took a bottle of full-strength carbolic and using a small amount of it mixed a solution with water and alcohol in the hand washbasin on a nearby stand. After immersing his hands in the solution, vigorously scrubbing them together and then shaking them as dry as possible— scorning the folded towel on the stand—he proceeded to mix a smaller amount of the same solution in a small container taken from one of his bags. Into this solution he dropped several linen compresses of Paul's own manufacture.

"And what, may I ask, is the chemical you are using?" asked Dr. Burrelle.

When Paul told him, the director's nose wrinkled fastidiously. "But that's the same stuff that some cities use to kill the stink of their sewage drainage systems!"

"Has it ever occurred to you that the stink of suppurating

flesh is very similar to the stink of the decomposing matter in sewers?" said Paul, continuing to work.

He worked carefully, cleansing away the bits of decomposing flesh around the edges of the bullet wound with a knife, which had also been immersed in carbolic. Then he sponged the area clean with more of the solution and taped over it a square of lead foil with a hole cut through it along with the carbolic-soaked linen compresses.

"Fortunately the infection hasn't gone on too long," he said. "I think the fever will subside fairly soon now, and by tomorrow the infection should be clearing up."

Dr. Burrelle shrugged with obvious disbelief. "It will be interesting to watch. . . . I would also be interested in getting your opinions regarding our other patients. Dr. Landau is now going through the wards on his rounds, and perhaps you would care to join him as an observer?"

"I would be delighted, but—" Paul looked questioningly at Pierre, who was now engaged in quiet conversation with Etienne.

Pierre waved at Paul in a gesture of dismissal. "Do go with the good doctor, Paul. Etienne and I have many business matters to discuss and prefer to be left alone. . . ."

iii

Dr. Claude Landau, the head surgeon, was a baldish, smallish, slender man but with a feral intensity that somehow transmitted a warning that he was not one to be trifled with. His darting dark eyes instantly took Paul's measure during the introductions while one slim white hand fingered at his pencil-thin mustache.

"So you too are a surgeon," he said, smiling thinly. "It should please you to know that this is one hospital where surgeons are recognized as of paramount importance. Most of the patients in the wards, as you shall soon see, are those requiring surgical attention. . . . "

A retinue of obsequious younger doctors followed as Landau led the way down a corridor with Paul beside him.

The stench in the wards was overpowering. Emaciated patients lay in their beds shivering with fever, and all those who had been in the operating rooms had pus flowing from their wounds, forming crusts on the bandages and bed linens. Landau checked one bed after another. Men with amputations or other surgical damage usually had a cradle over the wounded member to keep the bedclothes away from the wound. All of them without exception were flushed with the usual postoperational fever.

"May I ask what steps you take to alleviate the fever?" said Paul.

"None are necessary, Doctor. Fever is a natural phenomenon."

"Still, it has been demonstrated by Semmelweiss in Vienna that symptomatic and puerperal fevers can be avoided by a thorough washing of the hands in a chloride solution prior to an operation."

Landau waved his hands in disgust. "Nonsense! As any properly trained physician knows, fever is part of the healing process."

"Yet in most hospitals only about twenty percent of the patients survive after an operation, so plainly nature's healing process is not enough."

"The percentage is quite normal. Do you know of any hospitals with a better average?"

Paul couldn't debate this. "However," he said, "more and more doctors abroad are beginning to accept the fact that sepsis is the big danger that prevents healing."

Landau made a snort of impatience. "That is hardly a new theory. We too fumigate the rooms with sulphur, and as you may note the walls are whitewashed. The floors are mopped weekly with a chloride solution, though it is of doubtful value. For the floors of our operating rooms we use tar. We have also improved the ventilation, and we relieve our most serious cases with daily bleedings and purges. We are very modern and are proud of our high rate of cures."

With difficulty Paul repressed an angry desire to argue, knowing it would be to no avail.

As he checked the patients, Landau frequently poked his forefinger into suppurating wounds without so much as first washing his hands, and afterward merely wiping the finger on a towel which he tossed to an attendant before going to the next patient.

"Have you no fear that hospital gangrene might be transmitted in that way, Doctor?" Paul asked.

The head surgeon laughed. "Gangrene is not transmitted. It comes from the suppuration."

"But suppuration is transmitted. Isn't it the same thing?"

"Not at all. Suppuration is not caused or transmitted by human hands but is mainly caused by the trauma of the injury itself. Other of the causes are locked within the patient's own mental attitude, such as anxiety about his family if he dies, and so forth."

"Then you make no effort to suppress the suppuration?"

"On the contrary, we use the most effective means known to science. I will show you. . . . "

First giving an attendant orders to bring the "iron," Landau led the way into a ward filled with the sickly stench of gangrene. The patient was on his back, face turned sideways, eyes closed and features contorted into a permanent grimace of agony. He had been amputated just below the knee, and the stump of leg was elevated slightly, resting on a bunching of towels and rags on the bed placed there to absorb the continuous watery discharge seeping from the suppurating mess of gangrene and rotting flesh. Above the knee and halfway up the thigh, the flesh was swollen and inflamed an angry red.

The attendant arrived, pushing a metal cart filled with glowing coals from which protruded a black iron poker.

"I was able to get the leg off in less than two minutes," Landau said with obvious pride as he reached for the poker. "Unfortunately, the gangrene is now above the knee, and of course another amputation is not possible." No surgeon would attempt an amputation above the knee, because the arteries were too large to close by cautery and the blood would pump out too fast, bringing on the patient's death before the arteries could be tied.

Suddenly the red-glowing end of the poker lifted and plunged into the gruesome mass of gangrene. The patient gave a muffled scream and an acrid odor of burnt flesh rose up to mingle with the nauseous stink of gangrene. Mercifully, the patient fainted.

"That won't stop the gangrene," said Paul.

"No, but it will abate the sepsis."

"The man will die nevertheless."

Landau shrugged. "Of course, but it is still our duty to do all we can for him while he still lives."

In this charnel house? Paul thought, glancing around at the ward crowded with dying bodies. It was more of a virtual torture chamber. There was probably not a patient in the entire hospital who would not have preferred a quick dignified death to this slow continuous nightmare of prolonged torment.

Drawing a golden watch from a vest pocket, Dr. Landau

checked the time. "It is almost time for an operation I have scheduled for this afternoon. If you wish, Dr. Abbott, you are welcome to watch. . . . "

The operating theater had bare whitewashed walls, a floor of coarse boards mopped with tar and a rough wooden table in the center darkened with countless bloodstains. Against one wall was a cupboard where the instruments were kept: saws, bistouries, scissors, forceps and scalpels—all with scored wooden handles, like kitchen tools. Germ traps. Beside the operating table was a stand on which had been placed a tin washbasin and a hand towel.

The patient, who was soon wheeled in on an invalid's chair, was a good-looking young man with a mass of blond hair. His face was contorted with fright and reddened from his vociferous objections:

"I told ye I don't want my leg cut off! All I want is the hell outta this place! When they brought me in last night, I didn't know—they told me they could fix my leg—and nobody's done a fuckin' thing about it yet. Ye gotta let me outta—"

"Have no worries," said Landau, his voice suddenly silken and soothing. He walked over to look down at the frightened lad. "We're going to fix your leg. You're going to be fine."

"Please don't take off my leg," the young man begged. "I got me a wife an' kids to support, an' the old lady's pregnant again. . . . If I'm crippled—"

Paul stepped over. "May I examine the leg?"

"Of course. As you can see, the poor wretch has a compound fracture of the tibia caused, as I understand, by some sort of farm accident. Obviously there is only one prognosis possible. . . . "

Paul crouched to examine the leg, which had been wrapped in a bloodied towel, and saw at once that the break in front of the leg between the knee and ankle had originally been a simple fracture, a complete break of the tibia bone on such a slanting angle that careless handling—either by those who had brought him here or by hospital aides—had caused the upper section of broken bone to slide downward and outward a bit, breaking through the skin and thus turning a relatively simple break into a compound fracture—one of the most serious of all fractures. It was almost hospital gospel that a patient with a compound fracture was invariably eighty percent dead. A simple splint could have prevented the additional damage when the patient had been brought in last night, but the average nurse would not have known how to do it properly. And hospital doctors didn't work at night, except for wealthy patients.

Paul looked at the surgical director. "You have considered no alternative but to operate?"

"There is no other. Amputation is the only possible procedure."

Hearing this, the patient suddenly let out a sobbing wail.

Landau gave a signal to an attendant standing behind the patient, all readied with preparations very familiar to Paul: the face cone, the chloroform, the saturated compresses. At once the attendant brought the chloroform-soaked compresses down over the patient's nose and held it there with the aid of another attendant against the patient's strugglings, which soon ceased.

"Dr. Landau," Paul said, "will you permit me to demonstrate my procedure on the patient?"

"I would be delighted, Dr. Abbott. If you can beat my record of removing a limb in less than two minutes, then I shall indeed say you are a surgeon worthy of the highest respect."

By this time the unconscious patient had been lifted to the operating table and was being strapped down.

"I have no intention of removing the limb," said Paul. "I wish only to cleanse the suppuration with my disinfectant, then set the leg and put it in splints."

Landau's eyes iced with sudden hostility. "Dr. Abbott, I have studied under the most eminent surgeons of the day. I have performed hundreds of operations in a manner no one can criticize. My judgment is based on broad experience as well as the collective wisdom of the entire medical profession. For you to have the temerity to question it—"

"I meant no offense. I request only the opportunity to proceed with my treatment. If it fails, the patient will be no worse off."

"I forbid it! I would be derelict in my duty to allow frivolous experimentation on my helpless patients. . . . " As he spoke, the surgical director was carefully removing his fine frock coat, which he hung on a wall hook. "I shall proceed with the amputation as I had planned."

Turning up the sleeves of his spotless white shirt, he put on another coat. The garment, a lightweight greatcoat, was encrusted with so many layers of dried blood and pus from hundreds of operations that it had grown stiff from the accumulations. But as Paul well knew, it was his badge of honor in the eyes of other doctors. The gruesome accretions had the value of decorations. The proud wearer of such a garment looked down contemptuously at the clean coats of beginning doctors, who for the most part were only too eager to get their own coats covered as quickly as possible with a worthy crust of blood and pus.

Meanwhile an attendant had pushed a tub-like container up beside the operating table to catch the splashing blood and the severed limb. Another rolled up the metal cart with the glowing coals and redhot poker. Since the cauterizing poker could close off only the smaller severed blood vessels, the surgeon would use thin leather whipcord thongs—a dozen or so of which hung within easy reach from his coat lapels— to tie off the larger ones. The leg would come off fast enough —Paul had no doubt about that—but by tomorrow infection would be rampant with flowing pus along with a high fever, and hospital gangrene was almost sure to follow.

"The saw—" Landau held out his hand to receive the eighteen-inch flesh and bone saw that one of the younger doctors was quick to hand him.

This is murder, Paul thought fiercely. Licensed murder! The phrase Lister had used had been none too harsh: *Jus impune necandi*—"The right to kill unpunished."

Landau smiled thinly at Paul. "My invitation still stands, Dr. Abbott. . . . " He extended the saw. "You are still welcome to see if you can beat my record—or do you prefer to watch me exhibit my skill?"

"No thank you. I care neither to participate in nor witness an execution."

He turned, but not before glimpsing such a look of hatred on Landau's face that he knew he'd only added another to his growing list of enemies, and strode out.

iv

Back in Etienne's room, Pierre faced Paul with a worried expression.

"Etienne and I have been discussing the plantation problems, which are very serious," he said. "It is imperative that we get back as soon as possible. Tell me, Paul, how soon do you think it will be safe to move Etienne from this hospital without endangering his condition?"

"I'll be blunt. It was a mistake to bring him here in the

first place. I should have known better than to think that a hospital so fresh and clean on the outside would be the same inside. The sooner we get him out of this pesthouse, the better."

Pierre looked surprised. "Your words confirm my general feeling about hospitals, but I had considered this one superior. I myself have contributed generously to its improvement funds."

"To be fair, it's no worse than most hospitals anywhere else in the world—they're all breeding grounds of disease bacteria spread from patient to patient by doctors and nurses. Etienne would be safer in a woodshed. If he stays here there's no guarantee that he won't become infected with something far more dangerous than a bullet."

"Then you think he can be safely moved today?"

"He can be moved by stretcher in complete safety. If you're anxious to return to the plantation, you can just as well take him there. I will remain close to give him more of my personal attention and supervise the nursing care."

"Excellent! Then we can proceed as previously planned and leave for the plantation by steamer tomorrow. I will make arrangements for moving Etienne immediately."

v

In the carriage, several minutes passed before Pierre broke the somber silence.

"Paul, I've decided that you should know the reason for Etienne's duel. It involves a personal confession on my part. . . . "

"If you find it embarrassing, Pierre, there's no need."

"Dammit, Paul! I consider you a friend as well as my doctor! If I'm mistaken, say so and I'll not speak another word."

"I misspoke myself, Pierre. I'm honored that you think of me as a friend, and you have certainly proved yourself one to me. Any personal matters you care to reveal, I will hold in deepest confidence."

"The fact is, I've just become enamored of a most extra-ordinarily beautiful young lady. . . . "

Paul thought instantly of Syl. Pierre's words dashed the theory that he might be in love with his cousin.

"Someone you met recently?"

"Only yesterday evening at the quadroon ball. I was

smitten on first sight." He smiled at Paul, a bit shamefaced. "I told a little white lie to Syl. It was ungentlemanly of me to abandon her temporarily at the ball last night, but I had little choice, as earlier that day I had received a special message from Madame Silkwood concerning a young lady she wished me to meet—"

"Madame Silkwood!"

Pierre showed surprise. "You know of her?"

"Uh, the name was mentioned at the hotel. I understand that she runs an exclusive finishing school for young ladies."

Pierre chuckled. "Exclusive, I grant you. Madame Silkwood is the best-known and most expensive procuress in all Louisiana. A young courtesan trained by Madame Silkwood is a delight beyond compare. She has known me for years, and knows of my taste in females, and was therefore anxious for me to meet Micaela—"

"Micaela!"

"That name too is familiar?"

Paul made a tremendous effort to mask his feelings, but could not control tremblings of hot and cold rage. So that was where he had delivered the saucy young virgin—to a high-class whorehouse!

"I once met a young lady of that name, but of course it could not be the same one."

"Hardly, my friend. This one has been reared so carefully, so properly, so shielded from men, that she virtually blushed and the lashes of her lovely big eyes drooped in modesty when we were first introduced. Ah, what a tender, innocent young flower! One so beautiful, naturally, was the center of male admiration at the ball, and the trouble started when Domergue attempted to appropriate her for himself. Doubtless he mistook my arm in a sling as license for doing as he wished without risk and had not expected Etienne to step in as my surrogate."

Pierre sighed. "However, all has turned out well. Domergue got his just due. Etienne has proven his bravery and will heal under your care. And as for me—" He smiled.

"All of us, including you, Paul, will be embarking by steamer tomorrow morning for the plantation. Micaela will move into my Pontalba apartment soon after you vacate. Meanwhile Madame Silkwood will conduct the proper negotiations for the monetary arrangement, and if all parties are satisfied I will purchase or build a little home for Micaela in the Rampart area. I think she will bring me luck. . . . "

The carriage soon arrived at the Pontalba Apartments and the two parted. Paul was feeling sick at heart.

vi

The moment he unlocked the apartment door he caught the whiff of cigar smoke. One of Pierre's expensive cigars, no doubt, he thought. He pushed in, prepared to scold the gambler if had presumed to help himself to his host's cigars.

But the person seated in a chair absorbed in a book while exhaling great plumes of blue cigar smoke had dark hair severely combed back from her center part in shiny wings, ravenlike, and caught in a chignon, netted, at the neck. She wore a voluminous skirt, beneath which her legs were crossed with one booted foot tapping on the floor, signaling the impatience of her waiting.

"Fern—how the hell did you get in?"

She let the book fall to her lap and looked up in feigned surprise. Her full-lipped mouth opened and blew another cloud of smoke in his direction, and her even white teeth bared in a reproving smile.

"Is that any way to greet a lady?"

He strode over and snatched the cigar from between her fingers. "A lady doesn't smoke cigars—particularly those that don't belong to her." He snuffed it out in an ashtray on a nearby table and left it there.

"I thought you'd be pleased to see me," she said. "It's been quite a while since we've been alone together. . . . "

"You haven't answered me—how did you get in?"

She smiled archly. "Why do you think so many fine Creole gentlemen maintain apartments like this? It makes it so convenient for entertaining their *filles de joie*. Many single, respectable young ladies do not wish to be seen entering, however, in which case they sneak in by the back entrance with the cooperation of an obliging concierge who with his master key will also let them into the apartment they are to visit."

Suddenly he noted the title of the book in her lap. *Armance*, by Stendhal—the same book that Syl had been reading on the ship.

"May I ask where you got that book?"

"Surely, Paul, you're not going to accuse me of stealing Pierre's books as well as his cigars? Though I'm sure he'd allow me to help myself to either."

"Not that book he wouldn't."

"That's an odd thing to say!"

Briefly Paul told of the shipboard incident and how per-
turbed Pierre had been, but he omitted mention of the inscription in the flyleaf.

Fern's forehead puckered in thought. "Something similar
happened to me. I saw Syl reading *Armance*, and thinking
to practice my French, asked her to lend it to me when she
was finished. She actually blushed and appeared as upset as
you've described Pierre and refused to let me borrow it. I
assumed it was French pornography—of course Syl would
rather die than be caught reading anything like that—so yesterday I went hunting in the local bookshops and found a
copy. The bookseller knew nothing about Stendhal except
that he's a new writer, and he doubted that any translations
would would be available in English."

"And is it pornography?"

Fern shook her head dolefully. "Of course I'm just a plodding reader in French, requiring a French dictionary for
every other sentence, and I've just begun it, but thus far it
seems like nothing more than a not very exciting love
story. . . . However, as soon as I find out what it's all about,
I'll let you know."

"There's no need," Paul said curtly. "If something of deep
personal significance to Syl and Pierre is locked away in the
pages of *Armance*—something they obviously wish to keep
secret—then I prefer to honor their wishes by not knowing
about it."

Fern dropped the book and stood up, frowning. "Your
tone of voice, Paul! You're really being very unfair and acting very grumpy for one who's been . . . so intimate. . . . "

"Should I be otherwise? You've avoided me like the plague
since I arrived. I had expected to see you at the ball, but Syl
told me you had another engagement."

She came close and put a hand on his arm. "Paul, as I've
told you many times, I think there's one thing in life more
important to me than love, or yes, even sex. I *am* a carnal
woman—I doubt that many females think of it, dream of it
or rise to more excitement over it than I do—but still this
other thing in my life comes first."

"I fail to grasp your meaning."

"I have to trust you in this, Paul, because we both share
secrets about each other that could send us to jail, or worse.
The fact is that my escort last night, Jason Moore, is one of

the crucial links in the Underground Railroad. My meeting with him last night was purely business. We met with the captain of a coastal schooner who has agreed to carry slave escapees to the North by a water route for one hundred dollars a head. Our contacts in the North will provide the money. But we still need certain communication links to the slaves, and that's where I shall need your help—"

"And I refuse! I don't give a damn about slavery one way or another. I've seen worse, and personally have known worse. I've known fear, injustice and damned-to-hell poverty—and that's the worst kind of slavery in the world."

"That's hardly true. However terrible your experiences may have been, you're still a free man."

He grinned humorlessly. "There's a sword hanging over my head and you know it."

"But you're being helped. Don't you think the black people deserve a chance such as you've been given?"

"Sure, but not from me. What makes you think I could ever be an abolitionist?"

Her eyes were scornful. "Because you're a Yankee, like me. I thought any true Yankee who understood the meaning of freedom would be ready to fight for it for those to whom it is denied!"

His eyes slashed back at her. "Then you have misguessed, Miss Venable. I am a Yankee, yes. I believe in freedom. I care not whether skin is black or white. But I have been helped, indeed have been *given* my present freedom by one of the very slaveholders you detest. He has been more than generous. He's honest, decent and kind—and you expect me to turn on him as you have? You can go your way, do as you wish, but I'll have nothing to do with robbing my employer!"

For a few moments she glared at him with hatred; then her expression softened.

"Perhaps I have misjudged," she said gently. "I had forgotten the tensions you've been forced to live under since your escape from Scotland, then from the *Cly*, and the beastly duel you had to witness this morning. . . . It is something I should understand because my own tensions are something I have to contend with constantly. . . . "

Her eyes were bright as she began unfastening her blouse, and her full lips, faintly smiling, seemed to have added a new dimension of sensuous appeal.

Her blouse fell away and she began tugging at the camisole, pulling it over her head; then the voluminous skirt was unfastened and dropped, rustling, to the floor. She wore nothing under the camisole, and her full breasts joggled a bit as she bent to begin removing the petticoats.

The excruciatingly sweet *frisson* was suddenly a rising fever in his loins. My God, she was right! He hadn't realized how starved he was for female flesh until she'd made her first move to disrobe. To hell with the rights and wrongs of the world; now was not the time for argument. Before she finished undressing he strode forward and swooped her up in his arms and carried her into the bedroom. Together they pulled off his clothes and the rest of hers.

"You're a devil!" she whispered close to his face as he embraced her nakedness fiercely and began kissing her lips, ears, breasts. "But my kind of devil . . . we're so much alike. It was stupid of me to waste any time talking."

"Devil I may be," he said when finally he had rolled her on her back, parted her legs and begun the plunge into her, "but don't for a moment think this changes my thinking by one iota. Fucking you is a supreme pleasure, but never could it induce me to agree with your abolitionist ideas."

Her sensuous, writhing movements ceased. "You think I offered my body in exchange for cooperation I hope to get from you?"

"It's hardly original thinking. All through history women have traded their bodies for what they hope to gain from men."

"Damn you, oh damn you, you arrogant male bastard!" She slapped at him and tried to roll away from beneath him. "Like all men you think of women as scheming bitches on a much lower level—except for the empty-headed sugary ones like Syl posing as angels on a pedestal!"

Smiling, he held her in place with his strong arms, and despite her struggles continued his steady deep thrusts. His hands played over her breasts, down her sides, hooked under her buttocks, and he could feel her starting to respond again in defiance of her own will.

"It was a . . . mistake," she gasped, "to let my emotions get mixed up with my intellect. . . . I should never have allowed—"

"Your intellect may be mixed up with crazy ideas," he said, feeling her hips arching up in a resurge of passion to meet his thrusts, "but your body knows the truth."

Indeed she was like two women, both trapped in the same

identity and each seeking supremacy over the other. Her body was like a wild animal, separate from the other half of her, which was her brain, struggling to escape while at the same time seeking with a feverish passion to join with him; more than to join, to devour him with upthrusts of her crotch in such fury as to sometimes almost lift him from the bed. Simultaneously he could feel the fiery slashes of her nails, claws of hatred, down his back while her arms were hugging him ever more tightly in possessive embrace. Like a half-tame, half-wild puma, a strange sort of female guerrilla at war with all social conventions and traditions, paying lip service to them only to gain her ends, and in a way encased in her own set of rigid ethics quite outside the social scheme —but ethics that could be toppled when the wild, wanton passions of her body took over.

She was everything that he had ever hoped for in the purely sexual experience—lewd, lustful, utterly uninhibited, wondrously inventive in the sensual uses of her body. Sometimes the very quivering of her pelvis excited him beyond bearing—and yet . . . he knew that he was not in love with her and never could be.

The crescendo of their fused passions exploded into climax.

Paul, sated and content, was once again aware of his surroundings and had heard the opening of the apartment door. . . .

"Quick!" he whispered. "Get something on. Someone has just entered the apartment and I don't want to cause you embarrassment."

Then as he hurriedly began dressing, he remembered that it was too late: most of the items of Fern's apparel lay strewn over the living-room floor.

vii

Fully dressed, albeit carelessly, Paul emerged into the living room just in time to see someone stealthily headed for the door.

"Mike—!"

The gambler turned with an embarrassed grin on his face.

"Ah, Paul . . . you must forgive me. Had I noticed the feminine garments on the floor sooner, I would have left immediately. As it was, my mind was on other matters, and it was not until a moment ago that I noticed—"

"I will appreciate it if you leave now," Paul said without

anger—after all, the gambler had no way of knowing. "And return in an hour or so."

Mike turned to leave, but was stopped by Fern's voice: "There's no need to leave on *my* account, Mr. Quinn." She stood outside the bedroom wrapped in a sheet. "After all, if Paul's not ashamed—men never are—why should I be?"

Paul was annoyed. "What are you trying to do, Fern— brand yourself as a wanton?"

"I'm no more a wanton than you are!" she shot back.

Mike made a low, sweeping bow. "Ah, Miss Venable— please be assured that never will a whisper of what I have observed pass my lips."

"And just what *have* you observed, Mr. Quinn?" Fern said with acerbity.

"Uh . . . I am deeply sorry if I have misspoke myself," he said quickly. "I was only meaning, in all respect, that there are some who would, of course . . . uh, jump to false conclusions, which I realize are unjustified."

"Unjustified? Let me make it very clear to you, Mr. Quinn, whether the conclusions that you or anybody else jump to are false or not, I don't give a fig. To put it another way, why should men preen themselves and act so proud about their conquests with the ladies and expect women to be deeply ashamed of the very same act they engaged in together? Fie on you, Mr. Quinn, and the whole caboodle of you hypocritical men!"

Mike actually blushed and began backing away, his head bobbing up and down in hasty bows. "As I said, I misunderstood . . . and again I apologize deeply. I shall be leaving—"

"No," Fern said firmly. "You stay. I insist. I want no show of false gallantry on my account. I myself am leaving as soon as I gather my garments together. . . . " Quickly she gathered up her various items of clothing and vanished into the bedroom.

Mike stared at Paul, shaking his head in wonderment while mopping at his brow with a handkerchief. Then he crossed over to one of Pierre's cigar boxes and helped himself. Saying nothing, Paul went over and also took a cigar. Mike took a big sulphur match and struck a light for both of them.

Fern emerged, fully dressed, a contented smile now on her lips. "Paul, dear, it has been a most pleasant interlude, and there's only one more token of affection I'd like from you before I leave. . . . "

She walked toward him with her lips pursed, and feeling somewhat embarrassed, Paul readied himself for a parting kiss.

Instead, she took the lighted cigar from between his fingers, thrust it between her pursed lips and took a deep puff.

"*Au revoir,* gentlemen," she said airily, and went out, smoking.

Mike gazed after her as if awestruck. His voice lowered to a whisper: "A most fantastic female! In my wildest fancies I could never have dreamed up such a strange one!"

"Nor could I."

"And not a wee bit bothered when I showed up at such an awkward moment. I vow, she must be the first lady of quality in all history not to be embarrassed in such a situation."

"Speaking of showing up, how did *you* get in without a key?"

Mike grinned guiltily. "It was just a little trick, my friend. Locks are of great interest to me, and on examining the wondrous new modern one installed on the door I could not help but note that it takes but a playing card inserted in the crack to depress the latch, so—" He spread his hands in a gesture of innocence. "It saves me the trouble of asking you for a spare key."

"You wouldn't need a key in any case. I'll allow you to stay one more night, but tomorrow morning I'm leaving, early, and I'll expect you to clear out at the same time. And don't you dare try your lock trick after I'm gone! The concierge will have orders to see that you are not admitted."

Mike drew himself up to his fullest height, his face showing hurt. "I am sorry that you have such a low opinion of my integrity, Sir Doctor. I hope someday to prove to you that I am a gentleman of honor. . . . "

BOOK FOUR

The Triangle

ONE: *Les Cypres*

THE boat traffic at the port of La Nouvelle Orléans was busy as usual. As far as vision could reach, almost every type of floating craft could be seen gliding about or at anchor: great white-winged clippers, sturdy tramps and frigates from other nations; river luggers, steam tugs and sternwheelers arriving and departing. Boats tootled and whistled signals back and forth. Occasionally the peaceful activity was startled, to no visible effect, by the pistol-like crack of an overseer's whip along the quay where endless queues of blacks labored at loading and unloading cargo, their sweating torsos glistening like polished ebony under an omnipresent sun.

Aloof to all this, the *Bayou Queen* slid forward with majestic serenity as it left the quay and headed up the Mississippi. A fervent forenoon sun poured its white brilliance over the broad expanse of water, sending most male passengers to the salon for a smoke or drink and the ladies to their staterooms to preserve their pale complexions. Among the few who lingered at the railing to enjoy the view was Paul Abbott, a hand shielding his eyes against the hard sparkle of waves.

For the next several hours he remained at the railing, absorbed in the unrolling panorama on both sides of the river. Not once, it seemed, did he see a foot of ground that had not been groomed into sweeping lawns, colorful gardens or fresh green expanses of the "big grass," as cane was called. Frequently they passed grand homes set back from the river. Most were of dazzling white, some were of pale yellow or other rainbow shades. All had wide galleries and balconies and were fronted by ponderous columns that soared two or even three stories high. Under the passionate embrace of sun they had the look of splendid temples.

Adding to a sense of dreamy unreality was the illusion that the vessel at times seemed to be floating through the air. This was because the flood season was beginning; the water level was close to the top of the levee, lifting the ship higher than the flat greenlands below the embankment.

Finally surfeited with the parade of opulence, Paul went into the salon for a bite to eat. The place was crowded. His eyes searched among the sea of faces, but Pierre was nowhere in sight. Doubtless he would be in a stateroom with Etienne, who had been brought abroad on a stretcher, and the two would be in one of their eternal discussions of plantation plans and problems. Mostly problems, he suspected.

From the conversation in the coach that morning, Paul had gathered that Pierre, rich as he was, had been forced to take out huge loans for the payment of machinery and construction of his projected new sugar refinery and was skating on very thin financial ice. He had gambled heavily on a good cane crop this season—dependent not only on the vagaries of weather but on enough field hands for the harvesting.

And now the threat of spreading smallpox and slave runaways could spell disaster.

ii

Along the levee in the half-luminous glow of twilight, about a half-dozen of the Gayarre house servants waited with lanterns. Curling lines of vegetation along the river's edge had blurred into deep shadows, and in the bowl of darkening sky the last songbirds were sweeping in long flights toward nests in the distant swamp. Seated or crouching in the grass, the servants had been waiting patiently since sundown, eyes directed downstream in anticipation of that first dark spot of billowing smoke that would signal the steamboat's approach.

Now and then their glances roved nervously toward the shed known as the "pesthouse." Set back against a fringe of woods, it could scarcely be seen in the clotting darkness, but its location was indicated clearly enough by the low moans and wails that came from the slaves locked inside. With the fragrance of jasmines carried in the damp evening air were mingled the odors of sickness.

The boat was late, as they had expected it would be, since it stopped at any plantation where a bell clanged or a slave signaled with a cloth that his massa had passengers or goods to pick up. But they didn't mind the wait, no matter how long it might be. Patience was a trait they had in ample supply.

Besides, they were charged with suspense—and hope—

Massa Pierre comin' home! Him 'n' Missus Syl 'n' Missus Fern. Massa, he fix the sickness 'n' maybe drive 'way the voodoo curse. . . .

A small boy suddenly let out a happy screech:

"Dey come—dere dey come! Ah seed 'er light!"

He started racing toward the mansion to alert the other servants, and almost simultaneously candles began flickering in all the windows of the great white mansion.

iii

With a churning backwash the steamer nudged up to the wharf, which extended about forty feet out into the river. A gangplank was lowered. Baggage ticketed for the Gayarre plantation had already been piled near the gangplank by porters, who speedily began moving it to the quay.

While the ladies went ahead and Pierre busied himself with supervising the attendants with the stretcher bearing Etienne, Paul followed behind, staring in admiration at the enormous mansion rising with extraordinary whiteness against the dark sky.

Les Cypres, as its name suggested, was set amid a grove of cypress trees, about two hundred yards back from the river. Against the shifting clouds, its lofty pillars and roof lines glimmering in the rising moonlight, the majestic structure seemed bathed in a strange aura of mystery.

Meanwhile, after giving instructions to the head servant, an elderly Negro neatly dressed in frock-coated livery, Pierre turned to Paul.

"A carriage will drop you off at the guest house, Paul, and your baggage will be along in a few minutes, but for the rest of the evening I must beg your indulgence. I am exhausted, as I am sure you are. A girl will be sent over to attend to your needs. So if you'll excuse us for now, we'll call it a day and expect to see you at the manor tomorrow. . . . "

The guest house, of pristine white with a lawn and flowerbeds surrounding it, was in some ways a miniature reproduction of the big mansion. Although blocky in shape, it was two-storied and boasted four white wooden columns in front that supported the second story gallery, imparting a modest, templelike dignity. For Paul, it was luxury beyond any abode he had ever called home.

Wall oil lamps had already been lighted. He made a quick inspection, upstairs and down, and was increasingly pleased. There were several bedrooms, the largest of which was neatly furnished with chairs, stands, a desk, bookcase and a big bed so abnormally elevated that he checked and found it to have several mattresses, French style. It had been freshly made with clean sheets and was protected by a tent of mosquito bars and netting.

When he came downstairs again he found a golden-brown Negro girl waiting. The figure beneath her simple pale-blue cotton gown was lissom and shapely, and she was exceedingly pretty. She curtsied.

"Je m'appelle Céleste. . . . " she said shyly and stood as if awaiting orders.

"Uh, could you get me some water for a bath?"

"Oui, monsieur, certainement, monsieur." She glided toward the stairway, apparently headed for the upstairs bathroom.

"Just a moment, Céleste. . . . You do speak English, don't you?"

"Yes."

"Then let's stick to that, as I don't speak French. I was about to ask, how can you go to prepare a bath without first fetching the warm water?"

"Monsieur Gayarre has in his employ an engineer," she said in perfectly articulated English, "a most brilliant man who has devised a means of heating water in a central boiler and piping both hot and cold water throughout the manor and to all the cottages."

Paul's jaw almost dropped open, as much from her command of English as from the incredible luxury of running hot water in the cottage.

"In that case," he said, "there's no need for you to draw my bath. I can manage it myself."

She turned back from the stairs, her expression disappointed. "Is there anything else you wish, sir?"

"I'd like to know where you learned to speak such excellent English."

"I had an excellent tutor."

Indeed the tutor would have to be excellent, he thought, and probably from the North. Aurora, who had been raised in the Gayarre household, spoke little better than the slaves, with a broad slurred accent. This one, to Yankee ears, spoke with almost no trace of accent.

"Then you're not a slave?"

"Yes, I am a slave." Her head was bowed. "My mother is a slave and my white father never acknowledged me as his offspring."

Further questions were suspended by the sudden intrusion of a distant booming sound that quivered hollowly through the thick night air. Céleste's eyes, looking vaguely frightened, darted in the direction of the sound.

Toom-ti-ti-toom—
Toom-ti-ti-toom—

Then silence.

"What was that?" he asked.

"The voodoo drums."

Before he could ask more, the drums started again, this time with a faster rhythm, rattling out sharp staccato sounds accompanied by a deep pounding bass. They went on for several minutes with variations of cadence and pitch. Céleste was listening intently.

Then again, silence—

"What is it?" he said. "Some kind of voodoo ceremony?"

"No. The drums have sent a message that Massa Pierre is home."

"Is it in some kind of code, like the telegraph?"

"It is different. The drums speak a language that only black people can understand."

The drums erupted again with a very rapid, jerky, almost angry rhythm, growing steadily into an ever harsher, more jarring, broken rhythm—finally ending with a prolonged vibrating of sounds so fast that Paul felt a chill slither down his spine. To his frontier ears it had the sound of a giant diamondback coiled far off in the darkness somewhere rattling his warning. . . .

"What was the message that time?"

"That you are a Yankee doctor come to cure the sickness. . . . "

"How in the hell could they know that so soon?"

"The drums know everything."

"Well, I'm sure it can be explained easily enough."

Her eyelids dropped, screening her eyes. "If there is anything else you desire from me . . . anything at all . . . "

"I think not," he said, not missing her implication. "You can go now."

Silently she turned and glided away.

Alone, he wondered. Did Creole hospitality extend to sending seductively attractive colored girls to the quarters of male guests for amatory entertainment?

He was feeling strangely keyed up, restless, and knowing that tonight sleep would be difficult, decided to go out for a stroll in the cool night air. . . .

iv

There was a mist rising from the ground, and a somnolence hung in the breezeless atmosphere. Paul strolled about, surprised at the number and variety of buildings. Aside from the barns, sheds, stables, there were several largish cottages similar to his own, a screened summer house near the water, and closer to the manse long neat buildings he took to be for office use or other business purposes. Farther away loomed a huge plain structure with a tall smokestack that was probably the sugar house, and flanking it close rows of small shacks for the Negroes.

But always his eyes returned as if drawn by a magnet to the lofty mansion with its classic lines whitewashed into a kind of ghostly, ethereal beauty by the soft moonlight.

"Very impressive, *nein?*" came a deep gentle voice from behind him.

Turning, Paul saw a man almost as tall as he was, but heavier, with a soft pudginess from age or lack of exercise. His hair was graying, as was his neat mustache and pointed little chin beard. He wore rimless glasses and a somewhat slovenly linen suit, and was puffing on a pipe. He took the pipe from his mouth and smiled.

"My apology if I startled you," he said, holding out a hand. "I am Otto Guttmann, the plantation engineer. You are Dr. Abbott, I presume?" He had a faintly Germanic accent.

Paul shook the proffered hand. "Evidently my coming here has been well heralded," he said with a grin.

"There are very few secrets on a plantation. In your case I was advised by the manager of Terre Rouge—that's Etienne Troyonne's plantation, as you may know. We keep in close touch. And of course we're all scared out of our britches about the smallpox, so the arrival of a good doctor is an important event in our lives. To the managerial class, I mean. Some of the slaves, you can be sure, won't understand that certain of the white man's medical treatments are for their own good—"

A female scream suddenly rent the air, and was just as suddenly muffled into silence.

Paul's glance darted toward the slave shacks. "It sounds like someone's hurt."

Otto shrugged. "It's nothing to be concerned about."

"Don't you think we should investigate?"

"Sometimes it is better to play the part of the three monkeys—see nothing, hear nothing, say nothing."

"But it could be serious—"

"I venture that it's more than likely just one of the black wenches being taken down to Cantwell's Tavern for an evening of entertainment, and she doesn't relish the idea. . . . "

"Entertainment? Are the slaves allowed to go to town for entertainment?"

Otto chuckled. "Not entertainment for *her*. *She's* the entertainment for the customers willing to pay for it."

"A prostitute? They let her go to town for that?"

"*Nein*. You see, it's just a little sideline carried on by our overseer, a rather Neanderthal type who calls himself Zack Porter, though I suspect he has a few aliases up his sleeve. He spends a lot of time in Cantwell's, which is only a couple of miles from here. Hardly the sort of place you'd care to visit, I'm sure, Doctor. But boozing it up every night can be costly in the most sordid taverns, and the wenches pay for it. He takes one or two along, pays Cantwell for the use of a room upstairs, and the slave girls are kept busy while he's downstairs drinking and collecting the money from their customers."

Paul was appalled. "Is Mr. Gayarre aware of this?"

"This is a large plantation, Doctor. The owner can't know everything that's going on—it's the job of overseers to handle matters like this, and as a rule they're a bad sort. Our previous overseer was discharged, as a matter of fact, because he couldn't keep his hands off the attractive black girls. As a result, there are a lot of mulatto children around here, as you'll note after you've been here a bit. Our present overseer is certainly no better."

"Whoring helpless women out like that is despicable. I'm surprised that you, Mr. Guttmann, who seem to be an educated man, have done nothing to stop it."

"If you or I were to attempt righting wrongs insofar as the blacks are concerned," Guttmann said heavily, "it would be like shoveling against the tide. Utterly futile. As for the raw commodity of sex, it has always been in demand and always will be. And the sort of men who have the necessary streak of meanness to be good overseers are the very kind to exploit sex in one way or another. Nothing can change that."

"That's pure rationalizing."

"Call it what you wish, Doctor. But consider the fact that I am probably twice as old as you and have seen twice as much. My advice to you—it may be as useless as oxygen is to fish out of water—is to stick to the task where you know you can do some good—medicine—and otherwise remember what I said about the three monkeys. . . . "

Then, with a brief bow, he added, "Good night, Doctor. I hope to have the pleasure soon of your company at my little house."

v

Pierre Gayarre rose early. On this morning, his first day back in his own domain, he was eager to get out and ride over his greening acres to check the cane—the source of all his past and future wealth. His head was spinning with dreams.

He rang for a servant, gave his order for breakfast, and propped up against silken pillows on silken sheets began building again in his churning imagination what very soon he would begin building in reality. . . .

Meanwhile, in the kitchen—a separate building set off about fifty feet from the mansion in order to keep the home cooler and reduce the ever-present threat of fire—the head cook and her helper went energetically to work to prepare massa's *déjeuner*. They worked over a long brick structure, part of which was open fireplace, part enclosed stove with an iron top, the rest oven. The coals had long since been stoked into cherry-red heat in case the master should awaken early; the ingredients were all prepared and waiting to be cooked.

Breads and sweet rolls which had been kneaded and cut to size to rise during the night were now thrust into the oven in pans. Coffee and chocolate were started in pots. Eggs and meats were set to frying, along with fish, so that Miché Pierre would have an ample selection.

Within twenty minutes, four servants carrying covered silver casseroles, chafing dishes, urns and other service pieces were hastening toward Pierre's bedroom to serve his *petit déjeuner*.

Pierre ate slowly, savoring every morsel, but not once did his brain stop weaving new dreams.

It was true that he had inherited a thousand hectares of rich land that comprised *Les Cypres*—almost twenty-five hundred acres. Enough to make any planter rich. It had brought the plantation to its present splendor. But all of this had been accomplished by his father, and Pierre had a driving need to achieve great things on his own.

Part of his plan was a merger of the three plantations: Syl's Le Paradis and Etienne's Terre Rouge with his own Les Cypres. They were generally known as "the triangle," not only because of the close blood relationships of the owners but because they were nestled in the crescent of the river, embracing all three plantations in a roughly triangular section of about seven thousand acres. He had the legal power to do this with Le Paradis, as he had been appointed Syl's *guardien* since the death of her mother, the last of Syl's immediate family. Etienne had also approved of the merger.

But the major part of his new plans involved the miracle of the new steam machinery. Currently Les Cypres, as did most of the plantations, crushed their cane in grinders operated by mules plodding in endless circles hauling long spokelike oaken arms that turned the central grinders. The juice ran off in streams into a series of great kettles to be

boiled down over wood-burning furnaces. Then followed
separation of the molasses and the beginning of the granula-
tion process.

All this went at a slow pace. Sometimes the grinders
couldn't keep up and cane already cut soured quickly in the
sun.

The new refinery would change all that. Steam machinery could crush in one hour as much as now took
several days to be processed. He could easily handle all the
cane from Syl's and Etienne's arpents, and more. He had
hopes of buying new land up near Natchez. The more land,
the more riches he could garner. Hungry Northern markets
were waiting for all the sugar he could produce. He could
become the richest man in all Louisiana.

The undisputed Sugar King of the river!

Then he frowned, remembering. . . .

He had borrowed heavily, had mortgaged heavily on short-
term notes. The machinery had been incredibly costly; the
construction would be costly; his overhead was soaring. The
days when a good field nigger could be purchased for a mere
five hundred dollars were long gone. Inflation!

If for one reason or another he had a crop failure, if
illness or other causes seriously depleted his slave labor, his
dreams could collapse like a beautiful bubble. . . .

About an hour later, breakfasted, bathed, shaved and
dressed in riding clothes, he descended the wide staircase to
the first-floor level, crossed the banquet room and went out
onto the shaded gallery that encompassed the house. For a
few moments he stood there smiling fondly at the row of
lofty pillars that soared fully forty feet high. They were not
pure Doric, but they were immeasurably sturdy, built to last
forever, and at least presented the heavy simplicity of the
Doric style. Similarly the entablature that crowned the columns was massive and free of adornment. All in all, the
whole mansion might be called a monument to the Greek
Revival—in the Gayarre manner. Pierre could see his father's
heavy hand everywhere. The old man had known what he
wanted—the power of great bulk. And gazing upward between the massive pillars, Pierre knew his father had succeeded in getting what he wanted—the feeling of being an
emperor in his own realm.

It was what Pierre wanted too—but on a grander scale.

His normal routine after breakfast would be to visit the
office building on the other side of the manor to go over

the accounts, but that could wait until Etienne was up and around. Pierre's shrewdness in business was generally acknowledged, but he detested bookkeeping details. Etienne, with his tidy, methodical brain, on the other hand, had a talent for figures. For the present he was anxious to ride about on an inspection tour to see if the work crews had kept the ditches in repair, cut sufficient wood to be seasoning for lumber and fuel purposes, had taken care of the vegetable plots and, most important, had properly planted the cane cuttings.

A surprised groom at the stables quickly saddled a horse for him, and he was soon riding off toward the cane fields while the pinkish-gold rays of sunrise were still streaking through the morning mist.

As he rode an old tune from some forgotten days of the past began running through his head. He started to hum it, finally remembering the words:

> All I want in this creation
> is a little bitty wife
> and a big plantation

Abruptly he stopped humming. The little ditty reminded him too painfully of the major lack in his big dream, the ultimate joy of all—a wife.

He thought briefly of Syl and her loveliness, felt a sudden wince of pain and thrust the vision out of his head. *That* of course was impossible. . . .

He was still young, but he knew that many of his friends were beginning to wonder why he hadn't taken a wife. He could hardly lie to them and say he had no desire to marry— if they believed it they would think him abnormal.

That had been behind his decision to find a mistress, and by good fortune he had found Micaela. And what a beautiful creature she was! Well worth the rather dear price being extracted from him by Betsy Silkwood. Micaela would be a delight. Her saucy personality had enchanted him as much as her beauty—*and* it would certainly quell any rumors that he was an odd sort. With an octoroon mistress it would not be thought too strange if he never married.

As the first cane field came in view, he smiled. The long tender green shoots from the buried "joints" of cane were pushing up everywhere like a vast green carpet. But as he rode closer his smile faded. Between the rows weeds were leaping into vigorous, choking growth that should have been curbed. The overseer, Zack Porter, had been lax. The battle against weeds had to be unceasing until the cane rose thick and strong enough under the driving rains and steamy heat; not until about mid-July when it began tasseling above a man's head could it be "laid by" to continue packing juice into its stalks for the rest of the season without man's help.

Angry, he wheeled the horse about and started at a gallop on a shortcut toward the overseer's cottage.

vi

Feet barely touching the ground, Mally hung by her arms from a rope lashed around her wrists and suspended from the limb of a tree.

She had been there all night, but the arms had long since stopped hurting. The cord, cutting deeply into the swelling flesh around the wrists, had numbed them so they felt dead as sticks of wood. Her head was numb too, full of humming noises.

All she could still feel were the burning slashes on her back from the whip. Her dress was ripped down to the waist, exposing the bloodied streaks to the morning sun. And the bluebottle flies, drawn by the smell of blood. Their wings glistened and the greenish iridescence flashed as they swarmed around with an angry buzzing that mingled with the other sounds in her head.

She no longer cared; she expected to be dead soon.

After I daid, he take me to de ice house like he tooken the other girls. . . . They nebber come out again. He do bad things in the ice house. He say girls run away but us'n blacks know he lie. Dem girls daid. . . .

Last night he had come again to take her to the tavern. When she begged to stay because her baby needed her, he grabbed the baby and saw the sickness. Began shouting:

"Goddam rotten nigger whore—that's smallpox! Ya know all sick niggers belong in the pesthouse! Now mebby you caught it too an' I can't risk takin' any sick nigger over to Cantwell's!"

So mad he kick the door open and throw the baby somewhere in the bushes . . . slap her to the floor when she scream. Say he kill her 'less she quiet. Say he going to punish her. . . .

The noises in her head were growing to thunder . . . then crashing sounds. . . .

Silence.

The rope suddenly gave way and she was falling, but an arm caught at her shoulders, lowered her to the ground. She opened her eyes.

Massa Pierre!

"Mally!—what's this all about?"

His face was so wrathful, at first she was too terrified to talk. But his voice turned gentle:

"There's nothing to be afraid of now, Mally. I want you to tell me the whole story, *everything.* . . . "

vii

Pierre stared coldly and steadily down into Zack Porter's face.

"How long have you been whoring our black girls at Cantwell's Tavern?" he demanded.

The overseer's florid face began to blanch. Porter was a chunky, muscular man, balding at the temples. His most notable feature was the hot bullet eyes burning beneath the corrugation of scowl lines on his forehead—the eyes of a man possessed by a grudge against the whole world and quick to take it out on anyone weaker than he was. The face itself had been ravaged by a bout with smallpox years ago, leaving it pockmarked and disfigured for life. It might have aroused pity except for the hate and cruelty in his nature that had stamped the face with ugliness.

His eyes shifted away under Pierre's stare as he answered:

"Now looka here, Mista Gayarre, you been gettin' the wrong information. I ain't never done nothin' like that."

"Then explain why you tied Mally up by the hands on a branch from a tree!"

The overseer's eyes momentarily widened in surprise, and fear.

"Mally, why she's the lyin'est bitch on the plantation. Beggin' your pardon, sir, but only a fool would take her word against any white man's."

"You've never taken any of our female blacks over to the tavern?"

"Naw sir!"

"You didn't tie Mally to a tree?"

"I swear, Mista Gayarre, she's lyin' an' as soon's I get my hands on her, I'll—"

With a sudden spurt of rage, Pierre spurred the horse forward and with a vicious sweep of his good arm brought his riding quirt down across the overseer's face. Thin lines of blood oozed from the cuts across the man's shocked features.

"You'll never touch her again, Porter! As of now you're fired. In case you don't know, even the Black Code doesn't permit prostitution of slaves. If you're not off the plantation by noon, you'll be placed under arrest and I'll press charges until I'm satisfied you get your just punishment. Now go. . . . " Wheeling his horse around, Pierre rode away.

Zack Porter's bullet eyes glowered after him with malevolence.

viii

Paul smiled across the rough board table at Mally. He had cleansed her whip lacerations and rope abrasions, treating them with a soothing ointment, and to alleviate the pain as well as lift her from her depressed mental state had given her laudanum in a menstruum of syrup. Except for the inner pain reflected in her big, mournful, tear-sodden eyes, she seemed to have recovered remarkably. He had also examined and questioned her for symptoms of smallpox, finding none.

"You seem to be one of the lucky ones, Mally. You've been exposed to smallpox, yet show no signs of it. However, you've most certainly been infected and the onset could come very quickly. . . . "

There was no point in spelling out the grim story of what could happen, he decided. She'd already seen it in her own baby, and probably knew of the horrors afflicting the victims in the pesthouse. After the usual twelve-day incubation period, with few or no symptoms at all, it could strike suddenly with severe rigor, dangerously high fever, headaches, vomiting, back pains, convulsions; soon a rash would appear, pustules would erupt on most parts of the body; delirium and coma often followed. After untold agonies the victim more often than not died. The few who survived, after seeing the repelling reflections in a mirror that they would have to live with for the rest of their lives, sometimes wished they had died too.

"In any case," he went on, "we're not going to take any chances. I'm going to give you a vaccination—"

"No suh." She hunched lower in the chair, showing fright. "Ah don' wan' no vac'sashun."

"But Mally, a vaccination will protect you from smallpox

—and smallpox can either kill you or leave ugly scars on your face and body. You're a beautiful girl. You want to keep that beauty, don't you?"

Her tears increased. "Wha' good my beauty? My baby, she beautiful lak de moon in de sky. Now she daid. . . . "

The baby had been found dead in the bushes where Zack Porter had so callously flung it. One look at the disease-ravaged little face had told Paul that the infant would have died soon in any event. The disease was always most fatal to the very young or very old. He had noted too that the baby was a mulatto and wondered if Mally even knew which of her white customers was the father.

"You're still very young, Mally. You can have another—as many more beautiful babies as you want—if you keep yourself healthy."

"Paul—" Fern spoke quietly from the other end of the table where she sat near the array of needles immersed in carbolic solution, swabs, alcohol and the cowpox vaccine. Surprisingly enough, she had arrived early at Paul's cottage to volunteer her assistance with the vaccination program. Now she had risen and was rolling up a sleeve of her gown.

"I'd like to be the first one vaccinated, Paul. Then Mally can see how simple and painless it is. . . . "

Paul felt like a fool for not thinking of it himself. The word "vaccination" alone was enough to frighten a primitive, uneducated person who had every reason to fear the unknown.

First swabbing the skin of Fern's upper arm with alcohol, he took one of the needles from the carbolic solution and dipped it into the vial of inoculation mixture. It had been derived from the material taken from the vesicles that had erupted on a cow infected with cowpox, then dried and mixed with glycerol. A few short scratches in the skin were sufficient to transfer the bovine disease to a human recipient. It was the same inoculation material and simple vaccination procedure used by Edward Jenner in 1798 when he first published his discovery of a means of protecting people against smallpox that was virtually one hundred percent effective.

Jenner, like Lister and Pasteur, was among Paul's heroes —and also part of his general cynicism about the medical heirarchy. Like most great discoverers of new medical advances, Jenner had faced obstinate, hostile opposition to his new ideas. He had found the cure to smallpox, but it was too simple for the learned medical world to believe. Not until 1853—fifty-five years later—after Jenner had saved thousands of lives at his own expense did the English government finally enforce the inoculation of all British subjects against the dread disease. The United States had no such law.

"That's it," Paul said, putting the needle back in the carbolic solution.

Mally had been watching every move with fearful interest. "Dat all? Nothin' more?"

"Not a bit more, and it gives complete protection against smallpox for the next six or seven years. Now would you like to try?"

She submitted passively.

A chuckle of amusement drew Paul's attention, and he looked up to see Otto Guttmann, the plantation engineer, standing just inside the doorway.

"I came in just in time to see Miss Venable removing much of the mystery of inoculation, in Mally's eyes, by being your first patient," he said. "I think it's an excellent idea that may solve a little problem we're having outside. . . . "

Guttmann, Paul knew, had in the absence of an overseer been assigned by Pierre to rout out all the slaves and line them up in front of the shed that was to be used as a temporary infirmary until something better could be constructed.

"Most of our blacks," Guttmann went on, "put their faith in voodoo cures and distrust white medicine. They're strangely restive this morning and it's all our *estafette*, our boss of Negroes, can do to keep them in line. As a matter of fact, a few of them have run off into the swamp to hide, and I overheard one of them muttering that the new Yankee-doc's medicine would kill them."

Paul remembered the voodoo drums last night . . . the message Céleste claimed they were sending. . . .

Guttmann continued, "I have two suggestions. One, move your vaccination paraphernalia on the table outside in the wide open where everybody can see what's going on, that there's nothing to fear. My other suggestion, following Miss Venable's example, is that all white people on the plantation, including Mr. Gayarre himself, be the first to go through the inoculation procedure in full view of all the blacks. I think that will alleviate the fears."

"As you pointed out the other night, Mr. Guttmann," Paul

said, rising, "you've lived twice as long as I have, so you ought to be twice as smart. Let's get going. . . . "

ix

Guttmann's suggestions worked.

Pierre, not without a touch of the actor in his makeup, was quick to see the dramatic aspects and made quite a show of holding out his good left arm bared to the shoulder, laughing and joking while Paul went through the simple vaccination.

Syl followed, then Guttmann and Etienne, who was now able to walk. After that came Aurora and the house servants. Then the long line of fieldhand slaves.

It was Paul's first encounter with this class of slave, and he was surprised to find how much they differed from the house servants. The latter were cleaner, neatly dressed, well mannered—and haughtily snobbish toward their less-favored brethren who labored in the fields. For the most part the field workers wore battered, wide-brimmed palm-leaf hats, and were roughly garbed in loose cotton shirts and pants caught with rope or belts of snakeskin. Their attitudes were sullen, suspicious, but at the same time abject and fearful. They avoid looking directly at the house servants, showing awareness that even in their own black race they were at the bottom of the heap.

Nevertheless the vaccination program proceeded smoothly and by the end of the day everyone had been inoculated, but the vaccine material was almost used up. Inoculation of the slaves on Syl's and Etienne's plantations would have to await the new shipment of vaccine from Tureaud's apothecary.

Pierre reappeared. "I forgot to mention it earlier, Paul, but we want you to join us at dinner this evening in the manor." There was a subtle difference in Pierre's tone. "We shall expect you at seven."

It was not an invitation to a friend. It was an order to an employee.

x

Paul would never forget his first visit to Pierre's mansion.

From the first moment of entering—the wide glass door held open by a bowing black man in servant's livery—he was overwhelmed by the sumptuousness: a vista of space filled with grand tapestries, great sparkling chandeliers, silver girandoles set with candles, delicate rosewood paneling, fine carved furniture, low curved sofas of the Empire style imported from France, beautiful paintings, details of woodwork and a cypress ceiling fashioned with such exquisite care that the hairline joints could not be seen; everywhere he looked, something wondrous to behold.

Pierre rose from a deep comfortable chair across the vast living room and called a cordial greeting.

"The ladies are still in their rooms going through their mysterious rituals of primping," he said, rising, "and Etienne wishes to be excused so he can remain in his room to rest and browse through his latest shipment of books—he's quite a bookworm, as you'll discover. Meanwhile, it will give us an opportunity to go into the library for a chat and a drink or two before the ladies get here. Come. . . . "

When both were seated in luxurious brocaded chairs in the library, Pierre said, "What is your drink preference?"

Unfamiliar with the exotic liquors of the rich, Paul said whiskey would do him fine. Pierre passed the order in French to a servant standing nearby attentively. Another servant approached with a box of cigars, which he extended first to Pierre, who took one before offering it to Paul. Paul took one and bit off the end and had barely stuck it in his mouth before another servant was holding a lighted sulphur match for him. At almost the same moment the first servant returned with a heavy glass of whiskey, clinking with ice, and set it on the taboret beside his chair. Paul puffed deeply, reached for his drink and settled back in the chair with an expansive feeling of well-being. This was living!

"How do you manage to keep ice in this hot climate?" he said by way of small talk.

"We have quite a large icehouse near the river. The ice is shipped down from Illinois during the winter months, a whole boatload, at considerable expense. We keep it packed in sawdust and it usually lasts until the following winter months."

Pierre exhaled a plume of blue smoke. "From what you have seen and done here thus far, *Docteur,* how do you like your new job?"

"I think I can be very happy with it."

"I had in mind that your compensation should include of course your quarters and food, which will be supplied by the cook and servants assigned to that chore—plus a salary of three thousand dollars per annum. Is that satisfactory?"

Paul could scarcely believe it. Three thousand dollars! Even the most eminent surgeons at the Royal Academy did not make as much. Plus living expenses! With such a princely income he could afford books, experimental equipment, even some of the luxuries such as theater and opera usually reserved only for the rich.

"Such compensation I consider most generous, Pierre."

"However, I shall expect you, at times, to perform duties of an nonmedical nature."

"I shall be content to abide by any reasonable conditions or duties you care to impose in addition to my medical responsibilities."

"Splendid. Now on to the matter of the moment. . . . We need more niggers. Even without the loss from disease, we would be shorthanded for the coming cane-cutting season. Additionally, Etienne and I hope to acquire a great deal more land to put into cane and cotton production, for which we will require still more slaves. As it happens, the slave auctions in New Orleans begin in a few more days. Boatloads of fresh new niggers are beginning to arrive from Cuba. . . . "

Pierre paused to smile sardonically. "More correctly I should have said Africa. The truth is, as you may know, that our federal laws prohibit the importation of Africans for slavery in America, but like most laws it is full of loopholes. It permits us, for example, to buy slaves from Cuba. It follows, naturally, that the African slavers merely ship their niggers to the slavers' nests along the Cuban coast, and after going through a bit of legal hocus-pocus to get the necessary papers certifying them as bona-fide Cuban slaves from Cuban plantations, they are shipped on to New Orleans. We all know this and expect to get untrained niggers virtually straight from the Congo who will have to be trained by our own slaves. But by the same token we get them cheaper than the blacks sold down the river from the big nigger-breeding farms of Virginia."

"The slavery situation is far more complex than I had imagined."

"And getting more complex all the time," Pierre said, frowning, "what with increasing federal intervention, the criminal Underground Railroad activity and other such grossly unfair harassment that planters must cope with. Be that as it may . . . our present problem is that Etienne and I must leave for Natchez tomorrow to begin negotiations for a large tract of land. We will be gone a week. In the meantime Syl will go to New Orleans to the slave auctions and purchase the first batch of slaves. She has been on slave-purchasing excursions before and is very capable of handling all the details. However, I do not want her to go without a male escort, so I shall expect you to accompany her, for a dual reason. You will serve not only as her escort, but as a medical man you will briefly examine each nigger selected to ensure that we don't get stuck with any of the diseased and defectives."

Paul's passing moment of resentment over being assigned as a virtual assistant buyer of slaves was followed in the next moment by the more exhilarating thought of being for so long in Syl's company.

"I'll be glad to, Pierre."

xi

Never in his life had Paul dined so well. . . .

The four of them had finished with the meal but still sat around the large dining table of heavy carved mahogany covered with sparkling white napery and gleaming silver. Paul sipped at the final touch of the dinner, a brandy. The ladies were having coffee. Pierre puffed at a cigar. They had been served by a retinue of eight servants while a small black boy sat in a far corner holding a long string that stretched up to the "punkah"—a large fan that swung from a hinge on the ceiling above the dining table, its regular movements controlled by the boy tugging the string back and forth, thus keeping the air moving above the heads of the diners.

The first course had been a gumbo of crab and shrimp, dark-green okra and exotic spices served over snowy rice. Following had been a fricassee of terrapin, brown and aromatic; breasts of wild duck, snipe, delicate quail; enormous fish with flavors as rare as Pierre's wines, of which four or five piquant kinds accompanied the meal; mushrooms and platters of succulent greens flavored with bits of meat in the Louisiana style; and finally, a heady dessert of wild cherries and liqueur accompanied by various cheeses, hard, soft or ripely odorous.

Now Pierre rose from the table and asked to be excused. "I'm sure you will all forgive me," he said. "Etienne and I have many business matters to go over before our trip to Natchez. Syl, perhaps you and Fern could show Paul around the house."

Fern rose too. "I must also beg to be excused. I have been engrossed in a book that I find hard to put down, and I'm quite certain that you two will find enough to talk about without my company. . . . "

Her manner was a bit abrupt, Paul thought. Throughout dinner, too, Fern had seemed withdrawn, joining in the conversation only occasionally in a brief, perfunctory way. Was she restrained by the company of Pierre and Syl, he wondered, or was it because of him? Did she sense his admiration of Syl and feel jealousy?

"Come, Paul," said Syl, ignoring Fern as she would one of the servants. "I'll give you the *petit tour*. . . . "

For the next half-hour Syl, rather proudly, showed off Pierre's possessions: the fine Empire furniture from France; a Royal Commode inset with panels of pietra dura depicting flowers made and signed by Napoleon's own chief cabinet-maker, G. Beneman; the Sèvres porcelain, silver from England, tapestries, paintings and other *objets d'art*. With each item she gave its detailed history.

"How did you gain such extensive knowledge of all these objects?" Paul asked.

"After all, I grew up here. You see, my parents were in New Orleans on a visit when one of the terrible epidemics broke out. They didn't get out in time and died within a week after returning home. I was a small child then. Since there were no other close members of the family, our home was closed and I was raised in the Gayarre household."

"I'm sorry to hear that."

"Actually, this has been more of a home for me than the one I was born in. All that has been lacking for me is the sense of having a father, as Pierre's father also died within a year after mine—but from a different cause. I was brought up mostly by Pierre's mother, a sweet refined woman who taught me almost everything I know. She died of natural causes a couple of years ago, and then Pierre was appointed as my legal *gardien*." She laughed. "And he has performed his roles to perfection. He has been not only the stern, loving father but an indulgent brother and . . . dear, dear friend. . . . "

Her eyes took on a deeper glow as she spoke, or perhaps it was an illusion of the lighting, a reflection of the blue gown of some tenuous material that she wore. But Paul had noticed it before, the angelic smile, the softened voice whenever she spoke about Pierre. The inevitable insight pierced him like a sharp swift arrow.

My God, so that's it! he thought. She's in love with Pierre, and because they are cousins dares not admit it, perhaps not even to herself. . . .

The grand staircase was another item drawing her comment. As they ascended the wide steps her hand trailed lovingly over the polished banister. "Pierre's father brought thirty-three craftsmen over from England especially to carve the staircase. They also produced the doors, mantels, friezes and paneling—mostly out of brushed gnarled oak from England, teakwood from India and fine deal from Norway."

On the second floor she turned into a softly lighted bedroom. Paul was astonished. Was it not considered improper for an unmarried Creole lady to bring a gentlemen into a bedroom?

But her next words explained it:

"This was the master bedroom used only by Pierre's parents. Since their death it has become almost a shrine. Pierre worships their memory. Nobody else has been allowed to sleep here and nothing has been touched or changed since they last used it. . . . "

Paul glanced around the luxurious room, which seemed a strange combination of masculine Gallic simplicity, as exemplified in the heavy oaken paneling and muscular beamed ceiling, and delicate femininity: the satins and silk brocades in soft and muted tones, graceful chairs of carved rosewood, a fourposter bed with bedposts carved in a floral design and over it a lofty *ciel* or canopy lined with blue satin draped in a sunburst design caught in the center by a gold ornament. At the foot of the bed was a *lit de repos,* a reclining couch, and here and there a few marble-topped tables.

Syl was standing near. A wavering light from a girandole cast soft highlights on her profile and glinted in the reddish-gold of her hair. Whether from the magic of her beauty or the sensuous appeal of the bedroom, his head was suddenly flooded with unbidden thoughts. What must it be like to be the master of such a grand mansion, to have such a fine bedroom into which he could retire with a wife like Syl? Ecstasy beyond belief! He felt a powerful urge to crush her in his arms. . . .

He turned away and pretended to be admiring a large armoire while banishing the shameful visions.

" . . . and a candle is always kept burning there night and day, of course," she was saying, pointing at the boudoir altar in the corner, where a taper was flickering.

"They must have been wonderful parents to have won such devotion."

"Pierre couldn't have had finer parents, but unfortunately Uncle André was killed when Pierre was still a boy—"

André. Why was the name so familiar?

"You say he was killed?"

"Yes. In a duel. He was not much older than Pierre is now at the time it happened. There is a portrait of him in the front entry hall, and the resemblance to Pierre is remarkable. Would you care to see it?"

He murmured assent, but now his almost mirror-perfect memory was racing back to the night on Balize when Madame Charbaud had let slip the given name of her rich lover, her *protecteur*—André—and told of his being killed in a duel. . . .

Still, the name itself was common enough, and so were duels.

The portrait indeed had a remarkable resemblance to Pierre. André had been depicted by the artist seated in a curved chair near a window with the folds of curtain showing a vista of the estate outside. It was the same handsome, proud face; the same prominent but well-formed nose, the peregrine quality of profile, the same dark eyes under dark eyebrows arrogantly staring down the observer.

"It's a shame," Paul said, "that such a fine, healthy-looking man had to lose his life so prematurely because of a duel."

"Even more of a shame," she said bitterly, "because the duel was over one of those wanton quadroon women who entice so many of our men into corruption. Uncle André was a dear, wonderful man, but that was his one weakness. He kept a quadroon mistress. I am not giving away any family secrets, since it was common knowledge all around New Orleans. Creole men even seem proud of it! Thank God, Pierre is too sensitive and noble a person for that sort of thing. . . . "

"And what happened to the mistress?"

"Because of her savage blood, she shot and killed the man who had killed Uncle André—probably out of vexation over losing her luxurious way of living—and then disappeared. No one knows what ever happened to her."

As soon as he could politely manage, Paul bid her good night and left. His composure was too shaken.

The same man who had fathered Pierre had also fathered Madame Charbaud's daughter, Micaela—who was now Pierre's mistress.

Half-brother and -sister!

TWO: The Evils That Men Endure

IT was hate that kept Zambullah alive, brought back his strength. . . .

For the first few days after coming out of the blackness into which he had been clubbed once again by the white men, he had lain in agony, as much of the spirit as of the flesh. Grief and rage boiled silently inside as he lay unmoving, still seeing with the eyes of his memory as clearly as under a noon sun his wife Tembah writhing and thrashing about on the pallet with one white man holding her by the arms while another battered aside her kicking legs to violate her with his foul white man's lust.

The eruption of his rage had given him the strength of ten. Enough to break out of the cage, kill the two whites, break the arm of another, then snap the neck of the fat white chief who had peered in his cage as at an animal.

But his strength had not been enough. It could never be enough. The whites were as thick as flies swarming around rich garbage. Without spear or knife and slowed by the chain shackled to his ankles and wrists, he had been no match for the iron bars and clubs.

After awakening from the blackness, sore and sick and burning all over, the first thing he remembered was Tembah, and then the sickness entered his heart. The pain from the gashes and bruises on his body, from the swollen masses of flesh and tissue on his face and head, were as nothing to that deeper pain. He would never see Tembah again. She had come from a tribe where the women were noted for

2

chastity and virtue. Befouled before the eyes of her husband, she could not allow herself to live.

Nor did he, at first, want to live.

Until he had a strange dream. . . . Perhaps it grew out of the emptiness of his belly, for he had stopped eating and drinking, or it may have been generated only by his hurts and sickness, but it had all the power of a vision from heaven. Or hell. For a long time Zambullah, the killer of leopards, had not dreamed about them, but in this dream he was suddenly once again face to face with the largest of the leopards he had killed—his brother, for all leopards were his brothers.

In his sleep he tossed and turned, his muscles tensed and his belly clenched, for in his vivid dream the huge leopard was approaching as he lay shackled in chains with neither spear nor knife. Then, with a shuddering sigh, he relaxed and gave himself up to be eaten.

Instead, the leopard lay down beside him and began licking his wounds. In the mystical communion of dreams the leopard told him: *Fear not. I am your brother, your friend. I will fight for you. I will teach you cunning.*

Zambullah awakened refreshed, only half-believing the dream but aware of a tremendous new sense of force inside. And then he believed; he knew. He could feel the spirit of the leopard he had slain inside of him. The spirit of the leopard had entered into his body to feed on his hate, add strength to his muscles, sharpen his cunning.

He began to eat again. Hate again. He needed to build up his strength. The leopard inside had to be nourished.

One of the slaver's crew who fed him commented, "The big nigger's eatin' again! Like a starvin' wolf. Captain'll be happy to hear that. Bastard's been actin' kind of crazy, an' he was afeard we'd ruint his head."

"You can't hurt a nigger's head. They're made of solid bone."

"Well, whatever, it's still peculiar to see 'im lopin' around in that cage, draggin' them chains, bent over like some kinda ape. Come to think of it, I reckon that's what they really are when you git right down to it. Anyway, nothin' pure human. Came out here one night an' b'God his eyes were shinin' like a cat's. Gave me quite a turn for a moment there."

"Don't matter how peculiar he is. To sell him all that

matters is them big muscles. Let the fool that buys him worry about anything else."

"If he tears loose again at the slave auctions, nobody'll buy 'im."

The other laughed. "Hell, you still got a lot to learn about slavin'. Day before he gits unloaded in New Orleans they put somethin' in his food to put him to sleep. Before he wakes up they slip a spoonful of somethin' down his throat. After that he's gentle as a kitten. . . . "

ii

On the quay at the foot of French Street, the slaves were unloading. Line after line of almost naked blacks moved mournfully down the gangplank. Blacks from the Congo, Sudan, Senegal and Dahomey trudged on bare feet down the rough board planks—hapless humans who only a few weeks ago had been free men in the African bush. They came not willingly but with iron rings clamped around their necks and linked at intervals to a long chain that made lagging impossible. During the thousands of miles of journey—endless miles through Africa, across oceans, on and off ships several times—that chain had never left their necks. There were many who had been unable to keep up, nor could they drop out by the way. Dead or dying they were dragged along by their fellows, the dying ones galvanized into brief spurts of energy by the fiery lash of the overseer's whip until sooner or later they and the other dead ones were removed from the collars and thrown aside.

Until the survivors—powerful bush Negroes, women carrying babies, young girls and boys straggling along beside the chains—finally set foot on the free soil of America.

But as the chattel property of righteous churchgoing Christians who had stolen them from their homes and by whom they would for the rest of their lives be held in abject slavery, their whole futures, livelihoods, every action, their very lives henceforth dependent on the whim of whoever had purchased them.

Near the quay a carriage had stopped, and the three passengers within were watching. The big brown eyes of one of them were moist and fully as mournful as the unloading blacks. Aurora had seen many such unloadings, and they always filled her with sadness that never quite left her, though most of the time she managed to be laughing and gay. She knew what the fate of most of them would be. Only a few—a very few—would be lucky, as she had been. Of course she had been born on the plantation and as a child, being of the same age as Miz Syl, had been brought into the big house each day to be her playmate, later to become her personal maid. They had made a pet of her, treated her *almost* as if she were white. Yes, she was very lucky. Why then should she feel so sad?

Syl, noting Aurora's tears, said, "I know what you're thinking, Aurora, but most of them will be well treated. Certainly the ones I shall be buying today will be—"

But Aurora wasn't listening. Her lips had parted a little and her shining eyes widened. "Oh, looka, Miz Syl—looka dat one—!" She jabbed a finger excitedly.

A giant of a black man, separated from the others, was being brought ashore by two white men, each holding a chain on either side of him that was linked to a heavy collar around his neck. He wore leg irons which forced him to walk in a shuffle.

"Dey mean!" Aurora said indignantly. "Dat de kinda collar with spikes inside. See de blood comin' down his neck?"

"It's a shame," Syl agreed, "but perhaps it was because he wasn't behaving and they have to do it to control him. He's a very powerful man . . . a magnificent specimen."

A whip cracked behind the black giant. Aurora let out a little gasp of sorrow. The man wielding the whip cracked it again and then again, streaking it across the broad back of the big slave. The Negro's sluggish pace neither increased nor slowed. He shuffled on as if not feeling the stinging lashes, even though the blood was plainly to be seen dribbling down his back.

"He too proud to show it hurt," said Aurora, the tears beginning to glisten down her cheeks. "He a real man. You buy dat one, Miz Syl."

Syl looked thoughtful. "I have a feeling he must be very unruly and hard to manage. Otherwise they wouldn't have him chained so heavily."

"You buy him an' I make him behave! You can sho' bet on dat."

"We'll think about it, Aurora. . . . " She gave an order to the driver and the coach started ahead.

Aurora sniffled and wiped tears away with the back of a hand. "Oh dat man," she moaned, "dat man . . . "

Paul, seated in the back, drew his eyes away from the lines of chained men as the coach rolled past. Never had he felt more depressed.

iii

The slave auction mart was on a miserable side street just off the public square. Villainous-looking little shops and stores with roofs of dirty white tiles crowded both sides. Some of them had galleries on the second floor supported by posts that were nothing more than unpainted poles. The roadway itself was rutted, scalloped with potholes and obstructed here and there with heaps of firewood, paving stones or trash. Otherwise it was glutted with carriages and wagons of all descriptions tied to hitching racks.

Apparently quite familiar with the mart, Syl directed the driver to stop in front of a low wide building of the crudest construction which carried above the roof a large sign: BLACKWELL'S—*Only Slaves of the Highest Quality Handled Here*. This was obviously the center of the slave trade, for here the traffic was most congested. Here and there, wedged between the larger buildings, were smaller ones of brick with iron-barred windows that served as the slave barracoons.

Paul got out first and turned to help Syl down, after which she instructed the driver to move to the nearest hitching space he could find and ordered Aurora to wait in the carriage until their return.

"The auction has already started," Syl told Paul, "but they always try to sell the inferior ones first, so it doesn't matter that we're late."

She had taken his arm, and as he began guiding her among the noisy, cigar-smoking bystanders who clogged the streets Paul marveled at her composure, that one so dainty could be so calm and seemingly unbothered by the coarse hustle-bustle and redolent stench of animal excrement, urine and other unsavory odors that fouled the air.

The outer walls of Blackwell's were covered with scaling whitewash and faded sales posters. Inside, the air was laden with tobacco smoke and so crowded with slave buyers or the merely curious that it was difficult to get close to the auction block, which was simply an elevated wooden platform against one wall. On one side of the platform was a grouping of chairs interspersed with the inevitable spittoons, but from the brown splotches of tobacco juice mixed with the sawdust on the floor with flies buzzing around, it was plain that the patrons were indifferent to such sanitary concern.

" . . . and this is the big bargain of the day, ladies and gentlemen," the auctioneer was saying, including in his sales pitch the several ladies who, to Paul's surprise, were scattered among the buyers in addition to Syl. The auctioneer, a plump man of middle age with dark stringy hair plastered across his perspiring dome, continued with a merry chuckle in his voice:

"You might say the goods are slightly damaged, but a bargain is a bargain when you pay for less than you get." His plump figure turned toward the slave on the block. "Now, young man, stand up straight and tuck in that well-fed belly. Turn around so they can get a look at your back muscles— move sharp there! Show that you've got plenty of life in you!"

The slave, who was about eighteen, had only one eye and an ugly cavity where the other had been, half-closed by a sagging eyelid. His right arm hung useless, the muscles shriveled around a hideous scarring of flesh from shoulder to elbow. He stood in a slumped position, his one good eye looking as dead as mud. His movements were just as slow and dead.

There were a few snickers. One man called out: "What'd he do—jump under a cane chopper to get out of working?"

"No, my friend," assured the auctioneer. "This is a hard-working nigger who got hurt under a load of logs that busted loose when a chain broke. Wasn't his fault at all. Now look at those back muscles and that strong right arm— that shows he's a good worker—and both legs are as good as ever. Now I ain't claiming this nigger's perfect, but the price is right. Instead of a thousand dollars I'm only asking five hundred for this one. . . . "

He paused a few moments, and when no offer was made, said, "Any reasonable bids, gentlemen? Somebody make an offer. Just for a starter, how about four hundred?"

"I'll go fifty cents," shouted someone from the rear, eliciting a few guffaws.

"I will appreciate no jokes," said the auctioneer, frowning. "Jokes will only hold up bids on this valuable piece of merchandise and delay the showing of the guaranteed great bargains I have yet to bring out. But to make it a little easier, to prime the pump so to speak, we'll lower the starting price to three hundred. Make an offer, somebody. . . . "

Dead silence. The auctioneer's expression turned to a petulant frown. "I'm afraid you ladies and gentlemen don't realize that you've just missed a rare bargain, a chance to get for just a mere fraction of his true worth a good hard worker. . . . "

He waited another few moments for a bid, then nodded to the Negro to leave. The black looked around, confused, not knowing what to do, until a mulatto assistant who carried a record book stepped up and led him away.

Paul watched him shuffle away tiredly, like a man of eighty who had lived his life and was only looking for a place to die. His depression was growing into sickness.

Next on the block was a matronly black woman in a clean frock of pink cotton with a blue turban wrapped around her hair. She was accompanied by two children, a boy and a girl.

"Now here's something superlative," said the auctioneer, and to the black woman: "Tell them your names and ages. . . . "

"My name's Monda and I'se nearly thutty," she said, and then proudly pointed at the children. "This 'un's Kissie"— indicating the shy, brightly smiling girl—"and my boy's Wilfred. They tell you how old they is."

"I'se nine," Kissie said, showing shining teeth in a wide smile.

The boy was sullen. "I gwine on 'leven."

The auctioneer beamed at them. "Kissie and Wilfred—hop up and down to show the audience that you're full of ginger."

The little girl started hopping around gaily in a series of little grasshoppery jumps. The boy complied with reluctance, barely more than lifting one foot, then the other.

"Faster, boy!"

The boy increased his movements only slightly.

"Smile wide when you're doing it—let everybody see your teeth!"

The black boy grimaced in a way that was more like the ferocious snarl of a cornered animal, but revealing a set of good white teeth.

"You see, ladies and gentlemen? I promised you quality and here it is. These niggers are in the pink of condition, straight down from Virginia. It's plain they've been treated well. You can see the mother's a fine, fertile wench. She's been trained to cook and clean house and she's good for giving birth to a dozen more healthy little niggers. Just look at those hips and that belly—she could turn one out every ten months if you wanted her to."

As he talked, the little girl kept hopping up and down gaily, and the boy continued his sluggish movements.

"I won't linger too long on this great opportunity to acquire a whole family, except I want you to notice that we're kind to niggers here—kinder than the law expects. We like to keep families together. They work harder that way, 'cause they're happier. You heard the boy say he was eleven. According to the Code we can take children from their parents at the age of ten, but we ain't a-doin' that. That don't mean that anybody who buys them in one lot at a bargain price can't break them up an' sell the boy at a profit. That little boy will be grown up very soon. Another couple years he'll be doin' a man's work. And this little girl here in a few years will grow up an' fill out an' can be taught to make beds and be a good housekeeper for any of you bachelors out there. . . . " He paused and winked knowingly, to be sure his meaning sank in. "An' this boy here will be a fifteen-hundred-dollar nigger in another couple years. Now let's not waste any more of our valuable time. Who'll give me a start on the bidding?"

"Five hundred."

"Please, folks, let's forego the joking. Nine hundred as a starter. How about it, somebody?"

"Seven-fifty."

"Seven hundred and fifty is the offer. Who'll make it nine hundred?"

Nobody spoke. The little girl kept hopping, her smile gone. The boy lifted one leg after another. The mother's head was bowed, tears streaming down her cheeks.

"Oh come on now, ladies and gentlemen, we have no time for haggling. You all know the mother alone is worth a thousand. When she isn't cleaning house and cooking you can put her in the fields and she can work as hard as any man. The boy can start workin' right away. And it's plain to see the girl's going to grow up into a real beauty."

"Eight-fifty."

"Eight hundred and fifty is the offer. Make it a thousand and we'll close it."

Soon after the sale closed at nine hundred and a prosperous-looking farmer came forward to claim his purchase. As the three were led away for the bill of sale to be drawn up, the little girl trailed along behind, still hopping tiredly. The boy gave weary little jumps between each step.

" . . . and now," the auctioneer was continuing briskly, "we're going to bring out what you've all been waiting for—

prime breeding stock just arrived from the jungles. These are all hand-picked niggers selected from thousands, the healthiest, best-quality merchandise you'll ever see. You all know that the best stock is usually snapped up by breeding farms in Virginia that sell the issue back down the river at double the price. Now here's a rare opportunity to get your own breeding stock—all ready for training. Just mix 'em in with your own best niggers to learn 'em the ropes."

He stopped a moment to mop sweat from his face before continuing. "We're going to bring out a batch of the prettiest females first. Some have babies, some are pregnant, and the ones who aren't"—he paused again to wink—"soon will be."

A dozen or so shy and frightened girls ranging in age from about fourteen to twenty were guided to the platform by the mulatto record keeper. They wore colorful but cheap cotton dresses, some with dangling price tags, obviously purchased just for display purposes.

"I know the gentlemen particularly will appreciate these fine wenches. Coming straight from the wild jungles, they might be a trifle spirited, but all they'll need is a touch of the blacksnake laid on in just the right places an' that'll learn 'em to jump quick as a wink an' do anything you ask— *anything* at all, gentlemen. . . . "

His perspiring face gave way to a sly grin. "But I know you'll want to see the goods you'll be getting before making your bids, so as a special accommodation to our customers all the girls will go into the little room adjacent to the auction block and divest themselves of their garments— absolutely *everything*—so that the merchandise can be examined thoroughly. But hurry before the room is so crowded you can't squeeze in. . . . "

As the girls were herded into the room there was a general movement of the majority of the audience to follow. Syl was blushing, but several of the other women present were among the customers surging toward the back room, their eyes bright with interest.

iv

By midafternoon Syl had purchased a dozen of the newly arrived blacks.

"I think that will be enough for today," she told Paul, who had briefly examined the slaves of her choice and found them apparently sound and free of disease. "We will need many more, but Pierre is so much better at this. He will attend the next auctions and buy the others. Aurora will be disappointed that the big black man wasn't on the block today, but—" Her attention was diverted by a special new note of importance in the auctioneer's latest sales pitch:

". . . and this one is our biggest buy of the day, the most valuable nigger ever to be handled in Blackwell's famous auction room! Ladies and gentlemen, feast your eyes on the finest physical specimen of black flesh that ever set foot in this country. . . ."

The huge man shuffling onto the platform wore leg irons and a collar around his neck linked to chains held by this two white guides.

There was a leopard skin around his flat waist, and the bunched muscles of his broad shoulders, chest, arms and thighs rippled with each movement, gleaming with oil.

"And furthermore, folks, you are now gazing at an African prince, the son of a king. His name is Zambullah, the first nigger of royal blood we've ever handled. Just think of what he could do as a stud, gentlemen! Why with his seed planted in all your nigger wenches you could begin a real race of superior niggers. And don't forget—a nigger with the size and muscles of this one could work twice as hard and twice as long as any of your best fifteen-hundred-dollar niggers."

A voice rose from the audience: "If he's royalty like you say, why've you got him chained like a wild beast?"

"Just precaution, gentlemen, just precaution. . . . As you can see, muscles like that could tear two or three average men apart. Remember he's just in from the jungle and naturally a little confused. Might get a little skittish, you understand, and not knowing his own strength might do a little harm without intending to atall. Fact is, as you can plainly see, he's by nature gentle as a lamb. I've been assured that he's not made one whit of trouble since he left Africa. Whoever's lucky enough to get him can be sure that a slave of this royal quality will be faithful, and God help any man who ever tries to harm his master when this loyal nigger is there protecting him."

"If he's so gentle, why's all that dried blood on his head and back? Looks to me he's been banged around a lot like he wasn't behaving."

"The slight damage was caused by an unfortunate accident when the ship was unloading. One of the bales fell on the poor man. Would have killed any normal man, but nothing can really hurt this one. He was treated and examined by a fine doctor who pronounced him in perfect shape. All our slaves are certified healthy and sound."

"He acts stupid. He ain't hardly moved since he's been here. How do we know he's all right in the head?"

"Royal blood," said the auctioneer, "is never stupid. He might be a mite none too smart, but that's a real advantage. Get a nigger too sharp, he can be trouble. All you want from a nigger is plenty of muscle and just enough brains to take orders quick, and that's exactly the qualities this one has to offer. Now please, folks, no more of these time-wasting questions that don't amount to a hill of beans. Let's get the bidding started. How about three thousand just for a starter?"

During the silence that followed, Paul studied the Negro intently, sensing something wrong. Had there not been a slight stagger in his shuffling steps? That of course could be due to the chain on his leg irons, but what about the undue listlessness, the apathetic slump of posture for such a beautifully developed body? The reddened, watering eyes, confused air, the sense of disorientation?

Paul's guess was that the man had been doped with laudanum, morphine or one of the other tinctures of opium—and the only plausible reason would be that otherwise the slave was too intractably violent to risk bringing into the market.

He was about to whisper his suspicions to Syl when the auctioneer spoke again, peevishly:

"Folks, I must confess I am astounded that you haven't jumped at the opportunity of a lifetime to acquire the finest nigger that ever walked the face of the earth. Since the fault must lie with me for failing to convince you that this nigger of royal blood is the bargain of the century at any price, I'll try again. . . ."

Stepping over to Zambullah, the auctioneer grasped one of the great black arms and tried to lift it. He could barely budge it more than an inch or two, not only because of its heft but because the wrist was linked to the other wrist by a chain.

"You see, folks? His arms are like side of mutton. I myself am considered a strong man, but look at the difference. . . ." He rolled up a shirtsleeve and held a burly, hairy white arm beside Zambullah's. It looked half the size, puny.

Circling the Negro, he slapped at him here and there, praising the huge muscles, then suddenly pulled aside the leopard skin that covered his loins and cupped a hand under the black man's testicles. He grinned lewdly.

"The ladies present will have to excuse me, but we're also talking about breeding stock here, and I want you to get a look at the size of these—"

With a movement so sudden that Paul could only liken it to the pounce of a wildcat, the black man's shackled fists made an upward sideswipe at the auctioneer's head. The man yelped in pain and went tumbling off the platform. The mulatto and a white man rushed to help him to his feet. He got up cursing and holding a hand to one side of his face, which was beginning to bleed.

"Get rid of that nigger bastard!" he shouted at the white man who had helped him up. "Whatever you can get—anything to get him off our hands!"

The auctioneer's assistant, a thin, worried-looking man, stepped onto the platform nervously but seemed reassured by the way the two men who had guided Zambullah to the block were now tightly holding the chains linked to his neck. The big black was relaxed, making no show of resistance.

"This unfortunate incident," said the thin man, keeping his distance, "was plainly unintentional. The nigger is still a little confused. Ain't quite got over what fell on his head. But that don't reflect on his value. Any owner could set him right in no time at all with a few whops of the blacksnake. 'Course we expect you to be kinda leery, so how about startin' all over again with a low bid of only fifteen hundred?"

"Why hell," said one man, "you couldn't give that bugger away for a plugged penny unless you threw in a couple guards to ride shotgun on him."

There was a scattering of guffaws that instantly silenced when Syl spoke up loudly:

"Five hundred dollars."

Some of the audience stared at her as if she were crazy; a few put on knowing leers. They had heard of the kind of white woman who preferred black men over whites, and after what she'd just got a look at . . .

"One thousand," came another voice.

"One thousand from the gentleman in the rear," said the surprised auctioneer. "Now who'll make it two thousand?"

"Fifteen hundred," said Syl.

"Three thousand," said the man in the rear.

The assistant auctioneer was overjoyed. "Now there's a

sharp gentleman who knows a bargain! The offer stands at three thousand. Now if there are no further—"

Syl didn't hesitate. "Thirty-five hundred."

"Five thousand," came an instant later.

The audience was turning, craning their necks to get a look at this rash bidder, as did both Paul and Syl.

Leon Jacquard!

Jacquard, smiling triumphantly, bowed in Syl's direction. "Mademoiselle Beauvais, to make it easier on your pride as well as my purse, I feel it only fair to advise you that no matter how high you care to bid, I am prepared to go higher."

Tight-lipped, Syl turned and walked out. Paul followed.

V

In the small slave-auction office Syl made arrangements for delivery of the slaves she had purchased. Then, escorted by Paul, she started back toward the carriage. They had gone scarcely a score of feet when their way was blocked by Jacquard. He was faultlessly garbed in the latest style; the sun flashed from jeweled rings on his fingers, a breastpin and bracelets. He made a low sweeping bow.

"Mademoiselle . . . a word with you, please. . . ."

"I have neither the time nor desire to converse with you, Monsieur Jacquard."

"It will take but a few moments. I wish to offer my apology for any offense you may have felt because of my determination to outbid you."

"And what, may I ask, was the pleasure you seemed to derive from denying me the purchase?"

"The greatest of pleasures, *mademoiselle.* It was my way of demonstrating to you that I consider no price too high to pay for winning at least a smile from you. I purchased the slave only as a gift to you. All I ask in return is that you do me the honor of dining with me this evening, at which time the deed to the nigger will be turned over to you, made out in your name."

She let out a small gasp. "I could not possibly accept such a gift!"

His eyebrows arched. "And why not, *mademoiselle?* Surely you cannot take offense at an invitation to dine with me."

Syl flushed. "It should not be necessary to explain. A gentleman would understand."

An angry red spread over Jacquard's handsome face. "Your allusion is most unkind."

"I am sorry. Now if you will excuse me—" She started away.

"Another moment, please—" Jacquard's tone was almost beseeching. Syl hesitated. He put a hand gently on her arm and spoke rapidly:

"I am an impulsive man. I speak my feelings without thought. If I have offended, it was without intention, due to the rashness of my heart. Can you condemn me for that? I beg you to give me an opportunity to make amends."

"But for what purpose, *monsieur*? As I have tried to tell you, I have no desire for a friendship between us."

"But why?" His tone was angrily accusing. "What do you hold against me?"

Too upset to answer, she turned away. "Paul, please escort me to the carriage."

Jacquard's hand caught at her wrist. "But you have not answered my question!"

Paul roughly knocked the man's hand away. "The lady has had enough of your rudeness, sir. Out of our way, please."

Jacquard whirled toward him, eyes suddenly hot and glittering. "I have no intention of stepping aside for a fool!"

"Then we shall," Paul said agreeably, and taking Syl's arm started to bypass the man.

Jacquard quickly stepped directly in Paul's path. "Again you dare to interfere in a matter that concerns only Mademoiselle Beauvais and me. The last time I chose to let you hide behind her skirts, but this time you will not get off so easily." Reaching into a vest pocket, he flicked out a card and extended it.

"The choice of weapons is yours, sir!"

At that moment Paul realized that the man's persistence and rudeness toward Syl had been a deliberate ploy to provoke him into a duel. He was the type of man who would believe that all women are enthralled by men fighting over them—and would be attracted to the winner.

Taking the card, Paul tore it in two. "Duels are only for fools. Now for the last time—"

There was a stinging sensation as Jacquard suddenly flicked a pair of white gloves against his face. It was only a symbolic blow intended to avenge an insult and force the one receiving the blow to seek a duel—or be branded a coward.

It galled Paul beyond bearing, stirred a depth of rage in him that he had not suspected existed. Almost as a reflex action he stepped forward with catlike speed, at the same time swinging up with a left hook that jolted Jacquard's head back and following with a driving right that sent him staggering backward before falling with blood dribbling from his mouth.

Had he wished, Paul could have made it a knockout blow. He was adept at boxing. Following a fight with Jack Fordyce in Scotland, in which he had nearly killed his opponent with his rough-and-tumble frontier tactics—frowned on in Scotland—Paul's friend Alex Ushant had induced him to take boxing lessons. Thus he had received instruction and workouts with the great Tim Hopley and the Cardiff Strong Boy, showing surprising aptitude for the sport. As Alex put it, Paul was "demned dicey with his fists."

But Jacquard, excellent a duelist as he might be, was clearly not a boxer. Fists were not a gentleman's way of fighting.

Sitting up, holding a handkerchief to his bleeding mouth, Jacquard glared at Paul. The fury in his eyes was raw and deadly. Turning his head, he called out:

"Zack—teach this cur a lesson!"

A man emerged from the group of gaping bystanders. He was a chunky, powerful man with an ugly, pockmarked face. He wore a smug nasty grin.

"You damn bet I will, Mr. Jacquard!"

Paul heard a gasp from Syl. "Why that's Zack Porter—our overseer that Pierre just fired!"

Fists poised, Porter came in a rush. Paul crouched to meet him. At the last moment Porter stopped and with incredible speed his right boot shot out in a vicious kick. Unprepared for such a dirty tactic, Paul tried to sidestep. Too late. The heavy swamp boot caught him in the crotch, though thanks to Paul's quick move, with lessened impact. Fiery pain jolted upward from his testicles, brought nausea to his head. He staggered; his vision clouded.

"Since yer so all-fired hot to fight," snarled Porter, "I'm goin' to l'arn you how it's done. . . ."

Again he rushed, and this time Paul saw the glint of metal across Porter's right fist. Iron knuckles! The fist shot out.

Paul jerked his head aside. The knobbed metal scraped his cheek. By now Paul had his opponent tabbed: his manner of speech, the twang in his voice was that of one who had lived long on the Western frontier, perhaps as a trapper, soldier or Indian fighter. He was an experienced gut-fighter: hands, feet, biting, iron knuckles—anything to win. To *kill*—

Polite boxing, all rules of fair play could be forgotten.

He slammed back, missing. His head was still fogged.

Porter, pushing his advantage, grasped at Paul's jacket collar with his left hand to prevent dodging. The iron knuckles on his right hand flashed in a mighty swing—

Paul kneed upward at Porter's genitals, bringing a yelp of pain. At the same instant Paul's right hand, fingers pronged out stiffly, stabbed at Porter's eyeballs. Porter screamed and his swing with his iron knuckles feebly brushed past Paul's shoulder.

Porter backed away, fingering at a bleeding, blinded eye. Paul followed.

"You damned bastard—" Porter squalled at him. "I'll kill you for that!"

Paul slammed a hard right that sent his adversary floundering another few feet backward before falling. Dropping to his knees, he pinned the man down. Porter's good eye was rolling wildly. His breathing was hard; warm, alcoholic breath. If the man was carrying a hidden gun, as Paul suspected, his next move would be an attempt to shoot.

As coldly and methodically as if he were destroying a rattlesnake, he thrust Porter's iron-knuckled right hand on an angle against a loose cobblestone that lay nearby in the roadway. Then, keeping the wrist trapped under one boot, he rose up and brought his other one down with all his weight. Bone crunched. Porter howled.

It would be a long time, if ever, before Porter could use iron knuckles on that hand again. Or pull a trigger.

When he looked up, he saw Syl walking away rapidly. Jacquard was not in sight.

As Paul strode after Syl, the clustering of bystanders made way for him with alacrity.

As if I'm some sort of wild maniac, he thought morosely.

In the carriage, Syl added to his raging sense of futility.

"Oh I'm so humiliated," she moaned, holding hands over her face. "Why couldn't you have accepted Jacquard's *cartel* like a gentleman, Paul, instead of getting involved in such a vulgar display of brutality with a lowly overseer?"

"Because," he snapped back, "by your definition I'm not a gentleman." Then, remembering the big Negro Zambullah and the other slaves, he added bitterly:

"You see, I'm just beginning to understand how you exalted rich people think. Brutality to an innocent black person can be overlooked. Brutality repaid in kind to a brutal white person is unpardonable."

She slapped him stingingly across the face.

vi

The immensity of Paul's defection from high Creole standards of gentlemanly behavior was even greater than he knew, as he was to discover a few days later when Pierre and Etienne returned from Natchez.

It was early evening and a red sun was just sinking beyond the fringe of trees in the swamp when he was summoned by one of the servants with the message that "Massa Pierre" wished to see him.

Pierre met him in a cool but courteous manner at the door and bid him be seated in the library where it would be more private. Pierre was no longer carrying his arm in a sling. Partially paralyzed, it hung stiffly at his side, though he could move some of his fingers. In his other hand he held a newspaper.

"Before we discuss the matter," Pierre said coldly, "I would like to hear your side of the story."

"What matter are you referring to, Pierre?"

Pierre held up the paper and spoke with controlled anger. "The scandal you created in New Orleans is on the front page of *Le Moniteur*. I also heard about it from some of my planter friends on the boat. I feel deeply embarrassed and ashamed for you."

"I feel neither shame nor embarrassment. Under the same circumstances I would do the same again in defense of Syl and myself."

Pierre's control began to slip. "Defense of Syl? That was never in question! But if you felt her honor was impugned, there was but one way to settle it."

"By means of some silly duel?"

"Silly, you call it!" Pierre shook the newspaper in the air, his hand trembling. "In the words of *Le Moniteur*, your 'barbarian resort to fists was a public outrage to good manners.' Do you realize you have been publicly posted as a coward in New Orleans? A signed statement by Jacquard will now be legally affixed to public places and by a notice in the newspaper."

Paul shot to his feet. "I am a coward for defending myself against a ruffian using iron knuckles?"

"But in response to Jacquard's *cartel* you struck blows intended to inflict injury! The punctilio in such matters provides that a man guilty of such crude behavior is subject to horsewhipping or other physical punishment by any agent designated by the offended person."

"I don't give a damn about your stupid rules! Why should I change my own beliefs to conform to yours? You call this idiotic farce of killing or being killed a matter of honor! I call it murder or suicide—it's one or the other. Jacquard probably thinks I know little or nothing about firearms, whereas he's a skilled marksman who obviously wouldn't hesitate to gun me down, which would be murder. What's honorable about that? It happens that I grew up with a rifle, and am tolerably expert with a pistol, so I could probably acquit myself well enough. But I am neither a coward nor a fool, and have no desire to kill or be killed."

"That's quite enough, Paul! I don't care to hear any—"

"But I haven't finished!"

"As your employer, I order you to—"

"You may be my employer, but I'm not your slave. You hired me to perform medical services—not to fight duels. Nor do my duties include taking insults."

Pierre's face flamed. "If it weren't for my arm I'd call you out here and now, and if you dared refuse—!"

"How very honorable of you," Paul shot back. "It's only because of me that you're fortunate enough to be alive to even think of calling me out—and even more fortunate that with a useless arm it's quite safe to insult me!"

Even as he spoke, Paul began feeling shame for the hurtful words bursting from him in wrath. It was like the dirty fighting he had been forced into with Zack Porter, kicking below the belt.

Pierre's face turned a deathly white. He pointed a shaking finger at the door. His voice quivered:

"Get out—!"

vii

Paul was downstairs in his cottage with clothes and possessions strewn around him in the midst of packing when the front door quietly opened behind him.

"Docteur, may I have a word with you?"

Paul turned. It was Etienne Troyonne. He was looking quite recovered from his wound. Fern, who had become skilled in the use of the carbolic solution and bandaging under Paul's teachings, had accompanied the two cousins to

Natchez to attend to Etienne's wound dressings daily, and apparently had done a good job.

Paul shrugged. "I'm in no particular rush. I have all night to pack, since I can't catch a boat before morning."

"Why are you leaving, Paul?"

"I have no choice."

"But you weren't fired."

"I took that to be Pierre's intent. But regardless, I can no longer work for an arrogant employer who feels free to insult me for acting in accordance with my own beliefs."

"You made an agreement to be the plantation doctor. Do you feel it is right to leave before the smallpox is completely cleared up?"

"The agreement was terminated not by me, but by Pierre's manner of calling me down. If he wishes to apologize, I will consider staying."

Etienne shook his head. "It happened that I was in an adjoining room and quite by accident overheard some of the strong words spoken. I fear that Pierre is not at the moment in a forgiving mood."

Paul's anger rose again. "And do you too think I acted dishonorably?"

"No, Paul. I believe that under the circumstances you acted in the only way possible in accordance with your Yankee standards. But you can't expect Pierre to understand that—not immediately. However, I think that even he will realize sooner or later that he has made a mountain out of a molehill. Pierre has a magniloquent side that at times overcomes his common sense, and while he's still on his high horse I must ask you to be patient for a few more days before expecting a change in his attitude."

"I can't wait several days, for you see I too ride on a high horse."

Etienne smiled sadly. "Such are the evils of pride. Pride has no discrimination. A thief can be as proud of his thieving skills as an artist is of creating a masterpiece, or a child of making a mud pie. I can speak from the vantage point of having lost my own pride many years ago. I was a sickly child, later was rejected by the military, and have always been an object more of ridicule or sympathy than of respect. Thus I turned inward to my books, music and other inner worlds. There are more important values than pride. What of the sick slaves and your hard-earned abilities to cure them? Does that mean less to you than your false pride?"

"Of course that's important to me! It's my whole life."

"But you are leaving with no thought for those who need your help. Surely such pride is as foolish and false as the dueling you are so opposed to."

"You may be right, but since the smallpox outbreak is already under control, I won't be needed. Fern has acquired as much skill as I have for performing the simple vaccination procedure, and when the new shipment of vaccine arrives, she can complete the inoculation of Syl's and your slaves."

"Unfortunately, there are reports of new smallpox outbreaks on other plantations, including my own. A communication has arrived from the apothecary in New Orleans that there is a state of panic among the planters and townspeople, and under law all available vaccine must be divided equitably among all the physicians who are screaming for it. Since we have already received more than our share, no more can be shipped to us in time to do any good. We shall have to depend on you to do the best you can under the circumstances."

For a moment Paul wondered if Etienne's whole reason for coming to the cottage was really out of concern for Paul's feelings and the sick slaves—or solely for the money they represented. Then he thrust the mean thought aside. The slaves' lives were all that really mattered.

When Paul hesitated, Etienne added, "Don't think of it as staying for Pierre's sake, but for the slaves—and for yourself."

"But I can hardly stay if Pierre doesn't want—"

"I will undertake to speak for Pierre, as well as myself. . . . I beg you to stay."

"All right, Etienne—but only for as long as I feel there is a real need." Even an apology from Pierre would not change that decision, he vowed to himself.

The real sting had not been so much the affront from Pierre, but the hurts and continued silence from Syl.

THREE: The *Marangouins*

THE days slipped by as smoothly and ineluctably as the mighty river, whose rushing sounds, like time speeding past, were with Paul night and day. He immersed himself in work, oblivious of nearly everything else beyond the ailments of the black people, which were more numerous than he had imagined.

Inoculation of the slaves from Etienne's and Syl's plantations took priority, and was a relatively simple matter despite the lack of vaccine from the apothecary.

Long lines of Pierre's inoculated slaves and long lines of slaves from the other plantations were paraded past the medical work tables set up by Paul and Fern outside of the infirmary. A tiny bit of infectious matter from a vaccination sore was scratched into the arm of an unvaccinated Negro. One sore easily supplied enough material for several other vaccinations. Great care was taken to disinfect the needle used with carbolic between each vaccination, as syphilis or other infections might otherwise be transferred.

All blacks showing symptoms of the disease were immediately consigned to the pesthouse, where four more victims had died since Paul's arrival. Those who survived, who were in the majority and were now immune, were assigned the chores of caring for the sick ones, keeping the pesthouse clean and burying the dead.

Not one of the inoculated slaves developed symptoms of the disease, and apparently this news spread through the black grapevine, for the ones who had run away out of fear began trickling back. Some could barely walk because of the painful vesicles on the soles of their feet. One was bandaged over half his body with compresses of leaves from some unknown tree that he had obtained from a voodoo conjure woman known as Momselle Delphine, but despite his copious applications the rash worsened. He soon after died in the pesthouse. Some had escaped infection; some died in the swamp.

Fern Venable, who had been an able and dedicated assistant in all this, commented, "Are you aware that the blacks have stopped calling you Yankeedoc? You're now their Massadoc."

"What's the difference?"

"It means that you've won their trust. But I think what really did it was the way you cured little Angie. . . . "

Her reference was to a small girl, normally sweet and tractable, who had begun acting crazy. She flew into fits of temper, refused food and water, and was even cast out of the cabin by her own parents because they believed she was under a voodoo curse. Paul examined her carefully. The clue came when he noted that frequently she scratched her head in the same place. Carefully he shaved away the hair from that portion of her head and under a magnifying glass found the deteriorating head of a wood tick buried in her scalp. The body had been torn away by her scratching. He extracted the infected matter, disinfected the scalp, and the next day Angie was completely normal, happy and cheerful as ever. This much impressed the slaves. Massadoc's magic was more powerful than the conjure woman's.

Although Fern worked with him some of the time, their relationship was strained. Paul attributed it to his ungallant response when once she had asked him why he had not yet invited her to visit his cottage. Exhausted, at the end of a hard day's work, he had brusquely replied that he had no time for frivolity. The truth was that even though he hungered for a woman, he had lost his desire for Fern because Syl dominated his thoughts. It was illogical, for he found much to admire about Fern and little to admire about Syl—the latter seemed superficial, insensitive, even a bit cruel, little more than a beautiful ornament—yet he couldn't help himself. He could forget when working, but she intruded into his thoughts at night, filled his dreams as if he were an infatuated schoolboy.

He brooded too over his falling out with Pierre, who like Syl had not come near the infirmary. Etienne confided, however, that Pierre was very pleased with Paul's success in ending the smallpox epidemic. Etienne was sure that as soon as Pierre found a way to get off his limb of Creole pride he would find a way to mend matters with Paul.

But I won't be around if that day ever comes, Paul thought angrily. He had promised Etienne and vowed to himself that he would stay only as long as he felt there was a need for his services. That day would soon come.

But the medical problems seemed endless. The blacks, because of their faith in his powers, were now coming daily with new or long-hidden ailments: rashes that looked a little like smallpox but turned out to be scabies, a parasitic disease to be treated with an ointment containing slaked lime, ground mandrake root and rosewater; several cases of Q-fever, transmitted by raw milk or ticks; a run of ague, a form of malaria; snakebites; pyemia; tumors to be surgically excised; various itches for which he used a paste of camphor and sulphur, and when the sulphur ran out, substituted gunpower instead. He treated a few cases of syphilis with mercury but mostly hope; and yaws, another venereal dis-

ease which was curable, as syphilis was not. Some he could
help, others he couldn't. There was even a case of tetanus
and one of epilepsy, against which he was powerless but administered innocuous medicaments anyway for the value it
would have in bolstering their hopes.

The weeks slid by like days. April merged into May, and
suddenly it was June with the advent of the rains and soon
after, overnight invasions of hordes of mosquitoes, or as the
Creoles called them, the *marangouins.*

ii

Never in his life had Paul ever seen or imagined such incredible swarms of the tiny insects as now appeared, increasing daily. As the rains turned the day hot and steaming
and everything grew sticky to the touch, black clouds of
winged pests seemed to take over the earth. From sunset
until dawn their nasty buzzing sounds filled the air, the noise
so loud that Paul was at first startled until he grew accustomed to its daily reoccurrence.

Otto Guttmann, who had turned out to be a friendly sort
with whom Paul chatted occasionally, commented with a
chuckle: "From now on until the weather cools in October
or November, we'll be at the mercy of those pestiferous little
beasts. They will regulate family arrangements, prescribe the
employment and distribution of time, and essentially affect
the comfort and enjoyments of every individual in Louisiana.
The blacks don't seem much troubled by them, however, and
for my part I find a dollop or two of rum makes them easier
to bear."

Being of an inquisitive turn of mind, Paul began observing
them minutely. What became of them in the daytime he
didn't know, but their evidence, in the form of innumerable
eggs, could be found wherever there was even a drop of
moisture. A water pitcher that had passed through the drip
stone in the evening and appeared dry would by dawn have
on the bottom a sediment of the appearance of black mud.
In a day this mud would assume the character of sand, and
in another day or two would be living larvae. There was no
small hollow in the ground, a rock or scrap of wood containing as little as a teaspoon of water that was not wriggling
thickly with these things. It staggered Paul's imagination to
visualize the vast hordes hatching daily in the numerous
pools, ditches, streams and wide stretches of swamp. Certainly

it was beyond the realm of possibility that they could ever be extirpated by human effort!

He now appreciated the mosquito bar that protected his bed. It consisted of a linen netting completely covering and surrounding the bed like a tent. The numbers, minuteness and activity of the winged enemies rendered any warfare against them impossible, but defensive tactics were mandatory. The business of greatest importance each evening was to secure himself against attacks by proper arrangement of the netting—and by a swift slipping beneath it when retiring without admitting any of the devils. Once inside it gave him an indescribably pleasant sense of security to hear their clamor outside without the possibility of being annoyed by them.

Paul's interest in the insects was not entirely idle. He had long speculated on the possibility that mosquitoes were in some way connected to certain diseases. Such a theory had first been advanced in 1848 by Dr. Josiah Knott, who had noted the prevalence of mosquitoes wherever there was yellow fever and suspected it was due to the insects. Again in 1853, Dr. Louis Beauperthuy more specifically stated that "the disease develops under conditions which favor the development of mosquitoes. The mosquito plunges its proboscis into the skin and introduces a poison which has properties akin to snake venom."

Almost all the medical profession scoffed at such "wild" theories. The prevailing view was that yellow fever, malaria and such diseases sprang from the miasmas arising from foul water and heat, notably in the vicinity of tropical swamps, and that mosquitoes had nothing to do with disease.

But Paul had learned to distrust or at least question entrenched medical opinion and continued his observations, filling a notebook with details.

One unscientific aspect of his fascination with the pests was their nightly serenade, which grew to be truly musical in his ears. The tiny voices swelled and ebbed and intermitted in unanimous concert as if indeed the music were being performed by a most accomplished chorus. Having learned to identify the different notes, he was charmed with how their varying sonances were always in perfect harmony, and he even began to pick out four or five of the leading voices that sang with greater gusto. The shrillest he named Clementine, a more pleasing soprano was Suzette, the deepest buzzing he attributed to Antoine. . . .

This is childish, he decided one night. Overwork, too much solitude and the heat driving me crazy.

The next day he made his decision. He had done all he could for the blacks, fulfilled his promise to Etienne. He would stay only a day or two more to tie up loose strings, and then he would leave.

That evening his meal was brought by Céleste, the mulatto who had first told him about the voodoo drums. On the large tray of covered dishes was also a bottle of fine brandy.

"With the compliments of Monsieur Gayarre," she said in her excellent English.

Was this supposed to be a token apology? Paul wondered with a touch of anger. If so, why couldn't Pierre have come himself? Well, he could respond in the same coin:

"Please convey my thanks to Mr. Gayarre for his most gracious gift, and tell him also that I shall be leaving in a couple of days."

The attractive golden face showed surprise. "You are leaving? There will be many who will be very unhappy to know that."

Her soft voice held a genuine note of regret. His eyes had sought her face, again noting the strange beauty that came from her Negroid features blended with an infusion of white characteristics from the unknown white father. Her shapely figure was sheathed in a simple apple-green frock, and quite suddenly he was aware of a rising *frisson* in his loins.

At once he was shamed. Of course he had been long without a woman, and he had heard that the lassitude of hot climates had a way of heightening the erotic promptings, but one thing he vowed he would never do, *could* never do, was take advantage of a servant.

Perhaps it was part of the strange malaise he felt was creeping over him. He had been feeling more lethargic lately, sometimes with touches of dizziness. Was he coming down with a fever?

Fever . . . mosquitoes? Was there really a connection? He had been bitten often enough. At this season of the year it could be malaria . . . and he had no quinine. It had not been in stock at the apothecary's, but he had been advised that the voodoo women would know where to find the cinchona bark from which quinine was extracted.

"Céleste, where can I find Momselle Delphine, the conjure woman?"

The large limpid eyes widened. "I do not know."

"What do the black folks do when they want a voodoo cure? How do they find the voodoo doctors?"

She smiled. "Just follow the drums. . . . "

She turned and went out with the smoothness of a cat.

FOUR: Voodoo

OTTO Guttmann lived near the slave quarters at the edge of the woods in a humbler cottage than Paul's—possibly an indication of the German's lower status in the eyes of Pierre. Fern had confided to Paul that originally Otto, a virtual genius with machinery, had been brought over from Germany by Pierre's father to supervise the cane mills and keep them in proper operating order. A highly educated man, Otto had brought crates of books with him—also a beautiful young wife and a child. Tragedy struck a couple of years later when wife and child were carried away during an epidemic of yellow fever. Thereafter Otto seemed to lose his stiff Germanic self-respect, began slipping downward by steady boozing, just keeping sober enough to make him worth the modest salary Pierre paid him. Pierre considered him a necessary evil, detested him for his alcoholism and weakness of character and never accorded him the courtesy of invitations to the manor.

Otto, dressed in a creased, soiled white suit, opened the door. The big man's bushy black eyebrows, contrasting strangely with his tousled gray hair and slim gray mustache, arched while the pale-blue eyes behind rimless spectacles stared at Paul dully. In one hand he held a glass.

"Ah, Herr Doctor! So you have finally decided to call on me? What an unexpected pleasure. Do come in. . . . "

Paul was surprised at the neatness of the house. A mat rug covered the plank floor, the furniture was of woven cane, there was even a vase of flowers on a center table. Dominating it all were shelves of books from floor to ceiling, most of them in German, some in French and English.

"I regret to hear," Otto went on when Paul was seated in the small living room, "that you plan to leave us. . . . "

Paul was astonished. "But how can you possibly know?

I've told nobody." Except Céleste of course, he added silently, but that had been only minutes ago.

Otto chuckled. "I found out from my housekeeper. How she knows I won't venture to guess. You must understand that the blacks have their own grapevine. They know everything that goes on just as soon as it happens, if not sooner."

A distant throbbing of drums began.

Otto laughed again. "That's probably the news coming hot off the press right now. Those drums are the slaves' newspaper." Then, turning his head, he called out: "Callie—come out here and prepare a drink for the doctor!"

Callie was a plumpish, pleasant-faced black woman of middle age wearing a crimson turban and a striped cotton dress. She stood silently waiting as Otto went on:

"We only have a choice of dark Cuban rum and passable whiskey, but thanks to Pierre's gourmet tastes, plenty of ice."

"Whiskey," said Paul, and as the black woman went to fetch it he decided to come out with his real reason for the visit.

"Otto, I have been unable to procure quinine. I have heard of the bark that the voodoo doctors use to subdue fevers, and since you seem on familiar terms with the black people, I am wondering if you can help me get some of the bark."

Otto's pale blue eyes twinkled. "Ah yes, I think I could be of some help. Callie brings me some of the bark every season and makes an effusion of it which I drink. Thus far I have avoided the fevers. So you too, Doctor, are beginning to have some respect for voodoo medicine?"

"If it's cinchona bark from which quinine is derived, as I think it is, then it's no different from white medicine."

"True. It does happen to be one of the species of cinchona." Otto waved at his bookshelves. "You see, Doctor, I do considerable reading, and sometimes dabble into medicine. Quinine was not isolated by our medical profession until 1820—whereas the voodoo priests and priestesses have been using it for the same curative purposes for untold ages."

Paul's drink had arrived, and he swallowed some of it thirstily. Before leaving his cottage he had gulped down some of Pierre's fine brandy to alleviate the sense of beginning fever. It had helped, but now it was returning.

"Are you feeling quite all right, Doctor? Your face seems a bit flushed—"

"I think I may have a fever, which is why I am anxious to get some of the bark."

"I will send Callie to Momselle Delphine tomorrow to get you the bark."

"I would like to get it sooner, Otto. If you could give me directions for finding Momselle Delphine tonight—"

"I'm afraid that will be impossible. Momselle, I'm sure, is off somewhere in the swamps involved in one of her infernal voodoo rites. I could not in good conscience allow Callie to go there tonight, nor advise you to try. I would not try it myself. But come—drink up and let me offer you the next best curative, rum. That will hold the fever in abeyance until tomorrow. . . . " Twisting his head again, he called, "Callie—fix one of your rum drinks for the doctor!"

One or two drinks later—Paul couldn't recall how many times Callie had refilled his glass—Paul was feeling much better but having a little difficulty following the course of Otto's conversation.

" . . . what surprises me, Doctor," Otto was saying, "is how you as a medical man can remain so skeptical of voodoo cures. . . . "

"Obviously the voodoo priests know a number of herbs and roots and bark such as cinchona that are effective for certain ailments, but certainly only the most ignorant sort of people can believe in superstitious stuff like amulets, spells and that sort of magic."

"Ignorant?" Otto said musingly. "I never considered myself to be an ignorant person. . . . "

"Are you telling me *you* believe in such hocus-pocus?"

Otto regarded him with solemn eyes. "I would be ignorant if I didn't. I have been here twenty years—and keep in mind that I have the typical German's pragmatic mind that must always know the cause and effect of everything—yet I have observed and experienced enough of the so-called 'voodoo magic' so that I can no longer deny its existence as a reality and potent force beyond our understanding. And I venture to say some of it is in many ways superior in effectiveness to much of our white medicine."

The man was only spouting words out of his rum bottle, Paul thought indulgently. He reached for his own glass for another swallow and was surprised to find it had been again filled to the brim. He gulped some of it.

"Can your pragmatic brain give me an example?" he said.

"Many. For one, my own countryman, Mesmer, first introduced hypnotism to our medical fraternity only about a dozen years ago. Black witch doctors have been using hypnotism to achieve cures for hundreds of years. The only difference is that when a black medicine man hypnotizes another black it is called 'magic.' When a white physician finally got around to doing the same thing it is called a startling new medical discovery."

Paul could think of nothing to say, perhaps because his brain was getting too fogged. He had some more of his drink.

Otto leaned forward, his face very serious. "Frankly, Doctor, I have nothing but the greatest respect for the black man. They were brought here chained neck to neck, and among them were medicine men who had received their sacred inheritance in an unbroken line from their fathers and forefathers before them. They have preserved their jungle heritage, and it has enabled them to survive. They know how to submit to life as they find it and thus achieve a harmonious approach to nature that I myself am trying to achieve."

He waved disdainfully at his books. "I am supposed to be something of a scholar, and perhaps something of a philosopher, but I tell you this, my friend: I would trade it all if I could achieve the happiness of a simple black man. Show me an uneducated man with a woman, a place to sleep, enough to eat, and I'll show you a happy man. Books can be a curse. A man with too many books loses his joy in such elemental things, his juices dry up . . . and so I drink. . . . " Otto picked up his glass and drained it.

Paul was beginning to think that the German was far drunker than he appeared, and perhaps a little deranged. He firmly decided it was time to leave, that he would refuse any more liquor.

Otto was rapping his empty glass on the stand beside his chair. "Callie! Our guest's glass is empty!"

"No more for me, thanks," Paul said quickly.

Otto looked at him through blinking eyes. "As I was saying, I am but a poor example of my own philosophical beliefs. . . . " He made a disgusted gesture toward his potty stomach and the general flab of his body. "As you can see, I am beset with all the earthly lusts that are not in harmony with nature. . . . Flesh, food, drink—against these enemies even my intelligence cannot prevail. . . . "

He paused for a while, looking at the floor, bemused. Meanwhile Callie had reappeared to deftly exchange Paul's empty glass for a filled one before he could object, and then did the same for Otto.

Otto's head jerked up and his fathomless eyes stared at Paul. "We were discussing hypnotism, were we not? Of course. So I must warn you. . . . The drums you hear can more than talk—they can hypnotize you into doing things that . . . " He paused briefly to listen to the faint distant throbbing that had started again before going on.

"What I am trying to tell you, Doctor, is that after a time the bayous will swallow you, as they have me. . . . You'll become a part of them. Either that or you die. There's no escape. Just as water and oil mixed together sooner or later seek their own level, so you will sooner or later become a part of this damned swamp down here and be no better or no worse than I am, or any of the blacks, for that matter. . . . "

By this time Paul had decided the man was out of his mind and he rose to take his leave, but Otto was talking again:

"If I seem to get off the subject now and then, it's because of what this goddamn fever hole has done to me . . . because I've got too much inside of me trying to come out. . . . Never get much chance to talk to anyone . . . anyone intelligent, that is. Now you show me an ignorant man with a woman—oh hell, I already said that. . . . " He wobbled to his feet and blinked at Paul. "What were we talking about, Doctor? Voodoo? Yah? Someday I will tell you more about it, but for now . . . " He dismissed the subject to make a mighty slap at his neck with one hand.

It was all beginning to seem like some weird dream to Paul, something caused by drink. There was a sense of sickness in the air, something palpable and sordid. His head was throbbing. Or was it thrumming of distant drums?

"Got the little bugger!" said Otto, holding out something tiny squeezed between forefinger and thumb. "These goddamn pests are one part of harmonious nature I could do without."

Paul took his opportunity to escape without further amenities. Otto was obviously too drunk to notice or care.

ii

Gusts of driving moist air cooled his cheeks as he plunged into outside darkness. He was shaking with an uncontrollable sense of terror as if the man he'd just left inside were dead, a walking corpse. Though he knew it was really only fever filling his head with delusions, the fright persisted. Swarms of mosquitoes buzzed around his head, but he ignored them.

They were the lesser danger. In his feverish brain Otto suddenly seemed like a fat black hairy spider who had been winding him into his vast spiderweb of drab gray thoughts, winding and winding them around to make him captive, trying to pull him down to his level. His heart was pounding.

Somewhere in his whirling thoughts was still that solid bedrock of medical knowledge that told him it was he who was becoming crazed, his own mind creating the delusions. Not Otto.

But still his mind was trapped in these strange fantasies. One was a sensation that seemed to be reaching out from the bottomless depths of the swamp. The fantasy was impossible to cast aside: it was he, not Otto, who was a dead man walking. He was almost on the verge of screaming from the ghastly realization, but at the same time one small part of his mind retained enough objectivity to know that the rest of his mind was crazed—it was all delirium—but still sweat oozed in great drops from every pore. His shirt clung to his back from sweat that made his skin clammy. The fetid night air sucked into his lungs, clogged them; his breath was coming in thick short gasps. Gasping for fresh cool air that was not to be had.

He became aware that the ground was growing spongy and wet beneath his boots, that he didn't know where he was going. . . .

Something weird and frightening was pulling him. His first realization that he was running was when strange brush and undergrowth began snapping and snagging at his legs. His pulse was throbbing fiercely, pounding through his veins. An illusion. A corpse has no heart. His heart was elsewhere . . . beating, beating alone out there in the bayous, lost in the swamp, beating madly and relentlessly. He floundered on through the darkness, bumping against trees, slogging through water, tearing through brush, hearing his heart out there again and again.

It was booming hollowly now, quivering through the heavy swamp air. He plunged on. Sometimes the beating ceased and he would flounder aimlessly. Then he would hear it again, change direction. . . .

He was being held in thrall, pulled by some force that had invaded him, something deep and irresistible. The throbbing was changing to a new rhythm. Wilder. Reaching to him with harsh vibrations that drummed through his flesh like flicks of a whip. A crazy rhythm adding fire to the blood pounding through his veins, erasing his tiredness. . . .

He felt a surge of glorious new strength. He was suddenly like a king beast roving rampant through the jungle, seeking . . . seeking what? Sometimes he ran; sometimes he strode like a giant. Exultant. Then again running through open space. He had surrendered completely to the exotic pounding that was calling him on and had not even the slightest desire to resist.

The fear, the terror, were gone; only exultation remained. And anticipation. Of what he knew not. His hot flushed face was soothed by a tepid breeze. The whirling fantasies in his head were beginning to take vague shape in reality. . . . Shadowy silhouettes of trees and bushes around him had started undulating to the rhythm of the beat that was drawing him on.

During a few lucid moments he wondered if he were asleep and dreaming, wondering if this was reality or crazed delusion. If so, he didn't want to awaken, he didn't want to think. If it was only a fever-heated dream, he didn't want it to end. . . .

He crashed through thick brush, and all at once a brilliance of yellowish-orange light flared around him.

In front of him was a roaring fire.

iii

Assembled around the fire was an undulating mass of black bodies, men and women. Naked. Oiled skin glistened like polished ebony, splashed with crimson reflections from the ruddy glow of fire. From two crossbars supported by rows of stakes driven into the ground were suspended a series of drums—hollow sections of logs of varying sizes, the ends taut-stretched with animal skins. Each with its own drummer using fingers, hands, sticks, bones. The throbbing beat was thunderous.

> *BOOM-BOOM-BOOM—*
> *Tum-ti-ti-tum—*
> *Tum-ti-ti-tum—*
> *BOOM-BOOM-BOOM—*

He crouched down in the shadow of bushes, suddenly wary of the menace in the deep, lunging boom of the big

drums—at the same time drawn by the fast staccato pulsa-
tions of the small ones. There were two sets of drums, two
levels of sonance: the one sullen, fierce, aggressive, heavily
masculine; the other delicately chittering, flirtatious, luring,
feminine. All primal, inflaming . . .

The hot heavy air pulsed with a frenzy of concussions, now
rising in fury, now falling in seductive, subtle cadences.

Hypnotic.

The swaying dancers were spreading into two groups, following two different rhythms: the movements of the females
supple and alluring; the males tense and powerful. Now
approaching, then withdrawing . . . back and forth. . . .
The women danced with wide-spread legs, smooth satiny
torsoes rippling, twirling to the beat. Teasing. The men
stamped and leaped to the heavy booming, answering with
muscular pelvic thrusts to the coquettish twitchings of female
buttocks.

Pure sexuality.

He felt scorching heat; sweat dribbled down his cheeks.
The frenzied medley of sounds coursed through his veins
like a fulminating fever. The insidious power of the drums
was pulling at him. Giddiness swam in his head.

From somewhere the sleek, slim body of a girl sprang into
view. Stark naked like the others, arms writhing sinuously
above her head. Against the background of leaping flames
her skin shone a golden amber. Her eyes gleamed like liquid
fire. A red flower was pinned above one ear in the mass of
her wild, tossing hair. She danced closer, blood-red lips
parted around shining white teeth.

"Do you wish me to dance for you, *Docteur?*"

Céleste! Only by her voice would he have recognized her,
because of the shadows and fiery reflections rippling across
her face.

He rose to his feet and moved toward her, pushed by
uncontrollable emotions. It was as if he were floating outside
of himself looking down from somewhere above, laughing at
his clumsy antics but at the same time melding into the
swaying group, surrendering to the savagery of drums.
Around him feet stamped and pounded. The thick hot air
was filled with funky sweat mingled with perfumed musk.
The raging drums were deafening. Everything was a crazed
blur. . . .

"Come. . . . " She was leading him by the hand. The

drums were suddenly silent. In the shadows he saw couples wrestling on the ground.

They sank down into darkness.

"I knew you would come. . . . " Her whisper was inexpressibly tender, but the eyes flamed with passion. A heavy scent, sweet and molten as honey, came from the flower in her hair. Her fingers gently trailed down his chest, unfastening his shirt, probing lower. . . . The beautiful pear-shaped breasts pressed against his cheeks, and as he felt the heat of her body against his he began trembling in a violent fit of lust. A seething swept through him as if the roaring fire itself had entered his body, and the thunder of drums started again.

But it came from inside now; it was his own heart pounding frenziedly in his ears. . . .

iv

A jolting impact against one leg awakened him. Paul opened his eyes and saw the girl on her feet, cowering, one arm in the rough grasp of the large, booted man who had apparently kicked him awake.

"I should have known—" he said in a harsh, scolding voice. "I should have come sooner. . . . "

She cuddled closer to the big man, her free hand stroking his cheek, crooning in his ear: " . . . as soon as we get home I'll go to bed with you. . . . "

He pushed her aside and kicked again at Paul's leg. "Are you sober enough to stand up, Doctor?"

Paul struggled to a sitting position. His head throbbed with pain, his face burned, but he had begun shaking from a bone-deep coldness. The eastern fringe of night sky was a murky gray, which meant he had been lying here for hours. He wobbled to his feet.

Otto Guttmann frowned at him. "It will be dawn in another hour or so, so try to hurry. My daughter will guide you back."

Through his pain and fever Paul stared at him stupidly. "Your daughter—"

"Yes," Otto said harshly. "I spawned her. . . . " He turned away and his massive shoulders slumped. Wearily he added:

"I tried to warn you . . . you should never listen to the drums. . . . "

FIVE: Fever

. . . nakedness swam in his head, voluptuous limbs, breasts and eel-smooth torsos that swayed and swirled about him in slow motion as if underwater in a molten elixir of brilliant colorations . . . crimson tongues of liquid flame, fingers of lambent gold that stroked him pleasurably, incited him to unholy madness . . . pear-shaped breasts pressed against his chest, honey-sweet kisses burned his lips, a fiery tongue darted into his mouth. . . . "You are beautiful, Docteur," whispered Céleste. . . . Hips arched, thighs parted, and as golden flesh began to engulf him the face dissolved, transmuted into Fern. . . .

Fern's smile was unutterably lascivious. Her arms pulled him toward the dark vortex of her passion and he was at once caught in a strange conflict of wanting fervidly to possess her but at the same time sickened, repelled . . . sensual greed without love, without sweetness. . . .

At that moment a pert young face floated near, a saucy, laughing face of fresh innocence. . . . Micaela! Eagerly he strove to capture her slender nakedness, to shower her with kisses, for she was suddenly excruciatingly desirable, but she remained tantalizingly out of reach, evading him with teasing laughter. Then when he almost caught her, a whip cracked and Pierre's arrogant face, ugly with anger and contempt, came between them. Micaela ran submissively into Pierre's arms before the two dissolved into darkness. . . .

. . . darkness in a humble bed with a mattress of straw . . . a small child again, lonely and confused . . . lantern light flickered. A woman appeared in the doorway. She approached . . . a sweet face, luminous eyes. Kneeling, she kissed his cheek. "I am your new mother, Sarah," she whispered. . . .

As he soared with happiness, the bed scrunched under her weight. She slid under the covers. . . .

"No, no . . . you're not my mother!" he called in anguish as their bodies fused. "You're not my mother. . . ."

A pleasant stroking sensation was cooling his face when

his eyes opened. He was surrounded by gauzy white clouds through which slanted a bright rectangle of sun. A blurred silhouette, decidedly feminine, was bending over him.

"Thank God you're awake . . . your fever's dropping," she said, continuing to sponge his forehead and cheeks with cool water. "How are you feeling now, Paul?"

That familiar, precious voice!

"I feel foggy, unreal. How long have you been here, Syl?"

She laughed. "Off and on for five days."

"Five days! But it was only last night—"

"You've had a high fever and have been unconscious, in delirium, for most of the time. Pierre sent for Dr. Bender in New Orleans, who has had much experience with fevers. He came yesterday. Your fever almost rose to one hundred and six degrees at one point, which he said was very dangerous. He said the best we could do was sponge you down with cold water now and then, and he bled you—"

"He bled me!"

"Yes. He said it would reduce the heat in your blood."

"The idiot! Didn't he mention quinine?"

"He said there is fever everywhere in the South and there's no quinine available for love or money. They're hoping for a supply on the next packet from New York."

Paul sank back weakly against his pillow, exhausted by the brief flurry of anger and wondering who had disrobed him to sponge down his nude body. Céleste? Aurora? One of the other slave women? Certainly not fastidious, virginal Syl. . . .

"He said it was a very acute attack and the worst of it is past, but there's no telling when it will flare up again. . . . "

"If only I had been able to locate Momselle Delphine," he murmured half to himself.

"Momselle Delphine—that old fraud? Céleste brought you a package wrapped in dirty old rags that she said was from the conjure woman—some of that mumbo-jumbo voodoo stuff I think. I wanted to throw it out."

"Did you?"

"No. Céleste insisted it was some kind of herb you wanted."

"If it's what I hope it is . . . may I see it, please?"

Syl turned and called sharply: "Céleste, bring the *Docteur* the package from the conjure woman."

Céleste appeared. She was wearing a plain white cotton frock that swirled to her ankles. Her hair had been tightly drawn back, sleek and oiled close to her head. She withdrew a fragment of brown spongy bark from the bundle she held under an arm.

"The medicine you were looking for, *Docteur*," she said, extending the fragment.

Taking the bark, he wondered, had it all been just an erotic nightmare? Had there actually been the hypnotic voodoo drums? Had he really known Céleste as a wild, sexually savage animal? Or was it just a result of fevered imagination, pure delirium? Looking at her now, she seemed so cool, so objective. It seemed impossible that she could be the same person he had either known in lust or imagined in delirium.

He examined the bark, smelled it, took a bit and chewed it. Smiled.

"Please make a strong effusion of this, Céleste," he said, handing it back. "You know how it's done. . . . Take great care of the rest of it to be sure it isn't thrown out. And if you see Momselle Delphine, thank her for me."

And to Syl, who'd listened with a wondering frown, he explained: "It's cinchona bark, from which quinine is extracted. It will suppress reoccurence of the fever."

"I will pray that it works, Paul."

It was still hard for him to believe—that she had helped nurse him, perhaps did most of it. That she had cared enough.

"Syl, I can't express how grateful I am for what you've done."

The luxuriant lashes lowered over her brilliant blue-green eyes and the rays of sun glistened on the rich red-gold of hair that cascaded to her shoulders. "I was trying to make amends. . . . "

"For what? You owed me nothing."

"I was unpardonably unkind, as I soon came to realize, but couldn't bring myself to apologize. Whatever else I may be or seem to be, I am not really an unkind person. I know I lack understanding of many other kinds of people and other ways of thinking, but I cannot bear to think that I have ever hurt anyone. . . . "

"If I felt any small hurt, your presence here so far outweighs it that I shall be forever in your debt."

She gave him a teasing smile. "Perhaps I am beginning to understand more than you realize. . . . During your delirium you said certain things. . . . "

Paul was horrified. Certain erotic, shocking portions of his delirious visions still lingered in his head. If words he had unknowingly uttered had at all reflected his sick imaginings . . .

"I hope you realize that in high fever men are apt to say terrible things that are not really a part of their nature."

She stood up with a gay laugh. "You said nothing that was so terrible, though you did say something about your mother that I couldn't quite make out. . . . Is she still alive, by the way?"

A gloom fell over him. "She died when I was a baby."

"I'm sorry. I am in complete ignorance of your background, of course. But that reminds me. . . . A letter for you from Council Bluffs arrived a few days ago. I must go now but I will have one of the servants bring the letter, and I'll be back to see you again tomorrow. . . . "

ii

The letter was from Jere:

Dear Paul,

I am sorry if my writing is hard to make out, but I am not quite up to myself these days. Being a doctor, it is hard to get used to feeling like one of my own patients, but I fear that is the truth. It is not my wish to start this off with bad news, but I think it better to get down some of the things I think you would want to know before my strength gives out, as I tire easily. What is wrong with me I can only guess, though I am convinced it is nothing that my poor medical talents can cure. I doubt that any doctor in the world, no matter how great, could benefit me.

I spend most of my time at home now, much of it in bed resting. I regret to admit that whiskey has become the sedative that seems most beneficial. Meanwhile some of my neglected patients have been drifting away—where to, I can't imagine, unless it's to one of the Potawatomi Indian medicine men, as there's not another white doctor within a hundred miles. It is no great loss, since money is hard to come by and I am lucky to get payment even with dried corn, animal skins or wretched chickens.

But enough of the bad news, Paul. Your letter was welcome and the enclosed money a godsend. I am happy to know you are back in America doing so well. It makes it more difficult to ask what I most want to hear. When can you come home? I don't like writing on such a melancholy note, Paul, but I have a terrible fear if you don't come home soon I may never see you again.

I trust and hope this missive won't distress you too much, and if your present situation makes it impossible for you to visit home, please believe that I understand and more than anything else in the world want to know that you are happy and successful.

But if you are able to come, please advise me by the next post so that I shall have something to look forward to.

                              Your foster father,
                              Jeremiah

Paul's eyes were wet when he finished reading the letter.

iii

In the swaying, joggling coach, Fern Venable fumed with spiteful thoughts. They centered around her annoyance at the way that Syl had taken over the nursing of Paul. Once, when Fern had tried to help with her more experienced nursing abilities, Syl had made it very clear that Fern's help was neither required nor wanted—that she, Syl, was quite capable of supervising matters with the help of Aurora and Céleste.

Shit! It was a most unladylike word that Fern sometimes uttered silently as a release for frustrations of a magnitude almost too great to bear. For Syl—too dainty to ever touch a bedpan—to put on a pretense of being a Florence Nightingale was hypocrisy beyond belief! It was enough to make Fern feel disgusted with her own sex. Syl had put on the same kind of act with Pierre—winning most of his thanks for her devotion in nursing him on the boat when it was really she and Aurora who had performed all the dirty work while Syl provided nothing but her smiles and damnable charm.

That it was an irrational jealousy Fern was feeling she would not concede even to herself. No man could affect her that strongly!

But Syl probably thought so. A number of times Syl had teased her about her apparent interest in Paul, and quite likely she derived a certain pleasure from proving how easily she could take Paul away from her.

Well, she too could play *that* game! Not on Syl's terms, but on her own. Of one thing Fern was supremely convinced: that she possessed in abundance the one ultimate quality that no man could resist—pure sexuality. Whereas Syl was only a beautiful package—empty inside.

Fern allowed herself to smile. Her own bold, honest approach to sex was such that Syl—or any woman she'd ever known—could not compete. She could, if she wished, lure and capture almost any man in the chains of her sensuality.

She would take Paul again, she decided, make a point of *flaunting* her physical conquest so that Syl would know—and then drop him back in Syl's lap. If she still wanted him. . . .

"Miz Fern," said Aurora, who was seated on the back seat of the coach with Fern, "I sure wish you could see dat man. You swoon, I do swear!"

Fern laughed. "All you've been chattering about is 'that man.' I do hope you're not going to be disappointed, but please try to be realistic about it, Aurora. After all, you've never met him—he's never even seen you—and the chances of ever meeting are, well . . . to be truthful, hardly likely."

"Oh, it goin' be likely, Miz Fern. It goin' happen. Soon's after I git my love fetish from Momselle Delphine."

Fern smiled tolerantly. Aurora was absolutely certain that she and "dat man" were destined for each other and that God would somehow manage to get them together. However, with God so busy with other problems, Aurora was anxious to hurry things along with help from the conjure woman. Momselle Delphine's amulets and love fetishes never failed. Many an indifferent swain turned suddenly into an ardent lover after Momselle, for a fee, used her magic to open his eyes to the one who desired him. Some said it was only because the reluctant lover, once he knew that the powerful Momselle was interceding on behalf of the hopeful female, became too terrified of her voodoo powers to offer resistance and gladly succumbed to charms that heretofore he had overlooked.

The ostensible reason for this carriage trip was Fern's pretext of wanting to shop for dress material in the tiny village of Five Corners. Her real reason was to visit Momselle Delphine—but for a purpose far different from Aurora's. . . .

"All I'm trying to caution you about, Aurora, is that even if Momselle succeeds in this . . . miracle of bringing about the impossible—making your Zambullah aware of your existence and fired with a passion to become your man—your chances of getting together are hardly likely because his owner and your owner won't let it happen."

"But *you* can make it happen, Miz Fern."

"Me? How?"

"Help him escape in nex' buncha slaves you send North. I run off with 'im."

"But this man is just in from Africa—he probably doesn't

know a word of English. My rule is that I can help only those who speak enough English so that they can adjust to new surroundings in the North."

"He learn quick! I promise. I learn him my goodest English."

Fern shook her head sadly. "There are other reasons, Aurora. You're too inexperienced to understand. Infatuations always doom one to disappointment—take my word for it —and I don't want to see you get hurt as I have been. The really attractive men never belong to any one woman— they're too selfish. A man like the one you describe will only break your heart."

"But it my heart, Miz Fern! Lemme break it my own way!"

Fern sighed and didn't answer. None was required. How wonderful it would be, she thought wistfully, if love could really be as simple as Aurora believed it to be.

"Miz Fern—" Aurora called out. "We here! The rest the way jus' a li'l walk. . . . "

iv

The narrow road through the woods had come to a dead end. None but the initiated would have dreamed that any human habitation could exist beyond this point, because ahead was only the soggy fringe of swamp.

Leaving the driver, Jehu, behind with the carriage, Fern and Aurora set out. They had worn old boots for the purpose and for the first hundred yards had to hold their skirts up to wade through ankle-deep greenish-scummed water. Around them were the great writhing roots of giant moss-bearded cypresses that soared massively to shut out the sky. Now and then long-legged herons in the shallows ahead of them were startled into ungainly flight. Occasionally a snake skimmed over the water or went winding sinuously up tree trunks and branches. Fern was cautious, but Aurora was utterly unafraid. Momselle's magic pervaded all the wildlife through here and would protect them.

Momselle Delphine's shack, erected several feet above the water level on boards nailed to roots within a quadrangle of cypress trees, was an architectural impossibility. A monstrosity of warped boards, jagged strips of tin and patches of old canvas fitted together piecemeal, overlapping, comprised the walls and roof. A pathway of rotting boards placed over elevated roots led the last hundred feet or so to a rough stairway up to the door, which was a ragged blanket hanging from a crossbar above a lopsided opening. Hooked over a pole thrusting above the roof was the bleached white skull of a horse—the symbol of her witchcraft powers.

Inside the lighting was murky. Dried plants, roots, leaves and indefinable smelly objects hung in such profusion from the ceiling that Fern had to duck her head and weave about to approach the conjure woman. She was in her usual position at the rear of the shack seated crosslegged on the floor sorting through a pile of miscellaneous items heaped in front of her.

Momselle was reputed to be one hundred and four years old—and looked every bit of it. Her skeleton-thin body was garbed in several layers of drab, colorless dresses that hung from her frail shoulders as from a scarecrow. Her face was as wizened and wrinkled as a dried prune, and about the same color, and above that cottony white hair frizzed out like a halo. Her toothless blue gums munched steadily on a cud of something that now and then leaked dribbles of greenish-brown spittle down over a shriveled chin. She stank in an indefinable, moldy way.

As far as was known, she belonged to nobody. At least no planter cared to claim her. Too old to work, she would be just another mouth to feed. Her shack was on Pierre's land, and he knew about it but didn't mind. He was one of the few planters who made no attempt to suppress the voodoo cult, reasoning that it was an impossibility to stamp out anyway so he might better benefit by whatever goodwill might be won by his indulgence.

Aurora kneeled in front of the crone, at the same time placing a basket of foodstuffs from Pierre's pantry on the floor near the conjure woman. Momselle continued pawing through the assortment on her lap, which included little dried snakes, several dead toads, broken bits of colored glass, a bent horseshoe nail and a collection of leaves and roots. After a while she looked up.

"What do you want, girl?"

Aurora held out a small bottle which contained a little of her menstrual fluid, for she knew all about the ritual. It would take but a drop of the fluid to be touched against the man of her desires, in a way which Momselle would contrive, and the proper contact would be made. As she handed the bottle to the old woman, Aurora burst into a spate of im-

passioned Creole patois, pleading and wringing her hands
pitifully.

Momselle peered and poked around in the gift basket, and,
apparently satisfied, reached for a bag at her side to with-
draw two sewing needles, some yellow wool and a few pieces
of leather. Holding the two needles together, eye against
point, she bound them tightly with threads of the yellow
wool, after which she wrapped them with a layer of medicine
leaves from yet another bag. This she wrapped in an oblong
of leather already cut to proper size, and with another needle
deftly stitched it tight, then handed it to Aurora, who took
it eagerly. The amulet was to be worn around her neck night
and day, and she was to pray silently to the love gods several
times daily to make it work. Aurora was ecstatic.

And now Fern got around to the reason for her visit.
Walking close, she dropped a handful of silver coins in the
old woman's lap.

"The next boat will leave one week from tonight, Momselle, and we can carry one dozen of your people on this
trip. They are to meet under the same big cypress at the bend
of the river before midnight."

Momselle nodded. The message would travel rapidly. The
conjure woman had endless ways of communication, and
there wasn't a slave on any of the plantations who wouldn't
jump to do her bidding. It had been one of Fern's biggest
successes, enlisting the powerful old woman in her cause with
the help of some of her black friends. Fern had originally
hoped that Paul Abbott might serve as a message center
through his infirmary contacts with the slaves, but his refusal
had forced her to seek another method, and the conjure
woman was the perfect solution.

As they were leaving, the cracked old voice called after
them:

"White girl—"

Fern turned and saw a bony finger pointing, the toothless
mouth grinning at her.

"You are foolish, white girl. One day the swamp will eat
you." With that, Momselle broke into cackling laughter that
to Fern's ears sounded more like a death rattle than amusement.

She went out feeling chilled to the bone.

v

The cinchona quelled recurrences of Paul's fever, and within another week he was up and around. But instead of feeling the usual euphoria of recovery from sickness, he was filled with a sadness he could not dispel. Jere was dying.

He had at once answered Jere's letter to say he would return soon, then announced to Syl that because of the illness of his foster father he would have to leave for Council Bluffs as soon as he was able to travel.

On the day before his departure Syl came to say that Pierre wished him to join them that evening for a farewell dinner.

"Why doesn't Pierre come and invite me personally?"

"I think Pierre has too much pride to admit he's wrong, even when in his own heart he knows he's made a mistake. And there's another reason—"

"I don't need any more reasons. . . . " He had in fact had much time to think about matters during his recovery in bed, and it shamed him. He owed his freedom and much more to Pierre. What an ungrateful wretch Pierre must think him to be!

"In that case," said Syl, tossing her head as if piqued, "I'll say nothing more. . . . "

"Please forgive my careless words—I want very much to hear the other reason."

"I would feel terribly hurt if on your last evening here you cared so little about my company that—"

"But Syl, there's nothing more in the world that I would rather do than be with—" He broke off, wanting to pour out words of love, but he didn't dare.

She seemed to sense his intensity and backed away a bit, as if fearful of passion.

"Then we'll be expecting you at the manor at about seven. . . . "

vi

The dinner was as lavish and elegant as the last time Paul had dined in the manor. As Syl had predicted, Pierre's manner toward Paul was as cordial as if angry words had never been spoken.

Only one thing flawed the evening: Fern's friend Jason Moore was also a dinner guest, introduced to Paul as a cotton and sugar broker from the North.

During the dinner Moore dominated the conversation. Although it relieved some of the constraint for Paul, it also irritated him, because obviously the man was doing all possible to win over Pierre by presenting himself as a very pro-Southern type of Yankee, as one whose sympathies lay with the planters. This was the same man Fern had once revealed as part of her Underground Railroad organization. The deceit, the dishonesty of his pretense, galled Paul and kindled his anger toward Fern for bringing a virtual enemy into Pierre's household.

"However critical you may be of our populist-controlled Congress," Moore was saying to Pierre, "you will at least have to concede that they have taken all steps possible to protect your property rights. I refer specifically, sir, to the Fugitive Slave Act."

His reference was to a stringent federal law passed in 1850 that guaranteed slaveholders' property rights over their slaves by allowing them to follow escapee slaves into any part of the United States and bring them back, just as they would if it were a horse or money that had been stolen.

"I concede nothing of the sort," Pierre said tartly. "It is only proper that the rights of Southerners to recover property for which they have paid good money should be recognized and upheld by law. But in actuality the law has turned out to be quite different from its intended purpose—almost useless in fact—and has done a great deal of damage in other ways."

"Damage, sir?" Moore's eyebrows lifted. "I had thought that all Southerners were heartily in favor of its provisions."

"Apparently you have listened to a few misled or unthinking Southerners. The truth is that this federal law—this monstrosity of legislation—has submerged the whole issue of States' Rights. Here we are caught in the peculiar position of having supported a piece of legislation which is successful only in enlarging the powers of the federal government! It is true that many Southerners, in the urgency of our contest with the detestable abolitionists of the North, have lost sight of the larger principle we have been battling for. Only the blindest of Southerners fail to see that we have gained nothing but an elusive triumph when we permit the federal government to assume a power not even conferred by the instrument of its creation—our Constitution."

"I had assumed that all planters were pleased to have the federally guaranteed right of ownership of escaped slaves—"

"As for recovery of escaped slaves, experience shows that it is impractical. Payments to bounty hunters, the expense of bringing them back, the wasted time, make the whole effort virtually worthless. Meanwhile the federal government con-

tinues its intervention in Southern affairs and nibbles away
at our own self-determination." Anger was beginning to flush
Pierre's face.

A chord of music disrupted the conversation. Fern had
taken it on herself to break the growing tension by going to
the new pianoforte, a beautiful instrument handmade by a
Mr. Henry Englehardt Steinway and his sons. Syl had purchased it in New York and it had only recently arrived.

"I dedicate this little ditty to you, Pierre, but I'll have to
make it up as I go—" In a bright, sweet voice she began
singing:

> "Ça ira, ça ira,
> Les aristocrates à la lanterne—"

Pierre laughed uproariously. "You ungrateful vixen—trying your impossible French on me like that! I don't deserve
such punishment."

Getting up from the piano, Fern danced over to him and
kissed him lightly on the cheek. "All I wanted was to get a
smile out of you, Pierre. . . . "

The dinner ended on a more relaxed note. Pierre was the
first to rise.

"If you will all excuse me, I would like to have a little chat
alone with Paul in the library. . . . "

In the library both men ordered brandy from the servant
who hovered near. Pierre extended a box of his fine cigars
to Paul, who took one. Pierre waited until he had lighted
his cigar and was puffing contentedly before speaking:

"I trust, Paul, that our friendship is mended."

"As far as I'm concerned, it was never damaged."

"I hoped that was the case. Now about your trip to Council
Bluffs—I was distressed to hear of your foster parent's ill-
ness and offer my heartfelt wishes for his speedy recovery.
In any event, I am counting on your eventual return to Les
Cypres."

"I hadn't really planned that far ahead, Pierre."

"Then let me help your planning. I am fully aware of your
dreams, Paul—Syl made mention of your desire, ultimately,
to do research in medicine. I applaud such ambitions and am
prepared to help. I have in mind the construction of a small
infirmary and clinical laboratory on the plantation. It would
be built of the finest materials designed to your specifications,
stocked with all the medicaments you need and equipped with

the most modern medical paraphernalia. All I request in exchange is your return and resumption of the responsibility of handling medical problems in the Triangle."

Paul was deeply touched. Pierre's generosity knew no bounds.

"There's no need to go to all that expense," he said. "The present infirmary, with some improvements and new equipment will do me fine. In any case I promise to come back as soon as I can."

"Splendid! Then I shall look forward to your early return." Rising from his chair, Pierre walked over with his left hand extended. "Now that we are in agreement, I'll bid you *au revoir*. I wish to retire early, as I plan a trip to New Orleans tomorrow. Godspeed to you, Paul, and I pray that under your expert care your foster father will soon be well. . . . "

As Paul was somewhat clumsily shaking Pierre's left hand, the disconcerting thought flashed through his head that Pierre's New Orleans trip was probably for the purpose of seeing Micaela. The secret knowledge that he carried troubled him greatly. He had debated with himself as to whether he should speak out about it. But since he had not found out until it was too late, after Micaela had already become her brother's mistress, he felt it was now impossible. It could be devastating to both of them.

In the living room he found Syl alone.

"Mr. Moore asked me to convey his apologies for leaving without saying goodbye," she said, "but he had urgent business matters to attend to. And Fern came down with a sudden headache. . . . "

Paul ignored what Fern probably intended as a snub. "As a matter of fact, I too will have to leave early, as I have much packing to do."

Syl rose from her chair. "I'll accompany you to the door."

To his surprise she accompanied him out onto the moonlit gallery.

"By the way," she said, "I sent one of the servants over to your cottage with a parting gift."

"Syl, your generosity—and Pierre's—overwhelms me. I have done so little to warrant it."

"Nonsense. You have done so much for us both, and the gift it but a token of our regard." She strolled ahead in the darkness and turned, leaning against one of the great pillars.

"But such talk is trivial," she went on, "since this will

probably be the last time we see each other for heaven only knows how long. . . . "

He approached, almost feeling her nearness in the muffled moonlight. The soft night breeze was rich with the scents of jasmine and her delicate perfume.

"Syl—you know how inarticulate I am—"

"There's no need to talk, Paul. You already told me much more than you realize while you were in fever, in delirium. . . . "

Remembering bits of his erotic, fevered visions, he was grateful for the darkness that masked his flush.

"But I'd rather say it while I'm in full command of my senses."

Her luminous eyes and lips smiled up at him. "Then why don't you?"

"Syl—" The words that were to follow choked in his throat; they were the hardest words he would ever speak, and the first time he had ever uttered them:

"I love you. . . . "

Inexplicably, tears sprang to her eyes. Swiftly her hands drew his head down to kiss him briefly on the lips before running lightly to the door. There she turned and added:

"Paul, please write. . . . "

vii

The wrappings fell away and he stared entranced at the beautiful case of fine polished wood. On his return from the manor he had found it on the living room table handsomely wrapped, with an attached card on which was written: *"For Paul—may this be a first step toward the glorious future you have envisioned. Affectionately, Syl."*

With eager fingers he undid the latch and folded back the top. Inside, encased in a velveteen lining, was the most magnificent microscope he had ever seen.

It was of the finest German manufacture, of the highest power, the most versatile instrument of its kind currently available.

What a lavish gift! So she hadn't forgotten their conversation that night at the Grand Bal Paré about his dream of doing medical research. The costly gift could open up whole new worlds for him, help him delve into the hidden mysteries of bacteria and baffling diseases. He had been unfair to think of Syl as too superficial, too insensitive to doctors and those who were not a part of her privileged world.

His absorption in his new acquisition was broken off by a rapping on the door. He went over and opened it. Fern Venable was standing outside.

"May I come in, Paul?"

He frowned. "I thought you had a headache?"

"I feigned that to get rid of Jason—and to give me a chance to slip over here without being seen." Without waiting for an invitation, she stepped inside.

"It's a bit late, Fern, and I'm very busy—"

She looked at him steadily. "You're really angry at me, aren't you?"

"Disgusted would be a more appropriate word."

Her eyes flared. "Because of Jason Moore?"

"Because of your complete lack of ethics. How in the world could you find the gall to bring a co-conspirator to dinner as a guest to be showered with hospitality by the very people you plan to rob?"

"You don't understand—you don't understand at all!"

"I understand only too well that you've betrayed and continue to betray Syl and Pierre, who trust you implicitly."

"But such trust is absolutely *essential* to my work! I admit it's shameful that I must lie—it's an evil, but a smaller evil and a necessary one to help cure the much larger evil, the horrible evil of enslaved humans. It's no different or worse than being a spy for your country. Any means I am forced to use against a few is more than justified by the greater good achieved for everybody."

"For everybody? Aren't you excluding fine people like Syl and Pierre from that greater good?"

"Oh, you're so blind, Paul! You can't see the forest for the trees! You have no real compassion for the blacks."

Stung, he lashed back: "You're the one who doesn't understand compassion! Compassion should be for everybody—for whites as well as blacks; for red people or yellow or any other color. Perhaps I can't prove that compassion for black people is involved in my medical treatment of them, since I am being paid for it, but neither do your thieving activities prove that *you* have any."

She stared at him with hurt eyes. "I keep making the same mistake. Words are a trap. There's only one way you and I can really communicate. . . . "

She started unbuttoning her blouse. She wasn't wearing

a camisole under it. The blouse slid away from her shoulders, exposing naked breasts.

His gaze slid to the breasts, their ruby tips standing out. Her brown eyes were burning and she began unfastening her skirt. He felt the familiar *frisson* in his loins. It took a tremendous effort to speak:

"No, Fern—" Feeling a strange sense of sorrow, he walked over and pulled her blouse back up around her shoulders. "It wouldn't be good—for either of us. . . . "

Her eyes hardened.

"It's Syl, isn't it? She's got you hypnotized! And she's a nothing—*nothing* when it comes to knowing how to please a man!"

"There's no need to be insulting."

"Insulting? I haven't even begun to tell you the contempt I suddenly feel for you, Paul, but this might give you the idea—!"

Leaning close, she spat full in his face. Then twisting away from him like an outraged cat, tail lashing, she gave him a look of virulent hatred. Her voice was iced venom:

"You're going to rue this, Paul. I always even the score. . . . "

Whirling, she went to the door and out into the night, leaving him sick at heart, her spittle still burning on his face.

BOOK FIVE

Council Bluffs

ONE: King of the Mountain Men

IN the spring of 1855, a man garbed in the worn, fringed buckskins of a frontiersman rode a fine chestnut horse up a winding trail toward an Indian encampment on the bluffs overlooking the Neosho River in lower Kansas. The astonished eyes of two Indian sentries, observing his approach over the sights of their rifles, noted that the rider was not armed, nor did he display any sign of fear or caution.

Who was this white man who dared ride so openly under the very noses of the great chief Half-Horse and his band of braves? Did not any fool know that they raided and robbed farms, and killed as many of the hated whites as possible? His dress and easy manner of riding showed he was not a stupid farmer. An advance scout for the yellow-leg soldiers? A trapper? What was it that he carried folded over one shoulder?

One of the sentries lifted his "looking glass," which had been taken from one of the yellow-legs years ago, along with his scalp, and peered through it.

Hoeee—it was a white animal skin folded over the rider's shoulder—the hide of the sacred white buffalo!

The sentry hastened away to inform Chief Half-Horse.

ii

The buckskin-clad man rode slowly past the first row of tepees, unchallenged except by a few yapping mongrels. Here and there young braves stared at him in open hostility. A fat squaw engaged in cutting long thin strips of red meat from the suspended carcass of a deer paused in her work to gaze expressionlessly. A young squaw beside her unconsciously lifted a hand to primp at her hair. There was something about the looks and bearing of the rider with the stabbing blue eyes that had always turned the heads of females and gave subtle warning to men.

Christopher (Kit) Carson, at forty-six, was still as lithe and muscular as he had ever been, and his light brown hair was untouched by gray. Although below average height— even termed by his tall father "the runt of the litter" in a large family of strapping big brothers and buxom sisters—Kit Carson had grown a giant reputation during his past thirty years as a hunter, trapper, guide for exploring parties, army scout and Indian fighter in the great Southwest. Known everywhere as the "king of the mountain men," Carson could neither read nor write, except to scrawl his signature. Yet he had been on speaking terms with Presidents James Polk and Zachary Taylor, and had, in fact, recently returned from a conference in Washington with the current president, Franklin Pierce, and Secretary of War Jefferson Davis concerning the Indian wars.

But his present mission was a personal matter, something he felt he owed to the memory of his favorite older sister, Elizabeth Ann Carson Dixon, who in 1831 had vanished somewhere in the wilds of the Missouri-Kansas Territory. The trail had been long, and by necessity followed only during brief periods of respite in his action-packed life, but now the end was in sight. . . .

Chief Half-Horse and his council of warriors came out to greet him. The chief, a Sioux, had been banished from his tribe years ago by a more powerful rival chief because of

Half-Horse's raids on palefaces at a time when the Sioux were under solemn agreement to aid the whites in bitter fights against their mutual enemy, the Sacs, during the Black Hawk War. Since then he had collected an outlaw band of about a hundred outcasts from various tribes to continue warfare against palefaces who had usurped their ancestral lands.

They sat in a circle around a fire while the chief took out the peace pipe, which had a long stem of hollowed willow and a bowl of clay decorated with colorful paints and feathers. He held it over the glowing coals. When it ignited, he puffed on it deeply and passed it to Carson, who puffed on the pipe gently and offered it to the next man. After it had gone full-circle back to the chief, Carson produced a bottle of whiskey. Although a nondrinker, he opened it, wiped the lip in the approved fashion with a circular motion of his hand, and tilted it to wet his mouth before handing it to the chief. Half-Horse also wiped the lip, took a long generous swallow and passed it to a brave.

"Good firewater," he said.

"I have come in friendship. It would be an insult to bring cheap whiskey unless I could get none better."

"Kit Carson's friendship is welcome."

"The chief's eyes see well indeed to know who I am."

"It is known by all the tribes across the plains that only Kit Carson among all the palefaces possesses a robe of the sacred white buffalo." The chief's eyes had a covetous gleam as he admired the skin over Carson's shoulder. "Tribute to your prowess as a mighty hunter and fighter is heard in many tepees. It is said that no Indian can follow a trail better or is braver in battle. Even the Apaches admit this. It is also known that unlike most palefaces, Kit Carson does not speak with a forked tongue."

"The chief is generous with his words. I too have heard much about the prowess of Chief Half-Horse and his brave warriors. It is an honor to sit here with my red brothers and talk in peace."

The bottle had again returned to the chief. He took a long deep swallow. Then:

"What is it you seek from us?"

"I seek information about my sister, who was of a party of three wagons that were ambushed near the Little Sioux River about twenty-four years ago. All were killed except for one small child. I have no hate in my heart for acts of warfare that happened long ago, but wish only to know if the child was that of my sister."

"What you ask would not be possible for me to know."

"There were scalps taken. I would know the hair of my sister. Books of the white man's powerful religion were taken. My sister's Bible has my name written in it, and the name of her child."

The face of the chief, who looked to be past sixty, was expressionless as graven stone.

"I have led many attacks, taken many scalps, but I am no longer young. My memory does not serve me well after so many moons have passed. I remember nothing of what you speak."

Carson knew he was lying. He had never met an Indian without an excellent memory. He had researched the massacre as thoroughly as any detective. Lizzie's last letter to a sister in 1831 gave her last point of departure into the Territory. Records at the nearest army post, Fort Atkinson, provided a report on the three-wagon massacre. He had queried Hank Talbot, head scout of the discovery party, and had gotten nothing but opinions. Dr. Jeremiah Abbott, foster father of the surviving infant, knew even less. But the fact that the foster son was now grown up and studying to be a surgeon in Scotland was of much interest to Carson. Could he possibly be Lizzie's offspring?

It was the Indians who provided the best clues. From Chief Keokuk of the Sacs, from the Sioux Chief Inkpaduta, from the Mandans, Crows and Fox, he gathered the threads of information that pieced together—conclusively—all the evidence pointing to Half-Horse.

"Yet it is possible," said Carson, "that my memory would be better than yours in respect to my sister. Her hair was of a glossy brown with a sheen of red. I would recognize it instantly. In exchange for her scalp and the Bible, I am prepared to give this—" He took the white buffalo robe from his shoulder and spread it over his knees.

The chief's eyes gleamed greedily. The albino buffalo was one of the rarest of animals. Chief Half-Horse, like most Indians, had never seen one. Their skins hung in the tepees of only the most powerful chiefs, who were thereby protected by the Great Spirit and assured that after death their own spirit would enter the happy hunting grounds.

Half-Horse slowly rose. "Come with me to my tepee. . . ."

iii

Less than an hour later, Kit Carson rode out of the village with a scalp and a Bible in his saddlebag. He was heavy with sorrow. Lizzie had been his favorite sister. Though he had not expected better, the grim finale was hard to bear.

But the long search into the past had not been in vain. Inscribed in the front of Lizzie's Bible was the name and birthdate of her only child, Paul, now proved to be the one who had survived.

When asked why he had spared the infant, Half-Horse had answered:

"I was weak. In my own tepee was a son of about the same age, the joy of my life, and the white man's book of the Great Spirit was wedged under the cover of the trunk where the white child was hidden to protect him. Now my son is dead—murdered by the palefaces. Had I known the future, I would have killed the white child."

The scalp and Bible, Carson decided, would be turned over to Dr. Jeremiah Abbott, with instructions to give them to Dr. Paul Abbott—whose real name was Paul Carson Dixon— when he returned from Scotland.

It would have pleased Lizzie to know that her son had grown up to become a real doctor.

Kit Carson hoped someday to meet his nephew.

TWO: Jere

P AUL walked with misgivings toward the cottage. There was a general air of dilapidation about the old homestead. Tufts of grass erupted here and there amid the graveled path, and bordering clumps of Sweet William were in battle with encroaching prairie weeds. Close to the home itself, which was of native split cottonwood, a thick growth of old clinging woodbine reached up to obscure portions of the windows.

Even the unpainted door squeaked on neglected hinges when it opened to his knock.

The lank old man who stood in the opening was almost as tall as Paul, but because of stooped shoulders seemed much shorter. Frowsy gray hair encircled the mostly bald dome, and the sunken cheeks of the once weather-reddened face were now pale, splotched with large brownish liver marks. His dark frock coat and trousers were threadbare in spots, the shirt would never again look completely white, the black string tie hung as limply and dismal as its wearer. He peered up through rimless spectacles perched on his nose.

"Can I help you, sir?"

A mist gathered in Paul's eyes. His voice was thick:

"Jere, it's me—Paul. . . . "

He had an impulse to embrace the old fellow who for so long he had been longing to see. In Louisiana among the Creoles and perhaps in many other parts of the world, it would be considered normal for men to embrace after a long absence. But he knew Jere would be horrified.

Jere continued to stare as if he hadn't heard, or as if not believing that this well-dressed young man was really the same raw backwoods boy who had left some four and a half years ago. Then the old man's withered face convulsed in a frown. Or was it fear?

"You can't come in here, Paul—! Go! Go quickly!"

For a moment Paul stared back in stunned silence. Jere's mind was addled! Perhaps it was his sickness. He noted now the slightly yellowish tinge of his pale skin, the translucent look of faded parchment, and recognized it at once—the dread disease that no doctor could help, cancer in an advanced stage that may have reached the brain.

"I'm coming in anyway. . . . " He pushed in past the feebly protesting old man. He had come from the steamboat landing in a hired dray for the two miles to Jere's place. His luggage was still out by the road where it had been unloaded, but that could wait.

The smallish living room had the same faded brown carpet he remembered from boyhood days. The rough table of ax-hewn boards, the chairs with seats of wickerwork woven by a Potawatomi squaw, were the same. In the adjacent kitchen he could hear sounds of pots rattling. At least the old fellow had a housekeeper. He swung around to face his foster father.

"Now tell me what it's all about, Jere."

Jere blinked. Tears swam in his eyes.

"They're waitin' to arrest you, Paul! Maybe it was my fault for braggin' that you were comin' back from Scotland. Loy Stringer—he's the town sheriff now—heard about it. Claims he's got a 'wanted' circular for your arrest that was sent here all the way from England 'cause this is your home town. Loy's been boastin' around that he's fixin' to put the cuffs on you the moment you hit town."

Loy Stringer was an old enemy, a bully that Paul had once beaten up ferociously for attempting to rape Deerfoot's young sister. Loy was the kind who would never forget, never overlook an opportunity for revenge.

Paul took a deep breath, made his decision.

"The charge isn't true, Jere. In any case, I'm not running. If I did, I'd be running all my life. Right now I'm going out to bring in my bags—"

"No need. If you're of a mind to stay, Kahkomi will get 'em." Jere raised his voice: "Kahkomi! Go out an' fetch in my son's duffle!"

Kahkomi was a fat but comely squaw wearing a black dress and moccasins. She waddled into the living room without a glance at Paul—frontier etiquette didn't require an introduction—and went outside.

"Don't know what I'd do without her," said Jere. "Her husband died, an' not having any particular place to go, she figured she owed it to me to come work for me, since for years I treated most of her family without takin' any money in return. 'Course it's rumored around that I took in a squaw woman to replace Sarah. . . . " He shrugged and forced a sour grin. "Would likely be the truth, too, if I was still up to it. Fact is, even with Sarah, years back, I had trouble tryin' to satisfy her once a fortnight or so. Couldn't hardly blame her for runnin' off. . . . " A tremble had come to his voice. A gnarled hand wiped at his eyes.

Paul sought to change the subject. "How are you keeping up with your patients these days, Jere?"

"Can't say I'm exactly overworked. . . . But before we go on gabbin' like this, let me round us up a couple drinks. Got no choice but plain whiskey, I'm afraid."

"Suits me fine."

Jere got two tumblers and a bottle from the kitchen. Meanwhile, Kahkomi came waddling in with some of the luggage.

"Fact is," Jere said, handing Paul a half-filled tumbler, "I've given up my rounds. Got to be too much for me. Only take patients able to come to me."

Paul took a sip from his glass. The cheap raw whiskey burned down his throat.

"But there's not another doctor within a hundred miles.

What will folks too sick to travel do if there's no doctor to come to them?"

Jere shrugged. "What they always did before doctors came along, I reckon. Pray and hope for the best. 'Course I was figuring you might take over when you came back. Now I see I figured wrong. You look like you been doin' all right for yourself, what with all those fancy duds, the money you sent me. . . . Truth is, Paul, you'd be a fool to come back here, when you don't have to, and work for next to nothing. And don't you go worryin' about the folks back there in the woods. I'll tell you plain, you can ride your ass off tryin' to save a life and be lucky to get so much as a 'thank you.' Most of them, any cash they get goes first for booze and geegaws. 'Tain't worth it, Paul. You go back to wherever you were and stay where the money is."

"Nevertheless, I've decided to stay here."

Jere's tired old eyes showed a momentary flare of anger. "You're an even bigger fool than I figured, Paul. With any sense you'd be out in the barn saddlin' up one of the horses to hightail it the hell out of here while you still can—if it ain't already too late. Loy Stringer could be ridin' out here to arrest you this very minute."

"I'll worry about that when the time comes. At the moment, I'm less concerned about Loy Stringer than I am about you. What would you do if I left now?"

Jere's shoulders slumped. "I can manage. Always have."

"For how much longer?"

"Long as the Lord intends it, I reckon. A man gets used up, he lays back and dies."

"A man shouldn't be thinking of dying before his time."

"Dammit, Paul—let's be honest with each other! You know and I know what's wrong with me—any fool quack could take one look and make the right diagnosis. I don't have much time left in this world."

"Jere," Paul said softly, "nobody really knows enough about the disease to predict how much time you have. It could be many more good years."

Jere snorted. "Can't exactly recall I ever had many good years in the past and got no reason to expect any in the future."

"Jere, the important thing is that you're still alive. You can still walk. You've still got your doctor's knowledge and skills that took many long years to acquire. And there are lots of people around who need that kind of help."

"Why should I give a damn about them? Most of them aren't worth two beans in a pisspot. Nobody gives a damn about me facing the last sunset, except maybe you. So why should I give a damn about other people expectin' me to cure them when I can't even cure myself?"

Paul was making another diagnosis that went beyond bodily sickness into an area of medicine not yet explored by any doctor, as far as he knew—the trackless jungle of the mind. Jere's primary ailment was physical—there was no denying that—but what made it unbearably worse was sickness in the brain. His thinking was warped. He had lost his sense of worth. He felt his skills were unappreciated, that most of his life—often fogged with alcohol—had been wasted, and probably was haunted with the specters of past failures. How did one go about giving him back a true sense of values?

"Forget the ignorant people who don't appreciate or pay for your doctoring, Jere. Help them anyway—if not for their sake, then for your own. Maybe you'll never get any rewards in money or thanks, but you'll be doing what God put you on earth to do. You'll be able to hold your head high until that moment when you have no more to give."

Jere took a swallow of booze and lowered his head. "Ain't got it anymore, Paul. Lost my balls when Sarah left me. . . ."

"I refuse to accept that, Jere! That's water under the bridge. We can't change what happened yesterday, but we can sure as hell make a good try at deciding on tomorrow. Remember the days when you used to yank me out of bed at five in the morning to go on the rounds with you? Well, now it's my turn. Tomorrow we're starting on the rounds again, and I'll be yanking *you* out of bed at five to go with me—"

Outside, a fast staccato of hoofbeats was approaching. Jere got up and hurried to a window. The hoofbeats stopped.

"Could be Loy. . . ." Jere muttered.

The door pushed open and Kahkomi came in.

"Stover boy outside," she said indifferently. "He say his mama goin' die. . . ."

ii

Lenny Stover, a lad of about fifteen, led the way on an old plowhorse over unfenced prairie land. Paul, with a sour-faced Jere riding beside him, followed. It was about an hour's ride to the cabin, Lenny had said, where his mother was in bad pain, afraid she was dying because she was supposed to have a baby that was already two months overdue. She complained it was growing so big it would never come out. She would have sent for him sooner, but her husband didn't believe in doctors. Said only God should decide when and how a baby was to be born. But now Lenny's father was away setting out a new trap line and would be gone overnight, so she'd sent Lenny in for Dr. Abbott because she knew she'd die soon without help.

For a while they followed the old river trail that was so familiar to Paul, except that now it had grown to be almost a road, hard-packed by countless iron-rimmed wagon wheels. Then, at a point where the river sprawled into wide shallows— the same place where as a boy Paul used to come with Deerfoot to pick off a half-dozen or more of the plump ducks that used to collect there in the spring—they rode down the bank and forded the shallow water. Beyond that was deep woods. Another fifteen minutes of riding brought them to the small, two-room cabin.

iii

Elcene Stover, not yet forty but looking past fifty, was the mother of four sons and two daughters. She had delivered them with relative ease, without help from a doctor, and had then considered her childbearing obligations to God and her husband finished for this lifetime. Thus her latest pregnancy had dismayed her, though it had pleased her husband Earl, whose own sense of worth and future security was increased by the numbers of sons he could produce. It was like no other pregnancy she had ever had, she told Jere and Paul, because it felt different. She couldn't feel any life stirring inside, yet it kept growing, and hurting. . . .

"What do you think, Jere?" Paul said, after their first brief examination of the woman, who was lying fully clothed on a bed in the only bedroom. In her eyes it was not seemly for any man other than her husband, even a doctor, to see her in a nightgown.

"I'm afraid it's not what she thinks it is," said Jere.

Paul had known at once that it wasn't a pregnancy, but wanted Jere to say so first to avoid offending him. He turned to face Mrs. Stover. Her prematurely graying hair, once blond, hung in stringy wisps about her face. The skin was seamed with the early wrinkles of worry and weariness. Her pale blue eyes looked up at him anxiously.

"You're not pregnant, Mrs. Stover."

She nodded. "I was afeard it was somethin' worse."

"You're suffering from an ovarian tumor. A very large one."

She accepted that calmly. "How long have I got to live?"

"It's still growing. Unless it's taken out soon, it will kill you within a few more months, a year at the most."

"Kin you take it out?"

Paul hesitated. He knew of only a few attempts at such an operation, most of them failing, but it was best to offer some hope:

"I can take it out, Mrs. Stover, but it would be a very serious operation and there's no guarantee that you would recover."

"What chance you think I got?"

"I can't say. I can only say that you have but two choices: the probability of dying at once from an operation, or the absolute certainty of death a few months later without an operation."

"Kin you start now?" she said nervously. "I'd want it over with before Earl gits home, because he'd raise the roof if'n he found anything like that goin' on."

Paul glanced around at the slovenly, primitive surroundings. He couldn't risk such an operation here. Back at Jere's place they had anesthesia, a passable operating table and all the medications needed.

He told the woman this, adding: "When your husband returns, tell him what I've told you and I'm sure he'll understand it's the only chance of saving your life. Have him bring you in a day or two ahead of time when you're ready. We'll fix a bed for you and give you a sedative so we can be sure you'll have a long sleep and be well rested the night before we operate."

"I'll put my mind on it, Doctor, an' I thank ye kindly for puttin' yerself out so much. . . ."

On the ride back, Jere expressed his displeasure: "That was a damnfool waste of our time, Paul, and it was a mistake, you tellin' her what you did. You can be thankful Elcene's not fool enough to ever let us go cuttin' up her belly. If she died on the table, which in my opinion she would, we would be charged with murder."

Paul silently agreed. Perhaps it was just as well that his blunt words had thoroughly frightened the poor woman.

But both were wrong. A couple of hours after they had returned, as darkness was falling, there was a peremptory knocking on the front door.

Kahkomi opened it and Elcene Stover stood there, supporting her protruding abdomen with both hands.

"I thunk it over," she said, "an' made up my mind it's me, not Earl, who oughter have the last say over my own body."

The heroic woman, not having a wagon, had ridden all the way in on the old plowhorse with her swollen belly resting on the pommel of the saddle.

iv

At ten o'clock on the following forenoon, Elcene Stover lay on the stout wooden operating table draped with a sheet. A pillow had been placed under her head, but that did nothing to alleviate the pain and fear that paled her face. Her teeth were gritted and her eyes strained heavenward while she recited the Psalms.

Paul took a last look at the preparations: a nearby table with the muslin cone and chloroform, basins, compresses, bandages, towels, surgical instruments, the carbolic solution. Jere, looking worried, stood on the opposite side of the operating table. He and Kahkomi would help.

"We're ready, Kahkomi," Paul said. "Bring in the first pot of hot water." There would be an ample amount of that. Kahkomi had the flat top of the wood-burning range in the kitchen covered with heating kettles of water and another large one suspended over a blazing fire in the stone fireplace.

Kahkomi was long in returning, and when she did it was without water.

"Much trouble," she said gravely. "Sheriff come to get young doctor. Many people outside, much mad."

Striding from Jere's little office and operating room, which was a separate wing that had been added to the rear of the cottage, Paul went into the living room. He could now hear the ominous sounds of angry voices outside. A visit from the sheriff he had expected, and was prepared for. He had enough money left to hire the best lawyer available and had decided to take his chances in court. He couldn't keep running all his life. But why the angry crowd?

He opened the door and at once was confronted by the face of his old enemy.

Loy Stringer was little changed from the last time he'd seen him except for a thickening of flab in the jowls and beneath the chin. There was added girth in the waist, too, but the hefty figure, over six feet, looked as powerful as ever. His little porcine eyes had a mean glitter; the mouth was quirked with a nasty grin.

"You made a plumb bad mistake comin' back here, Abbott," he said lazily, and tapped a finger on the shiny star on his vest. "Now hold out your hands, quiet-like, while I put on the cuffs."

"What is the charge?"

"Wanted for a little murder in Scotland."

"That's ridiculous! I'm completely innocent, and only wanted for questioning."

Stringer's expression oozed sarcasm. "Like you're innocent of sweet-talkin' Earl's wife into comin' here so you could git under her skirt to deliver a baby?"

An angry muttering swept among the onlookers. Nothing was more jealously guarded by husbands on the frontier than the privacy of a wife's body. Deliveries of infants by doctors were almost unheard of. There were always midwives or a neighbor's wife to help. Only in the event of a crisis when it seemed that the expectant mother might die—often not even then—was a doctor sent for. In such a dire siuation the patient remained fully clothed, the skirts rolled back just enough so that the doctor could do his work without seeing an inch more than absolutely necessary.

"Mrs. Stover isn't going to have a baby," said Paul. "She's suffering from a massive tumor in her abdominal area that must be taken out—"

"He's lyin', Sheriff—" A thin man with an intensity of anger in his voice and manner hopped onto the porch. Of small stature, he had the bright, darting eyes of a fox. He wore knee-high boots, woolen pants, a deerskin jacket and a fur cap. He ranted on:

"Nobody kin tell me my Elcene ain't fixin' to have a whoppin' boy! I oughta know after havin' me four sons an' two daughters, thanks to the Almighty. Now He's blessin' me with the biggest one yet, an' He don't want no fool doctor messin' around with His work. He always took care of us good—nary any trouble. Them babies just pop outta Elcene easy as pie." He paused to point a trembling finger at Paul:

"And him a-wanting to take over the Lord's work an' turn my wife over to the devil! Effen I hadn't been off on my trap line yestiday when he come around to talk pretty to Elcene, I'd'a druv 'im off with a gun. Wasn't till I got back this mornin', my boys told me how she snuck off to come here." He turned toward the listeners around the porch and his voice rose almost to a scream:

"Effen he's harmed one hair of my wife's head, I want 'im strung up here an' now!"

There was an answering chorus of growls and mutterings. Paul overheard snatches: " . . . *butcherin' a woman*" . . . "*got her nakkid in there, too, I bet*" . . . "*any man try that with my woman, I'd kill 'im.*" Ignorance, misinformation, plus frontier sexual taboos and superstitions had made the crowd's mood ugly. And it was growing. A few riders, carriages, and some straggling along on foot were still arriving.

Forefront in the crowd was a group of tight-lipped women whose prim faces made Paul's heart quail. They had the look of churchy activists led by some fanatic. Religious fanaticism —an insult to any decent religion—sometimes added a false veneer of righteousness to the primitive emotions of a gathering of ignorant but otherwise respectable people that could transform them into an unthinking brutal mob.

Paul raised his arms for attention.

"Let me repeat—Mrs. Stover *is not* pregnant. She has an enormous ovarian tumor that will continue to grow until it kills her, unless it is taken out. I explained this to Mrs. Stover yesterday. I even warned that I couldn't guarantee that she would survive such an operation, but it was her only chance. She thought it over and came here of her own accord. Now since it was her own decision—"

"Don't matter what she said or what lies you told her!" howled Earl Stover. "I'm the one that runs my family! Nobody but me an' the Almighty got any say in the matter. Whatever's the will of the Lord, no man dast try change it."

A murmur of approval ran through the audience. Stover was speaking for every male present, upholding man's sacred right to control every thought and act of his woman.

"Nevertheless," Paul went on, "I intend to go ahead with the operation."

"Ain't gonna be none," said Loy Stringer. "Already wasted too much time puttin' you under arrest—"

"You've got no authority to arrest me for an alleged crime committed in another country!"

"This here's all the 'thority I need." Stringer's right hand slid down to the butt of his six-shooter. "Now you goin' to come easy, or do I got to—"

"Hold it, Sheriff!"

Stringer's eyes flicked toward the voice, and turning, Paul saw Jere emerge with a shotgun held at shoulder level.

"Jere—" said Paul. "Don't you get mixed up in this."

Jere ignored Paul. His old eyes, shining like blue flame, focused on Stringer.

"Make one move for that gun of yours, Loy, I'll blast your head off!"

"Jere, Jere—!"

"I got nothing to lose. I'd sooner be hung by the neck than die from what's growing inside of me, an' if I could take a skunk along with me, it'd be worth it." Jere's head swerved slightly toward the crowd as he continued:

"Most of you folks have come to me, one time or another, with broken bones, cuts, all kinds of sickness. You know I'm a fair-to-middlin' doctor, but my son Paul here, I can't hold a candle to him. He's one of the best surgeons there is, trained in the best medical college in the world. If there's anybody can save Mrs. Stover, he's the one who can do it." He paused to take a deep breath.

"I know I'm breakin' the law, holdin' a gun like this, but it would be a bigger crime—an' I figure the Almighty would agree with that—not to give Mrs. Stover a chance to live. So I want Paul to get on with the operation—an' I'm warnin' all of you, anyone tries to interfere, I'll shoot, begad!"

The uneasy, sullen silence that followed was broken by a strident female voice:

"I've heard enough to convince me—" A steely-eyed woman detached herself from the crowd and with a determined set to her jaw came briskly up the porch steps.

"Put down that gun, you old fool," she told Jere, and then ignoring the sheriff, she whirled toward Earl Stover.

"A fine husband you are!" she raged at him. "You ought to be ashamed of yourself, not caring whether or not your wife lives, and defiling the name of the Lord by saying he would condone the death of a good woman because you forbid her to go to a healer. Did he not send Jesus into the world as the Great Healer? For the likes of you, without an ounce of charity in your heart, to profess to be a man of God is worse than heresy!"

Stover hung his head. One of his boots scuffed at the porch floor, like a chastened schoolboy.

She skimmed a glance at the crowd.

"You there, Mart Doane—you come with me and we'll go in and get it straight from Elcene Stover how she feels about all this."

Mart Doane, a plump man with silvery muttonchops, and the only one present showing the affluence of a beaver, frock coat and stock, looked startled. "Now Mrs. Bloomer, this is no concern of mine."

"It better be! You're the mayor, and I'm making this a public issue. As the elected representative of the people, it's your duty to be concerned with everything affecting the good of our community. You get up here now, hear?"

Now she swiveled her wrathful face at the sheriff, who backed away a step, his whole attitude cringing with respect.

"Sheriff Stringer, while the mayor and I are inside talking to Mrs. Stover, don't you dare do any arresting, or we'll run you out of office."

"But Mrs. Bloomer—"

"You've been warned!" she snapped, and turned to enter the house while the embarrassed mayor shuffled up the steps to follow. The redoubtable Amelia Jenks Bloomer was a woman no man cared to tangle with.

She had moved into the community about a year before— the most astonishing female ever to settle in Council Bluffs— at first provoking shock and ridicule because of her garb of trouserlike pantalets gathered in ruffles just above the shoes, and over that a simple short skirt. "Her skirt reaches *scarcely to her knees!*" was a typical reaction. "Brazen" and "shameless" were other words used.

Little did the provincial citizens realize that Amelia Bloomer, thirty-seven at the time, had already won her spurs— and worldwide notoriety—for her rebellion against the domination of men, particularly in the matter of clothes. It was senseless, she had decided, for women to be forced to wear clothing so uncomfortable as sometimes actually to deform the wearer. Thus as the editor of her temperance paper, *The Lily*, published in Seneca Falls, New York, she startled the world by bringing out a full-page picture of herself in the simpler new style that gave women greater comfort and freedom of movement. Before long, women all over the world began to wear it. Even Empress Eugenie adopted the Bloomer style.

But Council Bluffs quickly came to respect Mrs. Bloomer as a sensible and sincere woman. As an activist for women's rights, she soon became one of the most powerful leaders in the state. Men quailed before her fiery words; women applauded.

Paul, watching and listening to all this, could only marvel. A man could scarcely reason with an angry crowd, yet this woman by her very presence had tamed and shamed them all.

Presently, Mrs. Bloomer emerged from the house.

"Dr. Abbott," she said, "your patient is waiting for you to begin the operation. . . . "

v

The chloroform had been administered; Elcene Stover was unconscious. The moment had come.

Lowering the razor-sharp scalpel to the taut skin of the swollen abdomen, Paul swiftly made a foot-long incision— and at once there was a crisis. Kahkomi made a hissing sound of surprise. Jere's jaw dropped open.

Mrs. Stover's intestines were spilling out.

"Quick!" said Paul. "Turn her on her side!"

While the others were rolling the patient on her side toward Paul, he worked at sponging away frothing blood, cutting, spreading aside the sprawling intestines so they would not block his view. The massive lesion filled the abdominal cavity so completely that it would be impossible to replace the intestines until the tumor was excised.

Carefully he reached in between the wet and glistening loops of pinkish, slippery alimentary ducts. His face was hot; he could feel perspiration trickling down his cheeks, but fortunately his hands were marvelously steady. Speed and delicacy would be all-important factors in minimizing the patient's postoperative battle to survive. He started cutting. . . .

vi

Twenty-six minutes later he began sewing her up. On a nearby stand was the bloodied tumor. While Kahkomi stared at it in wonder, Jere went to get the scales.

It weighed out at twenty-two pounds.

In removing it Paul had been forced to sever the Fallopian tubes, which gave him a wry sense of satisfaction. If the woman lived, at least her overworked body would never again have to submit to more childbearing.

Later, after having been advised of the successful outcome of the operation, Amelia Bloomer insisted that Earl Stover be shown what had been taken out of his wife.

Stover was aghast, disbelieving.

"Yep, that's right, Earl," Mayor Doane assured him. "That's what was took out of her."

Stover was not listening. A retching sound started in his throat and he ran outside to be sick, as discreetly as possible, over the edge of the front porch.

Mrs. Bloomer favored Paul with one of her sweetest smiles. "On behalf of women everywhere, Dr. Abbott, I wish to thank you for your determined stand to operate on a hapless woman against so much husbandly and group resistance.

"But you still have a problem. One which I intend to solve. . . . " And taking Paul's arm, she led him out on the porch to confront the sheriff.

"Sheriff Stringer, what are your intentions regarding Dr. Abbott?"

"It's my duty to arrest 'im, Mrs. Bloomer. You see, I got this paper here from England—"

"I admire your sense of duty, Sheriff," Mrs. Bloomer said loudly, half-turning toward the onlookers, "although this is the first manifestation of it, to my knowledge, that you've shown in the past year. It is common knowledge, in fact, that you spend more time in barrooms, or consorting with prostitutes, than you do in your office."

Stringer's face reddened. "Now looky here, Mrs. Bloomer—"

"To put it succinctly, Sheriff Stringer, this community is far less in need of a mediocre sheriff than we are in need of a fine doctor like Dr. Paul Abbott. Therefore I suggest that you go back to your usual haunts and leave the doctor in peace to care for Mrs. Stover. And if you don't, we'll start a petition at once for your recall from office." She turned and spoke directly to the crowd:

"Isn't that right, ladies?"

"We're right with you, Amelia!" called one woman, amid a chorus of female assents.

With a look of intense disgust, Loy Stringer swung around and stalked off the porch.

Several days later, Paul looked in on Mrs. Stover for a morning checkup in the little bedroom adjacent to the operating room. To his astonishment, she was up and bustling about, making her bed. With difficulty, Paul coaxed her back into bed, cautioning that she must stay at least a month.

Elcene stuck it out for only half that time. Then one morning the hardy woman got up, dressed, and climbing on the old plowhorse, rode home for a happy reunion with her family.

THREE: The Loneliest Year

IT was the loneliest period of Paul's life. Making it worse was the daily misery of watching Jere's steady disintegration toward death, against which all his doctor's skills were helpless. Whether Jere had only weeks, months, or possibly still another year of life Paul could not predict. All he could do was try to make it more bearable for both of them with the only therapy left—the useful exercise of Jere's medical abilities.

To this end, he insisted that Jere begin riding the rounds again. Together they began the daily sweep on horseback through many miles of backwoods country, from one lonely dwelling to another. All the families greeted them eagerly with their backlogs of physical complaints. They had all heard about Elcene Stover and the miraculous operation that had saved her from death.

Fortunately, most of the ailments were relatively minor— pleurisy, diarrhea, blood poisoning from a deep hemlock splinter, carbuncles, constipation and the like. Paul made a point of letting Jere take the initiative. Jere's self-respect had been greatly improved by the action of asserting his manhood, in his own eyes, by confronting the sheriff with a shotgun. Now, Paul reasoned, the less time the old fellow had to brood about his own ailment and the more time he spent helping others, the happier he would be during his final days.

Jere made one demand of his own.

"If we're going to ride on rounds, Paul, we'll have to carry guns."

"A doctor doesn't have to carry a gun, Jere."

"Ain't like the old days when a man could walk through the woods unarmed an' not give a hoot. All sorts of lawlessness an' crimes been increasin' in these parts."

Paul agreed, mostly to humor Jere, who many years ago had given Paul as a birthday present a beautiful Colt's six-shooter, which had been put in storage. Once he had worn it proudly, become quite expert with it, and now he again strapped on the familiar old gun before the long rides into desolate country.

ii

But it couldn't last. . . .

Late summer burned itself out; then the swirling, colorful leaves of autumn were stripped away by the whistling gusts of wintry winds; soon, the deep, drifting snows.

Jere finally balked. "Just can't take it anymore, Paul," he said one late afternoon when they returned, half-frozen and abysmally exhausted. He was wheezing for breath. "I appreciate what you been up to—tryin' to make me feel like a man again. I did my best, but I'm plumb used up. God, I sure could use a drink."

That was the last of their rides together.

Now the full Iowan winter was upon them; harsh, moaning winds and drifts so high that neither man nor beast could expect to get through. The wise and provident had already stockpiled provender for the winter. In the backwoods, for any man who could shoot straight, fresh meat was available within a stone's throw of his doorstep. Except for serious illness that might lay them low, they would survive until spring.

Even though the rounds were discontinued, there was little letup in the work. Paul's reputation had spread. Patients were now coming in increasing numbers to see him, arriving by horseback or sleigh or slogging in on snowshoes. Paul welcomed the workload.

But most dreaded were the lonely nights and mournful, all-night winds that whistled and hissed an icy breath between the loose chinks of his log-walled small bedroom. Such nights only intensified the nostalgia for the languorous hot South he was missing more and more.

They brought back also warm memories of Syl; of Pierre's generous friendship; of the calm, level-headed Etienne, who had finally warmed up to him. Often he thought of Micaela—always with a touch of sadness—the lovable minx who had somehow, though he scarcely knew her, entwined herself around his heart.

The long, lonely nights were not entirely wasted. Under the glow of an oil lamp, he pored over his old medical tomes as well as new ones he had acquired. Frequently he got out the gift from Syl, the magnificent microscope, and began delving into the mysteries of sicknesses by learning to identify the bacteria that caused them, taking samples from many patients for examination under the powerful lens. He made endless sketches and innumerable notes.

At the height of his aloneness, he wrote a long letter to Syl, taking great care to express himself in unassuming terms of affection although bursting with passionate desire to express his hunger for her love.

In due time he got a response, a long but most perfunctory letter detailing their lives on the plantation, saying that he was much missed and hoping he would be able to return soon, adding that Pierre and Etienne sent their regards. No mention was made of Fern. She ended it: "Affectionately, Syl."

He read and reread it greedily, seeking clues that perhaps she shared some of the same strong feelings for him, but could find nothing to support such a hope.

Finally the days melted into moody spring, soon flashed into bright summer, again burned into autumn. Paul felt trapped. Time was slipping past with a dreadful sense of his life sinking into a vacuum of futility.

He was also much poorer. Typical fees charged to patients—even when hours of riding were involved—were twenty-five to fifty cents a visit, rarely received in cash. Bushels of corn, Indian squash and other vegetables paid for services were piled high in Jere's woodshed, mostly to be given away, Animal skins accumulated over the months could be sold for a few dollars. Chickens and fresh-killed game provided many a fine meal, but were a poor substitute for cash. The purchase of medical publications, instruments and medications—ordered from St. Louis via steamer—had to come from Paul's dwindling money reserve.

He continued infrequent letters to Syl, getting back responses that more and more were subdued with resignation, as if she now assumed that he would never be coming back.

Paul couldn't bring himself to write that all that was delaying his return was waiting for Jere to die.

iii

The winds of another winter in Council Bluffs were beginning to whine and whistle around the cottage when Jere finally could no longer rise from bed. His cheeks were sunken in from drastic weight loss, the withered skin had the look of parchment; his breath came with great difficulty, because of the ravages of the disease, which had spread to his lungs. At times the pain was so severe he would turn his face to the pillow to muffle his hoarse screams. Laudanum no longer helped.

Sometimes Jere pleaded, sometimes he howled at Paul to grab a gun and end it for him. Neither man nor beast should have to endure such torture afore getting to hell, he said. Paul's refusals brought curses and tears until the pain subsided, or until Paul could numb him into sleep with the only medication that still seemed to work—alcohol.

During periods of remission, he had a great desire to ramble on about memories of the past that haunted him. Most of it gravitated around the young wife, Sarah.

" . . . had no right marryin' anyone as young as Sarah, but I . . . I reckoned you needed a mother to raise you proper. Made a trip to St. Louis, special. . . . Found her in a sportin' house an' took her home to Council Bluffs. . . . Nobody around here knew about her past, or ever found out. For a long time it went well enough, but it wasn't what she wanted out of life, or what she thought she wanted. . . . In the end she ran away with another man. . . . "

He closed his eyes, which were streaming tears, and after a minute or so of heavy breathing, continued:

"Fact is, I could have found a good woman, I reckon . . . even old as I was. Plenty of young enough widows around. But the truth be told, I was lookin' for a woman like Sarah . . . someone with life to her, a woman who was experienced an' knew all the tricks. . . . Old fool that I was! Couldn't really give her much lovin' . . . had kind of outgrown that. Could hardly blame her when she started cattin' around on the sly. She never fooled me by wearin' makeup when I was away. . . . Come home, I could always see traces of it an' knew she'd been puttin' it on for other men. . . . "

For Paul, such revelations were painful to hear, and stirred afresh the deep secret guilts he had carried since boyhood.

" . . . thought of goin' down to St. Louis and lookin' for her. In a house, because that's where she was bound to end up after she took off with that drummer. . . . Never did, though. . . . "

He half-closed his eyes.

"Pour me some more whiskey, Paul . . . feel it comin' real bad again. . . . "

On another occasion, Jere's words startled Paul.

"Never did get around to tellin' you about your real mother. . . . "

Paul, seated beside the bed, leaned forward eagerly. "What about my mother?"

"Should have been said sooner, but it kept slippin' my mind . . . or maybe to be real honest, I never did want to tell you. But I reckon you got a right to know." He lay there for a few moments, making deep, sucking noises for more air before continuing:

"Feller by name of Kit Carson dropped by a while back . . . sort of trapper. Understand he's made quite a name for himself fightin' Indians an' that sort of thing. Claimed he's your uncle."

"Kit Carson—my uncle!"

"Had proof with him. Did a deal of trackin' down everyone had anything to do with the massacre . . . the ones still alive, that is . . . soldiers from the fort, an' the Indians . . . . "

A sudden nervous tremor seized Paul. "Go on," he whispered hoarsely.

In his halting, disconnected way, Jere told him the whole story of the massacre and everything that Carson had told him about the mystery of why Paul alone hadn't been killed, the part played by the Bible. . . .

"He brought back the Bible, with your name wrote in it. You'll find it over there in the bottom drawer of my dresser."

The Bible, although yellowing with age, was well preserved, and the faded inscriptions in the flyleaf were clearly legible. Among them he found his own name:

Paul Carson Dixon, born Sept. 17, 1829, Indianapolis, Ind.
Beneath it was the authenticating signature of the Rev. Amos Beechcraft.

Later, alone in his room, Paul looked through blurred eyes into a cracked mirror on the wall at the one whose heritage had for so long been a mystery.

Now he knew who he was.

iv

Jere died in mid-February, during the worst of the winter weather. The small cemetery was by then drifted high with snow and the ground so frozen that it took several workmen a half-day, using pick and shovel, to dig the grave. The coffin was conveyed there by horse and sleigh, followed by several other sleighs carrying about a dozen mourners. One of them was Mrs. Bloomer.

Later, after expressing her condolences, Amelia said worriedly, "Have you heard any word from Dr. Moss? I had thought he would have arrived before this."

Young Timothy Moss was the doctor who was to be trained as Paul's replacement. Back in September Paul had confided to Mrs. Bloomer that Jere's death was imminent, and that he planned to leave Council Bluffs as soon after as he was able to find an adequate doctor to take over the practice. The good woman, who traveled around the state frequently, lecturing on women's rights, knew of a young doctor in Des Moines who had recently graduated from a medical college and had intended to start his own practice in that town, but was encountering difficulties from the established doctors already there. Moss had visited Paul, was enthused, had quickly decided to come to Council Bluffs with his pregnant young wife as soon as he could settle personal matters. That had been several months ago.

"I'm sure we'll be hearing from him as soon as the mail gets through, Mrs. Bloomer." Due to the unusually harsh winter, and bad ice conditions on the river, the mail had been held up for nearly a month.

"I certainly hope so," said Mrs. Bloomer. "And I hope you will not consider leaving before we are assured of a replacement, Dr. Abbott."

"I give you my promise."

But Paul had misgivings. He feared that Moss, on thinking it over, had changed his mind. What young doctor fresh out of college with a bona-fide medical certificate would want to come to this outpost of civilization where chances of financial reward were so slim? If Moss had decided not to come, it would mean that he would have to stay, for Paul could not in good conscience walk out now without knowing that Jere's revived practice would be taken over by a competent man. He might well be trapped into something he desperately did not want.

The steamer arrived three days later, its way having been cleared by tugboat icebreakers. Hundreds of townsfolk collected at the docks to greet it, all hopeful of letters among the backlog of mail.

Paul's spirits soared to find that his small batch of mail included a missive from Syl. An added surprise was a letter from his old Scottish friend, Alex Ushant. Wishing to save the pleasure of Syl's letter for the last, he opened Alex's first. It began:

"The most esteemed Dr. Paul Abbott," followed by, "Hallo, Laddie buck." The brief letter, bubbling with exuberance, went on to say that Alex had gammoned the laird and her ladyship into sending him on a trip to America because the laird had invested money in a California gold mine and thought it might be a good idea for Alex to inspect the mine holdings. It might even, thought the laird, shape Alex up into more of a man and improve his sense of responsibility to travel through the wild and dangerous American continent. As for Alex, he could scarcely wait to see real Indian savages, fur-clad trappers, buffalos and all the other exciting frontier attractions he'd heard about. He planned to travel by canal, railroad and stage to St. Louis, which he understood to be a civilized town of sorts, no longer subject to Indian attacks. He would stop at the Jefferson Hotel, expecting to arrive the first week in February, and stay about a week in hopes of seeing Paul again before proceeding West. He closed with a teasing hint that he had a great surprise for Paul, which he would save until they met in St. Louis.

Paul glanced at the calendar. February 18! Alex would have arrived in St. Louis nearly two weeks ago, have already left for the West. He felt a crushing sense of disappointment. What a shame to have missed the only true friend he had ever had in Scotland.

His spirits rose a bit, however, as he tore open the letter from Syl, which was on thick, expensive paper folded to envelope size and sealed with her personal, circular red wax insignia. Unfolding the beautifully penned missive, he began to read:

My Dear Paul,

It is with great trepidation that I take pen in hand, for the events I am about to set to paper are not, I regret to say, tidings of happiness. Nonetheless, I feel it my duty to inform you of the afflictions that have overwhelmed us of late, and the thought of your firm friendship to us is one of my greatest consolations. Indeed, among all our friends and acquaintances, it was you who first sprang into my thoughts as one, and perhaps the only one, that I could turn to during this period of dreadful calamity that has befallen us.

The shock and pain we have endured makes it difficult for me to go on. Please forgive me if my tears, which are now spilling freely beyond my control, fall on the paper and blur the ink. I shall not have the heart to attempt another draft, so this will have to do. I will endeavor, my dear Paul, to collect my thoughts and draw them so far from my emotions as to enable me to give you some idea of the situation in which we are now entangled. I presume to do this only because I well know the interest you have taken in our concern and because I, and Pierre too, consider you one of our closest, most trusted friends.

I have no choice but to state the blunt facts: My friend and companion of several years' standing, Fern Venable, is now in jail on a charge of aiding and abetting the escape of slaves from their proper owners, and arranging for their passage North on the secret Underground Railroad. It would be inconceivable for me to believe this, except that the circumstances and facts permit no other conclusion. She was apprehended in the middle of the night after directing a group of escapee slaves into a small boat, which was then headed toward the mouth of the Mississippi for whatever passage of escape may have been planned for beyond that point. Moreover, I am informed that she had been under suspicion and observation for some period of time and there is indisputable evidence that she has been the brains behind many slave escapes. It is even rumored that she is actually the notorious Nora Starr, who is said to have been instrumental in effecting the escape of hundreds of slaves. Oh, how I wish it were not true! How I wish it could have been anyone other than the one I considered a dear friend!—one whom we sheltered under our roof and gave of our love as freely as if she had been one of the family. It is beyond my comprehension, and I am numbed with the pain of knowing that it is beyond doubt the truth.

As if this in itself were not enough to destroy the happy tranquility of our lives, poor Pierre has been so overcome by the terrible hurt to his loving nature that it has transformed him into another personality, one so unlike the sweet, kind Pierre I have always loved that he now seems more like a stranger. I must keep in mind that Fern's betrayal has been, to his sensitive nature, a most dreadful blow, and I cannot expect a quick recovery. But my concern for him grows. He had always been a moderate drinker; now he drinks to excess. Rarely had I known him to lose his temper; now at times his voice rages in such anger that I tremble, and even fear to be in his presence. All of the slaves are terrified. Meanwhile, plantation affairs suffer without the kind of proper supervision that can only come from the master himself. Etienne lacks such ability, though he has great talent in money matters. I feel so helpless. I am truly at a loss as to how I can help him.

Fern's trial, I understand, will not be brought before a judge before another fortnight. In the meantime there are nasty rumors that a group of rough men led by our former overseer, Zack Porter, are organizing others of their ilk to march upon the jail and take the law into their own hands and wreak their own kind of punishment on poor Fern. Though I can never fully forgive her for betraying our friendship, neither can I condone brutal mob violence. My own wish is that she be treated with full and compassionate justice in accordance with the laws.

If the threat of mob violence continues, as I believe it will, only Pierre and Etienne are in positions of enough power and influence to avert it. Etienne is cynical about the whole matter and would make no move to help, unless urged by Pierre, who flies into a fury at the very mention of her name. Perhaps nothing illustrates the situation between us better than the fact that I—who have always been so close to Pierre that his wish was mine and my wish was his— dare not utter a word to him in defense of Fern.

These are the reasons, my dear Paul, why I have taken the liberty of writing these things. Perhaps nothing you could say would change Pierre's mind one whit, but your presence would be a deeper consolation to me than I can ever express. So I implore you, if it is at all possible—please return at the very earliest opportunity.

Most affectionately yours,
Sylphide Beauvais

Paul let the letter drop away with a strange mingling of sorrow and an undercurrent of elation. It saddened him to think that Fern's life might be in jeopardy, yet she had long been aware of the risks involved in the dangerous course she had chosen—she had spoken of them often enough. So often that he had sometimes wondered if she had a martyr's mentality, was actually inviting and hoping for retribution for her rash acts, for complex personal reasons as well as to draw attention to the wrongness of slavery.

The elation came from the fact that Syl, who so often filled his dreams, and with whom he was hopelessly in love, had called upon him for help. He saw nothing he could do to mend the situation, but her plea was all that mattered. He would have circled the earth if possible to do her bidding.

Only minutes later, there was a rapping on the door. Paul went to open it. It was young Dr. Timothy Moss, accompanied by his pretty wife and their newborn baby.

A pleasant-faced, red-haired young man, Dr. Moss was most apologetic for not arriving weeks ago. They had decided, he said, to wait for their child to be born, and their arrival was further delayed by the ice-blocked steamer.

" . . . uh, I only heard about your sad news as I was coming through the town," he went on. "I do hope we haven't arrived at an inopportune moment."

Paul opened the door wider. "Your timing is perfect, Doctor. Please come in, folks, and make yourselves at home. . . . "

FOUR: Echoes of Scotland

A week later Paul embarked by river steamboat for St. Louis. He had wasted little time in dispatching a letter to Syl to inform her that he would be leaving within days for New Orleans. On the chance that his old friend Alex Ushant might still be at the Jefferson Hotel, he had also sent a telegraphic message advising him of the day and approximate hour of his arrival.

It was a bitterly cold afternoon when the steamboat left Council Bluffs. Paul stood at the railing with the collar of his greatcoat raised up around his ears against the freezing wind knifing through every bit of exposed flesh, but nevertheless enjoying the beauty of the world around him. Both shores of the river were piled high with great chunks of glittering ice that had been broken free by the icebreakers. Trees and shrubbery were bowed down under loads of shimmering snow. Frequently, deer and other wildlife stood deep in the snow watching the boat pass, unafraid. The hard afternoon sun glistened against the crystals of ice at the water's edge.

As he was turning to go to his stateroom, Paul felt a small shock. A man with a familiar face was strolling down the deck.

Loy Stringer, the sheriff.

For a moment their eyes clashed. Loy wore a smug grin.

The oddness of it struck Paul forcibly. Why should Loy Stringer be on the same boat with him headed for St. Louis? The man was wearing both his badge and holstered gun, yet he had no authority to arrest him beyond the limits of Council Bluffs.

Paul was suddenly filled with forebodings.

ii

The quay along the St. Louis waterfront was in remarkable contrast to Council Bluffs. The ice and snow, which had diminished rapidly as the steamboat proceeded downriver, was gone now except for a few chunks of gray ice that had floated down from colder climes. And all the primitive beauty was gone. Even before sighting the city, its presence was marked by a dense billowy black canopy of smoke that almost blocked out the sky—unhappily reminding Paul of "Auld Reekie," as smoke-poisoned Edinburgh had been called.

However, it was plainly a prosperous town. On the outskirts fine homes lined the riverbanks, all beautiful and of modern design, surrounded by extensive landscaped grounds. But in the distance beyond, whole sections of the town appeared to be dwellings for the poor, row upon row of humble houses packed together in blocks, all built to the same pattern, even the windows as alike as peas in a pod.

Along the levee, the back-door hustle-bustle of commerce that supported so many thousands of people was evident everywhere. At least a full mile of riverfront was crowded with steamboats, tugs and keelboats tied in abreast of each other, two and sometimes three tiers deep. The air vibrated with tootling, whistling and the snorting of engines; it stank of coal smoke, fish and less definable odors. Dreary warehouses lined the river as far as the eye could reach; in front of them horses, drays and queues of dockhands loading and unloading cargoes; and behind, the endless stacks of grimy factories spewing billowing black smoke into the sky.

A passage was cleared for the steamboat by tugs, and shortly it was eased into its berth.

With his greatcoat now over his arm, for the weather was mild, Paul joined the group of passengers waiting to debark. His bags were amid a big pile of luggage to be taken ashore by boat porters and retrieved from the steamship baggage room. Eagerly his glance skimmed over faces on the wharf, seeking Alex Ushant, but his friend was nowhere in sight.

The gangplank clunked into place. Then, as passengers began streaming off, two uniformed men came striding up. A hard object jammed against Paul's back and a harsh voice called out from directly behind him:

"This way, officers! I'm Sheriff Stringer from Council Bluffs, and here's the man I telegraphed you about. . . . "

Then the voice hissed in his ear, "All right, you bastard, turn an' hold your paws out so's I can put on the cuffs! Make one wrong move an' you can bet your ass I won't hesitate t' plug you for resisting arrest."

Minutes later, as Paul was being herded ashore, handcuffed and in the custody of the three officers, he spotted a familiar figure trudging toward him through the rich abundance of mud that lined the levee.

Alex Ushant! The smile on the genial Scotsman's face washed away on sighting Paul, and his eyebrows raised in astonishment.

Paul faced him with a wry grin. "This is a hell of a way to greet an old friend, Alex—as you can see, I can't even shake hands. It seems that old matter in Scotland has finally caught up with me."

Surprisingly, Alex gave him a cheerful smile.

"Don't ye fash yersel' o'er it, laddie buck. We've buggered 'em before and we can do it again. I'll gae along wi' you to the station and we'll put up the de'il's own fight to set things right. . . . "

iii

The magistrate was a short and broad man with a totally bald dome, sleepy buttonhook eyes and a wide mouth that gave him the look of a bullfrog. Even his voice came out as a hoarse croak:

"Hrrrmmmmmmph . . . " he croaked, looking down at Paul from his position of eminence while holding the paper given to him by Sheriff Loy Stringer. "Now what we have here appears to be a bona-fide police document from Scotland containing allegations that a certain Dr. Paul Abbott may have perpetrated the murder by poison of a certain female of feeble mind who was under the protection of the English crown, and it is requested of any police authorities anywhere in the world who may encounter and apprehend the said Dr. Abbott that they aid and expedite his extradition to Scotland. What do you have to say to that, Dr. Abbott?"

"Only that I am innocent, your honor."

From beside him, Alex spoke up: "I am also prepared to testify for and verify Dr. Abbott's complete innocence, your honor."

The magistrate rapped a gavel and scowled at Alex ferociously. "Interruptions will not be tolerated, under penalty of removal from the courtroom or an indeterminate stay in jail, at the discretion of this court!"

Alex glanced sideways at Paul, his face paled, his jaunty manner gone.

"Now then . . . " croaked the magistrate. "Whereas it is not within the jurisdiction of this court to try an alleged criminal for an alleged crime committed in another country, and whereas it is the duty of this court, under the provisions of certain treaties and statutes and the amenities of international law, to surrender the alleged criminal into the custody of the proper authorities of another country requesting his return, there appears in this particular instance to be a certain lack; to wit, not even a hint or whisper of from whom, or where, or whither shall come the necessary monies that must be expended for the subsistence and passage of the alleged criminal for his return to Scotland."

Frowning, the magistrate rustled the paper in his hands and cleared his throat:

"*Hrrrmmmmmphhh* . . . Whereas this court recognizes and applauds the well-known Scottish national trait of frugality and sensible reluctance to part with a half-pence, and whereas there is no question whatsoever of Scottish honesty nor their national readiness to pay just debts, in this instance their admirable trait is in contradiction with our own hard-nosed American practicality. In short this court is not authorized, nor deems it advisable, to expend American tax dollars for the return of an alleged criminal to a foreign country. Therefore—"

Paul's hopes had risen. Perhaps all was not lost, after all.

"—therefore, in pursuance of our international responsibility, it is the decision of the court that the alleged criminal will be held in custody here, pending communications to be established with Scots authorities regarding costs and the means of extradition. . . . "

Now Paul's hopes sank to rock bottom.

Catching his eye, Alex winked at him, then turned and looked boldly up at the magistrate.

"But there's no need of all this fash, your honorable worship," he said in his most respectful tone. "I myself am, ye might say, an unofficial sort of official, come direct from Scotland with the proof of Dr. Abbott's innocence." He had meanwhile withdrawn a sheaf of papers from a slim leather pouch and flourished them in the air.

The magistrate glared down at him. "Who are you, young man?"

"Alister Duncan Malcolm Ushant, the fourth son of Lord Craiglockhart of Scotland."

The magistrate's manner was considerably less truculent. "And what is your alleged proof that Dr. Abbott is innocent?"

"Clippings from English newspapers, your honorable worship, telling of how the confession of a certain Jack Fordyce has completely exonerated Dr. Abbott of any complicity in the crime for which he was wrongly accused. Also a document from the chief of Edinburgh police, officially stamped and certifying that Paul Abbott is innocent of the crime." Alex handed the sheaf of papers up to the magistrate, who began perusing them.

After a few minutes he looked up. "Why didn't you show these to the desk sergeant when the defendant was brought in?"

"I tried, your most worshipful honor, but the sergeant was not of a mind to listen. He told me to 'tell it to the judge,' which I also tried to do, but—"

"*Hrrrrmmmmmphh . . .*" The wide mouth tightened as the magistrate shifted his eyes toward Loy Stringer.

"Sheriff Stringer, for your failure to handle this matter in your own jurisdiction, you should be severely reprimanded. But since it is obvious that like most provincials who wear badges because nobody else will take the job, you lack police training, I will be lenient. You have your choice of paying court costs, plus compensation to the City of St. Louis for the waste of two of our officers' and my own time —which I will charitably set at thirty dollars—or spend a week in one of our prisoner work gangs."

As the red-faced Stringer began worriedly fumbling into his buckskin purse, the magistrate swung his forbidding gaze back at Paul and added, as if an afterthought:

"Case dismissed."

iv

In the Buckhorn Saloon, Alex grinned across a small table at Paul and hoisted his foaming schooner of Black Velvet, American-style. The bartender, never having heard of the drink, and not having the requisite stout ale to mix with the champagne, had in accordance with instructions substituted with German bock beer, which Alex later pronounced "demned bloody good."

"Ye been through the de'il's own gauntlet, laddie buck, but it's all over now. Ye're a free mon."

Paul raised his glass and clinked it against his friend's.

"Thanks to you, Alex. You've saved my hide twice over. I don't know how I'll ever be able to repay you."

"Goddemn it, Paul—have I ever asked for repayment?"

Which reminded Paul . . . his savings had been all but used up, but the amount received from Timothy Moss as a down payment for Jere's property that had been willed to Paul was equal to about a hundred pounds—only half of what Alex had loaned him. Now, producing the money in American bills, he tossed them on the table.

"Money alone can never repay you, Alex, and I'm not yet able to fully repay even the cash, but here's half of it. The rest will be repaid in a year from now, if not sooner. As for the rest that I owe you—your friendship, your generosity, and the cunning that saved my neck—I fear I will be forever in your debt."

Alex almost savagely scooped up the sheaf of bills and planted them back in front of Paul.

"I'll be demned if I take a farthing from you! I don't need it, and I've kenned by the look of your greatcoat and wee touches here and there that ye're not yet rolling in the quid. Ye've had a demned rum go of it for too long, laddie, and if it would make you feel the better, there's no harm in tellin' that the laird is rolling in the siller, and so is her ladyship. Enough of it trickles into my purse. So put the American dollars back in yer pocket, Paul, and if the de'il e'er clobbers me so I have nae a drop of dunkin durie, I'll come a-knocking." He paused to take a great gulp of his drink, then:

"Why don't ye come West with me and invest the quid in gold mines, and then we can all be rich?"

"I've found something greater than gold, Alex."

Alex sighed. " 'Tis as I feared. . . . "

"What do you mean?"

"I would ken from the loony light in yer eyes e'er time ye spoke the name 'Sylphide" that she's a bewitching lass that has ye twigged for the better or worse."

Paul laughed. "Syl's bewitching enough, but far too rich and fancy ever to think of marrying the likes of me."

"Ye're out of your pumpkin, mon! All the lassies e'er

think of is how to ensnare a good mon. Rich and fancy has nothing to do with it, except give them more time for the scheming. They're canny as the de'il, all of them, and once the notion gets stuck in their bonnet, there's naught for a mon to do but make a run for it."

"Not from this one. Even you, Alex, would go a little barmy if you ever met Syl. Her beauty is like . . . I can only think of the stars, a summer sky . . . her voice as soft and sweet as a spring breeze, and—" He broke off at the ludicrous expression on his friend's drop-jawed face. Alex made a groaning sound.

"Ne'er in my wildest dreams could I e'er have imagined sich blather coming from the lips of my old sober and sensible laddie buck, Paul Abbott! Ye're a goner, mon, and I much fear, so is our friendship. First thing a lass does, once a mon is snared, is come 'twixt him and his auld friends."

"It's not that way at all, Alex! She has only affection for me, I think, but not love. She can take her pick from any number of rich, handsome suitors and would be crazy even to think of me in that respect. In any event I have no desire to marry, and if I ever do, I vow that never would I allow it to spoil our friendship."

"I am nae convinced one way or the other," Alex said gloomily, "but since 'tis plain the Sylphide lass has stole your heart, I'll get on to another matter that I've been saving as a surprise—"

"But I thought the papers exonerating me of any guilt in the Edinburgh murder was the surprise."

"Only part of the surprise, laddie—" Alex lifted his slim leather case from the floor and after elaborately opening it, drew out a rolled document tied with a red ribbon. He handed it over with a flourish.

"Your Certificate of Surgery, Dr. Abbott. A bit delayed in the delivery, but still fresh as from the royal mint."

With trembling fingers, Paul unrolled the fine parchment. Avidly his eyes skimmed over the exquisite Gothic print. This was not just a mere medical certificate of the kind signed by some unknown frontier clerk—something almost any medical pretender could get. This was the real thing, signed by distinguished physicians from the world's finest medical college—one of the most revered documents any surgeon could ever hope to get. Paul was so overcome by emotion he could scarcely speak.

"But, how . . . ?"

Alex was self-deprecating. "I had little to do with it except reach the ear of the laird. He can be hard as iron, but none can be fairer when he kens the truth of a situation. Once the proof came of your innocence, he went directly to Syme, Sharpey, Holmes and Lister—more high mucks than ye can put a name to—and put pressure in the right places."

"I'll write at once to your father and express my everlasting gratitude, but had it not been for you—"

"Nae—" Alex said hastily. "Not another word! Drink up. It could be years before we meet again—or maybe never—so gie a smile, laddie buck, and we'll venture forth in this quaint town to seek what it offers in entertainment. . . . "

Many hours later, after a fine dinner at Herr Klein's very proper and *behaglich*—cozy—little saloon—followed by visits to every improper saloon they could find—the two ended up at the steamboat office where earlier Paul had taken the precaution to purchase his ticket for the next boat to New Orleans, which was leaving shortly after midnight. Both were a bit wobbly from all the Black Velvets and bourbon imbibed, but in the best of spirits. The *Delta Queen* was already tooting its boarding signal.

The two shook hands, and then embraced.

"Goddemn it, Paul—" Alex had begun shedding tears freely. "Take good care of yersel'."

Then he turned abruptly and without a backward glance strode away, somewhat unsteadily, toward the hansom cab waiting for him.

BOOK SIX

Days of Disaster

ONE: Fallen Star

ABOUT twenty-five mounted men galloped into Five Corners shortly after dark. Their thunderous approach was like that of a hundred-footed monster. Close-packed, the majority of the riders carried torches that lit up the sky, reflected redly on their faces. All carried guns; some had clubs, sabers, ropes and various other items strapped behind their saddles. That the townspeople were hardly surprised was evident because there was not a soul on the street, but every window and doorway was crammed with watching faces.

Stopping in front of the jail, three of the horsemen dismounted and went swaggering into the jail office.

Oral Tomkins, the undersheriff and sole individual on night duty, looked up from his small desk at the intruders with a sickly grin.

"Not gonna be necessary to make no fuss about it, boys," he said amiably. He picked up a single key on a big ring and extended it to one of the men. "You'll find 'er in the back cell. . . . "

The man who had taken the key and another one strode back to the cells. The third stayed behind.

"One other thing we hafta do, Oral. Now you jist stand up an' relax. . . . "

"Aw shit now, Zack, you don't need to—"

"We gotta make it look real. You ain't gonna feel a thing. . . . "

Nervously, Oral spat out a gob of chewing tobacco into a nearby spittoon and stood up. "Jist a light little tunk now—"

Zack brought the gun barrel down viciously against the man's head. He collapsed, blood already beginning to trickle down the side of his face.

ii

Somewhere at the edge of a swamp the horsemen stopped, and Fern—her dress and most of her undergarments already ripped off—was hauled roughly from the saddleless horse she had been tied to. Under the garish flare of torches her bare white limbs gleamed with reddish highlights as she tumbled back on the ground.

"Hey, looka them big tits on that nigra-fucker!"

"Yeah—bet she's took jism from every buck nigra on Gayarre's plantation."

"Seems a shame we-uns don't get some of that free stuff afore we mess it up."

"There's nobody says we cain't!"

"Shut up, you fools!" said a scrawny oldster. "We're a-wastin' time. Where we gonna build a fire t'melt the tar?"

"Ain't gonna be no tar-an'-featherin'," said Zack Porter, who was both the instigator and in nominal command of the group.

"What in hell ya mean, Zack? We-uns come out here to have a real ball."

"You'll have your ball, but no tarrin'."

"Why'n hell not? I been waitin' to hear that nigra-lover squealin' her head off."

"I been thinkin' it over. That Yankee bitch has money connections up North. Northern money, Southern money— it's all the same. That money's bound to stir up an investigation. We turn this bitch into a blackbird, they got enough evidence to make it a mite uncomfor'ble fer all of us."

"What you gittin' at, Zack?"

"I say hump 'er all ya want. Then I'll take 'er back inta the swamp an' get my share afore I git rid of the evidence."

A bald man let out a whoop. "Heah, lemme show y'all how it's done. . . . "

Fern was sitting up, listening. She suddenly leaped up and tried to dart away.

It took three men to subdue her frenzied resistance before she was flung back on the ground, kicked savagely until she lay still.

The bald man, amid crude calls of encouragement, unbuckled his pants and knelt down between the captive legs. . . .

iii

She knew she was being carried. The regular, jolting movement that had brought her back into a kind of gray semi-awareness seemed to have been going on for hours, or it could have been only minutes. The sense of time, like all of her senses except that of pain, was too numbed to be sure of anything except that she was being carried, most uncomfortably, over a man's shoulders. The hard boniness was jammed up against her belly, cutting off part of her wind. Her legs flopped helplessly against her captor's torso with each squishing step of his boots.

Mercifully, she had blanked out under the brutal assault of the rapists. How many had invaded her body or how long it had lasted, she didn't know. Nor did she care. She was beyond that. She was so aching, bruised, sore in every part of her body that no further degradation or punishment could make any difference.

Just so it ends soon. It didn't matter how. Let me be shot, drowned, buried or thrown to the alligators. Can you hear me, God?

The slogging steps stopped, and suddenly she was slipping, sliding, falling. . . . The spongy ground whumped against her back, bringing from her a whimpering little gasp.

"Chrissake," Zack Porter snarled at her, "I thought ya was already dead!" He crouched down.

Then the blows began. Slamming, crushing, jolting fists

against her stomach, breasts, head—but always above the pelvis, leaving the lower parts untouched. . . .

Now she understood. Mally and other of the slave girls had whispered the gruesome stories—how Porter had beaten some of them senseless, taken them into the icehouse to lay over the big blocks of ice until they were half-frozen, dying. Then to be sexually violated. Some of the women had been locked in there until they died, later buried in the dark of night. . . .

She'd read about this most detestable type of pervert, so rare that the name for them was scarcely known . . . a necrophiliac . . . one who was erotically aroused by a dead body. Some became undertakers; some murderers. . . .

She felt the huge, horrid entry into her lax body. Porter let out a groan of ecstasy.

Is this what you really wanted, Daddy? You who were always beating us with harsh words, degrading mother and me, hating us, hating all women . . .

Her consciousness was drifting back into grayness.

. . . or maybe this is the ultimate I have been seeking . . . the ultimate self-degradation at the hands of men . . . the thing I had to prove. . . .

The last wisp of consciousness was flickering out as she began sinking, sinking deep into blackness. . . .

. . . maybe this is

what I have wanted

all along. . . .

Fern died with a small smile on her lips.

TWO: The Last Goodbye

GRANDLY the *Delta Queen* nosed up to the dock at Les Cypres with a stately shudder and considerable backwash from reversed motors. Disembarking, Paul was surprised to find a carriage waiting for him.

"Miz Syl been 'spectin' you," said old Jehu, the driver. "Day after day she sen' me down heah t' meet ever' wheeler comin' downriver."

At the manor she rushed up to embrace him, her head against his chest.

"Oh Paul, I'm so glad you're back!"

"And I too am glad to be here, Syl."

She drew back and looked up at him with sad, misted eyes. "But unfortunately, I have dreadful news to impart. . . ."

Briefly she told him about Fern having been taken from the jail by a band of ruffians several days ago. Nobody had seen her since. She was believed to be dead.

"What a rotten—"

"Please, Paul—" She had started weeping freely. "I can't bear to talk about it any more right now. Etienne will tell you more of the details at dinner this evening."

ii

Dinner was a forlorn affair. Even the servants displayed grave deportment and doleful expressions. Pierre's chair at the head of the table was conspicuously empty.

"Pierre is not feeling well," Syl explained, "and asks to be excused."

Paul was vaguely offended. Could not Pierre at least have sent him some word of welcome?

Etienne, who had greeted Paul warmly enough but with funereal reserve, now spoke up quickly:

"Don't take it as a personal slight, Paul. Pierre's sensitivity and deep emotions are such that he is still, temporarily, unstrung by Fern's incredible betrayal of his trust. I think you are entitled to know how it came about. . . .

"A few months ago we had as a guest a Mr. Jaspar Bledsoe, a society reporter from *The New York Times* who was in the South doing a series of articles on the first families among the Creoles. To our surprise—and obviously to Fern's consternation—he recalled meeting her when we were in New York. At a social gathering at the Rhinelander residence in Washington Square. And of course the Rhinelanders are well-known abolitionists. At one point Bledsoe said jokingly, 'And do you recall, Miss Venable, the tipsy gentleman who stupidly mistook you for the notorious Nora Starr? I got quite a laugh out of that.'

"Fern explained that she'd run across the famous Harriet Beecher Stowe, who had once been Fern's schoolgirl teacher, and when Mrs. Stowe invited her to accompany her to the

Rhinelanders she went along simply for the pleasure of her former teacher's company.

"We believed her, but apparently Bledsoe told similar stories to other Planters, who alerted the Vigilante Committee to watch Fern's actions, and eventually she was trapped—"

" 'Scuse me, Miz Syl—" An elderly, white-haired servant had appeared.

"What is it, Jonas?"

"Marse Pierre ask fo' Massadoc come to his room. . . . "

ii

Through the narrow door opening, Pierre faced Paul with reddened eyes. Apparently he had no intention of inviting him in.

"A little memento I would like you to have," he said thickly, extending a small wrapped parcel. "It is from Fern. I request of you not to open it before morning."

Paul took the parcel while studying the agonized face. Pierre's face had a sick pallor, a several days' ragged beard growth, and his hair was untidy. He wore a red silk dressing robe.

"Pierre, may I come in and talk for a few moments? I know you've been through a hellish time, but if only for the sake of our old friendship, I think we should have a talk—"

"Dr. Abbott—" Pierre's dark haggard eyes turned hard as stone. "There is absolutely nothing I care to discuss with you now or ever! Good night, sir."

With that he slammed the door in Paul's face.

Downstairs he found Syl with tears glistening on her cheeks.

"I heard. . . . " she whispered. She looked very worried and dejected; the long strain of worry was taking its toll.

He wanted to reach out and hold her, comfort her, but Etienne and servants were within sight; she might take offense.

"You need a good sleep, Syl. Would you like me to bring you a sedative?"

"No, no . . . I sleep well enough. But you're right. I'm terribly exhausted. I'll have to bid you good night for now, Paul, and we can talk again tomorrow. . . . "

Giving one of his hands a quick squeeze, she turned and hurried away.

iii

Alone in his cottage, Paul inspected the flat little package given to him by Pierre with growing curiosity. Pierre had asked him not to open it before morning, but what possible difference could it make?

With a sudden yank he broke the string and unfolded the wrapping, disclosing a green-covered diary and a folded note. He opened the note and skimmed over the words.

> Paul—I once told you that if I was ever betrayed by either you or Fern—the only Yankees in whom I ever invested my fullest trust—I would lose all faith in my fellow men. Events have proved me to be a fool for having expected so much.
>
> However, I have not forgotten my debt to you for having once saved my life. The enclosed diary, which I found among Fern's effects, I am hereby turning over to you in repayment of that debt. Had I turned it over to the Vigilantes, you would without doubt soon be dead. . . .

Dropping the note, Paul seized the diary and began riffling through the pages. What was Pierre's meaning, the implication that he too had betrayed his trust?

His eyes raced over the entries, wincing several times when he found some mention of Fern's intimacies with him, but surely Pierre couldn't condemn him so severely for that.

Finally he found it. The date of the entry was his last night on the plantation before leaving for Council Bluffs. He read and reread it, unbelieving:

> Dear Diary . . . tonight has been a great success! Paul has now become a full-fledged member of the UGRR (perhaps thanks mostly to my sexual charms!). He will carry messages to some of our key stations on his trip to Council Bluffs, and on his return has agreed to cooperate fully in the use of the dispensary as a crucial communications center for keeping the blacks advised about the time, place, etc., concerning our plans for their escape. Paul has been most wonderful with his clever suggestions and help in the past, and I predict he will become our most valuable contact in the South. . . .

He dropped the diary, dumfounded.

Had Fern really hated him that much?

The only possible reason was that last night before he left for Council Bluffs when he had refused to help her anti-slavery activities. She had probably feared he might betray her. But most important was doubtless her female vanity—he had spurned her sexual advances; thus she had artfully contrived it so that if he gave her away and she was caught, he would be pulled down with her.

And Pierre had believed the lie.

He picked up the note again and saw at the bottom of the sheet a postscript he had overlooked:

> P.S. I wish to thank you again, my friend, for another great service you have done for me—although my arm and hand are so stiff I can scarcely move them, life has come back to my trigger finger. . . . "

Dropping the note, Paul rushed to the door, yanked it open and started running. How stupid of him not to have thought of it sooner!

The distant muffled shot came before he was halfway to the manor.

iv

With the help of a manservant, Paul broke the locked door open. Pierre was in the ornate marble bathroom. He had been thoughtful enough at the end to place a sheet on the floor beneath him. The dueling pistol was still in his grasp, looking huge against his pitifully shriveled right hand, with the ultimate success and defeat of Paul's operation—the usable trigger finger—still thrust through the trigger guard. Blood was streaming down his face dark and rich from a neat round hole in his temple, staining the sheet a vivid crimson.

"Close the door," Paul told the servant, "and don't allow anyone to enter—not even Miss Syl."

Leaving the corpse untouched, Paul quickly examined the room. The bed was still neatly made, the counterpane unrumpled. There were no loose articles of clothing lying around. Pierre's sense of tidy order was apparent everywhere. The only evidence of human activity was the opened desk, on which were spread sheets of stationery, inkstand and quill. Also a book with the cover folded open.

The book was *Armance* by Stendhal. A long inscription

had been penned on the flyleaf. Beside the book was an envelope addressed to Syl.

Paul slipped the envelope between flyleaf and cover, closed the book and went out.

THREE: Micaela

SYL lost track of the days of grayness. Her initial grief, mercifully, soon subsided into that kind of depthless despair that numbs thought and emotions. While the slaves lamented and wailed and made voodoo spells in the yard, and also tried Christian prayer, she remained most of the time in the solitude of her own rooms, scarcely aware of her surroundings. Aurora waited on her with solicitous care; Etienne was always near, and Paul came often. Sometimes Paul held her hand and the warmth of his hand enfolding her chilled one was her only sense of contact with life and the world outside. She tried to make conversation, to please him, but couldn't find the words. Sometimes she knelt before the altar in the little plantation church and tried to pray, but the words that murmured from her lips were mechanical. The funeral came and passed. Lines of shining coaches came from many miles around bearing mourners; some came by steamboat. All sought to offer comforting words. To Syl it was all like a vague dream.

Nearly two weeks passed before she felt strong enough to read again the last words that Pierre had penned for her eyes alone. Going to one of her bureaus, she unlocked a bottom drawer and withdrew the novel, *Armance*. The envelope with Pierre's note was still inside the cover.

Settled into a chair, she put the note aside and began re-reading the inscription on the flyleaf, part of which had been penned in Paris at the time Pierre had given her the book:

For my dearest Syl—
    Would that I had the courage to tell you *vis-à-vis,* but even had I the courage, my boundless love for you would in itself be an impediment to my poor efforts to properly explain, in a manner fit for your chaste ears, a matter of

such delicacy. . . . So I beg of you to read this novel and from it gain the understanding of that which I dare not express. . . .

Syl paused to dab at her eyes with a lacy Italian handkerchief. It was torturing herself to go on, but the compulsion was overpowering to read again the rest of the inscription that Pierre had added just before his suicide:

Nearly three years have passed, my darling, since the above lines were written, and you know now—from the message derived from reading *Armance*—why it is impossible in this world for us ever to find or achieve the fulfillment of our love. You understand now why I urged you, against your will, to marry Nicholas—which, alas, was prevented by tragedy, and I think would have been a mistake in any event. I have come to believe that never—as long as I am alive—can you find true happiness with another man. Nothing will set you free except my own act of taking the coward's way out. Were I not such a coward, I would have done so long ago. But recent events—Fern, plantation troubles, the collapse of all my dreams—now make it easy, even something I welcome. I can only beg that you forgive me and remember always that my love for you will remain locked in my heart for eternity—

She set the book down carefully. How stupid she'd been! The first portion of the inscription, written when Pierre had given her the book in Paris, should have been enough of a clue. The plot of the novel was simply the story of a young man who was much in love with the heroine, Armance, and who could not bring himself to tell her that he was impotent. Because of that, he had ended his life and left it to a friend to tell his beloved the reason.

What a silly reason for killing oneself, Syl had thought!

In truth, Syl was an innocent about all matters pertaining to sex. She wasn't even sure what the word "impotent" meant in its fullest sense. She thought in a vague way it meant simply that a man could not have children. To her that wouldn't have mattered; her love for Pierre was far greater than her desire to have children. But so great was reluctance to speak a word touching on the forbidden subject of sexual love that she could not bring herself to discuss the matter with Pierre. She could not even have uttered the word— "impotent." It had an aura of "dirtiness."

Any such discussion would have had to be initiated by

Pierre, and of course he had been too much of a gentleman. Now she forced herself to give her attention to the worst shock of all—the note that had been enclosed in an envelope:

My dearest—

The words that follow will be most upsetting to you, but I see no choice other than to inform you of all the shameful details.

For some time now I have been keeping an octoroon mistress (in name only!). It came about after I received an urgent message from that well-known procuress, Mme. Silkwood, advising that she had news of vital interest for me. The news, as it turned out, was a greater shock than I could possibly have anticipated. Mme. Silkwood had under her nefarious tutelage a young virginal female whom she knew to be the illicit offspring of my own father and a quadroon. Her desire to let me know—if one can imagine such gross insensitivity—was in hopes that I would use my influence with planter friends to help find the richest possible *protecteur* for her young ward—my own half-sister!

To me, my duty was clear. I at once advised Mme. Silkwood that I would myself become the girl's *protecteur*, and that of course her paternity was to be kept an inviolate secret. Whatever other flaws of character Mme. Silkwood may have, lack of discretion is not one of them. Nor would it matter to her in the slightest if incest had been my purpose, such is her immorality.

Only after exacting a vow of lifelong silence from my half-sister—whose name is Micaela—did I reveal my deepest secret—that I am incapable of sexual acts, and that our relationship was to be no more than that of brother and sister. Not wishing, however, to reveal our true relationship (Mme. Silkwood assured me that Micaela did not know) I explained that I was assuming the sham role as her *protecteur* only to conceal my sexual inadequacy from all my male friends, who might otherwise think me abnormal, or worse, pity me. This, I am ashamed to confess, was a large part of my motivation. Beyond that I wished to save Micaela from a life of prostitution and preserve her virginity, if possible, for a suitable husband of color that I would endeavor to find for her. It was also my intention to bestow on her a substantial sum of money.

Since at this point I cannot make a provision for Micaela in my will without causing embarrassment to you, dear Syl, and because recent events and financial problems have forestalled the alternative of a cash settlement, my last request

is that you make whatever monetary arrangements you think
to be proper for Micaela, who, after all, shares my father's
blood.

My eternal love,
Pierre

Syl was dry-eyed after reading the letter. She felt a sense
of returning strength that came from hardening resolve.

Give the young strumpet a substantial sum of money, indeed! Pierre had surely been mentally deranged when he
wrote such nonsense. He had no obligation whatsoever to a
woman of color merely because she had been conceived
illicitly by his father and a quadroon who sold her body for
gain. Pierre's will, quite rightly, had divided his entire estate
between herself and Etienne, and to share any of it with this
Micaela would be a sacrilege to the family.

However, she would honor Pierre's last request to the
extent of making the monetary arrangements she thought
proper. She would invite the girl to Les Cypres, offer her the
choice of respectable employment and a home at the manor
—in the servants' wing with Aurora, of course—or a modest
token amount of money in deference to Pierre's wishes. What
could be more fair?

She would ask Paul to go to New Orleans tomorrow and
invite Micaela to the plantation.

FOUR: Flood

PAUL peered morosely through the misted coach windows.
A hard, steamy drizzle murked the streets of New Orleans.
For endless days the spring rains, sometimes amounting to
a downpour, had been drenching the warm earth, flooding
streams and bogs and creating a morass of mud and brown
puddles everywhere. Soon, almost every drop of that water
would be swarming with mosquito larvae that virtually overnight would rise in black pestiferous clouds to harass the
human race. It was one aspect of Louisiana he could do
without.

The home Pierre had provided for Micaela on the Rue

de Rampart was of modest size, two stories high and of exquisite design, set amid flowering trees, colorful flowerbeds and neat green lawn.

A black maid admitted him. Scarcely had she taken his dripping hat and cape than he heard a squeal of delight. Micaela rushed up to fling her arms around him.

"Oh Paul! I'm so glad you've come!"

He bent to kiss her on the cheek, but she at once sought his mouth with her full red lips. The kiss was long and sweet.

After a few moments he drew back, unduly stirred, and surveyed her. The large, luminous eyes were misted, but the lovely face was vibrant, more beautiful than he remembered. Her stunning figure had improved, too, the seventeen-year-old slenderness curved out a trifle more with maturity. She would be all of nineteen now, perhaps twenty.

"Age certainly becomes you, Micaela."

"Let me return the compliment. You've lost that gaunt look you had. You look stronger, more assured. I can see life has been good to you. . . . "

"Not all that good, Micaela. I came here because of—but I see you already know. . . . "

She had bent her head as tears welled from her eyes. "I guessed the moment you arrived it was because of that. . . . Did *she* send you?"

"Yes, Miss Beauvais has concern for your welfare now that Pierre is gone. She asked me to extend her invitation to visit her at Les Cypres."

"Invite me to the plantation? Mademoiselle Beauvais must be crazy! Never have I heard of such a thing! I know her kind. I cannot believe that she has any true concern for an octoroon."

"Tell me, Micaela, did Pierre provide you with enough money so that you will have no worries?"

"Pierre was very generous. Even when his debts grew huge, he borrowed to pay for my home and servants. I know he intended to do more, but—"

"I think that is what Miss Beauvais wishes to discuss with you. She wants to be assured that you will not have to worry about the future."

"Hah—the future is the least of my worries. Since Pierre's death I am flooded with attentions from rich men everywhere who want to become my *protecteur*."

"Is that what you really want, Micaela?" To continue as an expensive whore, he added silently.

"What other choice do I have except to become a servant?"

"Why don't you come to Les Cypres and find out if Miss Beauvais has any other choice to offer?"

She looked at him probingly. "Is bringing such a message the only reason that you've come to see me after all this time?"

"I felt I had no right to come sooner. You belonged to my friend, so I didn't think it proper to call on you. But I've thought of you with deep affection many times. . . . "

She laughed. "All right, I will come with you. It will give me a chance to get away from my suitors for a while and decide for myself what I want out of life. . . . "

ii

The *Bayou Queen* nosed stubbornly against the rush of turgid brown river, raising a swirl of froth at the prow. Its motors thumped and labored; the great side paddles slapped rhythmically. The current was of such force that the mighty sidewheeler, at full throttle, was logging scarcely more than three miles per hour.

Paul stood at the bow, peering abstractedly into the angry waters. Droplets of rain fell steadily from the brim of his beaver, slid down the folds of his dark rain cape. He and Micaela had boarded about a half-hour before, and Micaela, smartly dressed beneath her dainty parasol and looking for all the world like an imperious daughter of some wealthy Creole planter, had at once repaired to her stateroom. Paul, more aroused than he cared to admit by the propinquity of her nubile charms, had remained on the near-deserted deck, wanting the chill of fine drizzle against his face to cool his overheated blood.

What kind of lustful beast am I? he thought savagely. I love Syl with all my heart; I would go to the ends of the earth for her; I would die for her.

Yet the physical presence of Micaela, whom he knew only as a playful and naughty young minx—and another man's mistress—had set his blood churning in a way more to be expected in an infatuated boy.

He saw but one solution to the inner turmoil. It would be presumptuous on his part, though Syl had indicated in many small ways that she returned his feelings, at least to some degree. He decided that as soon as Syl had returned to a reasonably normal state of mind, he would ask her hand in marriage.

In the meantime he would keep as far distant from the wickedly adorable Micaela as was discreetly possible.

iii

A couple of deep-throated hootings of the boat whistle signaled an impending stop. The steady throb of motors lessened and the steamer veered toward shore. Some of the crew went to the forecastle to run the broad stage far out over the port bow. A deck hand walked to the end of it, which because of the high water towered six or eight feet above dock level, and stood readied with a coil of rope in his hands.

A scattering of passengers, attracted to the deck as was usual whenever the steamer stopped, had come to the railing to stare through the mizzle at the bleak view. There was little to be seen except the wide, rotting dock and behind the levee, a cluster of dismal shacks, some of them elevated on pole stilts.

"What we stoppin' here for?" one of the passengers asked a passing deck hand.

"Don' know, suh. There's a boy an' a nigger asho' wavin' a flag an' it's the cap'n's orders we stop." It was the custom of most trade steamers to stop at any plantation dock or village landing whenever signaled from shore.

The captain lifted his hand. A bell rang; the wheels stopped, then reversed, churning the water to foam. Pent steam from the boilers hissed through the gaugecocks and the steamer came precisely to rest, almost touching the dock. A ladder was lowered from the stage and a boy of about twelve climbed nimbly to the deck. He wore an old slouch hat dripping with water and sopped clothing.

"Please sir," he blurted to the captain. "My maw, she's in trouble an' my old man sent me t'fetch a doctor from the first boat passin'."

"Where is your mother?"

" 'Bout a coupla miles back thar in the bayou. . . . " The boy pointed vaguely.

"Sorry, son, but it's agin' regulations for our boat physician to leave the ship while on duty. Now, if your mother could be brought here—"

"She can't git outta bed, sir, an' the old man said if thar hain't no doctor soon, she'll—" He began to cry.

Paul, who with Micaela had just come from the salon where they had lunched, stepped forward.

"I'm a doctor, son. I'll go with you to see what's wrong with your mother."

The captain eyed Paul sharply. "Beggin' your pardon, Doctor, but it's plain from your talk that you're not from these parts. You don't know what it's like back in the bayous in the flooded condition they're in now. I wouldn't advise any sensible man to—"

"If the lad was able to make it to here," Paul said pleasantly, "I'll take my chances of making it back with him." Then he turned to Micaela, who was clinging to his arm.

"You take the boat on to Les Cypres. There'll be a carriage waiting for you. Explain to Miss Beauvais that I'll catch the next boat and join you later."

"No! I will not go to the plantation alone!"

Paul tried to reason with her, but Micaela was adamant. The rain? Poof! She had her rain cape and parasol. The discomfort of riding in a pirogue? Poof again. She was used to bayous and pirogues.

Giving up, Paul scrawled a note to be given to Syl's coachman when his and Micaela's luggage was set ashore at the plantation.

iv

A black man wearing a drenched straw hat and soaked overalls was waiting by the pirogue that had brought the boy in. The pirogue, a canoe-shaped craft that had been hollowed out from a large log, looked sturdy enough, but was hardly suitable for a lady. It had only two low and wet wooden seats near the middle, and the half-rotted bottom, fragrant with the stench of dead fish, was awash with about an inch of water.

When the black man realized that Micaela was coming along, he looked askance at Paul. "'Gators in dere, Marse. Moccasin too. All kinds bitey things. Missy don' go."

Micaela's response was to step into the pirogue without waiting for assistance and seat herself. She looked a bit comical, Paul thought, so fancily dressed and holding a tiny parasol primly over her bonnet while the hem of her expensive gown languished in bilgewater. Plainly she had a mind of her own.

Paul took the other seat and the boy, Jess, kneeled on a saturated pad of old canvas at the prow with a pole in his hands, which he shoved in the water and pushed vigorously. The black man was similarly kneeling at the stern, wielding another pole. Both had paddles near them, but these were for use in calm water, or going downstream.

The pirogue slid smoothly over the ruffled water. On both sides of the swollen stream were endless squared-off fields of rice, most of them so flooded that only the tips of the young rice plants could be seen. Soon they were deeper into a web of inlets and bayous curving along dense growths of giant, moss-bearded cypresses that seemed to be wading in the sinister black swamp water. Occasionally a snake skimmed past, its jewel-eyed head held gracefully a few inches aloft like the lethal end of a spear, showing no fear. Now and then giant brown pelicans took off from the water and went thrashing ahead to alert swarms of harsh-crying seabirds. On the banks, logs that turned out to be alligators slid into the water with scarcely a ripple. The rain fell steadily.

Micaela's bravado seemed to be faltering. She had flung aside the tiny parasol in despair and was now hunched under the inadequate rain cape, water dribbling from her bonnet onto her pert nose. Paul wondered if she regretted this impulsive errand of mercy as much as he did. From the boy he had been able to elicit that his maw had a baby "stuck inside her" and his paw needed help getting it out. So it was just another faulty childbirth, another of the elemental dramas of motherhood that were the stuff of medicine everywhere.

It was almost a truism that the uneducated never sent for a doctor until it was already too late.

"We're thar—!" called Jess. "Paw's out thar in front a-wavin' at us."

The banks had risen to several feet above the water and flattened out to a stretch of cleared land. About a hundred feet back from a rickety little dock was a small cabin, and in front of it a tall, powerfully built man was gesticulating wildly with both arms and shouting something unintelligible. As Paul jumped from the pirogue and started toward the cabin, there were gunshots. He began running.

The tall man wasn't waving at them. He was shaking one fist at the dark heavens, and the other clutched a revolver pointed skyward.

"Goddamn you, God—!" he was howling. "Come on out from wherever yer hidin' an' fight like a man!"

He triggered off a couple more shots at the sky.

Jess ran forward and caught at his father's arm. "Paw—Paw—!"

The man shook the boy's hand away and continued shouting:

"Come on down hyar now, an' bring yer whole passel of angels! I want ya t'see what ya done to us. I drug her right out here in the rain so ya-all kin see—"

Just outside of the cabin doorway was a pallet on which lay the body of an almost naked woman smeared with mud and blood from head to feet. Beside her was a naked, dead baby. Grouped around were five ill-clad children wailing in the most abject grief. A butcher knife lay on the ground nearby.

It was pathetic, ghastly, soul-sickening.

A quick examination told part of the story. The husband, crazed by his wife's torment, had tried to enlarge the opening to get the baby out of her—with fatal results.

The tall man was still screaming a vituperative scream of blood-curdling profanity at the sky, challenging all the gods in Heaven and Jesus Christ Himself to come down to earth and fight. The revolver was now clicking on empty chambers.

Suddenly the man was silent. Micaela had approached to slide her arms tenderly around him. She began crooning words in his ear. He started bawling in great choking gasps, then dropped to his knees and bowed his head toward her. She crouched down too and his sobs muffled away as she cradled his head against her breasts.

Paul had a crazy thought: Maybe God *had* sent down an angel, after all. . . .

v

The pirogue, catching the center current, shot ahead with amazing speed. Paul sat near the front with a paddle, and Micaela—refusing to be merely a passenger this time—sat in the rear with the other paddle.

They had stayed to assist with the burial. Paul had given the husband a calming dose of laudanum, and later Micaela had gone into the cabin to tidy up. Paul, going to fetch her, quite by accident noted her taking some bills of large denomination from somewhere beneath the bosom of her gown, which she placed on the table. The amount was well over a hundred dollars. More, he was sure, than the man made in an entire year.

For a while, the pirogue sped along with ease, requiring no paddling and very little effort to steer. Except for the incessant rain and their wet clothes, Paul would have enjoyed it.

But soon the current slackened. Oddly, the banks seemed to be sinking into the water, melting away before their eyes.

"Juste ciel!" exclaimed Micaela. "The stream, it is suddenly so . . . *élargissement,* so wide!"

Paul was already worrying about it. Ahead, the shorelines had all but vanished, leaving only the cypresses. They had the look of great dark giants wading in the brackish water.

"I'm much afraid that the Mississippi must have burst through the levee at some point and we're headed into floodwaters."

Indeed, in the fast-rising water there was no longer any definable current to guide them; in some places there were even small eddies and whorls of back movement in the sluggish water. The boat drifted aimlessly.

"We are lost," Micaela wailed.

vi

After about a half-hour of hard paddling, the trees thinned and the boat emerged into a wide expanse of water that appeared to be inundated farm land. Micaela let out a cry of relief.

"Look! There's a man up ahead!"

A hunched figure stood beside a tree on a hillock thrusting above water like a tiny island about a thousand feet ahead. They paddled with renewed vigor.

The figure turned out to be a dejected-looking Negro, shivering in sopped clothing. Paul called out:

"What are you doing way out here?"

"Ah swear de Lawd, I swum mos' de way, Massa. Ah was walkin' by de ribber when dat levee broke an' dis is de first dry place ah find."

"You want to get in the boat with us?"

"Law' no, Massa. I stay right heah. Water git higher, I clim' de tree."

"Which way is it to the Mississippi?"

"Somewhar' ovah theah, Massa—" He pointed in a direction almost in reverse from where Paul thought it should be. Maybe, he thought in disgust, we've been paddling in circles.

They paddled off in the new direction. Paul tried to pick

out some fixed object ahead such as a tree to keep them on course, but could see nothing except murky water that blended in with the murky sky. A wind was coming up, making the water choppy and bringing cold rain stingingly against their faces.

A couple of wooden crates floated by, a barrel, a few soggy blobs of feathers that had once been chickens.

"I think we're getting close," said Paul. "There are more things floating around, and the current's getting stronger. . . . "

Glancing back, he felt a surge of sympathy. Micaela's bonnet, utterly ruined by the sluicing rain, was perched at a ridiculous angle on her head, a decorative feather sagging dismally. The dark hair was plastered down each side of her pale cheeks. Sopped clothing clung to every curve of her body.

"I'm sorry I didn't insist that you stay on the steamer. By this time you would be arriving at Les Cypres, where a fine dinner and comfortable quarters would be awaiting."

Micaela laughed. "Have you no romance in your soul, *Docteur?* Raw, wild nature is so *émouvant* . . . it brings you closer to life!"

A small shed floated past. On its roof was a lone rooster huddled mournfully against the driving rain. The forlorn blobs of chickens that had floated past, Paul thought, had probably been a part of his harem.

"There's another male," he said sourly, "who has no romance in his soul . . . or in prospect, for that matter."

"Good roosters live long and have many prospects because their meat is tough and not as savory as the hens."

"Dammit, Micaela! Must you be so bloody cheerful?"

A sudden swirl of current caught them and propelled the pirogue forward. A surge of crosscurrent slammed against the prow, veered the pirogue sideways, started it revolving in a frothing whirlpool. He paddled frantically, spurred by a sense of being trapped helplessly in a whirling limbo somewhere in the gray stratum of downpour from above and angry water beneath. The whole world seemed to be closing in on them.

During the turning, twisting moments that followed, the paddles were utterly useless. They were spinning inexorably in the direction of an uprooted tree lying aslant in the water. The boat was being sucked along in a powerful rush toward the black arm of a branch angling out of the water to about the height of Paul's head.

He made a desperate effort to duck. The branch whacked him across the temple like a club.

It was the last he remembered.

vii

A jarring, grating sensation brought him out of it and he opened his eyes into intense blackness. Groping upward, he felt wet cloth inches above his head. It fell away under his clawing fingers and cold rain slashed at his face. The cloth had been Micaela's cape. Apparently she had stretched it over the gunwales like a small tent to keep the driving rain out of his face.

A series of bumping impacts were shaking the pirogue. He pushed himself erect. His head throbbed with a rush of pain, and through blurred vision he saw Micaela standing erect in the boat pushing with her hands against the trunk of one of two large trees thrusting from the water like fat stilts. The boat was hung up crossways against them, roughly seesawing this way and then that way with the swirling current.

"Micaela—sit down!"

She darted a glance at him. The silly hat was gone; her hair was streaming wildly down her face and her sopped gown clung to her tightly.

"Oh Paul—there's a house up ahead! As soon as we can get loose from these terrible trees—" She went back to pushing.

Paul rose to his knees, seeking his oar. It had vanished. He began crawling. The shift of his weight changed the whole balance of things, and slowly, terrifyingly, the pirogue began swinging around.

It happened too fast for either of them to call out. The boat began rolling as it swung sideways, and in a fraction of a second was suddenly upturned. Micaela's scream abruptly sliced off as she went under.

Paul snatched at a low-hanging branch and hung there, feet dragging in the current, frantically looking around for her. The dark head bobbed above water about a dozen feet away and a choked wail burst from her lips.

"Paul, Paul—I can't swim!"

Having grown up near a river, Paul was fairly skilled as a swimmer, but skill might not be enough in such turbulent water. Especially when fully clothed.

Releasing his grip on the branch, he started out. His boots

dragged at his legs as if weighted with lead; his clothes impeded each movement. The upturned pirogue drifted past . . . out of reach. Micaela's head sank again and all he could see was some of her voluminous skirt, brought to the surface by trapped air. She was still nearly a dozen feet away, being carried by the current.

He stroked toward her furiously, closing the gap. Her head reappeared briefly, her arms flailing. She opened her mouth—

"Pau—!" Her voice gurgled away as water flooded into her mouth. Her head sank.

In several more strokes he was able to grab a handful of dress and began hauling with desperation. Her head reappeared. The face was oddly puffed out, the eyes bulging.

Dread seized him. "Micaela—!"

A gush of water spurted from her mouth. "I-I was trying . . . t-to hold my breath and not . . . swallow any more of this *exécrable* water . . . n-not fit for pigs to drink!"

His crazy urge to laugh was quelled by the struggle to keep from going under with her added weight. Various flotsam was gliding past: a broken crate, an empty bottle, fragments of timber. . . . He grasped wildly at the first thing within reach. It was a board. A long board.

Gratefully he hooked one arm over the board; the other was supporting Micaela. The board sank slightly beneath their combined weight, but was still buoyant enough to keep their heads barely above water.

"Le bon Dieu is looking out for us," she gasped.

A shuddering impact shook the length of the board, jarred it loose from his grip. The leading end of the board had struck a hard, immovable object. It began twisting, nosing downward. Again Paul was floundering wildly, trying to keep Micaela afloat.

Another hard object slammed from behind, knocking out his wind.

"Ah!" she cried. "The house I told you about!"

A wall of grayed wood rose from the water, a low roof, a window at water level. His fingers scrabbled at the unpainted wood of the window ledge. One pane was broken, water pouring in. Chunks of wooden debris had collected against the building. He grasped a club-sized piece.

"I'm going to knock the glass out," he warned, "so turn your face and close your eyes in case there are any flying splinters."

viii

Inside, they could barely see. Sloshing through cold water up to their knees, they began exploring. A floating object bumped gently against his leg. By the feel of it, he took it to be a chair.

"It seems to be an abandoned house," he said. "Let's look for a staircase leading up to where it's dry."

Feeling their way through a doorway and then along other walls, they soon located a narrow, steep flight of stairs. Paul started up.

At the top of the staircase the blackness was even more intense.

"Paul—hold my hand. I can't see a thing."

He located her wet, chilled hand. It was quivering.

"You're shaking like a leaf!"

"I thought it was you shaking."

Paul was in fact not only shivering, but his teeth were beginning to chatter. "I admit I'm cold, but you must be frozen. Maybe we can find some old blankets or something up here to help keep us warm."

Hand in hand they felt their way through what might have been a bedroom, or perhaps it was an attic. It seemed barren of furnishings until Micaela gave a little exclamation of discovery as she ran into some sort of obstruction.

"It's a bed! An iron cot, I think—" She bent to pat a hand over the object, let out a sound of disappointment.

"Only a lumpy old mattress! No sheets, no blankets. . . . "

Paul's shivering had become uncontrollable. He gritted his teeth so she wouldn't hear them chattering. What a way for a good physician to end up! He'd be down with pneumonia, at the very least, or drop dead from exhaustion. Now with the drowning crisis over, all his other pains and aching muscles were making themselves felt; the swelling on his forehead from the tree limb was throbbing.

"Paul—" her hands traveled over him lightly. "You *are* shaking. You're ill!"

"I'm sorry Micaela, but—" He slumped down to a sitting position on the bed. "I've simply got to rest."

"*Non, non*—not until you get those wet clothes off!"

She went to work unbuttoning his sopped jacket, shirt, unbuckling his belt—

"Micaela—this is embarrassing—"

"For you, a *docteur* who sees naked women all the time? Sometimes you are a very silly man."

Deftly she continued disrobing him, pulling off one garment after another. Then he lay back naked on the rough canvas mattress and tried to control his shaking. As from a distance he was aware of the slopping sounds of her water-soaked petticoat, pantalets and other items of clothing dropping to the floor.

Moments later she slid down behide him, her sleek wet flesh warm against his coldness. Her arms encircled him; her body rolled over until she lay atop him.

"I will be your warm blanket. . . . " she whispered.

ix

He slept. Whether for minutes or hours, he didn't know. He awakened into warmth. He was on his side, snug within her encircling arms, aware of the soft pressure of her breasts, her pelvis—

A fragment of a strange dream lingered . . . the poignance of his childhood yearning for the mother he had never known . . . then a taste of the bliss of being comforted under the maternal wings of love. . . .

Then the raw shock of forbidden sensuality.

It was that which had awakened him. The unexpected sexual arousal that had slipped past the guardians of his brain while he slept.

He was no longer chilled. He was infused with heat. All his tiredness, his aches and pains seemed to have dissipated under the speeded coursing of hot blood. From some unknown reservoir of life force in his exhausted, chilled body had come a new rush of strength.

The stirrings in his loins were causing discomfiture. He began to disentangle himself from her embrace.

"Micaela, I think I'd better—"

"*Mais non, bébé.* You are rested. It is your turn to comfort me."

"I don't think you understand—"

"Only too well I understand. . . . " she murmured, clinging to him. "It is as *le bon Dieu* ordained. . . . "

Le bon Dieu, he thought, certainly had nothing to do with the kind of thoughts that were now so urgently crowding his head.

He met her burning lips with his own burning lips. Moral

resistance melted away under the seething fire that possessed him.

He began showering kisses on her lips, cheeks, neck, down to her breasts. He wanted to love every inch of this slip of a girl whose fortitude and stamina had exceeded his own, this essence of full womanhood who out of the bowels of darkness, death and pain had created beauty, this wondrous thing. He wanted to devour her with his love. She was moaning softly, writhing in his arms, her hot moist kisses sliding over his face, arms, chest. . . .

Then he had misgivings. "Stop me, Micaela," he said huskily. "I don't want to do this—not with Pierre's woman. . . . "

"*Non, non,*" she said fiercely. "Never have I been any man's woman! I belong only to myself. I am offering myself to you. If you persist in being such a fool, neither *le bon Dieu* nor I shall ever forgive you!"

His weak obeisance to his puritan conscience dissolved. It had been hypocritical in any case, for his primal hunger, the quickening rise of passion was no longer to be denied. With a hoarse little cry he caught her again in his embrace. She squirmed sensuously against him, and in the darkness he could not see but feel the soft warm mounds of her breasts, the subtle curves and hollows, the movements of her writhing, spreading limbs. A trembling had seized him, but not from cold, as he began guiding his hard, jutting organ toward that dark and mysterious, honeyed focal point for which it had been destined. . . .

At the beginning of his penetration she gave a soft moan. Then he stopped—

His medical brain told him what he could not believe . . . something he had never before experienced. . . . He began again, gently, firmly . . . felt the delicate membrane give way. At the same instant a small birdlike cry burst from her; a mingling of anguish and joy.

Then the moments of extra heat; the virginal blood . . .

He continued, slowly and tenderly now, and she clung to him tightly, with increasing ardency in her responses, while sobbing softly for the loss—and the giving—of the most precious gift of her life. . . .

x

Toward morning, after sleeping, and more lovemaking, they finally relaxed in each other's arms and got around to talking. . . .

"You've got some tall explaining to do, my sweet," he said. "All this time you've been masquerading under false colors. How in the world could you have been Pierre's mistress when, until last night, you weren't even a beginner in the amatory arts?"

"Was I a disappointment?"

"You were a joy beyond belief—but that's not answering my question."

"I gave my vow never to tell, but since you are my lover, I have no choice but to explain. . . . "

She then told him the full story, how Pierre had taken her under his protection—but not for sexual reasons. He had told her that it was a matter of great delicacy, something she must never reveal: that it was impossible for him to have a sexual love relationship with a woman, but he wished to carry on such a pretense so that his friends and relatives would never find out.

Paul felt a rush of sympathy for poor Pierre. So that really explained the suicide. Impotence!

"And all that time, he didn't even kiss you?"

"Only on the cheek. Like a brother, a very loving brother —and I learned to love him as deeply as if I were really his sister."

So Pierre hadn't told her the full truth. It was better, perhaps, that she should never know.

"Still, since he made no sexual demands on you, and you had much time alone, why did you not find others?"

"Love and sex are two different things, *Docteur*. Sex without love is lust. I care nothing for lust—I grew up seeing too much of it. It is only for animals. Sex should be given only with love, and I was determined that my first time would be only with a worthy man of my own choice, one for whom I could feel deep love."

Paul was embarrassed. "But why me? There are so many worthy men to choose from. And you scarcely know me."

"Why? *Je ne sais pas.* Only *le bon Dieu* can answer that. When I first saw you on Balize, I knew at once that you were my choice. After you left, there was only Pierre, whom I loved deeply in spirit but not in flesh. There were many, yes, who wished to have me behind Pierre's back. I spit on them! I was prepared to give my body to a *protecteur* whom I could not fully love, because that is what has been planned for me, but never would I betray him! It was not until after Pierre's death, and you returned, that I knew you were still my choice. And *le bon Dieu* arranged for my wishes to be granted. . . . "

An oppressive sense of guilt settled over Paul. He loved Micaela, yes; he adored her.

But he also loved Syl. Though he had never spoken to her about it, she still had his prior emotional commitment; he had decided to ask for her hand.

"Micaela . . . " he began cautiously. "As you must know, I am a man of modest means, and you are accustomed to luxuries—"

"Please—" she said quickly. "I hope you did not misunderstand. . . . I love you deeply—I shall always love you —but to marry you would be impossible!"

He was taken back. "Uh, but I don't quite—"

"Ah, *chéri*—!" She pulled his head close and kissed him tenderly. "Do not feel hurt. My love will be yours forever, but we cannot marry. The Black Code sternly forbids marriage of a *gens de couleur* to either a white or a black. I am free to marry only one of my own kind, which I do not wish to do. It is my solemn obligation to Maman, as well as to myself, to find another rich *protecteur*."

"Is that what you really want, Micaela?"

She hesitated. Then, "One must be realistic. I will always treasure your love, but for many reasons I must be *riche, très riche*. I must have a great deal of money so that I can bring Maman back from Balize, where she has been banished from the life she loves. With money I can protect her from old enemies so she can return to her beloved New Orleans and again hold her head high."

"And do you think you can find such a *protecteur*?"

"Ah yes, with ease. I can pick from many. I have now decided to pick the one who has offered the most. He has promised to at once place a very large sum of money in my own name at the Banque des Citoyens and build me a grand new home."

"He must be very rich indeed."

"Yes. Even richer than Pierre. He is Leon Jacquard."

xi

As the gray dawn grew brighter under a cleared sky, they reluctantly dressed again in their cold, wet garments—with the exception of a pair of Micaela's lacy white pantalets.

With a knowing smile, she insisted that they be hung out of a window as a signal on the end of a pole they found in the attic.

By mid-forenoon they were picked up by a rescue party of eager males.

BOOK SEVEN

Distant Thunder

ONE: The Knight Takes the Queen

THE dinner was over and Syl, who had scarcely spoken throughout the meal, now rose.

"Gentlemen, if you will excuse me, I think I will repair to the sitting room and read."

Paul and Etienne rose to their feet as she left.

"Come, Paul," said Etienne. "Let me give you another lesson in chess. . . . " Fond of chess and in need of an opponent since Pierre's death, Etienne had volunteered to teach Paul, who quickly came to enjoy it. He had developed into a dogged, persevering player who never forgot a move or a defeat and did not repeat his mistakes.

But this evening as they proceeded to play, his thoughts drifted elsewhere. . . .

Syl's attitude. Why was she so restrained toward him? Was

it because he had, albeit by necessity, spent the night with Micaela during the flood? He had overheard some sly badinage passing among the rescue crew, a rough sort, in allusion to the lacy white pantalets that Micaela had hung outside the window of the abandoned house on a pole as a distress signal, and possibly such coarse rumors could have reached Syl's chaste ears.

When informed that Micaela had changed her mind about visiting Les Cypres, and instead was returning to New Orleans, Syl patently had been more pleased than disappointed at not having to go through with her intention to confront the octoroon who had been Pierre's mistress.

Since then the news had spread like a hot wind up the Mississippi that Leon Jacquard was enlarging his mansion, refurbishing it lavishly to make it the grandest home on the river for his new mistress—Micaela—who had already moved in with him.

"Disgusting!" had been Syl's comment.

But that had been weeks ago, and Syl was still keeping her aloof, cool distance. Could she have intuitively guessed what had happened between him and Micaela?

Certainly it was something he would never forget. Often he relived in imagination those wondrous hours spent with her, the love she had given so freely and spontaneously.

Love she had since bartered away for Jacquard's wealth.

Or was Syl's puzzling attitude really her way of telling him that she could never accept him as a husband? Enough time had passed. It was now midsummer. He had told himself he had been delaying his proposal of marriage until he could be sure that she was fully recovered from the shock of Pierre's suicide. In his heart he knew it was from cowardice.

Etienne looked up from the chessboard.

"Paul, for the past half-hour you have been playing by rote, following only the plays I have taught you. You have learned well—I commend you for that—but you are very slow to take the initiative in trying out moves of your own devising."

"Matched against a master like you, I don't like to take risks."

"Why not? The only way to win is not to be afraid of losing. If you are too cautious, you might lose a prize. . . . "

Paul laughed. "Fortunately, we're not playing for money."

"There are greater prizes than money. I am rarely blunt— my preference is oriental obliquity—but in this case I think a more forthright approach is in order. . . . " The heavy-browed eyes sternly scanned Paul's face.

"Paul, what are your intentions in regard to Syl?"

"I wasn't aware that I am suspected of harboring intentions."

"Naiveté won't ring any bells at the fair, Paul. I am not blind, nor is Syl. We are both quite aware of your feelings. You flatter me by calling me a master at chess—I concede to an adequate skill—so I am sure you will credit me with the capability, should I choose to use it, to easily frustrate your aspirations concerning Syl."

Paul reddened.

"I only wish you to know that I am stepping back at this point. . . . " Etienne stood up. "So if you will excuse me, I have matters to attend to in my study. The next move is up to you. . . . "

He started away, turned to add:

"By the way, Syl is still in the sitting room immersed in her Gothic romance. Most unusual for this late hour, don't you think?"

ii

The needle flashed. Seated demurely in her big Empire chair, Syl for the past fifteen minutes had been sewing steadily at the colorful fabric spread over her lap.

But now her nimble fingers ceased and with an air of decision she set aside her crewelwork. A tiny smile flitted across her lips.

"Paul, all this time you have been talking of nothing but how poor you are and your uncertain future, and how a doctor is not likely ever to get rich. I have no interest or concern in such boring matters. Have you nothing else to say?"

Paul felt heat rising to his face. He was seated somewhat stiffly in a heavy, carved chair of walnut regarding her with something akin to stage fright. Soft light from a chandelier brought out the reddish highlights in her golden hair, which had been pulled back sleekly and fastened behind, a mass of perfectly curled ringlets dangling down her back. She wore a pale-green organdy gown. Simple, unadorned with ruffles or ribbons. It was wonderfully elegant. An appropriate setting for the dazzling gem of her face. My God, he thought, how could a rough clod like me ever be so presumptuous as to think—

"I'm sorry if I bored you," he said stiffly. "I was only trying to find words to say . . . "

"Say what, Paul?"

"That a man without a personal fortune of his own should never dream of asking . . . "

"Asking what?"

"Asking one like you to marry."

She picked up her crewelwork and began working. With a kind of exquisite intensity. "And why not? I am a rich woman, so why should I care whether a suitor had a penny or not?"

He blurted it out: "Syl, I can think of no greater joy, no greater honor than if you would become my—"

Before the words were out of his mouth, she rose from the chair and flung herself into his arms. Tears streamed down her cheeks against his.

"Oh Paul—I was only waiting for you to ask!"

TWO: The Deflowering of a Lady

THE only gloom on Paul's bright horizon was the growing tension between the North and South. It had been brought to a high pitch in that year of 1857 by the Dred Scott decision of March 13 rendered by the U.S. Supreme Court— a decision that was to haunt that august body for generations to come as the most infamous blot on its judicial integrity since the court was created. A sectionally biased court—albeit sincere in its majority convictions and with the tacit support of President Buchanan—had ventured into political waters beyond judicial propriety and ruled that *no slave or slave descendant—in brief, no Negro—could ever be a citizen of the United States.*

Thus denying blacks forever the right of seeking justice in the courts; thus destroying the power of Congress to prohibit slavery; thus denying the antislavery states the right to set slaves free. Thus ruining the concept of popular sovereignty.

In their jubilance over their victory, the slaveholding states

failed to hear, or take heed of, the ominous distant thunder
of outrage that swept through the Northern states. . . .

Paul first sensed it through visiting planter friends of
Etienne's. Their courtesy toward Paul was as punctilious as
ever, but with an added aloofness—sometimes almost amounting to insult—and a complete avoidance of any political talk
in his presence.

But the newspapers were dominated by it, clearly pointing
up the frightening gulf that was growing between slavery and
antislavery forces. Even Abraham Lincoln, returning to
Illinois politics under the new Republican banner, and long
considered a moderate about slavery, began to speak out
strongly against it:

"The lot of the Negro," he told a Springfield audience, "is
steadily worsening. Far from easing the bonds of slavery, the
South is drawing them tighter than ever, sealing off all ave-
nues of escape. New state laws are being enacted in the South
to prohibit even the slaveholders from emancipating their
own slaves. . . . "

Paul, who read all the papers avidly, brought up the subject
one evening at dinner: "Has Louisiana enacted such a law
that would forbid you or Syl to free your slaves if you so
wished?" he asked Etienne. "It seems so incredibly unjust—"

He broke off at the sudden warning look that Etienne shot
from under his brooding black eyebrows, but Syl spoke up
sharply:

"I certainly hope such a law *is* passed. Aurora has pestered
me so often about whether or not I shall someday give her
freedom papers. With such a law, I could simply tell her I
can't because it is illegal."

Their different attitudes toward slavery was the only
bothersome wedge between them, but something that Paul
was determined to overlook, believing that with time she
would change.

The wedding had been set for the following May. Syl
wanted that much time to heal the melancholia caused by
the loss of Pierre and to adjust to the idea of marriage.

Paul was content to wait, for now with the impossible
dream approaching reality, his everyday life, inversely, had
taken on a dreamlike quality. Now of an evening when he
looked over the cypress swamps into a sky drenched in moist
sunset, he thought not of the swarms of mosquitoes soon to
rise from stagnant waters, but of the beauty of the steamy
reds, golds and lavenders that silhouetted the moss-bearded
trees against their molten colors. He listened with pleasure, as

if hearing it for the first time, the cooing of doves in the *pigeonnier,* from whence came the plump tender squabs that supplied so many delectable dinners. He began to notice small things such as the chameleons flittering up a camphor tree, finding amusement in the way the *piquininos,* as the black children were called, caught them to play with, using bright bits of colored cloth to bring out the shifting color changes in the little creatures.

Thus the days slipped one into another, for the most part deep with peace and happiness and bright hopes for the future. The weeks slipped into months; summer into fall; Christmas came and passed; then the jasmine bloomed and the magnolias flowered, and again it was a glorious spring. The wedding was only a month away.

ii

One afternoon in April a sidewheeler with the name *New Orleans Lady* painted gaudily on the bow nosed in at the quay. A flamboyantly dressed gentleman debarked. The slave assigned to be on the watch for visitors had a carriage rushed down to pick him up. The visitor, delivered to the infirmary where Paul was at work, moments later swaggered in with a broad grin on his face.

Paul looked up from his microscope. "Mike Quinn! What in the world are you doing here?"

"I just stepped off the boat to say hello to my old friend," said Mike as the two shook hands. His clothing, Paul noted, while flashy as ever, was plainly new and of expensive materials.

"But how did you know I was here?"

"From that delightful creature Micaela Delacroix."

Paul felt a moment of senseless jealousy. "I wasn't aware that she numbered you among her friends."

"Aye, and only in this great magical America could it happen. The tales I could tell of my adventures here would start even you believing in the leprechauns. Only a few months ago I arrived at Micaela's fine mansion down the river, like out of a fairy tale, wearing not a stitch but the bare skin God gave me, and that divine lady greeted me with open arms."

Paul grabbed the man's lapels in a sudden surge of anger. "Damn your lies, Mike! Don't be telling me that you, naked, and Micaela—"

Good-naturedly the big gambler gripped Paul's hands and pushed them aside. "Your temper, my friend, over Jacquard's mistress is unseemly." He grinned slyly. "The more so if the rumors floating up and down the river that a certain dour Yankee doctor is soon to wed the beautiful Sylphide Beauvais are true. . . . "

"That's another matter, Mike. But about you and Micaela—"

"The lass is an angel of purity, and just as pure are my feelings for her. But come, walk with me back to the boat, and I'll tell you the brief of it. . . . "

Mike's story smacked of invention and Paul listened with skepticism. He had, Mike recounted, been in a poker game with the captain-owner of a steamboat, winning heavily until the captain weaseled out by loudly proclaiming that Mike was cheating—an arrant lie!—and forthwith ordered his crew of bully boys to strip Mike of all his clothes and put him overboard in a tiny rowboat without oars. And then the guardian angel that Mike firmly believed would always sooner or later—though usually later—come to his aid directed the boat out of the swift current into the sidewaters. Close enough to shore so that when the first dock appeared, he risked the swim of about a hundred ells through icy water to reach it. It was the Leon Jacquard plantation.

"I'll never swallow that, Mike," said Paul. "Jacquard would have shot you on sight."

"I would agree on that, my doubting friend, but fortunately Jacquard was away. And fortunately, Micaela had visiting her a most lovely creature from New Orleans who was waiting for the next boat back to the city. Micaela remembered me, of course, and the two angels with their hearts of gold and wits of a fox quickly got me dressed in some of Jacquard's fine duds—an adequate fit they were, too—and well before the master of the manor was due back, there I was dressed like the finest gentleman, escorting Micaela's enchanting friend aboard the next steamer."

Paul laughed outright. "It's an entertaining tale, Mike, but a bit too fanciful."

"Don't ye want to hear the end of it?"

They had arrived at the dock. "Another time, Mike. Your boat is waiting, though I'm surprised it's still here."

"They wouldna' leave without Mike Quinn. That's part of the story. You see, Micaela's friend, whose name is Danielle D'Indy, was one of Madame Silkwood's girls—but not from need. Danielle's mother is one of the richest ladies in New Orleans, but Danielle went to Silkwood's because, like me, she has a great love for excitement and adventure. We took a great liking to each other, and it was she that supplied me with the cash to get started again."

He paused and clapped a hand on Paul's shoulder. "For the first time in my life, my friend, I am on the way to becoming rich, and I would like to do something to show that I never forget old friends. Have you and Miss Beauvais set your wedding date?"

"It is set for May fifteenth, Mike."

"Then would you do me the honor of allowing me to provide you a wedding gift of a week's tour in the finest suite on the *New Orleans Lady*. It is most luxurious, the food is the finest on the river, and it would not cost you a farthing."

"It is very generous of you," Paul said, surprised, "but we couldn't possibly accept—"

"But you must! It is a matter of pride with me, Paul. Once you mistrusted me, but still it was the twenty-five dollars I befooled from you that gave me my start in this wondrous country. As a gentleman, you cannot deny me the courtesy of repaying you in my own way."

The fact was that Syl, who loved boats and the river, had recently proposed, as a modest but delightful possibility for a brief honeymoon, a steamboat voyage up the Mississippi and back, and Paul had concurred. Within his means, he would have agreed with anything that she suggested.

"But such a lavish gift—"

Mike chuckled and drew himself up to his most impressive height.

"For me it would be but a trifle, for you see, I own the *New Orleans Lady*. . . . "

"You *own* that grand boat? You're joking!"

"The only joke, my friend, is at the expense of the former owner—the very same scoundrel who once put me adrift naked from this very same boat. After hearing my story, Danielle D'Indy set her wits to working—she's a bold and sharp lass, that one—and as I said, she has a great love for adventure. She hired her own crew of bully boys and put them aboard as passengers whilst I, flaunting a big roll of money, gammoned the rogue into tempting fortune again with the cards. He is of the kind, you understand, who gets seized with the fever of gambling worse than a sot with a jug of grog. All night the game lasted, me playing him gentle as a fish with the hook half in his mouth—" Mike broke into laughter.

"The short of it is that I won the *New Orleans Lady*, fair and square. The knave tried to weasel out by calling foul, but Danielle's bully boys stood firm two to one against his scalawags. She had brought along her attorney, who had the quit-claim papers all ready for the signing, proper and legal. So you see, my friend, my prediction that I would make my fortune on the river boats has come true."

"Truthfully, Mike, did you really win fair and square?"

"Blister my limbs if I lie! Never would I stoop to cheat— except against a cheat."

Paul grinned. "In that case, I will accept your magnanimous invitation—that is, if it is agreeable with Miss Beauvais —but only on the condition that you will be my best man at the wedding."

The big gambler's handsome face beamed with delight. Grasping Paul's hand, he shook it vigorously.

"It will be a great honor, my friend. You can count on me."

iii

There followed in the next several weeks a series of small parties and bridal showers, but Syl begged her friends to keep them to a minimum. The wedding she wished to keep small and simple. Only about sixty invitations were sent out to those friends she considered closest to the family.

During the last two weeks, there was a dismal turn of events. Notes of regret, excessively apologetic, began to arrive from a scattering of the guests who for one reason or another would be unable to attend the wedding. Syl was shocked. Such social snubs from her peers were unheard of, unpardonable.

She shed her tears secretly in her own rooms, not telling Paul, and during the wedding rehearsal in the small plantation chapel the day before the wedding, held her head high.

All through the night before the event, slaves worked feverishly preparing the food: hams, green and cured; roast beef, turkey, chicken; various kinds of grilled fish; quail, squabs, pheasant; shrimp, oysters, crayfish. Suckling pigs and calves were readied for grilling in open pits. The finest wines, whiskeys, brandies, rums, and punch were placed ready for the serving. The chapel was decorated with blooms of magnolia, boughs of flowering dogwood, woven ropes of purple bougainvillea.

On the afternoon of the wedding, barely more than half the invited guests were present.

Adding to Syl's distress, Mike had exceeded her worst fears with the expensive vulgarity of his attire—a brand-new wildly checkered suit, a garishly flowered waistcoat and a dazzling plethora of diamonds and other gems flashing from fingers and breastpin.

However, when she appeared coming down the aisle on Etienne's arm, she had all the proud poise and bearing of a queen. Her radiant beauty, set off in a gown of white satin and lace, drew involuntary gasps and whispers of admiration from all sides.

After the ring was placed on her finger and Paul kissed her, he had a terrible, disheartening sense that the hot tears on her cheeks were more of chagrin than of happiness.

iv

The *New Orleans Lady* was a handsome sight. Tied in at the Les Cypres quay, she lay long and trim and pretty in the water. On the paddleboxes above the boat's name, which was painted in red and gold, were seductive, gilded mermaids. Railings of pristine white fenced in the hurricane and texas decks. Atop the texas deck was perched the all-glass pilot house, glistening under the setting sun. A flag fluttered from the jackstaff. Volumes of black smoke rolled and poured from the stacks—a grand effect prepared especially for the arrival of the newlyweds by the addition of rosin and pitch pine in the furnaces.

The entire crew of firemen and deck hands along with the captain, mate and even the lordly pilot—all resplendent in fresh white uniforms reserved for gala events—stood loosely at attention as Paul and Syl came aboard.

"But where are the passengers?" Paul asked.

"Begad, and did ye expect that I would be carrying passengers on the day that I am the best man for a friend? Tomorrow is soon enough to be taking regular passengers again. For this day and night, the entire ship is reserved only for you and your bride."

"Mike, I'm overwhelmed!"

" 'Tis naught but a trifle . . . and now, if you like, I will give you a tour of this capital vessel, which was built in Pittsburgh after a design by the great steam engineer and inventor Robert Fulton. It has a keel length of—"

Syl interjected quickly. "If you will excuse me, Mr. Quinn, I am quite exhausted—"

"Ah, but of course—it was thoughtless of me to dis-remember female nature. The leddies, delicate angels that they are, have no interest in machinery. I venture to say you will find matters more to your liking in our finest suite, which was once occupied by President James Polk himself. Come I will guide you there straightaway. . . . " He gave Paul a huge wink, which brought a flush to Syl and grins from the crew, most of whom were staring enrapt at Syl as they were escorted past.

"And now, Sir Doctor and Mrs. Abbott," said Mike when they reached the suite, "I shall leave you lovebirds alone to your delights. The door is unlocked, the key is inside, and the blessings of the whole ship and meself go with you. Every hand aboard is at your service. All you need do is pull the bellcord and ask for whatever you desire. . . . " With a low bow, he strode away.

v

The lapping and purl of waters against the hull, the steady slap-slap of paddle wheels, the drone of motors vibrating through every molecule of the ship . . . all this was counter-point to the turmoil of Paul's feelings as he lay in bed on his wedding night beside his frightened bride. . . .

Though not as lavish, the suite was as clean and dainty as Syl's own bedroom, elegantly fitted out with a crimson carpet, velvet sofa, several chairs, a gilt-framed looking glass and fringed red-and-gold bombazette curtains. The bed itself was covered with handsomely flowered bedclothes, and over it a mosquito bar tastefully screened with lacy white netting. The mattress, as Paul was to discover, had been stuffed with Spanish moss, of which the woods of Louisiana abounded, and gave off a murky fragrance akin to a salt marsh.

But such details were of trivial concern to Paul and Syl, both of whom were in the grip of their separate emotions.

Earlier Syl had emerged from her private bath and dress-ing room into the darkened bedroom (for she had insisted that the whale-oil lamps first be extinguished) and moved timorously toward the large bed, which was barely visible in the muffled moonlight. When Paul, already garbed in his nightshirt, had reached out to guide her, she flinched from the touch on her silken nightgown and hastily sought con-cealment beneath the sheets.

Now as he gently slid an arm around her, he again felt the shrinking away, the stiffening of her body.

"Oh Paul . . . I just don't know what . . . to *do*. . . . "

"You have nothing to fear, my darling. . . . " He bent and kissed her lips lightly. The lips were cold, unresponding. "I would not cause you hurt for anything in the world."

Suddenly her arms encircled him and she clung to him tightly, frantically. "It's not that I don't love you, but I . . . I'm frightened. . . . "

"Would you rather just go to sleep and get a good rest?"

"No, it's not that. . . . I want to be everything you expect, but—"

He kissed her again on the forehead, cheeks, and lips, which were still cold. He sought to comfort her by drawing her rigid body closer, again felt her unconscious resistance. One of his hands, almost idly, began caressing her cheeks, shoulder, down the side of her torso; it brushed against the silk over one of her small tight breasts. She jerked away as if stung.

"I . . . I'm sorry, Paul. I didn't mean to—"

"It's perfectly natural. You've been under great strain, and the day has been overexciting. . . . "

More than that, he thought, she had been overly protected all her life. Her schooling had been mostly through private tutors. Her innocence and purity had been fiercely guarded by the men who had reared her, without even a mother to advise and prepare her with the skimpy knowledge that most maidens carry to the altar. From books only could she have gained a surely distorted idea of the marriage relationship. Her body had remained sacred and inviolate, untouched by any hands other than those of the nurses who had bathed her as a child.

His intense arousal began to subside.

"There will be other nights, my darling," he went on. "Many other nights in the lifetime ahead of us. It is my wish that for tonight and for as many nights as it takes to become accustomed to the strangeness of each other's body—we simply relax and hold each other in arms of love. . . . "

She turned and pressed her face forlornly against his chest.

vi

Deep mellow notes from a big bell awakened him. Then a shouting voice from the hurricane deck:

"Stabboard lead, there! . . . labboard lead! . . . labboard, labboard!"

Syl still slept. Paul dressed quickly, bent to implant a light kiss on the dear face, and went out.

He was astonished to find the bright sun already overhead. The shouting came from the watchman who stood spread-eagled on the elevated hurricane deck looking forward to the prow where the two leadsmen, one on either side, were bent over the railing with lead-weighted lines plumbing the depths.

"Nine-and-a-half! N-i-n-e feet! N-i-n-e feet! Eight-and-a-half, eight-and—"

The calls of the leadsmen were repeated along the deck by the word-passers with resounding vigor; the watchman pulled at his bell ropes—answered by faint jinglings deep below in the engine room—and bawled more precise instructions through the speaking tube.

"Ah, good day, Sir Doctor. . . . " Mike Quinn strolled up, grinning pleasantly. "As you can see, we're in the shoals, but never fear, we'll be back in deep water soon. I trust your enchanting lady love and you were not too disturbed by the shouting."

"Not at all, Mike. In fact, Mrs. Abbott is still sound asleep." The unfamiliar words, "Mrs. Abbott," rolled delightfully on his tongue.

"And wrapped in sweet dreams, I would venture, bless her soul. Will her preference be to dine in the salon, or be served in your suite?"

"I think Mrs. Abbott would prefer having her breakfast in the suite."

"You have but to pull the bellcord and you'll get service quick as a wink."

"Mike, I don't know how I can ever thank you enough—"

"Your friendship and trust are thanks enough. But to another subject . . . We are again picking up passengers, and toward evening shall be picking up a very special one—that most exciting young lady to whom I owe my present fortune, Danielle D'Indy, who has been visiting in Natchez. I wish very much for you to meet her. Would you and Mrs. Abbott do me the honor of joining us at dinner tonight?"

"With pleasure."

When he returned to the suite, Syl was up and fully dressed. Without makeup, which she abhorred as something only for women of easy morals, she looked as fresh and innocent as a child.

"I was beginning to fear that already I had lost my Yankee husband," she said as they embraced.

"I've been lost only in my dreams."

"Seriously, Paul, do you have any regrets?"

"I vow, I've never known such happiness in all my life!" He laughed, adding, "Mayhap romance is catching. In any case, it appears that our host is similarly enamored of a young lady who will be coming aboard at Natchez. Mike has asked us to join them at dinner this evening."

"I think that would be lovely," she said almost mechanically, but it was plain from the faraway look on her face that her thoughts were on other matters. "Paul—" She drew his head down and kissed him lightly. "About last night . . . Thanks for being so understanding. . . . "

He held her tight. "I think you are building up a mountain out of nothing."

She kissed him again, more fervently. "My fears are gone, dear husband," she whispered, "Tonight . . . it will be different. . . . "

vii

When Paul and Syl entered the salon that evening, it had been transformed into a room of splendor and gaiety. Whale-oil wall lamps cast a soft magical glow over their gilded bases and the row of polished brass spittoons below. From a series of prism-fringed chandeliers, glittering radiance fell over tables covered with sparkling white napery and glistening crystal. Nearly half the tables were already occupied, for many more passengers had been taken aboard, particularly at Natchez, and the air was thick with a fragrance of perfumes, cigar smoke and cooking odors mingled with the burnt smells of wax and oil from the lighting fixtures. A four-piece band was lustily imparting Dixieland verve into their version of a modern European waltz.

Mike Quinn spotted them and came forward to meet them with a sweeping bow.

"We will not be sitting at the captain's table tonight," he told them after their greetings. "I thought it would be cozier —loosen our tongues in their sockets as the Irish would put it—with jist the four of us. I am most anxious for you to meet my delightful lady friend. . . . "

Danielle D'Indy, toying with a thin-stemmed glass of wine, sat alone at a table decorated with a lavish centerpiece of colorful flowers. She was, Paul thought as Mike made the introductions, one of the most dazzling females he had ever seen. Her smile was dazzling; the sparkle of jewelry on her wrists, fingers, neck and ears was dazzling; and her gown of rich red velvet dazzled in a different way, quite boldly exposing more perfection of creamy shoulder and bosom than most ladies would have thought proper.

Her black hair was coiffed close to her head and a row of ringlets dangled over her forehead, beneath which a pair of amused dark eyes sparkled as brightly as any of her gems. Her white teeth flashed with a smile, producing dimples as she spoke:

"It is such a pleasure to meet you both. Mike speaks very highly of you, Dr. Abbott, and of course, Mrs. Abbott, your maiden name is well known everywhere in Louisiana."

With a fixed smile on her face, Syl responded with gracious words, but Paul noted how her eyelids had flickered briefly at the first moment of meeting. He took it as an involuntary sign of Syl's disapproval of the flamboyant low-cut dress, so markedly in contrast with Syl's own discreet one of green satin.

After they were seated, the cork was popped from a magnum of champagne that had been brought in a large silver ice bucket. A black waiter poured four glasses and Mike proposed a toast to the health and happiness of the newlyweds. Paul followed with a toast of similar sentiments for Mike and Miss D'Indy, to which all dutifully drank. There followed a lull of silence, which was broken by Syl:

"Miss D'Indy, your name is very unusual. Are you perchance from New Orleans?"

Mike cut in with obvious pride in his lady love, "Danielle is indeed from New Orleans, where the D'Indy name is most esteemed. Her mother is well known in the highest social circles—"

Danielle stopped him with a playful slap at his wrist. "Mike, why don't you shut up? Mrs. Abbott very well knows who my mother is." And turning to Syl, she added sweetly, "My mother, of course, is Corrine D'Indy. Have you made her acquaintance?"

"I—I'm afraid I have not had that pleasure," Syl stammered.

"Ah, but you should!" Mike again cut in, an extra loudness in his voice indicating that he had been imbibing more than champagne. "She is of the finest Creole blood, and though she looks upon me as a lowly Irish sod unworthy even of kissing her daughter's little toe—with which I agree heartily

—I would lay my life low for such a one who gave birth to my lovely, true-hearted Danielle." He let out a booming laugh and continued:

"You see, I've come to think the Creoles are the salt of the earth. You might say I am by way of becoming an Irish potato seasoned with Creole salt"—he paused to release another gust of laughter—"and a dash of black pepper."

Syl had put down her champagne glass, virtually untouched, and Paul noted that her face was unduly strained and pale. One of her hands moved to her forehead.

"I—I am afraid you must all excuse me. . . . " She stood up. "I have developed a most excruciating headache. . . . " And turning, she hurried away.

Paul, feeling an unprofessional tinge of panic, almost leaped to his feet. "Please forgive me, but I must attend to my wife—"

As he started away, Danielle D'Indy caught at his hand.

"Dr. Abbott—" Her dimpled smile was good-natured. "Please don't be embarrassed. I feel no offense whatsoever."

"But—"

"It is exactly what I expected. Any other Creole lady would have done the same thing. . . . "

"I thank you for your kind words," Paul mumbled, but utterly mystified, and rushed away after Syl.

In their suite, he was quickly enlightened.

"Paul, I'm so sorry, but—" She clasped her face in both hands. "Under the circumstances, I just *couldn't* remain at the table."

"I don't understand—"

"Miss D'Indy's mother was only the mistress of Marcel D'Indy, a very wealthy bachelor. When he died, he left his entire fortune to his mistress, who has no real right to his name."

"Should that matter? He must have loved the woman deeply, and Miss D'Indy seems to be a very nice person."

"Don't you understand? Her mother was an octoroon. Miss D'Indy has *black blood!*"

viii

Again the darkness of bedroom, the marital bed, the soft river sounds, the heavy pulsing of motors . . . and the restraint . . .

Paul was puzzled and troubled by the fact that Syl's bias

against black blood could be so deeply ingrained, but was resolved not to allow differences in attitudes to affect their relationship. In all other ways she was kind and considerate, even feeling sincere affection for her slaves. Perhaps with time and more understanding, she would change. Yet . . .

Determinedly, he pushed such broodings aside and tenderly kissed her on the cheek. She lay stiff in his arms.

"You are not relaxed. . . ."

"I sense that you are displeased with me."

"I could never be displeased with you, Syl. I love you too much. I can only strive to understand."

"That is my fervent hope, that someday you will truly understand that I am bound by birth and training to beliefs that only God Himself could change. . . ."

"I would prefer that we drop the subject and never again speak of it."

"Oh Paul—" she embraced him tightly and began raining kisses on his face and lips. "I will do anything possible not to spoil our honeymoon. . . ."

He began his lovemaking with the greatest delicacy, fearful of frightening her. His mouth touched her face and lips with butterfly kisses; he stroked her lightly as if she were the most fragile flower. She lay passive, seemingly relaxed. Yet, when he ventured to caress her breasts, she flinched and momentarily grasped his hand as if to halt him, but at once released it.

"It's . . . all right, Paul . . . I'll get used to it. . . ."

He continued slowly, gently, caressing and kissing. Her responses, though nervous and shy, seemed eager; the chill of her lips had by imperceptible degrees grown warm.

For the first time, his hand stroked lightly close to her pubic area.

Her body turned rigid and she made a twisting, rolling-away movement.

"My darling," he said. "You are still too tensed from anxieties and groundless fears. Perhaps it will be best if we wait until—"

"No! If we waited a week or a month, it would be no different. I cannot help my silly fears, but I have given my love to you and wish to be a full wife." She had rolled back to face him, clinging tight. "Please go ahead and do . . . what men do to their wives. . . ."

With some misgivings, he proceeded with his slow, tender lovemaking. However timid Syl seemed at times, he knew that she also had a will of iron and was now determined that the deflowering must take place.

Still, he limited his amorous acts to kisses and fondling for a timeless prelude, delaying any further move that might shock her virginal sensibilities, all the while keeping a tight rein on his soaring passions. Until he sensed in her a responsive urgency. Carefully he parted her legs and she made no resistance.

At the first touch of his hardened organ against her, she gasped. Again the involuntary stiffening of her body, a shrinking away. He hesitated.

"Please . . . don't stop. . . . " she whispered.

The beginning of penetration was difficult. Her aperture was smaller than normal, probably underdeveloped, with no real arousal. But perhaps with time. . . .

He gentled in a bit deeper, and suddenly felt the delicate rupturing of the hymen. She gave a birdlike cry, and at the same moment his long pent-up orgasm came gushing out to mix with her released virginal fluids. Quickly he withdrew.

Syl lay still, breathing heavily from the ordeal.

"I . . . tried," she said after a while. "Was it . . . all right?"

He cuddled her like a child, kissing her with tenderness. "Never have I known such joy and bliss," he lied.

He felt her relaxing in his arms. "I love you, my husband. . . . "

"I love you too, my dear wife. . . . "

THREE: The Leopard Grows Restless

ALL around him he heard the steady *slap, slap* of big knives slashing at the dense cane forest. Nearly five hundred blacks worked in unison: the cutters, the loaders and the haulers. The "big grass," some of it tasseling twelve feet high, had taken on a purplish tinge; the crucial harvest season had arrived. All available male and female slaves had been called out for this final race to cut the cane, then rush it to the sugar mills for processing before it soured in the steamy heat. The blacks wore red- or yellow-striped garments, making it easier for their masters to keep track of them in the cane jungle. Colorful bandannas on the heads of the women and straw hats on the men bobbed up and down with their movements. For weeks this would continue: the workers going forth each day with their big knives at murky dawn, the long scorching days filled with the sweetish odor of sweat and cane juices, the crack of overseers' whips, the call of the water boy: *"Kola . . . kola . . . kola!"*

Zambullah worked with speed and skill, for knives were second nature to him. First a quick stripping of leaves from the sides of each stalk; next a single cut through the stalk itself, close to the ground; then the unripened top joints lopped off to be tossed aside; finally, two or three more cuts to reduce the tall stalk into roughly three-foot lengths.

The knife gave him pleasure to use. It was about two feet long with a pronged end for stripping off leaves. A lethal weapon. A single jerk of the pronged end alone could rip neck arteries. In the hands of a strong man, the heavy blade could lop a man's head.

Hundreds of such knives flashing in the sun. . . .

Only five or six whites guarding them.

True, the whites were armed with guns, but they were far too few against so many blacks boiling over with hatred.

All they needed was a leader, and Zambullah had come to be that. There were other Ebos among the slaves; they knew of his exploits with leopards, that he was the son of a king. The word had flashed around.

A year or two ago he would not have hesitated to seize the first opportunity to wreak vengeance against the white devils. But that was before his brother the leopard had come to him in a dream and entered into his body to counsel him, to teach him patience and cunning.

Thereafter he bore his punishment meekly. The strongest of muscles were of no avail against chains and clubs and guns. Only cunning. Again and again his scarred back took whippings until the blood flowed. His very size stirred the bestial cruelty of the white jackals who sought to break his spirit, reduce him to a whimpering cur so that he would never be a danger. He endured it all in silence.

"Never seen nothin' like it," said the assistant overseer. "Black bastid's got the hide of a rhinoceros. I laid it on enough to put 'im out cold an' he just stood there like a fencepost."

"It's jes' dumbness," said Zack Porter. "Dumbes' nigra I

ever seen. Don't even know when he's hurt. So dumb he ain't hardly larned any English. Lucky thing, though. With a single brain in his head, he could be a mess of trouble."

Zambullah understood every word spoken. Since the time of his capture in Africa, his quick intelligence had been picking up words spoken by the whites, storing them away while pretending ignorance. It gave him a small advantage. But most of the white words had been taught to him by that strange, beautiful girl who had slipped out of the swamp one day and joined him when he was weeding in the cane fields. He was sure that she had been sent by his brother the leopard, for Aurora's cunning matched his. Many times she eluded the eyes of the overseer to work beside him. As they worked, she taught him more words of the whites. Without any words at all she had communicated to him that mystical love that had brought her to him out of nowhere.

Later she had visited him at night. They had made love. It brought him a new strength. It also added to his caution, for now he had Aurora's safety to consider. When in excitement she told of the plan of the white woman Fern, a friend of the blacks, to allow them to join a group of slaves that she was helping to escape to the free country of the North two weeks hence, he first consulted Nyanga, the plantation prophetess and "seer" of coming events.

Nyanga was also an Ebo and knew that Zambullah came from a royal blood line. She also had a daughter of just ripe enough age to make a fine wife for him. Yet despite all her secret voodoo conjuring tricks, he had failed to take interest in her daughter. Nyanga's pride was ruffled.

Her words, spoken in African dialect, were scornful.

"So the young *undlunkula,* Aurora, has made you soft in the head!" she said scathingly. "And perhaps too much *ukuhlobonga* has made you weak in the spine."

Undlunkula was a general term for a pretty girl, one who deliberately swung her hips and flaunted her charms, and *ukuhlobonga* was the term for mating outside of marriage.

Zambullah looked with astonishment at the grim female face, which was as rigid as if carved from mahogany. Woven into her hair was a strand of tiny blue-and-white beads—signifying to all blacks that she possessed voodoo powers.

"How could you know these things—even her name—that I have told no one?"

Nyanga's informant had been Momselle Delphine, who had told of giving her aid to the lovesick Aurora. This had pacified Nyanga's pride a bit, for she acknowledged Momselle's powers to be far greater than her own. Momselle, as a message center for the Underground Railroad, had also told her about the escape plan two weeks hence.

"I have the power to see into your thoughts," Nyanga said grandly. "I know you have come here to ask my advice about escaping with Aurora two weeks from now."

Zambullah's astonishment grew. "And what is your advice, Nyanga?"

She smiled, now to win him over, for she had not yet fully given up on the hope for him as a son-in-law and did not want him to leave. She placed a work-coarsened hand on his wrist.

"I have long known that you are the leader we have been waiting for. Therefore, I will give you warning: you must not attempt to escape with your woman until I tell you the time is right."

"But I care not to be a leader, so why should I wait?"

Nyanga let her eyes roll heavenward and her words came in the half-chant of a seer: "Because I see death for you and your Aurora if you do not wait until the right moment arrives."

"And how will I know when the right moment has arrived?"

"A vision will come to me, and you will be told. You will then know that the time has come for all of us to rise up and overthrow our masters and follow you to freedom. . . . "

Zambullah heeded her warning—and when two weeks later a group of slaves attempting escape with the white woman were caught, his respect for Nyanga's powers soared. The white woman was killed; some of the slaves were roasted to grotesque caricatures of charred flesh in roaring fires; some were skinned alive and their heads stuck on poles as warning to others.

But that had been over a year ago and Nyanga still told him the time was not right. Meanwhile he grew more restless with each passing day. Perhaps her powers were too weak and she would fail to have a vision. Perhaps—

Hearing the call of the approaching water boy, he slowly straightened to his full six feet six and signaled for a drink. The long hours of grueling work under a scorching sun had not fatigued him, but his great perspiring body could not go too long without water. Old Benji, two five-gallon buckets suspended from a pole balanced across one shoulder, trotted toward him.

Sipping from the tin dipper, his thoughts returned with resentment to the restraint Nyanga had imposed on him. How could she know of the leopard inside, growing impatient? What did an old woman know about battle? What better time for an uprising than now during the busy harvest season when they had so many knives?

Why wait for Nyanga's vision? He had his own vision:

Hundreds of big bright knives slashing in the sun, growing red with the blood of the white devils. . . .

Lost in his broodings, he again raised the dipper to drink, but before the metal touched his lips there was a whirring sound in the air behind him, followed instantly by something darting and snakelike that lashed against his hand with an explosive burst of pain. A red line of blood bubbled from the back of his hand; the dipper dropped from numbed fingers. He whirled.

"Goddamn lazy bastid—you been two minutes swillin' down that watuh—!"

Glaring at him from a dozen feet away was Lucas Mims, the assistant overseer. He was gripping a long, sinuous blacksnake whip that was coiling back over his arms. His florid face, half hidden by bristling black whiskers, was ugly with anger. He raised the whip in preparation for another swing. "Now you git—!"

Instinctively, Zambullah's hand holding the machete shot up in a self-defense gesture against the whip.

"Hey now—!" howled Mims. "You dast raise a knife agin me? I'll larn you—!"

The whip cracked as it lashed out again and tore the knife from Zambullah's suddenly nerveless right hand. The machete dropped to the ground.

A horse came galloping up. Zack Porter, his pocked face perspiring beneath the straw hat pulled low over his forehead, scowled down at them. He had a shotgun cradled in one arm.

"What'n hell's the trouble?"

"Bastid threatened me with his machete!"

The overseer slowly dismounted, holding the shotgun pointed at the big black man. Zambullah stared at the gun, expressionless except for the burning in his lidded eyes.

"Reckon it's been too long since the nigger's had a good lesson," said Zack. "Mims, you go fetch a coupla the other men while I keep 'im covered."

"Hell, I don't need no help. Ain't no man along the hull Mississippi can use a snake better'n me."

"Do like I say! Whippin' ain't enough for this nigger. He got to be learned proper. This time we gonna learn 'im to beg an' holler loud enough to wake the dead. . . . "

FOUR: Jealousy

IT took four husky Negroes to carry Zambullah into the infirmary and place him on the table indicated by Paul.

The wounds were appalling. Back, sides, arms and legs were criss-crossed with gruesome slashes that welled blood. Some were raw whip wounds; some, gaping open in places, apparently had been inflicted with a knife. All seemed to have been rubbed heavily with a whitish substance which in places had caked and darkened with coagulating blood. Paul rolled a bit of the material between his fingers, sniffed at it. His guess was that it was mixture of salt and flesh-burning lime. It seemed confirmed by the way the big man was squirming and writhing from what must be the most intolerable kind of agony, yet not a sound passed his lips.

Deliberate, sadistic torture.

As Paul began sponging the wounds with warm water, he looked up briefly at Micaela, who had brought Zambullah in a coach. "Who did this to him?"

"Our overseer and his assistants. It was fortunate that I was out riding in the fields and was able to stop him, or I fear he would have been killed."

"Does Mr. Jacquard condone such cruelty to slaves?"

Her lovely lips curled with contempt. "He thinks of all black people as less than animals."

"Does he know you brought the man here for treatment?"

"No. He is away on a business trip."

Finished cleansing the wounds, Paul applied an instant painkiller, which was also a disinfectant, mixed from equal parts of aqua-ammonia, sulphuric ether and alcohol. Then a soothing balm that Paul had learned about from the Indians: the buds of the weed tree known as balm of Gilead boiled down into a paste. Some of the deeper cuts had to be sutured to stanch the blood; others could be closed sufficiently with adhesive plaster.

At one point he became aware that the black man was continuously watching him, every move he made. Something about the hooded intensity of the eyes sent a chill down his spine.

"You work with such speed, such skill," said Micaela.

He looked up, allowing himself a small smile. He had been trying to remain indifferent to her presence. It had been over a year since that night of the flood, but at the first sight of her when she had arrived in a big black shining carriage with Zambullah, a great surge of pleasurable excitement had seized him. Expensively dressed, more mature in manner, she was also more beautiful than ever, still an enchantress who could stir his blood.

"I've had a lot of practice," he said.

"I have always had a great interest in medicine, but of course it is unthinkable for women or for *gens de couleur* to study to be doctors, or even nurses, so I would like to ask of you a great favor. . . . "

"Anything within my power."

"I am so bored at home. Would you permit me to come here on some days and help you give treatment to the slaves, so that I may learn?"

He hesitated. He was married to Syl, loved her deeply. Did he dare risk such exposure to Micaela's sensuous charms that could still, as he was now increasingly aware, ignite in him such heady excitement?

"You wouldn't like it," he said with a laugh. "It's messy, smelly, bloody and often sickening work."

"I would not mind, no matter how bloody, how sickening."

"But wouldn't your Jacquard object?"

Disdain touched her lips. "We are not married, nor have I sold myself to him. I have insisted that he must not order me to do things I do not wish to do or prevent me from following my own wishes of a reasonable nature."

"He must be very broadminded."

"On the contrary, he is stupidly jealous, without reason. I shall never knowingly embarrass him or give him true cause for jealousy, but I shall always insist on my right to engage in respectable activities of my own choosing. You will let me help you, *oui*?"

He sighed. "All right. . . . we'll give it a try. . . . "

"*Ah, bon!* Then I shall return soon and show you how

hard I can work!" Impulsively she embraced him and gave him a light kiss.

On the lips.

ii

At Les Colonnades, the master of the great plantation paced about in the spacious living room with angry strides. His swarthily handsome features were stormy. At the sound of the front door opening and light steps in the entry, he ceased pacing and stood with legs spread, hands clasped behind his back, facing the door.

When Micaela stepped into view, his scowl intensified.

"Where have you been?"

"What a silly question," she said with a laugh. "You know very well where I have been. Zack Porter wouldn't waste a moment telling you about it, I'm sure." She continued past him blithely toward the wide curved stairway leading to the next higher level.

"Stop! I haven't finished talking—"

She turned. "You needn't shout."

"When I speak, I demand that you listen! Yes, Zack told me about how you interfered wtih slave discipline, how you undermined his authority in the eyes of the slaves, how you insulted him—"

"Insulted *him!* A mere overseer? Since when is an overseer of more importance than the mistress of Les Colonnades?"

"How the plantation is run is no concern of yours. Zack was hired to do a job, and it is only for me to decide whether or not he's doing it right."

"Never will I stand by and see a man treated so brutally and not raise a hand to help!"

"Call it brutality, or whatever you wish. Blacks aren't human, and must be treated like animals to get any work out of them."

She looked at him long and steadily. "Have you forgotten that black blood runs in my veins too, Jac? Am I also an animal in your eyes, to be treated the way you treat your slaves and horses?"

He smiled sourly. "You'll learn how to behave, or suffer the consequences. . . . "

"Was it misbehaving on my part to save the most valuable slave you have on the plantation? I'm sure Zack would have killed him, or if not, damaged him so that he would be unable to work for many days."

His lips twisted into a sneer. "Was it the slave you were worried about—or was it just a pretext for visiting the doctor?"

"What are you implying?"

"I am not so easy to fool, Micaela. I am observant of small things, such as your undue interest in the social column of *Le Moniteur* when the marriage of your Dr. Abbott to Sylphide Beauvais was announced. There was a wetness in your eyes when you left the room."

"Dr. Abbott is a dear friend of mine who once saved my life. I am always moved by events, whether happy or sad, that happen to friends for whom I feel deep affection."

"Just affection? You spent the entire night alone in an abandoned house with him. . . . "

"Did I have any other choice?"

His smile couldn't have been nastier. "You didn't have to take off all your clothing for him. . . . "

"How silly you are! I was fully clothed when we were rescued."

"Except for your pantalets!" he shouted. "I was told they were fluttering on a pole outside the window—it was the joke of the whole rescue crew! It is one of the embarrassments I have been trying to live down!"

She laughed. "But Jac—why should it matter? You knew I wasn't a virgin when I came here."

"Damned slut—!" He lunged toward her with a clenched fist, but she nimbly sidestepped and retreated to the staircase. "So what everybody thinks about you and Abbott is true, after all! So now you go there and start tongues wagging again. I shall be a laughingstock!"

"I would promise never to go there again, Jac—on one condition. . . . "

"And what is that?"

"The security of marriage, and having legally the name of my husband."

He raised both fists and shook them in desperation. "But you well know that the Black Code forbids it!"

"We could take a trip abroad and marry. No one would have to know."

"Please try to understand, Micaela. . . . I love you and would wish nothing more than to call you my wife, but it could not be kept secret. I would be forever banished from

Creole society. I would cease to exist as a person of importance. The merchants I deal with, even the slaves who work for me, would hold me in contempt. What you ask is an impossibility."

She gave him a twisted smile. "And that is what you call love?"

"Have I not proved my love? A generous sum of money was deposited in the Banque des Citoyens in your own name. You are provided liberally with rich garments and all the folderols of a fine lady. I spent a fortune in enlarging Les Colonnades—new decorating, expensive new furnishings—all to please you. Is that not love?"

"If it is no more than that, then love is too cheap. As you know, I had many rich suitors to pick from. Since I am denied marriage, at least I am free to leave you at any time and choose from among those I find most pleasing."

His face darkened. "And you do not find me pleasing?"

"At the moment I do not."

He forced an ugly smile. "Perhaps you are overlooking the ways in which I can be most pleasing—many women have complimented me on certain of my capabilities. . . . Why don't we discontinue this profitless talk and go to the bedroom where we can resolve the present unpleasantness with a demonstration of those capabilities?"

He moved toward the staircase as he spoke and she backed away, retreating up the steps.

"I think not, Jac. Lovemaking should be loving, not something hateful. . . . "

His fury erupted. "Goddamn slut—married or not, you're mine! I paid plenty for you, and I'm goddamn well going to have what I want when I want it—!" He strode rapidly closer. "Get up into my bedroom!"

Lightly she ran up the stairway, but instead of going into the master bedroom—which she visited only during those times when he demanded lovemaking—she slipped into her own bedroom and slammed the door behind her, locking it.

Furiously, Jacquard pounded on the door. "Let me in! If you don't, I swear I'll break the door open and then I'll break your neck!"

Her voice drifted sweetly through the heavy oaken panels. "Your threats do not frighten me, Jac. If you try to hurt me, I shall leave immediately and return to New Orleans. If Madame Silkwood discovers that you have been cruel to me, you'll never be able to get another girl to come and live with you, and all Creole gentlemen will hold you in contempt."

For a moment he rested against the door, breathing heavily, feeling temporary defeat. What she said was only too true. It was almost unheard of for a mistress *de couleur* to leave her *protecteur;* nothing could be more humiliating.

He essayed a new approach. "Let's be reasonable, Micaela. Open the door so we can talk. You know I'm so hungry for you I can hardly think straight—" Indeed, anger always did this to him. Any of the aggressive emotions stirred his hair-trigger eroticism, which had now grown so great that he could feel his penis hardening painfully against the restraint of his tight trousers. The anger surged back into his voice: "Dammit, Micaela—open up right away!"

"No, Jac—not until you've cooled down long enough so that I can be sure that you will behave like a gentleman. . . . "

He stood there seething with frustrations, but remained silent. She had again touched his tenderest spot. To be considered a "gentleman" was one of his most fervid dreams. Creole society had never fully accepted him. All his past accomplishments, all his energies and undying determination to become rich—richer than any of his neighbors—had been in support of that even greater goal: to win such distinction that important people everywhere would look at him and speak to him with great respect, lofty ladies would curtsy.

Because he was a gentleman.

After a while he went back down to the library and poured himself a large goblet of brandy.

iii

In less than a week, Micaela returned. She arrived early, shortly before the usual morning lineup of sick slaves, or those who pretended sickness in hopes of avoiding work.

"Bonjour, Docteur," she greeted Paul cheerily. "I am here to help, as I promised."

Paul looked up from the table where he was mixing medicaments. He hadn't really expected her to return, and now he was filled with misgivings. Though he would never betray Syl, he knew that the very presence of Micaela would bring back unbidden memories of that night of the flood when he had held her nakedness hot and throbbing against his own nakedness. Even as she was dressed this morning—in a light claret frock of zinzolin with a very daring mid-calf skirt, knee-high

button-up gaiter boots and sleeve protectors of black bomba-
zine that reached half to her elbows—he felt an unwanted
warmth creep through him from his intimate knowledge of
the seductive figure beneath.

"All right," he said roughly. "Get that apron hanging on
the wall and put it on. We don't want that expensive dress
messed up."

Dutifully, she obeyed.

"Now wash your hands in that basin. Use lots of soap."

"You are insulting! Do you think I would allow myself
to come here with soiled hands?"

"Another thing—you must learn to follow instructions
without—"

"Wait! The galloping—" Her glance shot toward a window.
The sound of thundering hooves was rapidly approaching.
"Only Jac rides that way—like a madman—"

Moments later the infirmary door slammed open and Leon
Jacquard, wearing a dark cape, stood silhouetted in the doorway with the morning sun slanting in around him. The lines
of the swarthy face were tight as drawn wires, the dark eyes
flashed.

"I suspected," he said with a scornful glance at Micaela,
"that you would come here on the same day I usually spend
away on business matters."

"You have no cause for jealousy, Jac. I come here only
for the purpose of learning about medicine—"

"Shut up, slut!" Jacquard's burning glance swept toward
Paul. "What she sees in you, I cannot comprehend, but it is
a humiliation I will not tolerate. I could have prevented her
from coming here today, but that would have robbed me of
the satisfaction of having her witness your cowardice before
I kill you—"

He strode a few feet into the room and flung his cape
aside, exposing two pistols thrust under his belt. Yanking one
of them out, he tossed it with a heavy clattering sound on
the floor in front of Paul. His other hand moved to rest on
the butt of the pistol still under his belt.

"There, you *canaille*, is a loaded pistol! You may examine
it to suit yourself. Once you were too cowardly to accept my
cartel, but now you cannot escape—"

"Jac, Jac—!" Micaela rushed forward to placate the furious
man. "You are being very silly!"

Raising his left arm, Jacquard gave her a powerful back-handed slap that sent her staggering backward. He turned to face Paul.

"Either pick up the pistol so this can be settled in the manner of gentlemen, or I will shoot you down like a cowardly cur!" Smiling thinly, he took out a golden watch. "I will give you ten seconds to make your decision. . . . "

"My decision is already made—it was made the moment I saw how brutally you struck at Micaela." Going behind his desk, Paul yanked open a drawer and took out the holstered Colt's pistol and ammunition belt that long ago had been a gift from Jere.

"However, as the challenged party," he went on, "I reserve the right to choose my own weapon."

"Please, Jac—" Micaela appealed. "The *docteur* is not a fighting man, and you're an expert marksman. It would be murder!"

Ignoring her, Jacquard's hand darted to the gun under his belt, started raising it.

"Your last chance, Abbott!"

The roar of gunfire wiped all anger from Jacquard's face. His features contorted with astonishment and pain as he wobbled backward a few steps, the gun dropping from his grasp. His left hand rose to press against his right shoulder, came away stained red.

"I'm sorry I was forced to do that," Paul said, holstering his gun. "I too was an expert shot before I went abroad to study medicine, and could just as easily have put a bullet through your heart, but I had no desire to kill, only to disable."

There was a flurry of movement as Jobe, the muscular boss of slaves, rushed in, followed by several other husky blacks.

"Wha' da trouble, Massadoc?"

"Just a disagreement that's settled now. Put that man on the operating table and strap him down."

Jacquard struggled vainly as the men lifted him and strapped him to the table. He looked up wild-eyed at Paul. "Don't you dare touch me! I know what you crazy doctors can do to a man!"

Paul smiled coldly. "I won't touch you. Micaela came here to learn doctoring, so I'll leave it up to her to decide whether she wants to practice on you, under my supervision—or leave the bullet in there to start gangrene and bring on your death. . . . "

Her face paler than usual, Micaela came over and looked down at Jacquard's sweating face. "Jac, I will try to take out the bullet. On Balize, I always watched how Maman went about taking out bullets or pieces of broken glass from silly fighting men. Sometimes they even lived. Perhaps if you ask the *docteur*, he will first give you chloroform so you will not feel the pain."

He glared up at her. "I know you both wish me dead, and now that I am overpowered, you have your opportunity. No, I do not wish `chloroform. I prefer to watch you kill me."

"You tempt me very much, Jac!"

iv

Paul watched with approval as Micaela quickly cut away the bloodied shirt, swabbed the wound with alcohol to cleanse it, then selected a slender forceps and scalpel from among the instruments, medicaments and dressings that Paul had laid out.

For nearly five minutes she deftly cut and probed while Paul gave quiet directions. All the while Jac lay with clenched jaws, sweating profusely, not making a murmur.

Finally she gave a little cry of exultance and raised the forceps, which held a small, bloodied object.

"*Ughh*—what a nasty thing," she said with a grimace and dropped the bullet with a metallic *tunk* into the nearby kick bucket.

Now the job of disinfecting the wound, applying the carbolic-soaked dressings, the foil covering and final taping was swiftly completed under Paul's instructions.

"You have a great talent for doctoring, Micaela," he said. "I could certainly use somebody like you for an assistant."

"Never!" Jacquard howled at him. "I will kill her if she tries to come here again!"

Paul beckoned to Jobe. "Unstrap our ungrateful patient and load him into his carriage."

Then he turned and saw that Syl was standing just inside the opened doorway. Her face was tear-streaked, tormented. Before he could speak, she turned and fled.

v

In the living room, Syl sobbed softly.

"I—I saw the carriage arrive with *her* in it," she choked

out, "then Monsieur Jacquard on his horse . . . then I heard the shot—"

"But it's all over now, Syl, and no real harm had been done."

She looked at him through wet eyes. "But why would he be so jealous if there was not some cause for it?"

"Cause! I assure you, my darling, the only cause is Jacquard's jealous imagination—just as you are imagining things now."

"Paul, I never told you this before because I refused to believe it, but an acquaintance came to me shortly after the big flood to report indecent rumors about you and . . . that octoroon."

Paul, torn between guilts, embarrassment and shame, and knowing that never in a million years could he hope to tell Syl the truth and expect to be forgiven, spoke with undue heat:

"I didn't think you were the kind to listen to malicious talebearers."

"Nor am I. When my informant told of the pantalets hanging on a pole outside the window as proof that she had been unclothed alone in the same house with you"—Syl's face flushed a delicate pink—"I ordered her to leave as I did not wish to hear another word."

Tormented, Paul began pacing about with clenched fists. The rumors were true enough, but so unfair! For him that night with Micaela had been the most loving experience of his life; there had been a purity in his passion.

Adding to his present agitation was something he wished not to face: that his sex life with Syl had turned out to be a dismal affair. Poor innocent Syl had no inkling of what a glorious, soaring thing such love could be. Perhaps by physical or glandular inadequacy, Syl was not capable of anything more than weak arousal during the sex act. Or perhaps it was because of an ingrained attitude that sex was only a dreaded wifely burden that must be borne with fortitude, the best grace one could muster, something that husbands needed and expected. Quite bravely she endured their interludes of lovemaking—as infrequent as Paul's tensions could bear going without release—always in as ladylike a manner as any lady could possibly assume in such a situation.

But for all that, the very intensity of his love made her sexual shortcomings seem unimportant—certainly she could not be blamed for such lacks—and after each unsatisfactory sexual episode he went to great lengths to shower her with tenderness and expressions of his devotion.

"Tell me honestly, Paul—was there anything between you and the octoroon?"

"Syl, I vow—you're overwrought about nothing!"

A new welling of tears flooded her eyes and she bent her head.

Deeply touched, Paul went over and reached to embrace her. She shrank away.

"No, don't touch me! Not until I get over the idea that your arms may have touched *her*. . . . I just can't bear to think that—"

"Syl!—you're being irrational! Please believe me when I tell you that it's you and only you that I love!"

She slumped back in the chair and turned her face against the cushion. Her wet eyes closed tiredly. "I'm sorry, Paul . . . perhaps I am being irrational. I haven't been at all myself for several days now . . . my mind is so full of wild fancies and so many fears. . . . "

He kneeled beside her. "But darling, why didn't you tell me you weren't feeling well?" He leaned forward and she allowed him to kiss her wet cheeks.

"I wanted to be sure before I told you. . . . "

"Tell me what?"

She looked up at him with eyes suddenly showing fright. Her voice trembled.

"I've been feeling it coming on for days, and now there's no mistaking it. I'm going to have a baby."

BOOK EIGHT

Gathering Storm

ONE: The Birth

THE summer and fall of 1859 was a period of great happiness for Paul. Syl's pregnancy added a new dimension to their lives, a cementing matrix that brought into singleness the diversities of their separate personalities; it was that condition of grace growing out of love that creates a sense of home and family wherever it may occur and relegates all the past experiences, places and conditions of one's life to a level of secondary importance by comparison.

Without doubt Syl had blossomed into full womanhood, bringing out all the strength and sweetness of her nature. She had found in Paul not only that intangible thing she had lost with Pierre's death, but something even more than she had ever hoped to find. In Paul, she had at last found herself.

For his part, Paul loved her with an unswerving intensity

that pervaded every hour of the night and day. He sometimes felt that he did not love her with all the passion of which he was capable, but he saw it in the light that it was a deeper and more satisfying love, not requiring the fire of sexual excitement that had been aroused in him by Micaela, and to a lesser extent by Fern. He could not have felt a greater love for the woman who was to bear his child.

But as the sun slipped lower from its summer apex toward the cooler days of autumn, his happiness was eroded more and more by fears he tried to ignore.

For he knew beyond doubt that Syl would have a more difficult time than the average woman in giving birth. Her pelvic structure was too narrow for easy parturition. The best hope was that the child would be small enough so that delivery would be possible without surgical intervention. His biggest fear was that she might require a Caesarean, that ancient operation used only as a last-resort procedure to save the life of the infant—but with only the slimmest of hopes for the mother.

If surgery should be necessary, she was almost certain to hemorrhage. In that case, delicate creature that she was, she would need an ample supply of blood.

And what was the proper kind of blood? Most of the greatest professors in Edinburgh differed in their beliefs. Those who used sheep's blood invariably lost their patients; others, using human blood, had not much better luck. Paul recalled some of his discussions with learned medical men in which he had brought up his own theory that all human blood was different, and that only by finding another person with blood similar to or precisely like that of the patient could a transfusion be effective. A few others had already submitted such a theory, only to be scoffed at. It was a subject that medical men could laugh at or argue endlessly.

But with Syl's life at stake, Paul could take no chances.

Thus he carried on his blood experimentation with an almost frenzied zeal, working during all spare hours during the day and often far into the night in search of his elusive goal.

The key word of his research efforts was "agglutination." In the medical sense, it meant the act of blood adhering together in clumps—an abnormality that in excessive degree caused death. In his earlier experiments with the blood of slaves, Paul had proved that in the majority of cases the blood of one person mixed with that of another would agglutinate to a greater or lesser degree. He theorized that in those few cases where no agglutination occurred, there might well be enough similarity or compatibility so that the blood from one person could be transfused into the other person with similar blood and no unfavorable reactions would result.

Following this premise, he started a new series of experiments, collecting samples of blood with a syringe from Syl, Etienne, the new overseer, Otto Guttmann and himself, who were the only whites on the plantation. The logical assumption was that Etienne's blood—since he was related to Syl—would be most similar to hers.

That was not the case. Etienne's blood—as well as the blood of all the others—agglutinated excessively when mixed with Syl's.

Of an inquisitive turn of mind, Etienne frequently dropped in to observe Paul at work. Paul had confided his fears about Syl to Etienne, who heartily agreed that all possible steps should be taken in advance to preserve her health.

"What will you do now?" Etienne asked, when told of the dismal results. "I suppose I could call upon my friends. Most of them would be very willing to contribute their blood to Syl, if need be."

"That would be impractical. The blood would have to be fresh. Should the emergency arise, the blood donor would have to be close on hand at a moment's notice. I think we shall have to first look to the blood from our slaves. . . . "

Etienne was aghast. "*Black* blood? That would be impossible!"

"Come—" said Paul, "let me show you something. . . . "

Taking from a wall rack a sealed and labeled test tube containing blood, he extracted a few drops with a small syringe and put them on a glass slide, which he placed under the microscope that Syl had given him.

"Take a look at your own blood, Etienne, greatly magnified. . . . "

Etienne bent over the microscope. "It's really quite beautiful! Like roseate beads, a bit unstrung. I never dreamed that such a delightful landscape of all those well-defined, pretty shapes could exist in a mere drop of my blood!"

Paul replaced the slide with another one on which he had put a bit of blood taken from another test tube. "Now compare it with this sample. . . . "

Etienne's heavy brows scrunched in puzzlement as he

peered into the lens. "It looks like the same blood. I can detect nothing different."

"The only basic difference is that the blood you just looked at came from Jobe, our black slave boss."

"Amazing! I would have assumed that blood from a black person would look . . . well, somehow different."

"I assure you, Etienne, that the color of one's skin has nothing to do with what is underneath it. The blood, the brain, the organs of all humans, whatever their color, are essentially the same. In the matter of blood, I am convinced that the only differences are those invisible variables such as the ones that cause agglutination, and I am hopeful that among the hundreds of our slaves we will find at least one healthy specimen whose blood will be compatible with Syl's."

Etienne's agitation returned. "But surely you can't be seriously thinking of using black blood for Syl if—!"

Paul cut him off furiously. "Would you rather see her die? If only so-called black blood could save her, would you deny her that chance to survive?"

Etienne bowed his head. "I apologize," he said humbly. "Syl's life, of course, is the paramount consideration. . . ."

Within three days Paul found what he was looking for in a squat, heavy-set, coal-black field hand named Moses. Repeated tests with fresh blood from both Syl and Moses showed complete compatibility when mixed.

Moses was healthy enough, but as he might well become Syl's lifeline to survival, Paul had him transferred to help in the infirmary, where he could be frequently checked for disease and his diet supervised to assure that he would remain healthy.

ii

"Paul . . . I'm afraid. The hurting has been going on so long. . . . What's wrong?"

Paul took one of her cold hands between his. It was three a.m. and Syl had been in labor for nearly ten hours. In the background, shadowed behind the rays of oil lamps and candelabra having backdrops of mirrors and foil to reflect all rays on the bed, were the solemn faces of Aurora and "Auntie Nana," Syl's childhood nanny. She was also a midwife who would be helping Paul with the delivery.

"There's nothing wrong, my darling," he lied, "but it may

be necessary to administer anesthesia to help with the birth. . . . "

The truth was that Paul's worst fears had been realized. Syl's pregnancy had lasted longer than usual, and despite her dainty eating the fetus was large—too large to pass through the abnormally small pelvis. Yet hoping against hope he had no choice but to wait until the first stage of delivery to prove that he was right. Normally at this stage there would be dilation of the neck of the womb accompanied by powerful contractions of the muscular walls to aid in expulsion of the child. In Syl's case there had not been full dilation. The contractions were too weak. Her pains were increasing. As were Paul's fears.

"You will feel nothing," he went on, "and when you wake up you will be able to hold our child."

"Anything—do anything—!" she cried in near-hysteria. "Anything to stop the pain. . . . "

Paul glanced around to see that all was in readiness: the tables with pots and basins of hot water; the ligatures prepared by boiling in water for tying the umbilical cord—and possibly for stanching hemorrhage; pledgets of cotton wool in boiled clean water to be wrung dry for swabbing her clean after delivery—

He signaled to Aurora, who at once brought the cone of muslin and the chloroform. . . .

Perspiration formed on his face as he worked with delicate speed. The quick abdominal incision to the uterus; the surprising ease and wonder of finally getting his fingertips on the new life within her—his own child! A healthy boy! Then the cutting of the umbilical cord. Not a moment to be wasted. The child handed to experienced Auntie Nana, who would know what next to do while he concentrated on the next great danger—separating the afterbirth from the wall of the womb without causing postpartum hemorrhage before closing up the abdominal incision. . . .

iii

Her face pale and bloodless, Syl looked up at the child held by a grinning Aurora. She was too depleted of strength to hold her baby. There had been a dreadful loss of blood, and the aftereffects of anesthesia left her in a daze. She managed a weak smile.

"Carson—" she breathed. "Carson Dixon Abbott. . . . "

It was the name she and Paul had decided on in the event their child turned out to be a boy.

She raised her arms as if to take him, then let them drop to the bed and turned her face sideways against the pillow. Her eyes closed. "I—I must rest. . . . " she whispered.

Paul had difficulty feeling her pulse; it was so feeble. Her skin was cold. The cruel but necessary assault of the Caesarean on her delicate body had been too great; the loss of blood was more than she could spare; she had virtually no strength left. The time had come.

Raising a hand, he signaled to Etienne, who stood in the background, his heavy brows lowered in somber concern. At once Etienne went to the door and admitted Moses, who entered in awed silence, his eyes rolling about the rich room in fear and wonder as he took the seat indicated by Paul beside the bed.

Syl's eyes opened and her head turned just as Paul was filling the syringe with blood from the black man's arm.

"Who is that?" she said weakly. "What are you doing, Paul?"

"You need blood to replace what you lost, my darling, and this man has the right type that will bring you back to health—"

"B-but he's *black*—!" she said in growing horror, attempting to sit up in bed. "You—you *can't*—"

"I'm afraid I must be truthful, Syl—it's the only measure that will save your life."

"No, no—!" she screamed. "You're a Yankee—you don't understand—I'd rather be dead—!"

"But Syl—try to understand—"

With a last horrified look at the syringe of blood he was holding, she made a lurching, sideways rolling movement toward the far side of the bed, falling heavily to the carpet. Paul leaped up and raced around the bed to stop her.

But with a hysterical last burst of energy Syl was already scrabbling over the floor on hands and knees—trailing a fresh hemorrhaging of blood caused by her exertions. . . .

iv

Sylphide Beauvais Abbott died quietly just as a new dawn crept through the cypress swamp.

TWO: The Vision

Leon Claude Jacquard eyed his reflection in the large French mirror with displeasure, but not because of any flaws in his dress or appearance. Certainly the image was that of a strikingly handsome man with an abundance of groomed dark hair falling to his shoulders, a somewhat hawkish nose and hard lips capable of saturnine smiles that many women found singularly attractive. Nor was his garb much less than perfection. This morning he was wearing a fine suit of pale-beige linen, a ruffled shirt of pristine white, a gorgeous stock of lavender silk and an impressive assortment of adornments such as cameos, diamond rings, a golden bracelet, jeweled breastpin, and a delicate golden chain looped across his waistcoat for his watch. Elegance personified.

His displeasure came not from anything discernible to the eye, but for deeper reasons. . . .

One of them being that this same fine gentleman frowning back at him from the mirror was *persona non grata* in the highest social circles. For all his wealth, distinguished families such as the Gayarres, the Beauvaises and the Menières had snubbed him with polite but total rejection.

All because he was not a member of a well-known old family, because they knew nothing of his background. For which he was grateful. . . .

The fact was that Leon Jacquard had been born in Haiti, where the name "Jacquard" had once been among the *crème de la crème.* He was the son of a distinguished French artillery officer who had committed a most terrible social blunder, resulting in the father's resignation of his commission, after which he exploited his military expertise by joining Laffite, the pirate. The spoils of piracy had paid for Leon Jacquard's fine education in Paris, which fortunately was completed just before his father's death from the plague —leaving not a cent for his family.

Returning to Haiti, penniless and embittered that his family name had fallen into disrepute, Leon plunged into a wild new life of lawlessness. A young man of great strength,

417

quick-witted, an excellent swordsman and marksman, and fueled both by a thirst for wealth and anger at a society that had scorned him, he quickly rose to leadership of a band of cutthroats that made forays against rich mansions on the Haitian mainland. Looting, macheting prisoners and trafficking in stolen slaves earned him enormous profits—also the nickname "Bloody Jac."

Then came the great Haitian slave uprising in Santo Domingo, with Negro power taking over and a purging of all whites known to have been enemies of the blacks. Bloody Jac, hated and known by sight to almost every Haitian slave, topped the list. He barely managed to escape to New Orleans, where most of his loot was secreted.

There had been whisperings about his dubious background, but nothing could be proved. In any case it had not prevented his swift rise to wealth as a respectable sugar planter. The past was a closed book that no longer concerned him.

What still did concern him, haunted him unceasingly, was the sin and abomination visited upon him by his father, who, quite fashionably, had kept a Haitian quadroon—then had committed the unpardonable social blunder of falling in love with and marrying her. Resulting in the spawning of a son.

That was the deep secret that had plagued Leon Jacquard's life.

His black blood.

ii

The breakfast table had been set as usual with fine china and silver service over sparkling white napery. One of the servants, always on the alert for whenever the master might appear, rushed forward to serve him.

"Would Massa lak de grilled fish, sausages, eggs or—"

"Nothing, nothing—" he said irritably. "Just coffee until *mademoiselle* gets down. Go up and tell her to get down here right away—" He made an angry sweep of his arm to dismiss her, and at that moment felt a sudden scalding warmth spill over his lap. There was a clatter of a tray and a cup falling to the floor. A second maid had been setting a cup of hot coffee in front of him at exactly the wrong moment.

With a curse, Jacquard leaped to his feet. "You clumsy bitch!"

The maid, Emeline, a pretty and graceful girl of about

twenty, backed away in fright. Though the upset tray had
been the fault of his swinging arm, she knew she would be
blamed. "I'se sorry, Massa, I—"

She tried to twist away as Jacquard—now spiraling off into
one of his uncontrollable rages—seized his chair and swung.
It crashed against her head, knocking her to the floor. Still
unsatisfied, he struck her recumbent body twice more with
the chair, and for good measure kicked her in the abdomen.

"Juste ciel! What are you doing to that poor girl, Jac?"
Micaela stood at the base of the staircase, staring in horror.

Jacquard tossed the broken chair aside and taking another,
reseated himself, not deigning to answer.

"Aggie—!" he called to the first servant, who had retreated a dozen paces. "Bring me more coffee, sausages and
eggs."

Micaela, meanwhile, had rushed over to kneel beside
Emeline, who was unconscious, breathing raggedly.

"Jac—this is the most brutal thing I've ever seen you
do—and to one of our best servants!"

"Leave her alone," he snarled at her. "Sit down and join
me for breakfast."

"I will not! I will never again eat with you or sleep with
you until you apologize to Emeline."

Jacquard chortled with amusement and turned his attention to the food, which was now being placed in front of
him. He had heard all kinds of crazy, meaningless ravings
from all kinds of females. It was a waste of time to listen.

iii

Nyanga the seer was busy over a tub of soapy clothing in
the laundry room when she saw the limp body being carried
toward her cottage and with unerring maternal prescience
rushed toward the group just as they were carrying her
daughter Emeline inside.

"Dat's Emeline—!" she cried, her large lustrous eyes suddenly blazing. "De massa done hurt her—"

Micaela spoke soothingly. "She's going to be all right,
Nyanga. Her eyes are opening, and I'll send Aggie to take
care of her. She'll be as good as new in a day or two, and I
promise to see that the master never hurts her again."

Tears streaming down the seamed face, Nyanga knelt beside the cot where Emeline had been placed. The girl's eyes
had opened, were darting around in fright.

"Is you all right, Em'line?"

"I'se all right, Momma. Don' you worry."

Nyanga stood up and with hands clasped, looked heaven-ward.

"Oh Lor'," she intoned, "I thankee fer sendin' me the sign—"

With that, she rushed out of the cabin, and her wildly waving arms soon increased the number of somber-faced slaves who had already gathered outside. Eyes sparking fury, she raised her right fist and shook it at the mansion.

"Thar's a day a-comin'—" she screeched. "Thar's a day a-comin'! I see de flashin' ob guns. I hear de rumblin' ob de chariots. I see white folks' blood a-runnin' on de ground like a river an' de daid heaped like piles ob logs. Oh Lor'—hasten de day when de blows an' bruises an' de aches an' de pains shall all come back to de white folks an' de buzzards'll eat 'em as dey's daid in de streets. Oh Lor'! Start de chariots a-rollin' an' gib us black folks rest an' peace. Oh Lor'—don' make us wait no longer for dat day. Gib us de pleasure of seein' de white folks shot down like de wolves when dey comes hongry out o' de woods. Oh Lor'—"

She paused as the group of blacks in front of her suddenly cleaved aside to make way for three white men who were striding toward her. The foremost, carrying a shotgun, was Zack Porter. Following were the assistant overseer, Lucas Mims, with his long blacksnake whip coiled over one shoulder and a third man with a cat-o'-nine—a short whip with nine knotted thongs designed to cut flesh.

"Back to work, you bastids—" called Porter. "Afore we burn your stinkin' hides off!"

The slaves edged back a bit, but none made a move to leave. Other blacks were drifting in from the fields.

"You-all gone deef?" bellowed Porter.

"It's that crazy voodoo witch been spoutin' trouble-rousin' talk," said Mims. "Dumb jackasses think she's got some kinda great power that'll perfect 'em." He took the coiled whip from his shoulder. "Won't take Len an' me long to learn them different—"

Nyanga's voice rose stridently. "Oh Lor'—hasten an' bring punis'ment down on de white debbils—!"

Springing forward with a vile oath, Porter slapped her savagely. "Shut your mouth, old hag!"

Recovering her balance from the blow, Nyanga leaned forward and spat in his face.

"Why you batty old bitch—!" With a vicious swing he crashed the shotgun barrel down on her head. Nyanga collapsed.

An upsurge of angry shouts rose from the blacks. Mims called a warning:

"Watch behind, Zack—!"

Turning, a chill slithered down Porter's spine as he saw the giant slave Zambullah leaping toward him. Frantically, he raised the shotgun, took aim—

iv

Listening to Nyanga's wild gabble had at first confused Zambullah, for the timing was all wrong. At this time of the season the slaves had not knives, but only hoes, and there had been no chance to organize for battle. Yet the prophetess was clearly telling of her "vision"—the signal for the slaves to rise against their masters—and such was Zambullah's faith in the voodoo woman that he now was leaping forward to strike the first blow at the hated whites with complete confidence that others would follow him to victory.

His way was blocked by the man named Len, the cat-o'-nine raised.

It was Len's last act. With catlike speed Zambullah arrested the man's arm in the midst of its swing. His other huge hand caught Len by the neck and yanked him up off the ground. It was at this instant that the overseer chose to fire.

An instant too late—

The body that Zambullah still held above the ground by the neck as a shield was no longer kicking. A hideous hole of red gore had been blasted into Len's back.

Meanwhile, a cordon of clamoring blacks had encircled the other two whites and were closing in.

"My Gawd!" squawked Mims. "It's an uprisin'—!" He dropped his whip and tried to run.

With one leap Zambullah had him by the neck. Holding Mims aloft for a moment with both hands, he gave the dangling body a quick jerk that snapped the neck. He tossed the dead man aside and whirled toward the overseer.

Porter, trapped in the midst of a dozen angry men, had dropped his empty gun and was bellowing at the top of his lungs: "Ring the vigilante bell, somebody!—ring that goddamn bell—!"

"Leave him be," said Zambullah, pushing his way through

the slaves who had begun beating the overseer to the ground. "His punishment belongs to me—"

Porter squalled like a stuck boar when Zambullah caught him by the head, then bent him back over an outthrust knee. Porter's arms flailed wildly as the black man hooked his other powerful leg about the man's torso in a scissors' hold. With the overseer's head still locked between the vise of his great hands, Zambullah began twisting. A scream gurgled out of Porter's throat, abruptly sliced off, to be replaced by the crackling, snapping sounds of small neck bones breaking. The black man kept twisting. . . .

v

The frenzied clanging of the big bell on a hillock near the mansion began just as Zambullah finished his gruesome ritual of vengeance. He straightened, ripping the pop-eyed head from its gory stump of neck, and contemptuously tossed it rolling over the ground. The headless body lay softly gushing spurts of blood from the ragged dark hole between its shoulders.

On the hillock Jacquard was throwing all his weight on the bellcord while Micaela watched in horror and dismay as the flurries of violence sparked other slaves into action. A scattering of blacks were racing toward the barns, warehouses. She saw a burst of flame as one of them touched a torch to a pile of straw. Others seemed to be running in criss-cross directions. Aimless, uncoordinated.

Then she saw the big black man bounding toward them.

Jacquard saw him at the same moment and dropped the bellcord to reach for his pistol.

"Zambullah—!" she shrieked. "Go back—!"

The sharp crack of pistol came at the same moment Micaela struck wildly at Jacquard's arm to deflect the aim.

"Damn slut—!" Jacquard howled, and slashed at her with the gun barrel.

She dodged the blow, but Zambullah had not been so fortunate. The deflected bullet had smashed into his left thigh—but failed to halt him. In another great leap he had Jacquard imprisoned in his arms, the gun twisted from his grasp.

Micaela snatched at Zambullah's huge wrists as his hands closed around Jacquard's neck.

"Zambullah—for my sake, please don't kill him! He's my *protecteur*—!"

The burning brightness of the great dark eyes bored into her, his hands still around the neck of his gasping captive.

"You've got to stop all this—" she went on. "Stop the men before it's too late—! Don't you understand? The bell has called the vigilantes. They'll be here soon with guns—"

Zambullah let his hands drop away, and turning, went away with great, limping one-legged bounds, leaving a trail of blood. . . .

THREE: Jail

AWAKENING, Paul heard the distant baying of hounds off somewhere in the swamp and idly wondered who would be out this early hunting on his land.

His land! It had a strange sense of unreality, the knowledge that he was the owner of over a thousand acres of rich river land, all the plantation buildings, was now the new master of Les Cypres. Syl had left him everything.

But that other reality, the bitter irony that all his new affluence was only at the expense of losing the woman he loved, oppressed him like a dull sickness night and day. It gnawed at him all the worse because he, who deemed himself to be a skilled doctor, had been unable to prevent her death.

The only bright aspect of the whole tragedy was the child, who in spite of the traumatic birth was thriving, healthy and happy. Though little Carson Dixon Abbott lacked a mother, all the servants doted on him and there was no lack of loving hands to see to his welfare.

Etienne in particular was enchanted by the child, and his normally morose expression radiated with smiles whenever Auntie Nana allowed him to hold the infant. He was fond of kneeling beside the crib and making ridiculous sounds to amuse the baby; he brought him endless toys; at times he even brought out his rare Cremona violin and played soft melodies that would soon lull the child to sleep. Paul himself spent much time holding his son, and feeling the tiny heart-beat against his own, thinking of the pulsing new life as a part and continuation of the life Syl had left, often felt his eyes misting.

The baying of the hounds was louder, closer.

Sitting up in the great bed with its thick mattress of goose-down and sheets of finest silk, Paul pulled aside the netting hanging from the mosquito bars—without which he could not have slept comfortably, for the mosquito season had begun—and slid out of bed. His glance fell on one of the newspapers that had arrived yesterday by steamer and placed on a bedstand by one of the servants, but which he had not yet had time to read. The headline blared: "LINCOLN SPEECH INFLAMES NEW YORK RABBLE."

Paul turned the paper over; it was too disturbing to read, and he was already familiar enough with the new president's views about slavery. For the past year Lincoln had kept pounding away at the theme again and again. By upholding slavery, he pointed out, America was bartering away its heritage of freedom. The Declaration of Independence had been intended as a standard maxim for free society, ultimately applicable to all peoples of all colors everywhere. But now, he warned, that once sacred document was being cheapened and diluted and twisted into something unrecognizable, all to aid in making the bondage of the Negro universal and eternal.

Paul heartily agreed with the president, whose clear logic had laid bare the heart of the controversy with the statement, "If the Declaration of Independence is of limited application, it has no meaning at all."

Paul was deeply worried. Abraham Lincoln's inauguration as President of the United States earlier in that year of 1861 had been a serious blow to the Southerners, who saw him as a threat to their very livelihood. A fermenting sense of unease hovered over the land. Tempers in both the North and South were rising to a flashpoint. Already South Carolina and a half-dozen other states, including Louisiana, had seceded, electing Jefferson Davis as the provisional president of a provisional new republic. Where would it all end?

He feared to speculate. He could only hope that the cool reason of the new president would eventually prevail. In the meantime he knew that his own position as an alien Yankee in the heart of an increasingly Yankee-hating South was getting more precarious with each passing day.

There was an urgent knocking. Throwing on a robe, he went to the door.

It was a wild-eyed Aurora. "Oh Massadoc—" she said breathlessly. "Zambullah's in de infirm'ry wid a bullet in his laig. . . . "

ii

Zambullah lay on the floor, half on his side, his hooded eyes watching Paul warily. His striped bed-ticking trousers were sopped to the waist, fouled with swamp mud and fragments of vegetation—with the exception of the right pants leg, which was missing. It had been ripped off and torn into bandaging strips that were now wrapped around the upper thigh over a packing of clay and leaves, apparently in an effort to stanch the bleeding which had seeped through to the cloth.

"Who shot him?"

Aurora looked at Paul beseechingly, not answering. He was again aware of the baying of hounds, seemingly more distant than before.

"Is he an escaped slave?"

She threw herself down in front of Paul on her knees, eyes streaked with tears and hands clasped as if in prayer as she looked up at him.

"Please, Massadoc—dey kill him if he go back. Please don' turn him in—!"

"We'll decide about that later. Right now we'll have to get him on the table so I can examine him. . . . "

With Zambullah on the table, Paul sent Aurora to fetch hot water. Quickly he removed the crude bandaging and thick clay pack, admiring the ingenuity of it. It had all but stopped the bleeding and had prevented a serious loss of blood.

In about twenty minutes the bullet was removed, the wound cleansed and dressed. As Paul finished the final taping, the mournful wailing of hounds came again, more distant. Both Aurora's and Zambullah's eyes had darted toward the sounds. A tiny smile touched Aurora's lips.

"It appears that the hounds have lost Zambullah's trail," Paul said.

" Zam smart. He circle roun' an' roun', den go back on his own trail like de fox befo' he jump in swamp watah. Dem houn's go crazy when de trail ends nowheah. . . . "

Paul frowned. "You must understand, Aurora, that as a

doctor I can only treat Zambullah's wounds, not hide him. He is Jacquard's property and will have to be returned."

Aurora turned her head away and began weeping.

iii

It was about noon when he heard the hounds again, this time very close. Their howling had taken on a yapping, excited quality, and suddenly he realized they were just outside on the plantation grounds. Moments later came the thunderous approach of galloping horses.

Etienne came hurrying downstairs. "What in the world is that?"

Paul quickly told him about the wounded Zambullah, who was now resting on a cot in the infirmary, adding, "It must be Jacquard and the vigilantes who have trailed him here."

"According to the Black Code, Paul, an escaped slave must be turned over to the authorities or his owner immediately. . . . "

"But the man is wounded and shouldn't be moved until he's had a chance to recover."

"A slave is not entitled to such concerns. We'd better go out and do our best to explain to the vigilantes. . . . "

But already the vigilantes had taken matters into their own hands, having dismounted and entered the infirmary. Several of them were roughly hauling the limping big black man out of the building. One man held a rifle at Zambullah's head.

As Paul and Etienne approached, Leon Jacquard emerged. Sighting Paul, a smile of triumph creased the swarthy features and he turned to speak briefly to several of the vigilantes. As a group they strode toward Paul.

"Dr. Abbott," said Jacquard, "we are placing you under arrest."

"On what charge?"

"For giving medical treatment, aid and comfort to an escaped nigger felon, for failing to punish him and for failing to immediately return him to his owner."

"I am a doctor. A doctor's first duty is to treat any person who comes to him for help."

"The Black Code decrees that it is the responsibility of any white person encountering any slave beyond the place of his habitual labor without written permission from his owner to arrest him. Section 30 of the Code further decrees that the slave shall receive twenty lashes from the person arresting him and be promptly sent back to his master, who then is obliged to pay the arresting person one dollar for his trouble."

"That's utterly unjust! In all humanity it couldn't be expected of me to—"

"Paul, Paul—" Etienne said warningly. "Monsieur Jacquard is merely citing the law—"

"Moreover—" Jacquard went on in a tone of jubilance, "we have other evidence. . . . Since you had already broken the law, we made a quick search of your desk and files and found *this*—"

He held up a small green leather-bound book—Fern's diary that Paul had shoved away in a drawer and forgotten to destroy.

"It is a most interesting document," Jacquard continued, "written by that notorious abolitionist, Fern Venable—alias Nora Starr—and your possession of it indicates that you are also an abolitionist who has supported the Underground Railroad in the criminal activities of stealing our slaves and fomenting uprisings. It shall be read more carefully for additional proof."

Etienne regarded Paul in dismay. "Is it true, Paul? Were you ever involved with Fern's abolitionist activities?"

Paul felt a terrible sinking sensation of despair. How could he disprove the lies written by a person now dead? Who would believe him?

"Never!" he said. "Never for a moment did I aid, encourage or believe in her abolitionist activities."

Jacquard turned and signaled to several of the rougher-looking vigilantes. "Put this man under arrest!"

Paul was quickly surrounded and gripped in strong brutal arms.

"Hold it—!" Etienne said sharply. "Whether Dr. Abbott is innocent or guilty is still unproved. You can't take any action against him without allowing him access to the due process of law—"

"Never fear, Monsieur Troyonne. Dr. Abbott will receive the full benefit of Southern justice. In deference to your friendship with him, we will even make it as painless as possible—he shall have a choice of being shot or hung by the neck."

Etienne's angry eyes sought out one of the planters who had remained seated ramrod-straight in the saddle a dozen feet away, watching and listening. The distinguished-looking horseman was Sieur Armand de Menière, one of the most influential planters on the river.

"Armand," Etienne said heatedly, "I am sure you believe as deeply in the rule of law as I do. I demand that Dr. Abbott be taken in complete safety to a jail to be held with all possible courtesies until he has received a fair trial. And I demand that the slave be also confined in public jail until it has been determined whether he has received cruel punishments such as are expressly forbidden by the Black Code."

"That's nonsense!" Jacquard said, scowling furiously. "The nigger is my property—"

Sieur Armand de Menière waved Jacquard to silence.

Etienne continued: "As you well know, Armand, hotheaded acts of atrocity do a great injustice to the South. Northerners seize upon them as proof that we are all callous brutes with no regard for human dignity or rights. And knowing you for many years as a gentleman of highest integrity, I am asking your pledge that both of these men will be taken to jail in complete safety."

Menière hesitated, his eyes meeting Etienne's square on. He was obviously a man accustomed to authority over others. After a moment he nodded.

"You have my promise, Etienne. . . . "

iv

The jail was filthy, the floor encrusted with fragments of dried food and excrement, above which hovered nastily buzzing flies. It had no bunks, no furnishings, only a floor of heavy timbers, and in one corner a great iron bucket close to slopping over from urine and defecations from previous occupants.

As a show of utmost contempt they had thrown him into the same cell with Zambullah. The black man lay along one wall on his left side, favoring the wounded limb. He looked relaxed except for the hooded eyes, which were alert to every sound and movement.

Other manifestations of hate came from the citizens of Five Corners. A number of men and some women passing the cell window, which was on the ground level, paused to spew out oaths and insults. One man thrust his face close to the bars to spit inside. Children jeered, hurled stones and rotten vegetables at the bars.

Paul knew it was hopeless. He had seen the same blind mob hate, the same mob lust for blood among the ignorant in Scotland just before the hangings.

The damning lies in Fern's journal alone would be enough to convict him. It was as if she were taunting him from the grave, trapping him into the same fate she had suffered for his failure to submit to her wishes.

v

In late afternoon they had surprise visitors.

First, Etienne's voice:

"Unlock the cell, please."

"But Mr. Troyonne, I got my orders—"

"And I am ordering you, in accordance with state law, to give me immediate access to the prisoners. We wish only to exercise visitors' rights to speak to Dr. Abbott for a few minutes. Mademoiselle Delacroix will accompany me. You may lock the cell door behind us if you wish."

"That won't be necessary, sir. . . . " A key rattled in the lock. The door swung open.

Paul rose to his feet as they entered. His clothes had become soiled, rumpled, his hair untidy; he felt soiled, tainted. By comparison, Etienne and Micaela were meticulously garbed in the height of rich fashion. Some of the fragrance of Micaela's perfume invaded the stench of the cell as her eyes met with Paul's and she gave an encouraging smile. It had been nearly two years since he had last seen her and she looked more ravishing than ever.

Etienne came close to Paul and spoke fast, in a low voice:

"There's no time to waste on small talk, Paul, so I'll get right to the point. My hopes for getting you a fair trial appear very doubtful. Mob feelings are running so high that I much fear that neither I nor my most influential friends will be able to control any mob hysteria that may lead to violence. Micaela is in a better position to know, as she has heard Jacquard talk. Certain elements of the vigilantes are determined that you will never have a court trial. Which is why she came to me to discuss a plan she has devised for your release. I do not know what it is, nor do I wish to know. I am sure it involves breaking the laws, but in view of the fact that mob violence directed against you would also be breaking laws—and would surely mean your death—I will not oppose any plan to help you. I will therefore leave you alone with her to discuss what she has to say—except for one last word—" Etienne's frowning eyes, surprisingly, were suddenly misted.

"I just want you to know, Paul, that whatever happens,

please have no worries about your son. I will take full responsibility to see that he has a proper upbringing and the training he needs to cope in this difficult world—"

Etienne found Paul's hand, gave it a quick firm handshake, then went out.

Micaela's soft hand closed around his. "Paul, I shall whisper my plan close to your ear, and then I must rush away. There is yet much I must do. . . . "

Several minutes later she gave him a light parting kiss, adding:

"The rest is up to *le bon Dieu*. For now, I'll leave you in His hands."

vi

With darkness the cries of the gathering crowd grew more raucous, taunting, vicious. Men rode past the cell slamming the bars with clubs, shouting insults, threats—

"Hey, let's git that fuckin' nigra-lover an' that murderin' nigra outta there an' l'arn 'em how decent folks don't take their kinda shit—"

"Yeah, let's fry their hides an' hang that nigra's ugly head in the center of town as a warnin' to the other nigra bastids—"

"Hell, what we waitin' fer—?"

Peering through the barred opening, Paul saw that many of the surging crowd carried torches. Only a few of them were mounted. Most appeared to be of the poorer white class, the types who could not themselves afford to own slaves—laborers, tradesmen, drunks. . . . It seemed odd that their hatred of blacks was so intense.

Another bellowing voice from in front of the jail: "Open up that door, Oral—hear? We have t' bust it down, we'll bust your skull in—!"

"Hell, I ain't about to put up no fuss. Jes' a minute now—"

A sudden shout of delight burst from someone in the crowd. "Hey—looka what's comin'—back there on a hoss—!"

Following moments of silence, a beginning susurration of astonished whispers swelled to a surf of gleeful approval.

"Jee-zus—! Nakid as a pig's ass!"

"Who'n hell is she?"

"Only one way t' find out—me, I'm a-headin' over for a closer look—!"

At the window, Paul saw the object of their excitement.

A beautiful black horse had trotted into view at the rear of the crowd, bearing a shapely nude female with long black hair streaming down over her pale nakedness.

Micaela!

As the crowd turned and surged toward the incredible vision of unclothed beauty, she swerved the horse away—but just far enough to be safely out of reach. The clamoring rose to an uproar: shouts of lustful appreciation, obscene invitations.

Skillfully she kept the horse wending back and forth, smiling back at them, laughing, teasing.

"Christ—that's Jacquard's wench! She's gonna give it to all of us—"

"C'mon—let's grab 'er!"

A man ran out to catch at her reins. She swerved away just in time. Another darted out from another direction. She made the horse rear almost in his face, forcing the man to duck away from the deadly, churning hooves. Two mounted men suddenly started out from different directions to entrap her. Snorting, the spirited animal wheeled about and shot away between the two converging horses, which were soon in hot pursuit.

"They'll snag 'er down in the woods damn quick—!"

And now most of the mob, as if propelled by a single brain, began moving toward the woods where the riders had vanished. Under the red flare of torches, eyes shone with lust. In the crowd was a scattering of women. Children tagged along, now and then hopping up and down in joyful anticipation of excitements to come.

But a dozen or so men stayed behind. One of them spat in disgust. "Shit! That's the same bitch was picked up with nothin' on under her skirt after spending the whole night alone with the Yankee bastid durin' the flood. Any damn fool can see she was tryin' to trick us away from the jail."

"Ain't gonna do no good! We got plenty enough of us right here to git that Yankee an' the nigra out here an' give 'em the works—"

They converged toward the open jail door.

vii

From the cell, Paul could hear the whining voice of the jailer:

"Now looka here—ain't no need to go whoppin' me on the haid like Zack Porter done last time! I ain't a-tryin' to stop ya. Jes' go right ahead an' unlock the cell for yerselfs. Here's the key—"

In the darkened cell, lighted dimly only by a lantern hung on the corridor wall outside, Paul knelt beside the big black man and took out the small bottle that Micaela had slipped to him during her visit. He had already explained the purpose of the bottle to Zambullah, and what they had to do, but now he added:

"The moment that key turns in the lock, I'll drink half the bottle, then you swallow the rest. . . . "

Booted footsteps started down the corridor. The flouncing rays of lanterns threw grotesque shadows on the wall as they approached.

Moments later a key rattled in the lock.

In the dimness, Paul held the small bottle to his mouth, swallowed, passed it to the black man.

And instantly began coughing, gagging from the horrible taste of the stuff. It burned its way into his stomach, spread nauseously. Agonizing cramps seized him with such sudden severity that he toppled forward on the floor and began rolling around, arms clutched hard against his belly in a futile effort to quell the twisting pains and suppress moans that jerked convulsively from his lips. A vast growing sickness swelled inside until his stomach felt ready to burst. Violent tremors shook him; retching sensations started up his throat—

Came spewing out, his whole stomach turning inside-out in a gushing, foaming mess.

He lay in the stench and slime of his own regurgitations . . . ah, blessed relief! He became aware of Zambullah, still rolling around, moaning, his vomit beginning—

Aware, too, of the open cell door, the men crowding inside, the flood of lantern light, the muffled exclamations—

"My Gawd—it's the *black vomit*—!"

Nothing was more feared throughout the South than the black vomit—the most lethal symptom of yellowjack, as yellow fever was called—signaling a quick, agonizing and certain death. People fled in terror from their own mates, their closest loved one, at the first sign of the deadly disease that infected and killed all unfortunate enough to come within breathing distance of it.

And as they all knew, yellowjack had already started in New Orleans. The papers warned that it could turn out to be the worst outbreak of the dread disease in living memory, would soon start working its way up the river. . . .

"Outta my way—I'm a-gettin' outta this place—!"

There was a clumping and scrambling of booted feet in a rush to get out; then pounding footsteps down the corridor. . . .

Paul rose to his feet, lightheaded and weak, and for a moment rested against a wall. Micaela's plan had worked—so far. . . . The small bottle had contained ingredients that she had found in the infirmary—a mixture of liquid surgical soap that Paul had improvised for his own purposes and a black elixir of licorice. The noxious, sickening concoction—Micaela's own invention as a way of simulating the frothing black vomit of yellowjack—was a powerful emetic and relatively harmless.

"We've got to hurry, Zam. Follow me—"

With Zambullah hopping along on his one good leg, they hustled down the empty corridor to the back jail door.

Outside in the blackness, Aurora's voice called from a nearby clump of bushes. "Dis way, Massadoc—"

viii

Naked from the hips down, her torso above covered only by a man's cape, Micaela stumbled through the front door of Les Colonnades—shoved forcibly by Jacquard, who strode in after her, slamming the door shut behind.

The vicious shove sent her careening forward, to end up sprawled on the carpet. The cape flew open, exposing the rest of her nudity.

"Rotten whoring slut—!" he shouted. "If I hadn't gone chasing after you in time, half the men for twenty miles around would have been crawling over your belly! You've done nothing but humiliate me—I ought to take a whip—"

"I was only trying to save the lives of two innocent men—"

He stared at her, breathing heavily, still raging at the memory . . . the man who had snatched at her horse's bridle just as he had arrived . . . the other man . . . both like crazed beasts lusting for his woman. Only his pistol stopped them. He had been only too ready to shoot them both—and had they ravished her, she would have been shot too.

As his eyes clung to her sprawled nakedness, his loins,

acting against his will, were reacting with an urgency of desire. No matter how she infuriated him, her body still had that damnable power of inciting him to erotic passions almost beyond control. Even the thought of hundreds of men chasing and capturing her to have their way with her only added, perversely, to his growing concupiscence. He felt his male organ stiffening.

"Slut—! Cover yourself! Have you no shame? Do you want to be seen like a naked whore by one of the nigger servants?"

When she made no move to cover herself, he strode over to the wall where he kept the whip used to chastise slaves and took it down.

"You'll do as I say!" he howled at her, flourishing the whip.

Slowly she stood up, leaving the cape on the carpet.

"You dare to threaten me, Jac? Have you forgotten I am a free person? Even Louisiana law doesn't permit you to whip me."

Jacquard laughed harshly. "You have much to learn about the law, my ignorant little fool. However the law may read, I could whip every square inch of your body and there's not an authority in the whole South who would do a damn thing about it—because you're still a nigger!" Casually he let the whip swirl through the air, cracking it perilously close to her face.

"Now get up to my bedroom—" He was raging with sexual desire, fueled as much by his fury as by the sensual vision of her helpless nakedness. "Before any of the other niggers see you unclothed."

She didn't move. A small smile played over her full red lips.

"What other niggers are present besides you to see me this way, Jac?"

Jacquard stood as if paralyzed. A strange expression, a blend of humility and fear, momentarily shadowed his face. "What was that you said—?"

"Jac, I've known for a long time. Momselle Delphine is from Haiti, too. She knew your mother well . . . all the things you've done. So your pretense of being better than I am is meaningless. You're just as much of a nigger as I am. Your mother was a quadroon, just as mine is—and should you dare to whip me, everybody in Louisiana will be told what you really are. . . . "

He let the whip drop from his hands, his expression transformed by a strange smile.

"So now you know my secret—so surely you understand the necessities of discretion that rule my life—" He continued:

"No, my dear, after what you have just told me, I wouldn't dream of whipping you—now you leave me no choice but to—"

He lunged at her, his powerful hands clawing at her neck. With catlike speed, her agile dancer's body whirled and leaped aside, raced toward the staircase.

He charged after her. "I'll catch you, bitch—and when I do—!"

She fled up the steps, his boots pounding close behind. Darting into her own room, she slammed the door in his face and a key turned in the lock just as he threw his weight against it.

He pounded on the door. "Let me in, Micaela! I promise not to hurt you. I only want to discuss this matter."

"No, Jac. You are too cruel and dishonest. I have decided to leave you."

His voice softened. "What I say in anger is not to be taken seriously. Don't you understand that I love you? I wish only to make you happy. I will take you to Paris—we will marry—anything you want—"

"How can you expect me to trust you now, Jac? You lied before. You told me you were not free to marry me, yet even the Code allows *gens de couleur* to marry each other. Had you admitted to me the truth, we could have married in secret so nobody else would ever know. But your love was not strong enough—"

"Not strong enough?" he half-screamed. "My love is so strong that I am going out of my mind—I am crazed with desire for you! If you let me in I will prove it to you in a way that words can never express—"

Indeed, he was so in the grip of surging erotic passions that he could scarcely think straight. His hardened penis was trapped painfully under his tight trousers and against the oaken door.

Her tone was sad. "No, Jac—it is too late for that . . . even if I could believe you. . . . "

In another eruption of rage he beat his fists against the door until his knuckles bled. "Little fool—! Don't you know

you can never escape? I'll never let you out of this house!
Open up before I break the door down——!"

When there was no response, he delivered a final savage
kick at the door before turning away. Going downstairs, he
repaired to his study and took out a bottle of brandy from
a locked cabinet. Scorning a glass, he raised the bottle and
drank deeply.

The liquor rolled down his throat to settle in his stomach
like a pleasant little ball of fire, soothing his outraged sensory
system, giving resolution to his conflicting emotions. . . .

It was clear enough. The physical side of him craved her
like a drug—but that he could bear.

What he couldn't bear was the knowledge that now she
held a sword over his head, had the power to expose to all
the world the shame of his black blood. It could wreck his
career, all his dreams.

It left him no choice. . . .

With an ax he could easily chop the door open, then sate
himself with a final enjoyment of her flesh, and then—

He went to a wall and pulled the bellcord.

ix

In a few moments Emeline appeared. She was still limping,
her face swollen from the beating he had given her yesterday, and her eyes were wide with fright.

"What are you doing here? Where's Benjy?" Benjy was
the head house servant who normally would have answered
the bell call.

"Benjy can't walk, Massa, so he send me."

Now he remembered. The aborted black uprising yesterday had done no serious harm, except for the death of his
three top overseers. The vigilantes had arrived in time to put
out the fires before they were out of control. Then Benjy
and about a dozen of the other slave bosses had been flogged
into unconsciousness, as an object lesson to the others.
Jacquard would have preferred to kill them, but slaves were
too expensive.

"All right. Go to the tool shed and fetch me an ax."

"Yassuh, Massa . . . "

Waiting, he took a few more pulls at the brandy bottle.
Five minutes passed. What the hell was keeping Emeline?
Angry, he left the study and strode into the living room.

"Emeline!" he bellowed. "Come here at once!"

Even as he was shouting, he became aware of the faint, acrid odor of smoke. Alarmed, his glance darted around seeking the cause, stopped at the gallery windows. Outside he saw the jouncing flare of a torch. It reflected redly on the face of the one carrying it. Nyanga, the crazy voodoo woman.

With an oath, he started down a hallway to the locked gunrack, one hand searching in a pocket for the key. Then he heard Emeline's quiet voice from directly behind him.

"Here I am, Massa—"

He turned just in time to see the descending ax, but not quite soon enough to avoid it. . . .

FOUR: Exodus

WE almost dere, Massadoc. . . . " said Aurora. "We close to de ribber now. . . . "

Thank God, Paul thought as he sloshed the last few steps through sucking swamp waters to the rise of a low reedy bank that could barely be made out through the thick fog. He was beginning to stagger and reel from exhaustion. His head was full of dizziness and humming noises. Or was it the droning of those damnable hordes of mosquitoes? Hardly a square inch of his body had escaped their vicious little stings, even through his clothing. His body was a mass of welts and such relentless itching that it had even distracted him from the constant fear that every log was an alligator, every slithering movement a water moccasin.

He could only marvel at how Aurora had been able to guide them through the steamy, starless night. After finding her hidden in the bushes behind the jail, she had led them to a wagon and team of horses tethered among the trees about a hundred yards away. The next twenty minutes had been a fast, bumpy ride over an all but obscured old logging trail to the edge of a swamp. Then another fifteen minutes of slogging up to their knees across a section of swamp that Aurora explained was the fastest and would leave no trail in case they were followed.

As they approached the rush and gurgle of the Mississippi,

Paul saw the blur of the boat she had promised would be
waiting. It was a long rowboat at the river's edge, with two
men standing by. And beyond, the great murky silhouette
of a steamboat. Soon he was able to make out the name
on the side. It was the *New Orleans Lady*.

ii

When she heard the steamboat whistle at the river bend—the
prearranged signal she had worked out with Mike Quinn on
the previous day—Micaela let out a deep sigh of relief. It
meant that her plan was working!

It was the signal for Emeline to see that a fire was started
in the empty overseer's cottage. It would surely provide a
distraction that would draw Jac rushing away from the
manor, and also allow the twenty or so slaves who wished to
escape with her to slip down to the quay without being seen.

Already she was fully packed—only a small bag and a
purse containing her money and jewels—and the rope that
had been hidden under clothing in the armoire was securely
knotted to a bed post. The window was open—

A few minutes later she was on the ground hastening toward the quay with her bag and purse. Only then did she
become aware that it was the mansion, not the overseer's
cottage, that had been set afire. One whole wing was seething
and crackling with flames.

It distressed her to see the destruction of so beautiful a
house, but there was no time to worry and puzzle about it
now. Ahead she saw the slaves huddled at the end of the
quay, and out in the river the big paddlewheeler was beginning to nose in. . . .

iii

They came within sight of New Orleans about an hour after
dawn. Even at a distance it was ominous to see because of
the great clouds of black smoke boiling up from the main
streets to rise over the gilded spires and domes of the city.
For miles beyond the outskirts the black haze could be seen
floating in the red rays of morning sun.

"What in the world is all that smoke?" said Paul, who was
standing beside Mike Quinn at the railing of the hurricane
deck.

" 'Tis smoke from the tar barrels because of the plague.

The smoke, ye understand, is to purge the air of fever, which is killin' off people like flies. Bedad, even the rich nabobs who never died before are dyin'."

"Why don't they leave the city?"

"The time is too late. The nimble ones with enough shillings got out while they could. But now the railroad has stopped running and all the carts and carriages left in town are needed to carry off the dead. It's work only for the niggers an' the Irish, ye understand, for nobody else will touch it. The harbor, as ye'll soon see, is near empty because every tub that can carry human cargo has left, an' no ship will venture in."

"How about you, Mike? Aren't you afraid to risk it?"

Quinn laughed. "I am a gambler who puts his trust in Irish luck. I saw the plague by way of being a guarantee that none would dare give chase. And on my return trip, I can turn a tidy profit by picking up a load of passengers at triple the usual rate."

"How far are you taking us?"

"The nigger girl Aurora knows all of the Underground Railroad contacts, and I got a message to them yesterday. A schooner, I was promised, will be waiting to meet us a mile or two below New Orleans to take you aboard."

"Mike, I don't know how or when I can ever repay you, but—"

"Ye can best repay me, Sir Doctor, by repairing with me to the salon and partaking with me of a bottle of the Irish medication that I shall prescribe for you. From the wearied look of your face, I would venture that you need it sorely. . . . "

iv

Captain Carswell stood with his short legs braced wide and hands clasped behind his back as his eyes ran over the line of slaves boarding the schooner *Hope*. He was a stocky but powerful man with a heavy and bold head, built well onto a strong neck, and eyes that glinted like glass of palest blue. He knitted his forehead.

"That's twenty-four of ye," he grouched at Paul. "I only reckoned on twenty. It's chancy enough carrying runaways without overloadin' to boot."

"We're willing to pay extra," said Micaela. "At one

hundred a head we owe you twenty-four hundred dollars, but I have another three hundred that I will give you."

Carswell snorted. "Not enough, ma'am. This is my last trip an' I had to raise my rates. Gettin' too dangerous these days, an' carryin' abolitionists is a sight riskier than the niggers. I'll need another thousand."

Micaela bit her lip. "Dr. Abbott is without funds, and I have no more, but——" Quickly she slipped off a ring with a large glittering diamond and extended it. "I don't know how much it cost, but I can assure you it is very valuable. . . . "

The captain examined the ring briefly, thrust it in a pocket.

"The niggers can go below. You an' him can take a cabin——" His eyes rested on Paul, who despite his best efforts could not keep his head from nodding forward in weariness. Carswell's voice was harshly suspicious:

"Here now!—what's wrong with him? Don't like the look of this a-tall. He wouldn't be havin' a fever, would he now?"

"Oh no, no!" Micaela assured him quickly. "The poor man hasn't slept in twenty-four hours. All he needs is a good sleep."

"Waal . . . ye can take the cabin right behind mine."

"If you don't mind, Captain, we'd prefer to be down with the slaves."

Carswell scowled his disgust. "Ye abolitionists beat all! Waal . . . if it's the niggers ye prefer to be with, an' ye can stand the stink, it's your choice."

V

By evening Paul knew he was coming down with yellow fever. He had developed a severe headache, his face was hot and flushed, and he was so weak he could scarcely stand. When Micaela brought food, the sight of it nauseated him. She also brought down blankets, making a rough bed for him in a corner where it would not be so noticeable that he was sick if the captain or any of the crew came down. Sitting beside him, she bathed his face with cool salt water, then rubbed his skin with rum she had purchased from one of the seamen. But still the fever soared and during the night his mind began swirling with delirium . . .

. . . vividly colorful phantoms danced through his head. . . . The face of his foster mother, Sarah, as she had looked when he was a child, a handsome young woman with none

of the taint of her loose living in saloons apparent to his innocent childish eyes. . . . She was smiling at him through the haze of his fervid fancies . . . disrobing with an inviting smile . . . and he was suddenly no longer a child, but a man as she came perfumed and warm and naked into his arms. . . .

. . . then magically transforming into Fern, her live, silky-fleshed body writhing, soft breasts crushing against his chest as her limbs spread. . . .

In his high fever he groaned and rolled and sought to cling to the body which was already vanishing like smoke, and then was gone and he was left alone in the night with nothing but a most oppressive sense of guilt, dark feelings that slowly resolved into something familiar . . . a dear face. . . .

Syl's . . . She was looking at him through eyes luminous with tears . . . hurt eyes pleading with him to alleviate the torture behind her sweet smile. Her arms were outstretched, beckoning him as she drifted backward into blackness, and he began to follow, yearning to be lost in blackness with Syl away from all the pains and passions of living, to sink into that inviting, restful nothingness. . . .

Then suddenly the blackness cleaved away and bright light broke through. . . .

"I think you're going to be all right now, Paul. . . . "

He looked up at the face of the soft voice and her beauty was like the morning sun.

"Micaela . . . I must have fallen asleep. . . . How long has it been?"

"You have been in a terrible fever for three days, *mon cher,* but it is almost gone now."

"Three days! And you were the only one who attended me?"

"When they found you had yellow jack, no one would come near. The food and water was handed down to me in bowls."

"And you weren't afraid of contracting the fever?"

"Don't you remember, Doctor? You once told me that yellow fever is not contagious. It was your theory that it is carried only by mosquitoes."

He smiled feebly. "I've been bitten by the damned pests a thousand times in the past week—but that's still no proof that they caused the disease. . . . "

"For now you must forget it, *mon cher*. Just be grateful that you are still alive."

He twisted his head in the direction of the blacks he had briefly glimpsed while trying to sit up. He felt a surge of anger. "Why are they chained?"

Micaela frowned. "It was by the captain's orders. He said he always chains runaway slaves as a matter of safety because of the Southern gunboats that patrol the ocean lanes. In case one of them stops us, he can claim he is delivering the slaves to another buyer. He says he has falsified ownership papers to back up his story, so there is no danger."

"I don't like it."

"Don't fuss, *mon cher*." She placed a soft hand on his forehead. It is best that you rest and recover your strength."

The talk, his anger, had exhausted him. He closed his eyes and at once slipped back into sleep.

vi

"Cap'n Carswell," said the first mate, "I see smoke on the horizon off to the nor'east. Can't rightly make it out, but it has the look of a gunboat bearing hard on our course. . . . "

The captain snatched the glasses from the mate and held them to his eyes. He cursed softly. "It be a gunboat, sure enough. Plain as warts." He handed the glasses back.

"Mr. Slater, go below an' git the aft hatchway open an' the niggers lined up in case we have to dump 'em."

"Cap'n, I can't go down there an' risk the fever."

"Do I hear ye right, Mr. Slater?" The captain cupped a hand behind an ear. "Or is it my ears that are failin'?"

"But Cap'n—it's like a death sentence to git exposed. The niggers don't catch it, but us white folks pick it up quick as a wink from just a whiff of the air near wherever there's yellow jack."

The captain rubbed his chin thoughtfully while his bleak blue eyes stared off at the speck of approaching gunboat. "I be a fair man, Mr. Slater, so I'll give ye three choices. Ye can go down there an' carry out my orders, or we can wait to git picked up by the gunboat yonder an' taken back to be hung by the neck for runnin' stolen slaves—or if neither of those suit ye—" Carswell reached under his shirt and hauled out a derringer.

"I could shoot ye through the head here an' now an' save all the trouble."

"Aye, aye, sir. Whatever you say, sir."

"Then get down there an' stand by for further orders—take Mr. Judson and a seaman with you, if ye like—an' lively now. . . . "

vii

Micaela looked up with a sudden prescience of trouble when she saw the three crew members come down, one carrying a rifle. They glanced uneasily at Paul, who was napping beside her.

"Open the back hatch," one of them ordered.

The other two quickly released the latches securing the large hatch in the rear. It swung away on hinges, bringing into view the green frothy wake of ocean a couple of feet below.

"What is that for?" asked Micaela.

"Captain's orders, ma'am."

Roused from his stupor, Paul sat up. Another day—or had it been two?—of almost constant napping had restored some of his strength, but his head still swam with dizziness. He saw the open hatchway, the shackled slaves lined up along a bulkhead wall—each one linked to the next in a continuous chain. What was it all about?

From somewhere came the muffled boom of a small cannon.

Moments later a voice bellowed down from the upper hatchway: "They put a shot over the bow—unload the niggers—*fast*—!"

The boat rolled in the waves and from above came the sound of canvas crackling in the wind with the sound of a whiplash as the boom swung around to bring the boat about in obedience to the warning shot over its bow. A moaning rose up from the blacks.

Watching, seeing the first slave forced to the brink of the open hatchway with a rifle at his head and the two others roughly pushing him, Paul's fever-fogged brain finally grasped the situation. The blacks were chained ankle to ankle. Once the first one went overboard, his weight would drag at the next. The pull would increase with each man that followed until the multiplying weight of slaves overboard would haul along the rest as inexorably as falling dominoes.

The third black along the chain was resisting, flailing with his arms, scrabbling for a handhold to keep aboard. The man with the rifle slammed its barrel against his head and the slave went over. The other blacks were in turmoil, shouting, battling against the pull—

Paul struggled to his feet, swaying with dizziness. "You damned murderers—stop!"

The mate swung around, bringing his rifle to bear on Paul. "Don't take a step closer, mister, 'less ye want a rifle ball through your head."

Micaela's voice came like a swift echo:

"And you'll get a bullet through your head, *monsieur,* if you don't drop that rifle!" She was pointing a small pearl-handled pistol.

The rifle swiveled toward her. "No bitch ever tells me wha—"

His last word gurgled off into eternity as a section of his skull caved in. Zambullah, dragging along the other slaves chained to him, had leaped from behind, to bring the heavy iron of his wrist shackles down on the man's head. The rifle clattered to the floor.

Paul made a rush forward to get the rifle, stumbled as everything began tilting, swirling in front of his eyes; he fell sprawling on his face. . . .

One of the crewmen suddenly threw himself down to get the rifle, grasped it—

There was a small, cracking sound and the man let the rifle drop as if he'd been stung. He looked in astonishment at a round little dark hole in his forearm that was starting to dribble blood.

"Do not touch the rifle again," said Micaela, "or I shall kill you. And you, the other man—get back from the slaves."

Paul, his head clearing, rose to his knees and saw that at least a half-dozen of the slaves had gone overboard and their combined weight, linked by chain, was pulling the others after them, unable to resist the powerful force hauling them toward the ocean.

"Zambullah—!" he shouted. "Get the chain hooked around the stanchion—" The chain secured around the iron post would at least prevent more slaves from going overboard.

But his advice was needless. Gripping the chain in both muscular hands, Zambullah had braced his good foot against the stanchion and started hauling the chain backward. Slowly, inch by inch. The great muscles rippled and bulged from the strain, gleaming with sweat. Faster. . . . The last slave to go overboard reappeared in the opening, chained leg first, the other leg kicking wildly. An arm appeared and hooked over the edge of the hatch. He was adding his efforts to Zambullah's.

Paul wobbled to his feet and started forward to help, but the effort was too great. Blood pounded in his head, his eyes hazed, and after a few steps he fell again. Before sinking into blackness he could hear the captain's voice bellowing, as from a great distance:

"What in damnation be ye doin' below? Git the aft hatch closed, ye swabs, an' git back up here. Lively now! We're being boarded. . . . "

viii

Paul's eyes opened to the blurred vision of Micaela bending over him. She held a cool cloth against his forehead.

"Ah, you are awake, *mon cher?* I am so glad."

"What happened to the slaves?"

"It is sad. Two were drowned before they could be pulled from the water, but Zambullah saved the rest. He was *magnifique!*"

A stern voice in the background drew his attention, and he was startled to see a tall man in a navy officer's uniform interrogating the two crewmen who had been forcing the slaves overboard. Both men stood with hands bound behind them, responding sullenly to the questions. Paul looked questioningly at Micaela.

"Are we under arrest?"

"Mais non! We were stopped by a gunboat from the North, and we are now under the protection of the U.S. Navy. Only Captain Carswell and his crew are under arrest."

His first surge of jubilation faded. "Have you forgotten that the Fugitive Slave Act is a federal law? The U.S. Navy is obliged to enforce such laws—which means that the slaves must be returned as the rightful property of their owners, and when they find that we were instrumental in helping them escape—stealing in the eyes of federal law—we will be returned under arrest as well."

"Mais non—"

A new voice intruded:

"How are you feeling, Doctor?" It was the tall naval officer.

"That depends greatly on how soon we'll be shipped back to Louisiana. . . . "

The officer looked puzzled at first, then broke into a laugh.

"I'm afraid that won't be possible. You've been at sea for several days or more, so of course you're not up on the current news. I regret to inform you that two days ago—April twelfth—Confederate troops opened fire on Fort Sumter. . . . "

Paul thought he had misunderstood. "You're telling me that the South attacked a federal fort—?"

"Yes, Doctor—war has broken out between the North and the South. . . . " He turned to leave, then added:

"I'll have your ship physician look you over, but for the present it appears that you are in good hands."

After he was gone, Micaela said, "I am sorry that the war has come, but glad because it means freedom for you and freedom for the slaves."

"For us, yes," he said soberly, "but you are already free, Micaela. Why did you take such great risks to get involved?"

"Because you needed me."

"Without your help, I would certainly be dead—but you paid such a dear price to give me aid—aside from risking your life, you've given up all the comforts and security of a rich life—and I have not a cent to repay you. I don't know when, if ever, I can ever touch any of my possessions in Louisiana. And now that you have paid the last of your money and your ring for our passage—"

She laughed. "You need not worry. . . . I did not want the captain to know, as I knew he was not to be trusted, but I have more money and valuable jewels in my purse—enough for us to get started again in a new life. . . . "

"*Us*—?"

"Do you not want me as your woman?"

He averted his head, abashed by the weakness that had dampened his eyes. After a few moments he spoke:

"I could want nothing more than to have you as my woman—but I fear you would not want to be the wife of an army surgeon—"

She squealed with delight. "Your *wife*?"

"What I am trying to tell you is that I have no choice but to offer my services to the Union forces."

"But you would be a most admirable army surgeon, and I would be so proud to be your wife!"

"But—"

"And to show my full faith in your theory that yellow fever is not contagious, I am going to kiss you."

And she did.

BESTSELLERS

Historical Romance